THE BEAUTIFUL GAME

PETER MARTINUZZI

PublishAmerica
Baltimore

© 2013 by Peter Martinuzzi.
All rights reserved. No part of this book may be reproduced, stored in a retrieval system or transmitted in any form or by any means without the prior written permission of the publishers, except by a reviewer who may quote brief passages in a review to be printed in a newspaper, magazine or journal.

First printing

All characters in this book are fictitious, and any resemblance to real persons, living or dead, is coincidental.

PublishAmerica has allowed this work to remain exactly as the author intended, verbatim, without editorial input.

Softcover 9781629079851
PUBLISHED BY PUBLISHAMERICA, LLLP
www.publishamerica.com
Baltimore

Printed in the United States of America

To Janice

1

Red Card

Every house is the same. Minuscule front yards are hemmed in by oversized driveways leading to overstuffed garages. Immature landscaping adds insult to the cheap construction of a front porch so small it's rendered useless for anything but cosmetic appearance. The gauntlet of homes is arranged in an artificial maze to control traffic flow and give the illusion of safety. Constructed on the cheap by a single builder in a single summer, the neighborhood gives the appearance that the buildings were constructed not for families, but for the benefit of the almighty SUV. But the outdated word neighborhood implies that the houses are filled with neighbors, people who share something more in common than a mortgage they can't afford. The occupants are superfluous, it's the streets, driveways, and garages that matter. A knock on any door would be unlikely to produce a resident, let alone one who knew where the local greenbelt and park were located.

If the people in charge of children's athletic organizations really wanted parents to attend these summer soccer games, you'd think they'd provide a better map. The clock on the dashboard said 8:24am. The GPS was baffled but didn't have the humility or common decency to tell him he was on his own. Michael Johnson pulled his Ford F150 to the curb in the middle of the block and consulted his county street map. How tough could it be to find a public park the size of an airport? Apparently, the task was insurmountable. The housing development was so new, it didn't even count. Oak Park Drive was the address of the park field house. He'd already passed Oak Park Hill, Street, Trace, Chase, Court, Circle, Boulevard, and yes, Oak Park Drive. On what he thought was the proper street, Michael counted down the numbers. Before he reached the address of the field house the Drive ended at a T: Oak Park Lane. He drove what felt like a figure eight and swore he ended up at the exact spot but facing in the other direction.

At the end of a twelve-hour shift at St. Bernadette's hospital, Michael Johnson was exhausted. His sleep-deprived brain was betraying him. The July sun was already high in the sky and made him want to close his eyes. He felt like some combination of Winnie the Pooh lost in the Hundred Acre Wood, Alice in Wonderland, and Dorothy in the Poppy Fields of Oz. North, South, East and West lost their meaning in these ridiculous suburban developments. Why did they always name them after the habitat they'd just ruined? Pheasant Run meant there were guaranteed to be no pheasants for twenty square miles. He contemplated taking a quick nap, but his wife Jennifer insisted he attend this game and he had no guarantee when he might wake up. He couldn't remember why this particular game was so important or whether Jennifer had even mentioned the reason. Was it picture day? They didn't need the parents for that ritual humiliation. Hannah didn't much care, he thought. She was nine years old. For her, a soccer game was still about the halftime juice box and Rice Krispie bar.

The Luke Skywalker of the suburbs, he decided to trust the Force and turn off his navigator. Based on the position of the brutal Kansas sun and avoiding the streets he'd already driven twice, Michael turned down a random Oak Park that was guarded by not one, but two signs that said "Dead End" and "No Exit." As he drove the quarter mile spur, he noted the houses became larger and the landscaping more ostentatious. The street ended at a tasteful barricade of imported Italian limestone blocks, inscribed with the identical label announcing Oak Park. Together they had the effect of a row of tombstones in a military cemetery. He brought the F150 to a stop in defeat. Between him and the crowd gathered to watch the game was a half mile of neatly mowed lawn and a storm culvert six feet wide and just as deep. There must have a been a bridge for pedestrians nearby but his view was blocked up and down by privacy hedges of mature yew trees. The clock on the dashboard said 8:42am.

Michael put the truck in reverse and turned to head around to the other side of the park. Using only his sense of direction and ignoring every teasing street sign, he made a wide, mile-long arc he estimated would bring him to the proper location. How many trenches could the Death Star possibly have? His instincts served him well. Rounding a corner another pair of street signs read "Slow Children at Play" and "Oak Park Recreational Area." The first sign had always confused him. Did it mean that there was a mentally challenged child in the area? Should he drive more slowly because the kid didn't know *not* to run into the street? Or did the community actually think the kids would put down their video games long enough to play in the front yard? Such activity would likely be in violation of the homeowner's association covenants and subject to stiff fines. And why did a playground have to have a name? When he was young, anywhere beyond the front door of the farmhouse was a recreational area.

As usual at these events and despite the absurd amounts of acreage set aside for the greenbelt, no parking was provided. The street was clogged on both sides with parked cars as far as he could see, but Jennifer's Honda Civic was not among them. The clock on the dashboard said 8:51am. Rather than miss the start of the game or risk blocking someone's driveway, Michael pulled his truck part way into the approach ramp of a service drive, resting his bumper on a chain. The hanging sign read "No Parking" but he figured the warning must be for weekdays only. Out of choices and patience, he decided to risk the ticket.

Michael stepped from the truck and went to close the door, then remembered his drive-thru coffee sitting in its cup holder. He reached back to grab the door before it slammed, but misjudged the swing. He pulled back to avoid an amputation but not before the frame caught the middle fingernail of his right hand and tore it partly off. He put it to his mouth and tasted blood. When he removed it to survey the damage, he could see a fresh line of bright red forming at the tip. The nail showed a crease where the tip had bent back, but it was now back in place and unlikely to fall off.

With his fortifying coffee in hand, Michael scanned the rows of parents on both sides of the field looking for his wife, Jennifer Smith. The girls were still warming up, going through passing drills and kicking endless goals past the stationary goalie. Jennifer Smith was at the far end of the field, standing by herself, despite the gaggle of parents supporting both teams. Michael Johnson ran the gauntlet of disapproving eyes, nodding at faces he recognized, but not a single name came to his sleep-deprived cranium. Jennifer stood with her arms crossed, her face in a stern and determined frown. "Where the hell were you?" she said. It wasn't a question.

"Good morning, Honey," Michael said. "I've missed you too."

"Cut the crap. You were supposed to be here at 8:30am."

"They haven't started yet. What's the big deal?" Michael did a quick inventory of his mental calendar noting birthdays, anniversaries, Boxing Day. None of them seemed to be on the horizon. "Who are we playing today? The dreaded Ornate Box Turtles?"

Michael's joke fell flat. Hannah's team had flirted with naming themselves the Susan Bees, after Susan B. Anthony, Kansas's champion of women's suffrage. In the end they went for the more threatening Honeybees, named for the state insect.

"Not that you care, but they're playing the Sally's." Michael failed to suppress a laugh. Another absurd team name, this time for the State Amphibian, the Barred Tiger Salamander.

"Oh, that's classic. From what I've seen of warmups, they should call themselves The Cottonwoods, after the State Tree. Until it's time to pass out juice boxes they stand around like plants."

Jennifer Smith was not amused. "I was counting on you to do this one thing for me, and once again you screw it up."

"Am I missing something?"

"No, no. Nothing important. Only the end of our marriage."

"That's what I like about you, Sweets. Your sense of humor." Michael leaned towards his wife to give her a peck on the cheek. She recoiled but he persisted until his lips met her skin and he was able to produce an exaggerated smooching sound. He then took a long drag on his quickly cooling coffee and watched the girls line up for the opening kick. Hannah was still on the sideline, further evidence that for her soccer was a social event for fifth graders, not an Olympic sport. Michael felt Jennifer's eyes on him and turned to meet her scowl. "What?" he said, genuinely perplexed. "You know my shift doesn't end until 8:00am. Then I sign out to the day shift. There's that pesky issue of all the sick people that tend to hang out in hospitals. Thankfully, I was able to rush across town during the peak of weekend vacation traffic. What did you expect?"

"You're just lucky my lawyer is late."

"Very funny. What's this, like a yellow card?"

"Huh? What?"

"You know. Soccer." He gestured towards the field with his coffee, a fresh drop of blood forming at his fingertip. "When the referee gives a player a yellow card, a warning for unsportsmanlike conduct or a delay of game, or whining. I know I whine a bunch."

"I think we're beyond that point. More like a red card. You're out of the game. No substitute allowed."

2

THE LAWS OF THE GAME

"Uh, huh. You've got a lawyer," Michael Johnson said. "Next you'll tell me he's got the papers all drawn up and once I sign I'll get to see Hannah twice a month but still have the privilege of paying for your bimonthly hair color appointments."

"He's got the papers all drawn up and once you sign…" she started, then became distracted by the soccer game. "You know the rest. GO EMILY!"

Michael looked to the field. Emily was his friend Jason's daughter, but for the life of him, Michael couldn't tell them apart. They all wore the same royal blue ribbon in their nondescript hair, somewhere between sandy blonde and light brunette, to tie back a shoulder-length ponytail. The ribbon matched the blue shorts and socks. The short-sleeved T-shirts were all formless, baggy, and blinding white. The action on the field was so random, like water vapor particles coalescing around a dust mote to form a snowflake. He couldn't think of a single reason to cheer. It wasn't as if Emily was on a breakaway to the goal.

Michael's foggy mind was not prepared for this verbal exchange, especially after a full week of night shifts. The coffee wasn't helping to clear his head. He glanced at Jennifer Smith and searched for any sign that his wife of ten years was teasing. He was met with the same stern glare and folded arms. "Maybe you'd better tell me what this is all about."

"See? That's your problem," Jennifer said. "You're so clueless, you don't even know when I'm being serious."

"Sure, pull the other leg."

"James will be here any minute. Melissa was here on time to drop off Madison, and I guess he must have gone to the office to get the final notarized copies. Or something. I don't know, the point is, I'm serious." Jennifer pointed down the line of parents and Michael recognized Melissa. Of course, he couldn't have guessed her name, but she'd be easy to pick out of a police lineup. Melissa was the trophy second wife of James, the kind one apparently trades up for when he makes partner at the law firm. Michael didn't know her in the least, but imagined Melissa was the kind of woman who put on makeup before she went outside to exercise. She probably owned color-coordinated sweat suits that cost more than the monthly payment on his truck. Her perfect French manicure told the world she wasn't concerned with housework, let alone yard work, gardening or other potentially messy hobbies. Melissa couldn't have weighed much more than Madison. She had a cowbell and clanged it any time Madison came within twenty yards of the soccer ball.

"Hello? Michael?" Jennifer said. "I'm over here. Stop leering."

"What? I'm not leering, I'm half asleep. Gimme a break. And since when did you start using words like 'leering'?"

Jennifer ignored him and began to list her complaints with Michael. "The way you are with money is enough to ruin us."

"Not this discussion again…" Michael began.

"That's right," Jennifer interrupted. "We're not having a discussion. I'm telling you why you'll be signing the divorce papers."

"Money is just a tool," he continued. "If I have a nail to drive, I use a hammer. If I want to buy something, I use money."

Like a marital reflex, Jennifer couldn't help but argue the same old points. "No, it's not. How we live with money determines everything from when we can retire, to where and when we can vacation, it's how we provide for our daughter. It's why we're both working and why we decided to have only one child to raise her as comfortably as possible."

"No, that's what *you* decided. It's not like *I* can get pregnant. So we disagree about money. You knew that about me before we got married." The method of their marriage was still a sore spot for Michael. He'd wanted a big wedding, with all of the trimmings, fully knowing that the modern event is an invention of hollow symbols that have nothing to do with contemporary life. Ever the practical schoolmarm, Jennifer would have none of it. The discussions were heated, lengthy, and ruined much of what should have been a delightful engagement.

Michael Johnson had just finished nursing school and Jennifer Smith had obtained her teaching degree. He planned to work and save for a full year, even having money leftover for an exotic honeymoon. In the end, Jennifer won out and they had a simple ceremony, presided over by a friend in the city park and overlooking an historic, but sadly stagnant pond. Despite a guest list that could be counted on less than their combined fingers and toes, gifts rolled in from near and far. Without a registry, relatives just sent well wishes and cash. The five figure total would have easily covered the cost of a lavish wedding plus Michael's desired fantasy honeymoon. Rather than admit her frugality had stolen something from the event, Jennifer invested the entire amount in a jointly held mutual fund and wouldn't entertain another word about it.

The coach substituted in the third string, which meant Michael would have to pay more close attention to the game and his daughter's safety. Serious injuries were unheard of, but for reasons he couldn't divine, Jennifer insisted he rush out onto the field should any of the girls suffer so much as a loose ponytail. "Hannah's in. Pay attention," she said on cue.

"My pocket CT scanner is at the ready," Michael said with all the sarcasm he could muster. "I'll evacuate the subdural hematoma with my coffee straw and put the victim right back in for the crucial second half."

"You're an asshole."

"C'mon, Jennifer. You're asking me to care about a game between nine-year olds like I'm on some kind of NFL medical crew. If there were a real injury, forty parents would be on their cell phones calling 9-1-1 before you could toss your cookies." She kept her arms crossed and eyes on the field, maintaining her best defiant pose. "And you're telling me you want a divorce and I'm supposed to care if our team will end the season three and seven or two and eight."

"You just married the wrong girl."

"What's *that* supposed to mean?"

"We don't view money the same way, you want ten children and I'm happy with Hannah. You're happy sitting on the porch after work and I want to see the world."

"And?" Michael said. "That's what makes us cool together. We're not clones."

"That's not all, Michael," Jennifer said. She dropped her arms and turned to face him. With a straight face she added, "You load the dishwasher wrong. The knives are supposed to go blade up."

Michael laughed out loud. "Okay, good one. Where's James? I'll sign those papers right now. 'You see judge, we were doing fine until a piece of rice stuck to one of the knives. You can't imagine the pain and suffering.' I'd love to hear what your lawyer thinks that's worth in alimony."

Still facing him and not smiling Jennifer said, "I'm serious Michael."

"Then why didn't you accept The Dishwasher Challenge?" That's what Michael called his proposal to settle the argument over the proper way to load the dishwasher. First, he argued, you had to determine if there was even a difference between putting the knives and forks in the rack pointing up or down. If you couldn't tell the difference, then it didn't matter. They would load half the blades and tines facing up and half pointing down. After the wash cycle, they would need some neutral third party to lay out the dishes, say Hannah, who was old enough at the time to help, then they'd come back to see if they could tell the difference. Michael saw her refusal to consider the experiment as proof that he was right, that it didn't really matter and she should just be happy he helped with the housework at all.

"Living with you is unbearable. You're a slob. You throw your clothes everywhere. When you *do* change the toilet paper roll, it's upside down. It doesn't roll off down the wall, you know. It's supposed to come over the top."

"You're not serious?" Michael stammered. He looked around not sure if this scene could really be playing out in his own life. There must be hidden TV cameras somewhere. He recognized another father standing a head taller than the rest of the crowd and took a few steps in his direction. "Hey, Jason!" he shouted.

"Whaddya want, Michael? I'm watching the game here," Jason said. "Emily almost had a breakaway."

"How do you load the dishwasher?"

"What?" Jason gave Michael a look that one would give to a toddler who had just reached into a campfire for a dropped marshmallow. "Get real, Michael. That's women's work."

"No, I'm serious. What about loading the toilet paper dispenser?"

"Dude, that crap don't matter. Pick your battles." Jason went back to watching the game. Amy leaned forward from beside her husband's impressive bulk and gave Michael and Jennifer a pleasant smile and two-finger wave. Until that moment, Michael hadn't realized Amy was at the game, let alone holding Jason's hand, hidden by his formidable profile.

Michael turned his attention back to Jennifer. Her expression was grim as ever. "Why aren't we like them? Is that what you're asking?" Michael said.

"It's a slow death by a thousand tiny cuts, Michael. I'm bleeding here and you don't even notice."

Like all couples on their way to divorce, Michael and Jennifer didn't begin with petty bickering. It wasn't love at first sight, but more like a comfortable jog towards their inevitable union. They met at college.

If the main job of adolescence is to make friends, then the main job of young adulthood is to impress the hell out of them. On paper, we major in subjects like Biology, Economics and Political Science. In practice, we major in sarcasm, ego, and self-righteousness.

Michael and Jason applied to colleges as a team, promising the other they'd only attend a school to which they were both able to matriculate. Michael had the numbers to eventually fulfill his dream of attending medical school. His only limitation was choosing a school that his parents could afford without putting a third mortgage on the farmhouse. Jason had his wrestling scholarships all lined up, so grades weren't much of an issue. Most of the schools at which he interviewed asked if he'd be interested in adding "Outside Linebacker" to his resume, since there was no conflict with the wrestling season. Kansas State University fit the bill for both young men. It was far enough away that they didn't feel like they were still living at home. It was close enough that a weekend trip home could be had for less than a half tank of gas. Two months before graduation they were comfortably committed to become Wildcats following the summer work season.

The first half of their first semester was spent rehashing the subjects they'd dreaded but already mastered in high school. Grades came easy since there were no distractions other than the Xbox in the corner of their tiny dorm room. After October midterms the cabin fever put Michael past his breaking point. One Friday after dinner, the two young men sat in bean bag chairs fighting each other at virtual martial arts.

"Dude, we gotta get out of here. Get some fresh air, or something," Michael said.

"I'm not cheating on Amy," Jason said. "Plus, she might call tonight."

"Dude. You're not serious. And who said anything about cheating?"

"Prepare to be crushed." Jason's character performed an impossible move that caused the equivalent of a gallon of blood to spew from the face of Michael's warrior.

"She ain't gonna call until November. You said yourself, she's out of minutes. Besides, it's just a party. Mingle, have a lite beer, wander around. You might trip over a pile of angst and land on some fun."

"Look. You go ahead, Magellan. See the world, collect your treasures, report back in the morning. Just use a condom." Michael laughed since both he and Jason were virgins, though not for lack of trying. Jason had given Amy a Promise Ring at their high school graduation. He was as much a man of his word as he was a man of giant, size fourteen shoes. Jason only pressed Amy a little, and gently at that. After prom she'd consented to second base which at the time was like a trip to Paris for Jason. She told him to get a job, get her a ring, and a new last name, and she'd think about it.

Michael had remained unattached throughout high school. He'd put multiple girls on his bike route around town, yet they somehow failed to notice the impressive peacock feathers trailing his speeding Huffy bicycle. When they all hit puberty, the same women failed to notice the stationary rims on his ancient and battered Chevy S10. Since arriving on campus, he'd been mistaken for a high school senior on more than one occasion. Upperclassmen working in the administration office kept asking if he was lost or visiting for a tour of the campus. He knew without Jason as his wing man he was wallpaper at any frat party.

"If I win this round, you gotta come with me to the party. At least for an hour."

"How 'bout we arm wrestle, instead?" The proposal was ludicrous as Jason was easily double Michael's size, including biceps larger than his friend's puny thighs. Conversely, Jason was no match for Michael on the flat screen. It was no contest. Michael's warrior defeated Jason's in a puddle of blood. The character lifted his victim, threw him off a cliff, then did a silly victory dance.

The two men left the dorm and headed in the direction of fraternity row. It was like a new chapter of "Goldilocks and the Three Bears." The first house was dead quiet. The only thing missing from its mausoleum-like facade was an eviction notice on the door.

The second house had all the chaos of a street scene from Baghdad. The lawn was littered with the detritus of countless parties. Empty beer cans were strewn like confetti. The landscaping, if it could be termed as such, was beyond salvation. The lawn was represented by random tufts of grass strewn about the hard packed dirt. A tangle of waist-high weeds made a skirt around the foundation of the house. A water-logged plush sofa sat askew on the corner of the lot spilling its contents over like an exploded pumpkin. An oblique crack traversed up the poured concrete steps. The lower half sagged leaving a gap wide enough to lose your cell phone between the five steps. Boards were missing from the porch and those that remained didn't look sturdy enough to support the pile of empty kegs and overflowing garbage cans that were collected on one end. A love seat swing that was meant to be hanging was instead parked idly and leaned up against the front windowsill. Two fraternity brothers dressed in sagging pants and wife beaters, were sharing a bong in plain view of the street. Another with his dreadlocks tucked up into a giant Rastafarian crocheted cap, was passed out or dead. He was seated in a bucket seat, no doubt recycled from a long-defunct sports car, his head lolling off the inadequate headrest. Four other brothers sat on the roof with a water balloon launcher. Two held the high tension straps, one loaded the balloons and the last flung them over the house across the street to land somewhere on sorority row. They all wore the NFL jersey of their favorite football player. The deafening thump of rap music emanated from the two front windows, one ajar, the other broken with a threatening pane angled like the blade on a guillotine. Despite the cultural references, not a single black man could be seen through any of the windows, lounging on the porch or throwing the football around the front yard. "The only thing I'm gonna get in there is a black eye," Michael said.

The third house was just right. A tastefully painted butcher paper sign was taped along the length of the porch railing. It announced a meeting of two houses, one a sorority, both with Sigma in their name. Most importantly, the sign noted, "FRESHMAN WELCOME!" in block letters at the bottom, as if they were expecting a single student. It appeared to be painted with a full-sized paintbrush and was easily visible from across the street.

Despite a handful of people sitting on the grass, the two friends respected the tidy front lawn and took the flower-lined walkway to the fraternity house. Closer to the sign they could make out countless signatures in colored pen in the manner of a workplace birthday card. There was also the inevitable graffiti. "Free Tibet!" in red Sharpie was followed by "…with the purchase of any Pakistan" in green ink. It took Michael a second to get the joke but he smiled and pointed it out to Jason as if the sign alone proved they were in the right place.

Michael dragged Jason up the steps and the two men stopped at the open door to look inside. "Are you sure this is the place to find your destiny?" Jason said.

"Hmm. You may be right. This isn't a party, it's a painting." The room was shoulder-to-shoulder with an even number of men and women. A low hum of voices blended into a steady drone of white noise punctuated by the rare high-pitched giggle. There was no music, and most of the crowd was dressed like they were about to jump into a golf cart. To a person, they all held red plastic cups filled with beer, soft drinks, liquor, or in some cases, all three. "Let's find the kitchen. It's time I started learning how to drink."

Jason rolled his eyes. "Yeah. That'll impress the med schools."

The two men made their way through the crowd in the direction Michael thought the kitchen must be. Daylight failed to penetrate the room more than a couple of steps from the door and their eyes took a moment to adjust. Despite their size differences, it was Michael who did the pushing, excusing, and greeting. "Hey. How are you? Nice night, huh? Excuse me. Thanks. Alright, Sigma blah blah."

Half way across the living room he tripped over a lump and landed on all fours. Turning around to find the obstruction he was shocked to see a comely coed lying flat on her back. "What the…" he stammered. She wore penny loafers, a conservative hound's tooth skirt that reached to her kneecaps and a short-sleeved sweater, buttoned to the neck. Her medium-brown hair was all one length, smoothed to her head and pulled to the side in a severe, asymmetrical ponytail. Even in the dark room, with her eyes closed, Michael could see the excessive amount of blue eye shadow smeared on her upper lids.

Jason stood on the other side of the body shrugging his shoulders with his palms to the sky. Michael knelt down by her right shoulder and started his Basic Life Support protocol. If one thing would look good on a medical school application, it would be how he saved a choking coed during his freshman year. "Hey, does anyone know this girl? Somebody call 9-1-1!"

Michael tried to rouse her by shaking her shoulder. Not a single person in the roomed moved, including the girl on the floor. If anything, the noise became louder. "I can't believe you people," Michael shouted in exasperation.

He bent his head, put his ear to her mouth, and tried to see if her chest was rising but the noise in the room and the lack of light prevented him from making an accurate assessment. "She's got a pulse, but I don't know if she's breathing," he said to no one.

Michael pinched her nose, tilted her head back and her mouth flopped open. He attempted to give her a rescue breath, but no air went in. Her lip gloss tasted like fruity bubble gum. "I think she might be choking!" He looked in her mouth but couldn't see an obstruction. Rather than try to lift her and perform the Heimlich maneuver, he put his mouth to hers for another try. If he could force the obstruction down, probably a wad of gum, then she'd at least be able to breathe from one lung, just like they'd taught him in his certification class. He took a deeper breath this time, but was unable to exhale into her mouth. Instead of the passive stiffness of a resuscitation dummy, Michael was met with the mobile lips and then the searching tongue of the girl on the floor. He tried to pull away in surprise, but she caught him around the neck with one arm and pulled him in for another impromptu French kiss.

Under any other circumstance Michael would have been delighted with the interchange. As it was, he'd been played for a fool and was in no mood for jokes. His heart was pounding from the adrenaline of his attempted rescue and the embarrassment of being the butt of a joke. The din of voices in the room stopped long enough for every head to turn towards him and laugh. It lasted only a moment and everyone went back to their plastic cups and their deep discussions of Marxism. For Michael it felt like reliving his entire four years of high school in five seconds. The girl propped herself up on her elbows. She extended a hand to Michael, who was getting up to leave. "Help me up?" the girl said.

"I don't think so."

"Whatever. If it'll make you feel any better, I'll split the pot with you. Or, if you prefer, I'll go fuck off." She rose awkwardly to her feet with the skirt clinging to her thighs. She made a show of brushing herself off starting with her shoulders, then her chest, and finishing with smoothing the skirt over her thighs. She walked a few steps to the other side of the room where a gaggle of similarly dressed women was watching the scene with identical postures and red plastic cups. Michael watched her approach the group and saw that they all had the same double smear of blue eye shadow and jaunty ponytail. The former victim stopped in front of the group and held out her hand. There was much fumbling of cups and purses until each of the women had paid her share. She then returned to Michael and threw the wad of bills at him, showering him in green confetti. Indignant, she turned again, walked past the other women and into the kitchen.

Michael retrieved and pocketed the bills, then followed her, preparing to give her a piece of his mind. When he entered the kitchen she was emptying the last drops of a bottle of Manischewitz into three plastic cups. She handed one to Michael, and another to Jason who had followed them into the kitchen. "I once went to this pizza joint out in the middle of nowhere called Anthony's or Angela's or something. We were on a field trip to the geographical center of the country, up near Lebanon. We stop in this little hick town, 'cause there's nothing around for miles and the whole class is starving. Anyway, they've got a silver dollar nailed to the hardwood floor."

"Antonio's," Michael said.

"What?"

"Yeah, it's outside Bellaire," Jason said.

"So you've been there."

"We're *from* there," Michael said.

"Well. Then you know. Only a tourist would try to pick up the silver dollar. All the locals know it's nailed to the floor. Get it?"

"I fail to see your point."

"I made a bet. I told the sisters I could get someone to fall for the Silver Dollar trick. Didn't it strike you as a little odd that you were the only one who came to my rescue?" She looked from Michael to Jason. "And what about you? Don't you know to help a damsel in distress? You stood there like a totem pole."

"He's the premed stud. I'm just a lowly poly-sci major."

"Oh, god! No!" She covered her ears with one hand holding the cup of wine. "La la la la. Promise me, please. No talk of majors, high schools, or astrology, thank you. You've *got* to be more interesting than that, or I'm going to go back and lay down on the living room floor again."

"How 'bout we start over with introductions, then?" Michael Johnson said. They all stated their names and shifted cups to shake hands. Jennifer Smith raised hers to the center of the group and they bumped cups in a toast to nothing.

"L'chaim!" Jennifer said and took a big gulp. "To life!"

"Are you Jewish?"

"No, but this wine is." The men both choked down a tiny sip. Neither of them drank to any degree in high school.

Michael made a face when the alcohol vapor rose from his stomach to the back of his throat and then out his nose. "Yeesh. It starts all innocent like a juice box, then tears out your tonsils."

"It reminds me of working on my truck," Jason Williams said. "Brake fluid, oil, antifreeze. I can't quite place it."

"Oh man, you guys really are a couple of rookies, aren't you? I thought you back country hicks were all weaned from the teat straight to daddy's moonshine." The two men looked at each other. "This fine distilled beverage," she said holding her cup aloft, "is the cheapest buzz on the block."

"It tastes more like the Welch's company started making lighter fluid."

"And a fine palette you have, Dr. Michael. We're enjoying the kosher labors of the fine people at Manischewitz." She reached back to the counter to retrieve the empty bottle and held it aloft, showing them the label. "Not less than 51% Concord and a whopping twenty-two proof. Try finding a wine cooler half this potent at twice the price and I'll wash your socks."

"Is that Hebrew?" Michael said squinting at the label.

"You bet it is, my soon-to-be-drunk friend. The sure sign of a high quality beverage. Although I guess I should have asked you if you have any allergies. It contains sulfites. You're not allergic, are you?" The two men shook their heads. "Well, then, party on!" Jennifer said and raised her cup again, "To Bacchus!" The men looked at each other for the second time. "The god of wine? Oh, you newbies really are going to need a guide."

Jason Williams reached into his pocket and pulled out his cell phone. It was a text message from Amy. "Hey, guys. As much fun as I'm having, I'm gonna go find a quiet spot and give Amy a call. You're cool?" he said to Michael more as a statement than a question.

"Yeah, sure. I've got my very own guide," Michael said dripping sarcasm. He gestured to Jennifer with both hands, like a game show hostess presenting the grand prize. Jason thanked Jennifer for the drink but put his cup on the kitchen counter. He punched Michael in the shoulder much harder than was necessary and left through the living room.

"Well, this wine's not gonna drink itself," Jennifer said as she picked up Jason's drink and divided the contents between their cups. "Jason's a cute kid. Gonna make someone a fine wife one day."

"So, tell me, Jennifer. Can we drop the post-ironic banter and pretend we're real people?"

"Sure doc. But if at any time tonight you become a bore, I'm leaving to find someone else to resuscitate me."

"See? That's what I mean. Can't you just, I don't know, talk like a normal person?"

"Geez, doc, yeah. But if you're gonna get lucky tonight, you'll have to loosen up a little."

Michael looked at Jennifer and thought a minute. "You're doing it again. Can't you turn it off? I'm not a doctor. Not yet anyway. I don't appreciate being the butt of your little sorority pranks. And I didn't come here to be insulted. Jason was right." Michael poured the rest of his wine into her cup, threw his empty into the sink and turned to leave. Over his shoulder he said, "I thought it might just be the wine talking, but now, I'm not so sure. See you around."

Jennifer poured her cup in the sink and rushed out of the kitchen to catch Michael. She grabbed him by the arm in the middle of the living room and started making profuse apologies. She was sorry for insulting him and his friend. She admitted to being a little tipsy. She begged him for a second chance. She explained she was from a small Kansas town herself and meant nothing by the country hick remarks. "I just get a little nervous around new guys. Maybe I come on a little strong. I talk too much. I've got diarrhea of the mouth. But you're different. You're not like other guys. Mostly, they just go with it and try to outdo me. You seem really nice. You are nice, aren't you? I mean, you haven't been bragging about yourself, or trying to out-drink me or anything. Please give me another chance. Please, please, please."

Michael stared at her with pursed lips but didn't answer. He took her by the hand and led her to the porch. A couple was making out on one half of the porch swing like their lives depended on it, oblivious to the crowd seated around them, on the lawn and steps. "Hey, you guys," Michael said as he sat on the end of the swing. "Mind if we join you?"

The woman got up in an indignant huff, grabbed her boyfriend by the hand and stomped into the house. The crowd on the lawn and steps applauded as they left. Somebody said, "She's always doing that. Like she gets extra credit for Anthropology 101."

"Yeah, like she's majoring in Promiscuous."

"Last week it was some other guy," another co-ed said by way of explanation.

"But you gotta admit, Bookstore's got a nice rack."

"Bookstore?" Michael said.

"Yeah, she's got 'Used' written all over her."

"Yeah, and she's got extended weekend hours during home football games!"

The crowd laughed and went back to their previous conversations. Jennifer joined Michael on the porch swing, sitting a friendly distance apart. Without the pressure to perform on either side, the conversation flowed easily. They discovered that they had much more in common than their initial meeting would have suggested. Both came from small, blue collar towns of less than ten thousand in rural Kansas. Both had large families by modern standards and plenty of pets over the years. For vacations they had camped at some of the same state parks and reservoirs, in some cases during the same summers. Neither of them had been out of the country. Jennifer found herself talking freely about the forbidden topics of majors and high school. They were both freshman and wanted to help people in some capacity for a career. He wanted to be a doctor, he just didn't know what kind. She wanted to be a teacher, she just didn't know what kind. Jennifer was happy for the sincerity of his interest. Michael wasn't there to hook up, nor was he just nodding and waiting for his turn to brag about himself.

An hour into their conversation, Jennifer had a revelation. "You're completely without guile, aren't you? A wet-behind-the-ears, babe in the woods, pure as the driven snow."

"What's guile?"

"It's like you were dropped from an alien ship from the planet of Polite. Or a time machine sent you here from 1920. Or maybe 1967. You're not a hippie, are you?"

"Huh?"

Jennifer spelled the word guile for Michael. "It comes from the same root word as guilt. It means duplicity or cunning. You've got *none* of it."

"Just because I can carry on an intelligent conversation?"

"It's different. More than that."

"I can do Smart Ass, if you'd prefer."

"No. Please don't. You're not like any other guy I've ever met."

"Now I'm the one who's supposed to take two points off for cliche, right?"

"Sorry. But it's really true." Jennifer turned to face him and took his right hand in both of hers. She squinted directly into his hazel blue eyes as if she would be able to read some fine print written on his corneas. "I've got a theory about you," she said. Jennifer paused, then after a moment said, "Tell you later," but she kept a firm grip on his hand.

Michael pressed her about her high school achievements and she finally relented to list her many impressive accomplishments: class president, captain of the debate team, multiple Varsity letters in three sports, editor of the yearbook. Michael couldn't help himself and he told her how impressed he was, even calling her an overachiever and hinting that she might be out of his league.

"I've always hated that label. Overachiever, underachiever. Aren't we always taught that we all have the same potential? That we can all grow up to be president?" Michael shrugged, more or less in agreement. "Well, then, what's the big deal?"

"It's all semantics," Michael said. "I'm just saying good job. There's still sex-discrimination out there."

"Sure, I've got a two-page resume, but at least you went to prom."

"You're kidding. At our school it was like, mandatory. If you didn't have a steady girlfriend you were almost required by law to take your sister. I just went with Amy's best friend so we could double with Jason. What was your story? Some kind of political protest?"

"You might say that." When Michael didn't say anything, Jennifer felt forced to continue. "Okay, okay, twist my arm. He kept pressuring me to, you know, *do it* on Prom Night. So I cancelled on him. Watched old movies and ate junk food with my mom instead. Got a good night's rest."

"The cad!"

"Ugh. I'm no prude. I like a good kisser as much as the next girl, but I'll do it when I'm good and ready, you know? It's not like I'm waiting until I'm married, like those hypocrites in Celibacy Club. When they lost their virginity they found out it didn't live up to the hype or their period was late and it freaked 'em out. So they start a club, like it'll restore their hymens. I've just got a high standard, does that make me a nun?"

"I just don't understand why it's got to be such a public issue," Michael said. "Isn't anything private anymore? I'm not just talking about bragging rights, or the endless STD talks in Health Class. I'm talking about society in general."

"Well, that's another thing we have in common—our purity."

"I wouldn't have guessed as much after that stunt you pulled," Michael said, gesturing with a thumb back towards the house.

"You wouldn't believe the names I've been called. But trust me, I'll know when the time is right."

The evening gave way to twilight. A few scattered clouds reflected the waning of the sun, from orange to red, to a watery pink, then light gray. Stars began to show, but not enough to form any familiar constellations. "So. Tell me your theory?" Michael said it like a question.

"I've had another thought. I've been trying to figure out if my theory is right or not, but it's a hard hypothesis to test. Introducing the theory itself could disrupt the testing of its validity." Michael waited. "Just telling it to you could provoke a response that keeps me from finding out if I'm right. Then it occurred to me. Your response will give me the confirmation I need."

"I can wait."

"Oh. I think you may have just proven my theory. Darn it. I hate being right all the time."

"Ha, ha, you're hilarious," Michael giggled.

"Here's the theory. And as always, when talking to me, you'll find there's a prelude, okay?"

"Okay."

"Here goes: you know how everyone, and I mean *every*one, says they like people?" Michael nodded. "Like, who goes to a job interview and says, 'You know sir, I really *hate* people. I was hoping for a position away from humans in the dead letter department at the Post Office. That way I won't have to talk to anyone,'" Jennifer said in her male-sounding announcer's voice.

"Uh-huh."

"Well, I think you really. Like. People."

Michael shrugged. "Of course I like people. I've been one all my life. No one better to invite to a birthday party."

"I don't do birthday parties." Jennifer quickly put a hand to her mouth but the words were already out. She knew it made her sound crazy, but she had her reasons. She might tell him later in their relationship, but not likely.

"What? Are you Mormon? Jehovah's Witness? We know you're not Jewish."

"Never mind that. Back to people and your love of them. I mean more than that. Hundreds of guys at this school say they want to be doctors. They all wrote about helping humanity and saving lives in their admissions essays. But you really *do* like people. I hope Jason appreciates what a good friend you are. You haven't been bragging at all. You really do want to hear about me. It's beyond flattering. I'm stunned."

"Well, thank you. I guess I never thought about it."

"And there it is!" Jennifer exclaimed. "I was right! If I was wrong you would have said something ironic or cool, like, 'Yea, I'm the male Mother Teresa,' which would have completely ruined my night. But not you. You're nice like the sky is blue, it doesn't have to try. And it's because you really like other people. You're the last thing on your own mind. Fish don't think about swimming, they just do it. That's why I say you're guileless."

"Okay. What about you? Besides your constant metaphors and similes?"

"Hey, I thought you were a Biology major?"

"Never mind that. Answer the question."

"Ah, you'll find out plenty about me soon enough. I'm not done with you yet." Jennifer shifted her gaze from the stars back to Michael's face again. "Here's the kicker: You've let me hold your hand for over an hour and you're not even sweating. It's gotta be eighty degrees out still and your fingers are as dry as a baby's freshly dusted bottom."

"You have a point?"

"Yeah. You really *don't* have an ulterior motive. You're not trying to put any moves on me. Every guy who's come up those steps has tried to look up my skirt. You haven't even been staring at my sweater. Although I did catch you looking once, which was nice, because I was worried you might be gay." Michael laughed out loud. "See? If you had a plan, you'd be nervous and sweating. But it takes confidence to be yourself. Really, just to be yourself."

"Who am I going to impress? There's always someone taller, more handsome, richer, better grades. I'm just enjoying the moment, you know? Very Zen."

"That's what I mean. You're above temptation. You should run for office."

The night wore on but the conversation never lagged. After midnight a Sigma fraternity brother walked up the steps with a case full of Budweiser. He reached into the carton and passed the cans to anyone within arms reach, shouting "Go, Wildcats!" By his size and demeanor it was clear to all that he was on the football team. At the top of the porch steps he tossed a beer each to Jennifer and Michael on the swing. Jennifer had to release Michael's hand so they could catch their respective beers without injury. They giggled, cracked the cans in unison, clinked the rims and each took a sip. "I hate beer," Michael said and they both laughed again.

"First one, huh?"

"Yeah. How did you know?"

"Just a lucky guess. Hold on." Jennifer got up from the swing and disappeared into the front door. She came out a minute later with two pretzel rods in her hand. She slipped off her loafers and resumed her seat on the swing, curling up her legs like the Little Mermaid. "Here. These should help the beer. Pick one. Short pretzel has to take a dare."

Michael looked at her outstretched arm and the fist holding two pretzel rods. One pretzel was sticking up an inch higher, but she covered the bottoms with her delicate fingers. "Hmm. An interesting proposition. Do I know you well enough after four hours to make the right choice? If I do, will I use that knowledge to choose the short pretzel on purpose and let you choose the dare? Or will I choose the long one because I have something devious in mind that I'll dare you to perform? Is the short pretzel really the shorter of the two? Is Jennifer Smith the kind of girl who'd try to trick a guy?"

"I'll never lie to you," Jennifer said with a straight face.

Michael reached out and touched the pretzel that was sticking out higher, then grabbed the lower pretzel between his thumb and index finger. Jennifer kept her fist around both pretzels, not letting him see the bottoms. "Is that your final guess? I'm about to learn a lot more about you than your major."

Michael nodded and she released her grip. His pretzel was cracked at the bottom, a full inch shorter than hers. "What's my dare?"

"Kiss me."

"Really."

"Yeah." Jennifer put her beer on the porch and balanced her pretzel on top. She took Michael's beer and pretzel and did the same. In one deft maneuver she pulled out her ponytail holder and shook her hair out in a fragrant cascade. "I'm getting chilly. Hold my hand again."

She took his hand in hers and tucked it against her side like a running back would protect a football. Jennifer put her head on Michael's shoulder and waited. With his free hand, Michael raised her chin to look into her eyes. She gave him a slight, toothless smile, closed her eyes and pursed her lips. Michael lowered his kiss to meet hers like a butterfly landing on a rose. They stayed in that position, no tongues, no groping, for a full minute. When they broke, Michael saw that Jennifer's eyes were still closed, the same dreamy smile on her face. "I thought so," she said.

The rest of the night was spent in the same easy conversation. They finished their beers one sip at a time over four hours, sucking the pretzels like fine Cuban cigars. The crowd on the lawn and porch gradually dispersed leaving them to their whispered conversation. The two must have nodded off because the next thing Michael knew it was daylight and there was a spot of saliva on the front of his shirt. Jennifer was still holding his hand for warmth, her legs curled up on the porch swing. Not wanting to break the mood, he waited for Jennifer to wake on her own. He needn't have worried because her cell phone let out a tinkly jingle.

"What time is it?" Jennifer said, reaching for a slim phone tucked in her waistband.

"I don't know, but the amount of daylight would suggest that the night is over."

"Breakfast is on me," Jennifer said putting on her loafers. "C'mon." She got up off the swing, grabbed Michael's hand and bounded down the porch steps. She kept up her power walking pace and in a few blocks they reached the edge of the campus. She was dragging him with such gusto Michael didn't even have the breath to ask where she was taking him.

At the intersection of Second and Main, the idyllic tree-lined streets of the campus gave way to the anonymous retail environment of any suburb. Mature pine trees gave way to tall street lamps. Verdant lawns became parking lots and driveways. The regal administration and academic buildings became big box chain stores and fast food restaurants. The cool temperature of the shaded porch gave way to the building heat of a typical Kansas day. Near a driveway to the enormous parking lot of a discount store, three Sigma sorority sisters—a buxom blonde, a statuesque brunette, and a glowing redhead—were holding up hand-painted signs. They were wearing tiny Daisy Duke-style shorts and Sigma T-shirts torn in strategic locations and tied at the rib cage. The signs read "Truck Wash FREE!" and "Car Wash $5,000." A third banner sign was tied between chairs and announced the annual Sigma Sorority Charity Fund Raiser.

"The Kappas sold flowers at Homecoming, the game and dance. It was a joke. They raised, like, five hundred dollars. We're going to bury them."

"Yeah, all you need is one car to come and get washed."

"Overhead was ridiculous and their margin was puny. It was blistering hot at the game. Half the inventory wilted by noon."

"Sounds a bit pricy for a single car."

"Oh, that was my idea. Somebody wanted to put 'Donations Accepted' but you've got to be a little more imaginative. Obviously, we're not charging cars five grand, but they always stop and ask. The car wash is just a loss leader. Plus, everyone around here drives a truck. C'mon, I'm famished."

They walked past the driveway where a man was getting out of a gleaming, silver Chevy S10, a newer model than Michael's by a decade. He handed the car keys to another sorority sister, this one wearing electric pink hot pants. She sported the same jaunty, asymmetrical ponytail that Michael had seen on every woman at the mixer. Her Sigma shirt was torn in the general shape of a wife beater undershirt and showed most of her pink bra. She looked surprisingly graceful in her six-inch Plexiglas stripper heels. Jennifer and Michael watched her gesture to the owner of the truck who listened intently and watched her as she pointed out his entertainment options while the vehicle was being washed. She'd drive it to the cleaning crew, through the human car wash, then park it on the opposite side of the lot where he could pick it up at his convenience, donations gladly accepted. He helped her into the cab and she gave a perky wave, then put the truck in gear and eased it into the parking lot.

"Sort of obvious, isn't it," Michael said.

"What?"

"Sex sells."

"Remind me to have you fill out a comment card to help us plan future events."

Jennifer led Michael up the driveway of the parking lot and into the fracas. A dizzying array of booths was set up in the style of a street fair. There was a table set up selling discount subscriptions to men's magazines. A group of women dressed as NFL referees in black shorts was giving free hair cuts and neck massages. The retail store had a display where current and future hunters could augment their collections with a new rifle or shotgun. A state game warden was dressed in full uniform to answer questions. He was also overseeing the sale of permits for whatever a man might desire to shoot and kill, mount or eat: pheasant, duck, deer, doe, pronghorn, you name it. They had information on rifles, handguns large enough to take down an elk, muzzle loaders, bows, and shotguns. The next booth was all about fishing: river, lake, reservoir, live bait, lures, and fly. You could purchase a new rod, find a secret spot on a county map, buy a new boat or trolling motor, and exchange your favorite trout recipes. A car audio store had set up a display with huge speakers blaring nonstop country and western music. A local restaurant was selling their line of barbecue sauces specially formulated to complement your favorite game.

"It's like Disney World, except the all-male version," Michael said.

"Exactly."

At the back of the parking lot and near a small field, three long tables were set up for breakfast. Sorority sisters in aprons and little else were handing out paper plates and pancakes to a long line of hungry men. As they proceeded down the buffet, the plates were loaded with pancakes, maple syrup, strawberries and a mountain of whipped cream. The men were directed to a casual grouping of round tables under a tent. "Wait here, I'll cut the line and get us some food," Jennifer said.

Michael looked around and found the largest display of all, a triple-sized booth displaying the benefactor of the entire event, the local animal shelter. He perused the signs which could be easily read from yards away, extolling the virtues of the work done by the shelter. The display explained in only happy terms how donations were used to rescue, shelter, feed, and eventually find a suitable companion—not owner, since we don't *own* our pets—for the animals. They rescued mostly dogs, but also cats and exotic pets. Michael noted there was no mention of the fact that sometimes the most humane solution was to put the animal down, but he would admit, that procedure costs money, too.

Jennifer returned with the plates. "I hope you like strawberries. Let's have a seat."

"Hey, thanks. I didn't realize how hungry I was. Considering my last meal was a sip of Manischewitz, a soggy pretzel and one half of a flat beer."

They sat at an empty table and started in on breakfast. A few parking spots away, a lone sorority girl was throwing a soggy tennis ball onto the empty, adjacent field. With each throw a spastic border collie would rifle after it, catching it before it bounced three times. Jennifer explained that he was purebred. He had a shiny, healthy-looking black and white coat, but the darling look of a mutt with a black circle around one bright, blue eye. His energy was boundless. Despite her clumsy throws, sometimes only a few yards, the collie would dutifully retrieve the ball and drop it at her feet.

"Nice dog." Michael said between mouthfuls. "Maybe she should use a tennis racket so he could get a little more exercise."

"She's not left-handed."

"Huh?"

"That's Candy. She's a trip, right?" The woman was dressed similarly to the other sisters, but was even more at risk of falling out of both her top and bottom. Jennifer pointed her plastic fork to the pancake griddle. "I talked to Laura, our chapter president and she said Checkers is the third dog we've found a home for."

"Wow."

Jennifer consulted her cell phone. "Yeah. Not bad for 8:30am."

"Wow, again. I'm impressed."

"See, we had tryouts for Ball Girl. Candy's got the goods, if you know what I mean. Plus, she plays third base for the softball team.

Got a sixty mile-per-hour fastball, but no control underhand, so they put her at the hot corner. Anyway, her throw looked more like a major league bullpen ace. I suggested she try it left-handed. You can't argue with the results."

"Um," Michael looked around. Most of the other men were not eating their pancakes. Candy bent over at the waist. She wound up with the saliva-smeared ball in her wrong hand and heaved it towards the field. Her release was a tad early and the ball shot straight up in the air. She landed hard on her wrong foot and every curve of her young body went off in a different direction. Checkers caught it in mid-air without moving and dropped it on her foot for another throw. This time she over-corrected holding the ball too long. It hit the pavement with a loud, wet splat and bounced off into the field. The effect on her intimidating body was the same. Few if any pancakes were being consumed.

"Laura said guys are writing checks and asking about other breeds. It's a win-win."

"But don't you feel a little, I don't know, exploited?"

"Candy's got a 3.75 GPA. She aced the LSAT. Her biggest problem this year is deciding which law school she wants to go to. If you could get up the courage to talk to her, I'm sure she'd agree, there's no harm in our sales tactics." Michael put another bite of strawberry and pancake in his mouth and waited. "Those are the laws of the game, Michael. Men and women should be able to get along better than they do in all aspects of society. This is about more than voting rights. Any sane person who's paying attention will tell you that the world is an unfair place to women since the time of, oh, I don't know, forever. We're all feminists, yourself included. You love people, women are people. The fact that you're even worried about exploitation makes you all right in my book."

Michael had no answer. He looked around the parking lot. Women were washing cars, wet from head to toe. They were throwing soapy sponges at each other, seemingly oblivious to the stares of the men all around. The country music was blaring out a sing-along song and three girls stopped scrubbing, held up their brushes like microphones and sang the tune arm-in-arm. When the song was over, a chant went up, every woman including Candy stopped what they were doing and shouted what sounded like a mix of Greek, Spanish and Pig Latin. Hoots and hollers went up from all corners. "Go, Wildcats!" A new song started and they all returned to their various jobs. "Hey, how come you're not hosting a booth, or washing cars?"

"I worked my butt off to set this thing up."

"You did all this?"

"It took me a month and a million phone calls. 'Cause of my work on the high school yearbook I was volunteered to head the fund raiser. Someone said 'car wash' and it grew from there. I knew if we wanted to make any real money we couldn't work our collective ass off in the hot sun for three bucks a car. You ever try to get free use of a three acre parking lot from a headless—no, mindless—corporation? Even for charity?"

"I can't say I have," Michael said.

"Let me tell you, it ain't easy. I had to convince the manager *and* his accountant that any presumed sales losses during our event could be written off as a charitable donation. Truth is, they're probably above average today, because of all the guys we're bringing in. Then they tried to jam me on the water hook-up, until I promised them we'd keep in under one hundred thousand gallons and use biodegradable soap. And who would have thought the city would charge us a sewer surcharge?" Michael let out a whistle. "Look around, just count the tables, let alone the chairs. You think they walked here on their own while we were at the Sigma mixer? Laura couldn't believe my cell phone bill, but I think she'll be happy to help me pay it, when it's all said and done. I'll grab a towel for the last couple of hours, but mostly I just need to finish up the accounting when it's all over."

"You're the Donald Trump of charity events. No wonder you don't have a boyfriend." When Jennifer didn't answer right away, Michael turned his gaze from the car washing to his host. Her eyes were squinted and her lips were narrowed as if she were trying to decipher whether his comments were complimentary or not. Michael watched her face soften, but still she didn't speak. "I didn't mean anything by it. Sorry if it sounded insensitive. I'm really, really impressed. Really."

Another moment passed and Michael feared he'd ruined their wonderful evening and morning with his offhand remark. Finally she spoke. "You're absolutely right," Jennifer said. "There's a cliche that no great thing was ever accomplished by committee. Well, the other side of it is the people who get things done. That's me."

"They also say that well-behaved women rarely make history," Michael said trying to recover lost ground.

"Touche." Jennifer stirred her soggy pancakes and syrup in a lazy circle. "But that bumper sticker does nothing for those women after they're history themselves."

For Michael, her comment was the final puzzle piece to realizing her true nature. If light bulbs of insight were real, the spotlight above his head would have rivaled the Gotham City Bat Signal. Jennifer had it all, as they say; smarts, looks, and a future of unlimited possibility. Her success was only limited by where she chose to aim. The tragedy was that she had only one desire to fulfill but it had nothing to do with publicly recognized accomplishments. Despite all of her outward success, Jennifer still lacked that which she most needed to acquire: a deep and lasting human connection. To Michael, Jennifer possessed the kind of self-assurance he could only dream of having. Yet, this woman was lonely. There was a missing piece to her sense of self, and that piece depended on the connection to another person. It didn't have to be a boyfriend, lover, or husband, but another person who understood her need and was willing to be there for her.

After a moment of silence that was more comfortable than it should have been, he spoke. "I will be your friend." Then realizing how ridiculous it sounded, he made the corny declaration worse by trying to qualify the assertion. "I mean, if you want a friend, that is. Of course. But that's up to you."

"Shut up," Jennifer said giggling. She took Michael's right hand in her left and held it tightly by the fingertips, palm up, across the table. With her right hand she wiped up the remainders of their sodden, sticky breakfasts and smashed their palms together making an obscene noise and a gooey mess. Blobs of pancake residue and cold syrup dripped from their clenched hands onto the paper plates. She stared directly into Michael's eyes. "Friends," she said. "No bullshit. I said I'd never lie to you and I meant it. I still mean it. No matter where this goes, who you date, or get married to and have fifteen kids with, I'm going to remember this day for the rest of my life."

"Why is that?"

"Because for the first time ever, someone said it. People get married, wear rings, but then take them off when they go on a business trip to Vegas. High school friends sign yearbooks, but then give endless excuses about how life got too busy, or the kids take too much time or work is too demanding. It's only a marriage or friendship in theory, because they never say it. People never say it. But you said it. You said it. And what's more, I believe it. I believe you."

Jennifer Smith and Michael Johnson didn't date the rest of their undergraduate years, they simply were. It was never published in the

Campus newspaper, but their relationship was obvious to any casual observer even in the absence of any public displays of affection. That they would later have a long-lasting and fulfilling marriage was inevitable.

3

Penalty Kick

The soccer game proceeded despite the indifference of Michael and Jennifer. They both stared over the field as Hannah was substituted in, then out again, registering nothing of the action. Michael stood surrounded in a haze of disbelief. He couldn't imagine how they'd come to this place after such a short time. Ten years had passed like the blink of an eye.

Jennifer stood rock still, arms crossed and legs apart like the doorman for an exclusive night club. She knew her previous complaints were minor, even petty. Toilet paper rolls and dishwasher fights might break up a lesser marriage, or cause the rare tension around the time of her period, but theirs was on life support. Where other marriages might have a paper cut, theirs was bleeding from a major artery. If marriage counseling could fix marital heartburn, theirs was a Code Blue. Nothing short of a major resuscitation was going to save it. One element was gnawing at her daily since she found out about it over eight years prior. It made her sick to break the silence to remind Michael. "You had an affair."

"What? You're delusional," Michael said in his immediate defense mode. "I've put every spare minute into this marriage. This family. When did I have time for an affair?" The concept was ludicrous.

"That Katy slut, at the hospital. During the snowstorm."

"Huh?" Michael turned to face his accuser, but Jennifer spoke out of the side of her mouth pretending to watch the girls bounce the ball back and forth at midfield.

"Don't act so innocent. The nurse. The annoying, perky one. You know full well what I'm talking about. Kendra or Kelly. Whatever."

"You mean Kathy? Don't be ridiculous. She's a child. And even if I did, which I didn't, but let's suppose for the sake of argument, why bring it up now? That was eight, nine years ago."

"Exactly. Kathy. Just further proof that you know who I'm talking about and that I'm right," she said as if no evidence were needed for such an accusation. "You probably screwed her in a broom closet. Face it. Even you want it over. As much as I do."

"I can't believe what I'm hearing. How am I supposed to prove I'm innocent? Next you'll tell me I'm a Communist." For Michael it was one thing to accuse him of being difficult to live with. It was another to claim he'd had an affair. He loved Jennifer and only Jennifer. Their life together was beyond anything he could have imagined for himself. In the lottery of life he thought himself very lucky to be a four-time winner; great wife, wonderful daughter, excellent health and a good job. He turned to Jennifer and held her firmly by the shoulders forcing her to face him. "It's not fair to accuse me of something like that. I've never broken our vows. And who told you I did? I'll bust his nose."

It was Jennifer's turn to laugh. If ever there was an embodiment of the cliche, "I'm a lover, not a fighter" it was Michael. The idea of him defending his honor through physical means was comical. But she understood what he meant by making the claim. He had denied the event enough over the years it was as if it had never happened, so it was up to Jennifer to remind him. The affair was a scab on their marriage that had turned out to be cancerous. Now the cancer had become malignant, spread to the major organs and was killing its host. For Michael Johnson and Jennifer Smith, it was time to end it. The life support of their denial wasn't doing anything to save the marriage, only prolong its inevitable demise. "If you must know, it was Barbara Vickers who told me."

"Barbara Vickers…"

"Yes. Barbara Vickers."

"…of the sorghum dynasty?"

"Yes. Sorghum. Not to mention sunflowers and a little bit of wheat. More importantly, school board president since before we were born."

"…and nuttier than squirrel shit."

"Michael!" Jennifer scolded him for swearing and looked around to see if any other parents had heard.

"Oh, please. You couldn't come up with a better name? You do realize she's been dead for ten years, right?"

"Not exactly. She died the year I was pregnant with Hannah. Remember the big storm?"

"So?" Michael was making no effort to put the pieces together, he was so sure of his innocence that her argument couldn't possibly be going anywhere sane.

"Sure, she'd lost a step at the end, but she still attended every meeting of the board. She helped me get some ideas through committee and our daughter is benefitting from those changes as we speak."

Michael rolled his eyes. It was another of their fundamental disagreements. As an educator, Jennifer believed that even elementary school was crucial to one's future life. The better the foundation, the stronger the performance in high school, college and beyond. In fact, she argued, it was more important than college, since without a good foundation, the rest of the educational building couldn't even be finished. An exceptional student wasn't born and bred, they were created slowly by caring hands from the time the first bedtime story was recited. Nobody woke up in medical school and started saving lives.

In contrast, Michael believed that schools were interchangeable, after all, they all had access to the same books and common knowledge. Algebra in some swanky private school was the same as the algebra taught in some dirt-floored hut in middle Africa. It was how the student applied himself that made all the difference. And further, there were some kids who just weren't any good at math. Other students didn't like art or history. Expecting them all to excel at every subject matter would be like telling a lawyer he was no good if he couldn't also operate a tow truck.

Michael knew his wife's communication style well enough not to begin the education argument again. He knew Jennifer wasn't consciously trying to change the subject. Somewhere in her female mind, mentioning the fact that Jennifer's hard work on the board was benefitting their daughter added truth to the accusation that he'd had an affair. Saying that those benefits were in part bestowed by a now-deceased, deeply demented 90-year old figurehead on the school board, meant that anything else the crazy old lady said was also true. If Michael rose to the bait of her new topic, that would prove his guilt. He'd be ignoring the obvious topic of his infidelity in an attempt change the subject and avoid being caught. Such was the logic of being married. Her subconscious, emotion-based method of arguing was one reason Michael kept the date of her menstrual period in an email reminder to himself every month.

"I'm sure you and Mrs. Vickers together have revolutionized elementary education. That doesn't excuse the fact that she's accused me without proof. That's slander, hateful gossip."

"So. You deny it?"

"Of course I deny it. When have I ever lied to you? What if I said Jason told me you had an affair?"

"Don't change the subject. Mrs. Vickers and I were good friends. She was like a mother to me at times and I trust her word. The question is not why I'm bringing it up now. It's why you bothered to stay with me after obviously falling for that slut."

"Wait. That doesn't make any sense. If I didn't want you after that, why am I still here? Why wouldn't I just leave? By your logic, the fact that I didn't leave you should prove my innocence! Plus, I told you what happened, which was nothing. She was a confused kid. We were both stressed but nothing happened. You gotta trust me. Maybe there's a point where love comes with a little faith and trust in your partner."

Soon after Michael started his job at St. Bernadette's Hospital, he and Jennifer decided to have The Talk. It was the topic both were avoiding, but it qualified as the Official Elephant In The Room. When would they start their family planning? How many boys, girls, and Golden Retrievers would they have? Who would take off from work to raise the kids or could they, would they, want to afford to put them in day care? It seemed reasonable to the lovers that Jennifer should both get pregnant and have the babies. After that decision, the exact details were somewhat up in the air.

When Michael had plans to become a doctor, Jennifer had her own ideas about where and how they'd live. They married the summer after college. It was as easy as walking across the stage and accepting their diplomas. Jennifer had her teaching degree and was considered by most of the school districts she'd researched to be over-qualified. They suggested she get an advanced degree, become an administrator, even run for office. She told them she planned to change education in the United States one child at a time. One great student, she argued, could change a classroom. One classroom could change a school. One school could change a district. One district could change a state. One state could revolutionize the entire educational theory of the country. Her plans were to start at the foundation—the students themselves.

Michael applied to medical school and was accepted to the University of Kansas. For four years Michael had lived as a proud Kansas State Wildcat and developed a healthy distaste of all things Jayhawk. True, he'd freely admit, the in-state rivalry meant nothing when it came to helping patients, but imagine a Seminole cheering for a Gator, a Trojan siding with the Bruins, a Spartan moving to Ann Arbor and rooting for the Wolverines, or Army switching sides and pulling for Navy. His loyalty was unfortunately with a school that didn't offer the training he desired. What he didn't tell Jennifer was that he also applied to their nursing school.

In the end, Michael decided that the length of medical school, the on-call nights, the sheer duration of the training, was time he'd rather spend with Jennifer. Sure, every married couple pays lip service to the notion that the relationship is more important than the paycheck. Yet, how quickly we rationalize the time spent apart developing separate careers. Wouldn't the ideal marriage be one in which the spouses went into business together? Then work, play and family time would all be the same time. When it became clear that medical school and residency would only take him away from his future wife, Michael chose a shorter path to a parallel career. He could still help people and save the best years of their marriage from being lost under a pile of textbooks. He felt vindicated in his decision when Jennifer became pregnant soon after they graduated from their respective programs.

Being new to the seniority list at St. Bernadette's, he drew the short straw, the night shift. It was a rare career nurse who did the 8:00pm to 8:00am shift and stuck with it until retirement. For some nurses, it was convenient early on in their married lives to come home from work, get the kids off to school and sleep during the day. But chores in such families would invariably remain undone and the stress of trying to live a normal life on the weekends was too much to sustain over the length of a career in the field. A weekend was like two days of severe jet lag, trying to spend daytime hours with the family, only to have to repeat the cycle on Sunday night, spending two days getting back into the life of a vampire. By the time the kids were older, enough seniority was gained that nearly every nurse took the opportunity to switch to the day shift.

Michael enjoyed the night shift, if only for its variety. He would be assigned to more patients than the day shift nurses, but if he was lucky, the majority would sleep through the night and he could concentrate on helping those most in need. Some were general medical patients with infections or mild respiratory issues, but the easiest were the post-op patients. Mostly they were elective and so happy to have a new hip or knee, they'd just sleep through the night, blissful on pain medicines. If he were unlucky there would be multiple admissions of new and demanding patients and he'd sign out to the day shift nurse feeling as though he'd run a marathon. At least the shifts passed quickly on those nights.

Early in his career, Michael was buoyed by the freshness of it all, the excitement of mastering the procedures, computers and paperwork and the rare thrill of thanks he received from his patients. It was autumn, his newlywed wife was in her first trimester with their first child and the Kansas heat was finally showing signs of relenting. The sugar and red maples on the grounds of St. Bernadette's were beginning to change to their fire red and yellow displays. Michael bounced from the front seat of his trusty pickup truck, over the sidewalk and through security with its shiny, new post-9/11 metal detector. He gave a jaunty wave to his new friend from the Police Department, Officer Robert Miller who was new to the detail and took the job of National Security seriously. Mr. Miller was immune to barbs that a medium-sized, Catholic hospital in the middle of Kansas was not likely to be a terrorist target.

Michael took the stairs to the third floor nursing station, full of optimistic energy and ready to argue that the elevators were for sick people. He milled about the station while the day shift nurses finished their final duties and drug counts. At precisely 8:00pm, the head nurse, Shirley began distributing patients from the day shift to the night shift. Whether she was a no-nonsense woman from birth or not, her present occupation necessitated an efficient attitude. "Michael, you'll be helping Kathy get oriented," Shirley said handing him a short list of patients. The information was in columns starting with the room numbers, then the names and finally the major diagnoses or chief complaints. The spread sheet was designed with plenty of space for taking and making notes to optimize care and recall proper documentation at the ends of shifts. Michael's sheet was nearly blank.

"Kathy who?"

"Fresh out of school. Kathy Hall. You'll thank me later for the light load. Make sure she gets the paperwork down so we don't have to start over tomorrow morning."

"But only five? I'll be bored all night."

"Well, then, you can have The Dragon Lady." There were snickers and mumbles from the rest of the crew. "ER called up and said they're having the usual trouble getting her ready for the floor. In fact, it'll be the perfect chance for Kathy to learn the protocol. If she ever gets here."

As if on cue, Kathy rounded the corner at the far end of the hallway and started towards the nursing station. In the movie of Michael's life she would have been walking in slow motion, likely to a soundtrack of her own, heavy on guitar, a hard-driving blues tune. Most likely it would have been George Thorogood's "Bad To The Bone." She held her motorcycle gloves in one hand and walked like she owned the place. Kathy Hall took off her helmet and shook out a giant mane of perfectly straight hair like someone pouring out a five-gallon bucket of blonde. She stuffed the gloves in her helmet and tucked it under her left arm in one deft and familiar movement. Her jacket was open revealing a set of bright, hot pink scrubs like cotton candy on steroids. Necks were craned down the hallway and silence reigned until she arrived with a hand out to Shirley. "Kathy Hall. Sorry I'm late, it won't happen again."

"Be sure that it doesn't." Shirley ignored her hand and went back to distributing her lists of patients. The clock said three minutes past the hour.

"I'll do my best."

When the roll call was finished, Shirley introduced Kathy to Michael. "Why don't you show Kathy where she can stow her gear, then get down to ER. They tell me The Dragon Lady's in rare form tonight."

Kathy looked at Michael for an explanation. "Oh, you'll see. Better to let the mystery unfold on its own."

Michael led Kathy to the break room. It was tiny. Seeing Kathy's expression, he answered her unspoken question. "We call it the Broom Closet, although that's not entirely accurate, since the janitor's room is twice this size. I'm guessing they chose it to discourage us from taking too many breaks." A paired row of two dozen tiny lockers was bolted to the wall, each not more than one cubic foot in size. Keys were dangling from most of the cubicle doors. Some had bumper stickers or pictures of male models, mostly having lost their shirts, some in only underwear, but others were unadorned. None of the lockers had names or numbers. On the opposite side was a kitchenette with a galley sink and a miniature microwave oven which took up most of the counter space. Stuffed in the corner was a refrigerator that looked to be from the set of a 1950's TV sitcom, complete with a giant horizontal pull handle. It was decorated with magnets representing most of the States of the Union. Michael explained, "If you want to secure something for the shift, just lock it up and take the key with you. Anything you leave in the fridge is fair game, so I'd advise against it, unless you're trying to lose weight."

In the center of the room was a card table and three chairs. Kathy removed her backpack and sat in the nearest chair. She spun her golden tresses into an efficient bun and pinned it to her head. She swapped out her motorcycle boots and jacket for a pair of brand new running shoes and pinned her name tag over her left breast. She needed three lockers, one for her backpack, one for her boots and one for her jacket, but had to resort to leaving the helmet on top of the refrigerator. The entire procedure took less than a minute. With a pen in hand she turned to Michael, "Shall we?"

"Of course. Follow me." With his hand on the door of the Broom Closet Michael stopped and asked, "Why didn't you tell Shirley that you got held up by security? You were only three minutes late."

"What good would that have done? I should have planned better, what with all the terrorism alerts and whatnot."

"Good point." Michael liked her attitude and hoped it wasn't just for show.

"Shirley doesn't care and neither do the patients," Kathy added.

"Touche. Good point again."

Michael took the stairwell three floors down to the emergency room and made a mental note that Kathy didn't ask why they didn't take the elevator. At the door exiting the stairwell Michael stopped. "I should warn you, she's a pistol. Injuries are common, needle sticks are par for the course. Fortunately, she doesn't have any communicable diseases. The basic story is this; she starts to cause trouble at the assisted living home, wandering, banging on doors, picking fights. Truth be told, she should be in a nursing home. Anyway, the ambulance comes, loads her up and drops her off. They've stopped trying to start IV's in the field. Sometimes she'll take oxygen, but most of the time, not. The only thing we can be sure of is a fight." With that, Michael pushed the door open and entered the hallway.

As they rounded the corner to the din of the emergency room they were met with a shriek from one of the curtained bays. A nurse in wine-colored scrubs soon emerged with her head tilted backwards and a towel pressed to her bloody nose. "The bitch hit me again! That's it! Call the floor! I'm done with her!"

A surgical stand then came end-over-end through the curtain and landed with a crash spraying needles and IV tubing across the polished linoleum floor. Kathy turned to Michael. "I'm assuming that's our patient?"

"As you say, shall we?" Michael said and gestured with a dramatic flourish for her to walk into the fray. "Ladies first."

They approached the curtain and Michael reached up to pull it back so they could enter. Kathy caught his arm and whispered, "Wait. What's her name?"

"Mrs. Vickers. Mrs. Barbara Vickers, eighty-five years old. Strong as an ox, blind as a mole, crazy as an outhouse rat, and stone-deaf," Michael said in his regular voice.

"I can HEAR YOU!" came a shout from behind the curtain. Kathy gave Michael a stern look as if to say, *now* look what you've done.

"Beggin' your pardon Ma'am. My name is Kathy and I was jus' wonderin' if we might come into yer room for a spell?" No answer came from behind the curtain. Kathy looked to the nurses' station where the crew was tending to the nurse with the broken nose. The charge nurse waved her on as if to say, just walk in. Kathy motioned to Michael to right the tray and gather the IV supplies. "Mrs. Vickers, Ma'am? Are you there? I don't mean to intrude."

All they heard was a soft, gurgling sound, like a sleeping kitten with a bad head cold. To Michael she whispered again, "Could she be sleeping? That's not good." Kathy ventured a peek around the edge of the curtain, then reported her findings. Mrs. Vickers looked like she was laid out for her own funeral. She was covered from the waist down with a single sheet. Her upper half was immaculate in a houndstooth suit and black sweater. Across her lap she clutched a Louis Vuitton bag. On her head was a matching pillbox hat, slightly askew. It appeared her overly generous makeup was applied with a less than steady hand some days ago. The excessive rouge and lipstick failed to mask her ashen complexion and only made her purple lips look black. "Yep. She's out like a light. Get me a new IV kit, something small, 20-gauge."

"Small? Did you notice the one on the floor is a pediatric butterfly?" Kathy gave him the look that every married man knows, first from his mother, then from his wife. It means we're not having a discussion, just do as I say. "Okay, okay," he said and retreated to the nurses' station where a rolling cart was loaded with the most commonly used items.

When he returned with the cart and pulled back the curtain, Kathy was standing over Barbara blowing oxygen over her face from the canister under the bed. She held a face mask one inch from the old woman's lips and nose taking care not to touch her. She whispered again to Michael, "This tank's getting low. Be a dear, would you and hook me up to the wall?" Michael fished a new length of oxygen tubing from the supply cart and removed the plastic wrapping. He attached the female end to the oxygen on the wall supply spigot and turned the knob all the way. The indicator bubble rose up to fifteen liters per minute and a whistling sound came from the business end which he handed to Kathy. Rather than remove the tubing from the low tank or the mask, she simply inserted the tip under the edge of the mask and let both sources blow oxygen over Mrs. Vickers's mouth. "Close that curtain, would you? Less stimulation when she wakes up." Michael made a second mental note.

In a few moments, Mrs. Vickers's eyes began to flutter. The hint of a smile crossed her face, but as her eyes opened fully, the lips narrowed to a pale frown and her eyebrows knitted into a scowl. "Get away from me!" She flailed at Kathy and connected a bony forearm across the nurse's shoulder.

"Yes, Ma'am. Sorry to intrude on your sleep." Kathy removed the oxygen mask and hung it over the railing on the bed. She grabbed Michael by the arm and escorted him from the bay, closing the curtain behind her. Michael started to speak but Kathy shushed him by putting her finger to his lips.

After what seemed an eternity, a small voice called from behind the curtain, "Hello? Is there anybody there?" The nurses' station went quiet. Now that the bloody nose had stopped they had turned their attention to the bay to see what Kathy would do next. "Hello? What kind of place is this?"

"Mrs. Vickers? It's Kathy again. Were you needing some assistance?"

There was another pause and finally, "I think so."

"Well, you told me to get away from you, so I did."

"Oh."

"May I come in? Perhaps we could talk face to face? That's how I like it best." After a moment, Mrs. Vickers indicated that she would like Kathy to return, but *only* Kathy. Michael stayed behind the curtain and tried to offer mental support by telepathy. "Thank you for allowing me into your room," Kathy said. "My name is Kathy Hall and it's a pleasure to meet you." Mrs. Vickers gave her full name, including her maiden name, Epstein. Michael imagined them shaking hands as if they hadn't already met. "Wait. Did you say Barbara Vickers? *The* Barbara Vickers, of the Kansas Vickers? This is indeed an honor."

"Oh, stop bowing. There's no need for all that formality. We were always a humble family."

"Oh, but you're too modest. I repeat, it's an honor to have you. How may I assist you?"

"I want to go home."

"Okay. Did you park with the valet service? I can call the concierge and have them bring your car around. No? Shall we call you a cab? A family member perhaps?"

"You're going to let me go?"

"Sure. Why not? This isn't prison and you didn't commit a crime. Did you? You're free to go at any time. Of course, that's true for everyone, not just because you're a Vickers. Wow. Or do you have something to confess? I can have Officer Miller summoned, if you wish."

"Ha, ha, ha. Very funny."

"I'm being totally and completely serious, Mrs. Vickers. There is no law that says you have to stay here. You do know where you are, don't you?"

"Of course I do, silly child. St. Bernadette's. I was once on the Board of this hospital, I'll have you know."

"Very well. Then you should know you're free to leave at any time. Just tell me what you'd like to do. And I don't mean to press, but Michael and I have some very sick patients to tend to up on the floor, so if you could be a dear and let us know as soon as you can. I'll give you a moment to think about it." She exited the bay, closed the curtain behind her and stood next to Michael. Facing the nurses at the station she crossed the fingers of her left hand and put her right index finger to her lips to keep everyone quiet.

"I think I've made my decision," came a small voice from behind the curtain.

"Yes, Ma'am?"

"I'd like to stay."

"May I ask what made you change your mind?" Kathy said.

"I can't...I can't..." was the only sound she made followed by more soft snoring. Kathy entered the room again and placed the mask near her face. Mrs. Vickers soon woke up and this time the smile remained after she was aroused. "I can't breathe very well."

"Yes. I've noticed that. Would you like me to help? It's a pretty easy fix."

"Yes, please, Kathy. And…"

"Yes Mrs. Vickers?"

"I'm sorry I hit you before."

"That's alright. I'm tougher than I look. Besides you only did it because you were delirious." Mrs. Vickers gave her a confused look. "Your oxygen level was really low. Did you see or hear anything that probably wasn't there? Did you know you gave the other nurse a bloody nose?"

Barbara shook her head, eyes wide with a mortified look on her face. "The other nurse?"

"Yes. Well, you did. Maybe she's the one who really deserves an apology." Kathy gave Mrs. Vickers the mask to hold to her face. She soon grew annoyed having to hold it like a microphone and pulled the elastic strap over her cap. She folded her hands in her lap as if waiting to have her hair done. Kathy went about the business of examining Mrs. Vickers, explaining each step along the way in her happiest sing-song voice. "Your neck veins are all standing out like a bodybuilder. You lungs are full of water. It's no wonder you can't breathe. May I see your legs?"

Mrs. Vickers shook her head no. "I used to be a dancer. Ballet, tap, jazz. I had legs like a bird! Drove the servicemen crazy at the Veteran's Hall. You should have seen me at the Rotary Club!"

"Please?"

"Be nice," Mrs. Vickers said and with her bony fingers drew the sheet above her knees. The effect was like a magic trick. It took little imagination to envision a two hundred and fifty pound middle linebacker lying beneath the gurney with his legs coming through a hidden opening. Her real legs of course were under the table. Stuffed into her pointed-toe, three and a quarter inch Prada pumps were a pair of bulging black sausages the size telephone poles. Her silk stockings were drooping at the thigh where a clip had come loose, but at the location where her ankles should have been the fabric was split like she'd been forgotten on the backyard grill. Michael put his hand to his mouth in shock.

"May I remove your shoes? They're lovely. I'd hate for them to get scuffed up by our rough sheets." Mrs. Vickers nodded and Kathy removed the shoes as best she could without causing more damage to the stockings.

"Oh, that's heavenly. Thank you for not squeezing my ankles. Everybody always squeezes my ankles. Why do they always squeeze my ankles?"

"Mrs. Vickers? Do you know why you can't breathe? Has anyone ever explained it to you?" She shook her head. "How many times have you been here with this problem?" Mrs. Vickers shrugged her shoulders. "Ten times?" Kathy looked to Michael. He used his index finger to point to the sky. "Twenty? More?"

"Getting warm," Michael said.

"Oh, that's a shame. I'm assuming they've checked your heart, right?"

"They used to do lots of tests, now they just poke me and put tubes everywhere and send me home after a few days."

"Oh, I'm so sorry for you. Well, not this time. You're under my care now and we'll get you through this together." Kathy explained that her heart was no longer very strong and that's why the fluid was building up in her lungs and legs. It made her tired to carry around all that extra weight. It was the fluid that caused that annoying cough, too. But the real problem was that her heart had to pump two or three times just to circulate as much blood as it used to do with a single beat during her dancing days.

"My heart hasn't been the same since Mr. Vickers passed."

"He must have been some fella to have been able to get the likes of you to the altar."

"Oh, we weren't always having wings of hospitals named after us. We're what you call 'new money.' And anyway, sorghum isn't what it used to be either. Those sugar beets nearly put us right out of business. He tried to expand but nothing ever really took off. The mister even tried to convert a few fields to windmill farms and sell some electricity back to the power stations. Coal and gas were so cheap, we barely broke even. The tornado ended that venture, knocked 'em right off their bases. Thank goodness for ridiculous insurance policies. Imagine that, trying to harness the wind for clean energy—this was before that windbag Al Gore was so popular—and then it's wind that blows the farm away. Ha, ha! I made a pun, I called Gore a windbag! Oh, he was such a kind man when we met him at the fund-raiser, too bad the mister only votes Republican. Well, I'd have cancelled his vote again if he were still alive. And now we've got this whole 9/11 thing going on. Sort of puts the sorghum molasses futures on the back burner, huh? Oh, how he'd laugh at all the green this and environmental that. In the end, he decided to just retire, sold off the assets, donated the land and pond for a park. Such a shame. The Vickers's Company Headquarters building has been sitting idle ever since. They should make an orphanage out of it or something, but who listens to an old lady, anymore?" Mrs. Vickers looked up from the reverie of her trip down memory lane. "Have I been rambling? Oh, I'm so sorry. I haven't asked about you, dear. How long have you and Michael been dating?"

"That's okay, Mrs. Vickers. Now that your IV is started we can get you to a more comfortable bed up on the floor."

"What? You're done already?"

"Yes, sorry to have to pull rank on you, but they won't let me take you up without it. It'll be easier for you to not have to swallow all those nasty pills anyway."

"What about the other tube?"

"For the oxygen? I'm sorry, there's no way around that one, but we can probably get by without the mask and just use the nasal cannula. That okay?"

"No. I mean the other one." Mrs. Vickers pointed to her skirt.

"Oh. The catheter. Well, all that water is going to have to go somewhere. You can walk, right? Well, if you don't mind being up all night, then we'll leave it out. If you'd like a good night's rest and change your mind, I'll be happy to set you up. I'll only give you one chance to wet the bed. Deal?"

Up on the floor, Michael couldn't resist complimenting Kathy on her performance. "That. Was. Amazing."

"I've started more challenging IV lines."

"You know what I mean. But I have to ask. What's with the corny Southern accent?"

"Well, thanks, but our night is just getting started and I feel like I've run a marathon. You were right, too. That roundhouse she gave me is gonna leave a bruise" she said, rubbing her upper arm. "I guess the accent just comes out. Maybe it seems less threatening as I'm about to jab someone with a giant needle, to sound like an innocent Southern Belle, fresh off the plantation."

Michael helped her with the paperwork, which involved a five-minute call to IT to set Kathy up with a password. She had used the same electronic medical records in nursing school so the rest of the admission was a breeze. She called report to the admitting doctor and literally tucked Mrs. Barbara Vickers in for the night. "Just call me if you think you'd be more comfortable with the catheter. Or if you need help getting to the bathroom. There's a bed pan, but it's hardly worth the effort."

"I didn't get your name sonny. You've been so quiet."

"Michael, Ma'am."

"That's a funny name. I don't know any Ma'am family from Kansas."

"Michael Johnson. Let us know if you need anything."

"I'll try not to disturb you two love birds." The two nurses gave each other a look. Maybe Mrs. Vickers had a screw loose after all.

"Uh. We just met tonight, I'm giving Kathy her orientation. Besides, I can't speak for Nurse Kathy, but I'm married."

"Oh? What's your wife's name? And tell her if you were my fella I wouldn't let you out all hours of the night carousing with young single women."

"Jennifer. Jennifer Smith. And she doesn't consider my twelve-hour shifts to be any form of carousing, thank you very much."

"Well, what kind of name is Smith if your name is Johnson?"

"Long story short?"

"I've got all night, sonny."

"Well, we've got work to do, so I'll just say we're working on it. Her teaching degree was awarded under her maiden name—while we were engaged. Same with the business degree. She's never gotten around to changing it."

"Teaching degree, you say? She doesn't happen to teach 3rd grade at James Buchanan Elementary School, does she?"

"That's the one."

"Oh, well, you've got a keeper there. She's whip smart, and a real go-getter. She's only just started and really shaking things up on the school board."

"Well, uh, small world, I guess. You get some rest and ring us if you need anything. We'll check back later on our rounds."

"Good night, Nurse Kathy and *Mister* Johnson. Ha, ha."

The two nurses made quick work of the orders for their other five patients. There was a nighttime dose of insulin to be given, a few bags of antibiotics and one post-op transfusion unit to be hung. With time on their hands they asked the other nurses if they needed help, but all was under control. They retreated to the Broom Closet for a well-deserved minute off their feet. "Ugh," Michael sighed pushing open the door. He sat down heavily in one of the plastic chairs. "I feel like I'm halfway through a double."

Following him through the door, Kathy pulled a masculine-looking metal lunch box from her backpack in the first locker. Inside was a classic, metal thermos, with a lid that doubled as a cup. She poured a sip and gestured with it to Michael. "Take a snort of liquid courage. Beans from France. Twice the caffeine, better than Starbucks."

Michael took a sip. "Ooh. Too much for me." He shook his head. "Although my sinuses have never been so clear."

"Put a little hair on your chest, eh, Johnson?"

"I've got hair on my chest, I'll have you know."

"Prove it." In a goofy mood, Michael pulled down the V-collar of his scrubs to reveal a hint of sparse chest hair. "Oh, please. It looks like you dribbled some of Mrs. Vickers's beef broth down your chin. And a real man wouldn't let his wife keep her maiden name." All the air left the room. Despite their quick bonding over Mrs. Vickers, Kathy knew she'd crossed a line. Seeing Michael's hurt look, Kathy tried to backpedal. "Uh, what I mean is, a real woman would take her husband's name. Um, well, it's not about the chest hair anyway."

"I think I'll check on my patients," Michael said. He left Kathy at the card table.

The next few months Michael and Kathy shared most of their night shifts. By default, the low nurses on the totem pole took the majority of the weekend shifts in addition to their holiday coverage. Over coffee breaks and lunches at 3:00am they shared stories of their days in training and learned they had more in common than outward appearances would suggest. They agreed that the training to become a doctor was too long, not to mention the inevitable debt one incurred.

Add to that the length of residency training, even for a simple primary care specialty like Pediatrics and the choice was obvious. They had both opted for nursing school.

Autumn blended seamlessly with winter and before they knew it, Michael was celebrating his six-month anniversary at St. Bernadette's. It just so happened to coincide with Michael's birthday. No one noticed but Kathy, who marked the occasion by making him a cake from a Hostess Ding Dong and a single candle. She presented it to him in the Broom Closet and sang an *a cappella* solo to the tune of "Happy Birthday" changing and adding words to mark the event. "Oh, you got me a burning hockey puck. How thoughtful," Michael said.

"And a little bird told me there's some news at the Johnson/Smith household."

"Huh?"

"True or false: You knocked up Jennifer."

"You put it so gracefully. But yes, we're expecting. Too early to tell the sex and all that, but we're excited. Not even showing yet, but we're making plans, choosing names, getting a room ready. The whole bit."

"Hard to keep a secret if she's coming to the hospital for her prenatal appointments."

"Never mind patient confidentiality, I guess. No secrets around here," Michael said. "What's your news? I noticed you're not packing the helmet."

"Oh, no big deal, just too cold to ride. Without the helmet I get through security a lot faster. No thanks to that zealot, Officer Miller."

"C'mon, he's not so bad. Just doing his job."

"Got four wheels and a heater, now, too. Couldn't tell you the make and model." Kathy took a plastic knife from a tray by the microwave. "What? Did you think I'd wear a ski suit all winter? Put on some studded tires? Sorry to blow your image of the rebel nurse. I'll try to grow a mustache if that'll help. Now shut up and blow out your candle."

Michael gave a puff and removed the candle, presenting it to Kathy. Instead of taking it, she leaned forward and cleaned off the chocolate cake and creamy filling with her lips and tongue. Surprised, he let go of the candle and Kathy leaned back, twirling the candle with her fingers like a toothpick. "I'm glad you're here, Michael. Thanks for showing me the ropes and helping me pass the long shifts. I don't know what I'd do if I had to spend all my nights with Madge."

"Oh, go easy, she's mostly harmless," Michael said, trying to defend the veteran nurse. Madge was a white-haired grandmother type of indeterminate age, as round as she was tall. She insisted she'd switched back to nights since the kids were gone and she couldn't sleep anyway. Rumor had it that Shirley had relegated her to the night shift since demands were somewhat less than on the day shift. It was okay as a nurse, even beneficial, to be careful and meticulous, but one couldn't be slow during the day. Madge was from the old school, at a time when patient admissions went for weeks not days and the sickest patients from that time would likely be treated outside the hospital by today's standards. Then, there was the question of her accuracy. With fewer medications to be administered on the night shift, it was less likely that she'd make any further mistakes in her dosing. Everyone hoped for an early retirement. For some of her patients it was too late, but nothing was ever linked directly to her overlooking the allergy list or a drug interaction. Madge was losing it, but had nothing to retire to, so it was likely she'd work until she was fired or was physically unable.

Michael cut the Ding Dong, popped half into his mouth in one bite and pushed the remainder to Kathy. "No. It's for you," Kathy said. "Gotta watch my girlish figure."

Madge burst into the Broom Closet out of breath and one screech short of hysterical. "Oh, *there* you are! You guys have gotta come quick! The Dragon Lady's out of control and she's asking for one of you. I know I'm up for the next admission, but maybe I could trade you a patient?"

"I'll handle it, Madge," Kathy said. "I haven't seen Mrs. Vickers in months since she started taking her medicine. Did they try to put her on oxygen?"

"Yeah, well this time they found her wandering the grounds of the nursing home in her bare feet. It's gotta be ten degrees out—below zero with the wind chill—and the snow is really blowing."

"Let me know if you need any help," Michael said. "I'll watch the floor for now."

Madge and Kathy went to the Emergency Room, where the usually efficient chaos was replaced by an eerie calm. A radio at the nurses' station could be heard playing soft jazz. Two paramedics were flirting with one of the new staff members. Despite being bundled in their winter coats, hats and gloves, their noses were still Rudolph red. "Hey guys, thanks for bringing in Mrs. Vickers," Kathy said.

"No problem, er, that's not entirely true. It's brutal out there. We're just trying to warm up before we head back to the station. Had to chase this one all over the nursing home grounds." He pointed with a thumb over his shoulder to where Mrs. Vickers was lying on her gurney. The way she was lightly snoring gave no indication of the effort it had taken the men to bring her in. They gave a brief synopsis of their attempts and finally, Kathy waved them off realizing they'd not done a single thing for the poor woman.

She excused Madge, who retreated back to the third floor and went to the bedside to observe her client. Mrs. Vickers was breathing in shallow pants like the way a toddler would cry after dropping her ice cream cone. Kathy hooked some tubing and a mask to the oxygen supply on the wall and turned it up to the maximum fifteen liters per minute. She placed the mask in front of Mrs. Vickers's mouth and waited. In a minute, her eyes fluttered open and she smiled at Kathy. "Oh, how nice to see you dear."

"Likewise, I'm sure. How are you feeling?"

"Oh, splendid. I've just had a lovely walk in the park. You should have seen the flowers. Like a Monet painting, come to life."

"Mrs. Vickers? Do you know who I am?"

"Of course I do. You're Susie, my favorite daughter-in-law. Thanks for coming to visit. I'm sorry the place is such a mess." Kathy gave a look to the nurses' station that suggested they could all be in for a long night. She pulled back the sheet to reveal Mrs. Vickers's standard uniform. Madge's description of events was an obvious exaggeration. The same houndstooth skirt she'd seen before, the same ridiculous pumps. It was a miracle the woman hadn't fallen and broken a hip. There was one major difference in her appearance. Mrs. Vickers's ankles were as slender as the day of her last discharge.

"Have you been having any trouble breathing, ma'am?"

"Did you see the parade today? It was better than last year. No? Well, you should have seen Mr. Vickers on his horse. Such a handsome man. I felt like a queen, knowing he was all mine."

Mrs. Vickers didn't protest when Kathy started her IV line. She hardly seemed to notice. Due to the lateness of the hour, they decided to use the standard orders for her previous diagnoses and the doctor on call for the nursing home discussed the situation with Kathy over the phone. Nothing was typical about this admission, so Dr. Allen decided he'd brave the weather to come and assess the situation for himself. Mrs. Vickers was transferred to the floor and a battery of tests were ordered to be run while he made his way to St. Bernadette's.

On the floor, Mrs. Vickers was the talk of the ward. "None of this makes any sense," Dr. Allen remarked at the nurses' station on the ward.

"I don't get it either," Kathy said. "It's not like her last admission, or the one before that. With her congestive heart failure, she's always responded to the oxygen and the Lasix with no problem. Could it be just her dementia?"

"That's as good a guess as any. And between you and me," Dr. Allen said, "please don't tell anyone I'm just guessing."

"Mum's the word," Kathy said.

"Is there a place I can get some rest? The roads were treacherous and getting worse. No way I'm going out in that mess again, tonight. I'd rather wait here 'til they plow the roads. Something."

"Uh, not really, but there are some empty rooms. You can help yourself to a bed in any of the rooms on the south end. The ambulances aren't even able to get through this stuff, so something tells me we won't be seeing too many more admissions tonight."

From the perspective of patient care, the rest of the night passed without incident. All anyone talked about was the lousy weather. Local roads were impassable due to drifts. It wasn't so much the quantity of snow but the bitter cold and the wind. Plows were getting stuck. Due to high winds they closed I-70, the main artery through Kansas. Too dangerous for the truckers, they said on the news, especially the semis. The wind would blow them right over, if they didn't first slide off due to the ice. Locals were advised not to leave their homes. Even if they were able to get their cars started, the most minor inconvenience, say, a flat tire, would be life-threatening. It was too cold to risk a trip to the store for milk.

Around 4:00am the call lights in the nursing station began to light up. Dr. Allen came down the hall from the south wing with two blankets wrapped around his shoulders. A few nurses were finishing notes and arranging medicines for the morning rounds. "Is there any reason I can see my own breath?" Dr. Allen said.

The temperature in the south wing was a good twenty degrees below the rest of the hospital and dropping. Inquiries were made, maintenance was alerted, but no explanations or solutions were forthcoming. Despite his junior status overall, and lack of experience compared to Madge, the rest of the crew looked to Michael for guidance. "Any suggestions?" he asked the assembled crew. He was met with only blank stares. "Well, the only thing I can think of is to move the patients to the west wing for now. We'll put up some blankets to block the cold air and hope maintenance can figure it out tomorrow."

What should have been a relaxing shift was spent transferring patients from their single rooms to triple and quadruple rooms designed to hold at most, two beds. Any objections were met by wheeling the patients right back to the south wing to think it over. The patients quickly changed their tune and gladly agreed to be moved to the new wing. It was just for the night, after all.

When the time came to give their patients over to the day shift, the night shift nurses met as usual at the central nurses' station. They were met at half past the hour with the vision of Shirley dressed like a member of Shackleton's South Pole expedition. No other nurses scheduled for the day shift were able to get to the hospital to relieve the night shift. "Michael. Who have we got?"

"Only one new admission, the lovely Mrs. Vickers. We have a few that are ready to be discharged, but I guess that's not gonna happen."

"Sorry folks. I've got to ask you all to keep on for another twelve. Not like you've got anywhere to go. Any objections?" There was a stunned silence and a few murmurs, but no dissent. What could they say? "Would you all like to keep the patients you've got or switch it up for some variety?"

They decided to keep their current assignments, rather than learn the schedules of their new patients. By 9:00am, the nurse call light board was lit up like a Christmas tree on fire. The housekeeping and food service crews weren't able to make it to the hospital and their overnight skeleton crews couldn't handle the demands of the patients, let alone feed the hospital staff. Nurses were asked to help with housekeeping and distribution of food trays in addition to their more pressing duties of wound care, medication administration, and fielding phone calls from concerned family members. About noon, sleep deprivation was beginning to catch up with all of them. Passing in the hallway and with no prelude whatsoever, Michael said to Kathy, "What next? We'll have to do laundry?"

"Yeah, sure," Kathy said pushing an empty wheelchair. "I'll have to get out of these soon." She reached into the waistband of her scrubs as Michael walked past and hooked her thumb around the back of her thong, showing him its lacy edge.

"That's not what I meant and you know it," Michael said walking backwards and carrying a fresh bag of IV fluids.

"Suit yourself, Birthday Boy."

As soon as the breakfast mess was cleared, the second round of medicines needed to be administered. Medications were calculated and pushed, IV fluids were replenished. Shirley helped where she could but there was too much to do for anyone to get some rest. At noon, Shirley made an announcement overhead for the crew to meet at the central station. "Look, you guys are dragging. I get it. Let's be extra careful with our medications. Double check everything before you give it to the patients, please. Take the extra time. Trust me on this one, it'll save us work in the end. And document as you go. We don't have the manpower to do anything twice. Guess what? Time for lunch."

Three giant carts stacked with trays of hot food were delivered to the floor. A general groan went out from the crew. "That's the spirit!" Michael said, grabbing the trays for his patients.

Sometime around 3:00pm Shirley caught Michael at the nurses' station with his face plastered to a chart. His pen had run off the paper onto the table and he was drooling on the orders page. His arm hung limp off the table. Shirley cleared her throat loud enough to rouse him. He awoke with a start and the chart clattered to his lap, then the floor. "It's okay, Shirley. I got this."

"I see. Grab a couple of blankets and head to the south wing, last room. The sun has been warming it a bit and I had maintenance put a space heater in there. It's not perfect, but you should be able to get in a power nap. I'll wake you in an hour and we'll try and rotate the other nurses through."

"No, I'm okay. Thanks for offering."

"Who's offering? We're not trading cookies and pudding at lunch, here pal. That's an order."

Michael made the long walk to the last room in the south wing and did as he was told. He wrapped a towel around his head for warmth. The view out the window told nothing of the dangers of the weather. The sun was bright on the snow, but the parking lot was a static wasteland. He tried to pick out his car but all he saw were white lumps. Gusts of wind continued to blow drifts of snow up and over the parked vehicles. He shivered at the scene, climbed onto the gurney, and was asleep as soon as his head hit the pillow. He didn't even have the strength to draw the blinds.

After what seemed like only a moment, Michael was aware of an unusual warmth at his back. He was lying on his side and he let his dry eyes flicker open. Between his own two hands was a third hand, soft and dry. An arm was wrapped around under his waist. There was a warm breath on his neck. Michael jumped from the bed in surprise and looked back to the bed. He was expecting a call from Shirley, and his mind was reeling with confusion. In the bed was Kathy, smiling at him with droopy eyes and a warm smile. "What the hell?"

"Come back to bed, I was just warming up."

"Warming up to what?" Michael said. "Don't answer that. I've got work to do. I'll see you around."

"Aw, come on, I didn't mean anything by it. The next room is freezing. No sunlight at all." She stretched like a cat. "Please. We've got at least fifteen more minutes before afternoon rounds."

Michael looked at the clock. He read the numbers but they didn't make any sense. The sun was still out, but too high in the sky by the shadows. "What? No. This never happened." His mind gradually cleared and he realized the time meant his second shift was nearing its end. The odds of relief coming for their night shift was near zero. It would be thirty-six hours before the roads would be passable. Jennifer would be so pleased at the overtime on his next check. He thought all of these things while wandering out of the room and down the hall without another word to Kathy. Madge passed him with a blanket under her arm and they exchanged nods. He didn't look back, but overheard her interrupt Kathy, then excuse herself to find another room for a nap.

When dinner was served and the evening doses administered, Shirley called another meeting. "Good job, crew. What can I tell you?" She looked around the station. "Has anyone seen Madge? Oh, never mind. I'm staying. I'll cover. The good news is, some of the major roads are open. The bad news is, we're likely to get more patients before we get to discharge anyone. The other floors are in the same boat. Heat is on in the south wing, but it wasn't just our floor that got hit. It shouldn't take more than a couple of hours and we can start accepting more patients."

"Uh, are you hiding a dehydrated nurse in a closet somewhere?"

"Who's gonna take the new patients?"

"Yeah, we're all maxed out."

"Sorry. We'll rotate new admits. Family can't get here to take anyone home, but they're managing to get the sick ones in. Ambulances are filling up the ER again and I'll try to have them keep who they can until we can get some space. At least transfer our patients back to their own rooms in the south wing."

Groans erupted amongst the assembled staff. They rose from their chairs and went silently back to their duties, maintaining the same assignments. Meals were eaten hastily and on the run, if at all. Breaks were taken in brief snatches between new admissions and orders carried out for existing patients. Conversations were non-existent. Even the weather was a tired subject.

At 3:00am the call bell from Mrs. Vickers's room lit up the nurses' station. Michael was finishing his charting and answered the call. "Yes, Mrs. Vickers? How can I help you?"

"It's Kathy. I need you."

"Not appropriate," Michael said and turned off the call light.

The call came again. Michael thought twice before answering, but decided he could handle it by intercom better than in person. If he needed to get Shirley involved, he hoped she would understand. "This better be good," he said into the desktop microphone.

"Call a Code Blue, Michael. She's not responding." Michael made the call overhead and rushed to the room to find Kathy in tears, short of breath, and performing chest compressions. Mrs. Vickers was the color of the snow in the parking lot. A nasal cannula trickled oxygen over her nose and lips. He felt for a pulse and her arm was as cold as the rails on the bed. Michael set up the wall oxygen and a bag for ventilation, then handed it to Kathy so she could rest while he took over the chest compressions. Taking his position, he felt a warm spot where Kathy's hands had been massaging the pale chest of Mrs. Vickers. They made eye contact and he shook his head, which only brought a fresh set of tears from Kathy.

The rest of the Code team arrived led by Dr. Allen. Kathy tried to give him a summary of the incident but was unable to speak, so Michael took over the narrative. Medications were given and lines were started, all to no avail. The scrambling of the team came to a halt as Dr. Allen called the Code and made his pronouncement. The only remaining sound was Kathy, sniffling as she continued squeezing the ventilation bag and stroking Mrs. Vickers's hair. Michael brought her from her trance by placing a hand on hers. Without a word, the nurses left the room one by one to resume their other duties. Dr. Allen took it upon himself to locate and notify the family. Shirley told Kathy to take a break and pushed her out of the room towards the Broom Closet.

Michael assumed care of Kathy's other patients. A quick round of the floor showed them to be resting comfortably and the morning rounds were still a couple of hours away. Needing a break himself, Michael proceeded to the Broom Closet where he found Kathy slumped in a pile by the sink, sniffling and whimpering to herself. This was not the cocky motorcycle rider he'd first met. Where was the take-charge caregiver he'd come to admire? He found himself feeling a mixture of pity, sympathy, and not a small amount of admiration. After all, it wasn't just book smarts that made a good nurse. Michael believed you really had to love your work. "Hey, Kathy. It's alright."

He placed a hand on her shoulder and without a word she put her hand in his, then pressed it to her cheek. "She died alone."

"You can't change the weather. I'm sure her family would have been here if they could. Plus, she's been admitted so many times. How could you—how could anyone—have known this would be the one?"

"No. I should have been watching her more closely. I knew there was something different about her this time."

Michael knelt down next to her since Kathy showed no signs of releasing his hand. "We all have a double load of patients. You've got to give yourself a break. We're all stressed and overtired. You're a good nurse, Kathy." A thought occurred to Michael. "Have you ever had a patient die on you?"

"No."

"Well, it's going to be a long career if you take each one this hard."

"But, it was Mrs. Vickers. I feel like I knew her personally. We toured her family's home in middle school history class. The factory in high school. And here she is, my favorite patient. Now she's dead."

"I don't know what to say," Michael said.

"Then, just hold me."

Feeling a bit awkward, Michael gave her a hug, sitting behind her on the cold linoleum floor. Kathy put her arm in his and pulled him closer, tilting her head back and pulling his lips to hers. Confused, Michael tried to pull away but she pinned him with another hand on his neck and kissed him again. Madge burst into the Broom Closet with her hair done up in a fresh tease and new makeup. "Oh, *there* you are. Where have you guys been? I just wanted to tell you I'll take the next admission."

When she'd left, Michael extricated himself from Kathy's grasp and spoke first. "This never happened." He stood up and brushed off his scrubs, leaving Kathy on the floor by the sink.

"Yes, it did." She looked him in the eye, a direct challenge.

"No, it didn't. What are you expecting? I'm married. We have a daughter on the way."

"She won't even take your last name. She missed your birthday."

"She doesn't do birthdays."

"Why? Is she a Jehovah's Witness?"

"That's beside the point. There's nothing I can give you beyond support on the floor. I'm sorry about Mrs. Vickers, I really am. But beyond these hospital walls, I've got a life that can't include you."

"Okay, then let's just keep it in here."

"You're not hearing me. I like you, Kathy, you're a great nurse to work with, but that's the end of it for us. Don't make this more difficult for me. If I have to change shifts or move to another floor, that would look even worse. Got it?"

"So, what are you saying?"

"I'm saying, we have no future, so don't get any ideas. Promise me. Think of it from my perspective. If you really like me, don't ruin my life—our life, the life I have with Jennifer—by thinking this means more than it does."

Kathy got to her feet without a word and turned her back to Michael. She washed her hands at the sink, then dried them with a paper towel. Taking another towel from the dispenser, she moistened it with cold water and held it to her bloodshot eyes for thirty seconds. Satisfied that her appearance was acceptable, she left the Broom Closet without another word to Michael and walked to the nurses' station to seek further solace from her colleagues. The tears flowed again and the other women shared their stories of caring for and being abused by Mrs. Vickers. Soon, they all felt a little better and were even able to have a laugh or two before morning rounds began.

Michael took Madge aside at the end of the shift and tried to explain things, but the damage had already been done. No amount of argument could convince Madge that what she'd seen was an innocent moment of sympathy between colleagues. She just nodded her head to Michael and lied that she hadn't made anything of the kiss or that she'd told any of the other staff. As ineffectual as Madge was as a nurse, she was just as effective at spreading gossip. Kathy behaved herself as promised and in time, the rumors faded, but not the alleged history. It was simply assumed that the affair had ended amicably. It occurred to no one that one never existed in the first place.

4

ONE HALF OF INFINITY

Nearly a decade later, Michael still couldn't convince Jennifer of his once and ongoing fidelity. He scanned the row of parents again trying to come up with examples of less than perfect marriages that somehow appeared to be holding steady, if not thriving. "Would you like it better if I was the doting type? Always falling over myself to compliment you? Buying you roses all the time? Telling you how I couldn't live without you?"

"That might be nice, once in awhile. But it's got to be genuine. Otherwise it doesn't mean anything. You can't do it because I ask you to. It's like having to explain a joke. It just doesn't work."

"What about Jason? Should I be more like him?"

"Jason? Amy? Don't be ridiculous. They're pathetic."

"He's still my friend. Don't be rude. Plus, that's not what you mean. He's just not your type."

"True, I'm more impressed by an IQ above eighty," Jennifer snarled. "But I don't see what *any* woman would want with him." As far as Jennifer knew, Jason Williams had one of those nebulous corporate jobs that had to be explained even after he told you his career field. Jason was physically intimidating to say the least. The future Mr. Williams was born at St. Bernadette's, the hospital where Michael now worked. He still held the record for Biggest Baby at over fourteen pounds. The combined weights of most twins didn't approach that number. Meeting him was like trying to get your hand around a basket of cucumbers. In his day he was a champion heavyweight wrestler. He hadn't seen two hundred and forty pounds since he was an 8th grader. Talk with Jason Williams for too long and your neck would get a kink from looking up to his pumpkin-sized head.

"Maybe it's real love," Michael said. "Hold my hand." Jennifer gave him a look that could have reversed global warming. "Just try it. Maybe I'm not so repulsive."

"Get real. As lame as you are, Jason Williams is worse. Holding hands does not a gentleman make." Michael stared at Jennifer with his mouth agape. He couldn't believe the words that were coming out of her mouth. She continued to watch the soccer game. "GO EMILY!" Jennifer finally turned to meet his stare when the ball ricocheted to the other side of the field. "What? 'Love is blind' you're going to tell me?"

"You know what he did for Amy. Tell me that's not love."

"There's nothing romantic about jail time. Plus, he ruined his career before it even started. Not exactly the ideal provider." Jennifer was not a believer in any of the Hollywood versions of love. That's what she called them, "fake love," invented to sell movie tickets. The only thing more annoying to Jennifer than "love at first sight" was the "mortal enemies turned soul mates" version. Top it off with a ridiculous grand gesture and a cheesy literal sound track and it was more cliche than she could stand. The list of movies she hated was longer than the list of her favorites.

"He did it for Amy," Michael said. "You can't tell me it wouldn't have gotten your attention."

"What? Please. Committing a felony is hardly a selling point. And that engagement ring? Comical at best." Michael had to admit, like Jennifer, he was only vaguely aware of what Jason did for a living. He had no idea what Jason's annual salary might have been eleven years ago. Sure, Amy's ring had more gold than diamond, but any rational person had to admit, the engagement ring was the most oversold symbol in retail.

Another argument he'd lost with Jennifer during their courtship involved the importance of the ring. It wasn't just something to gawk at with her friends, it was an investment. Jennifer treated the ring as if she'd resell for a profit someday. She needed the absolute highest quality available, regardless of what Michael could afford at the time. When he proposed, she laughed at the ring he'd chosen as if he'd presented her with a necklace made of paper clips. She accepted his proposal at the time with all the grace she could muster, then immediately insisted they shop together for a new, loose stone of impeccable clarity and color, in a carat weight five times the budget Michael could afford. She insisted on designing the setting, adding countless melee. Her only concession to cost was admitting the white gold actually did look better than the platinum. Luckily for Michael, she was willing to use some of the wedding gift cash to avoid a decade of credit card debt.

Michael felt the need to defend himself, knowing that bringing up the old argument would only drive the wedge further. "It's not the size, you know. Every diamond is unique. Every love is unique. If one guy buys a two carat diamond and another buys a single carat, it doesn't mean the second loves his fiancé only half as much. One half of infinity is still infinity."

"Oh, spare me the boundless love crap. He could have made something of himself. He could have been famous, a legend. Then Jason could have gotten her a better ring. If he really loved her, I mean."

"Maybe Jason loves Amy more than money or fame," was all Michael could answer. The adverb "maybe" and his defeated tone was Michael's signal that he'd given up the fight. After ten years of marriage, it was an unspoken rule between them that the winner was not the person who had the last word. Jennifer returned to her defiant posture, occasionally looking from the game to the street, letting her silence tell Michael, he'd lost the "Jason and Amy" argument.

There is a logic which applies only to those in love. If not under its spell, one cannot comprehend its undeniable and irresistible force. When Paris decided that Helen was the gal for him, he went and got her. Never mind that she was married at the time. Further, every Spartan agreed it was a perfectly good reason to go to war. Not a single warrior suggested Menelaus go get her back himself. No, under the logic of those in love, a ten-year war and the sacking of Troy was the perfect response. It was this kind of thinking that led Jason to believe he knew just how to win Amy's heart. He wasn't going to let a couple of silly laws keep him from their shared destiny.

Jason and Michael were on the same high school wrestling team, though of vastly different talents. In addition to his cucumber fingers, Jason had quickness and size. He wrestled in the heavyweight division which had an upper weight limit of two hundred and eighty-five pounds. The other wrestlers on the team were in a season-long battle to make and maintain their weight class, while Jason ate huge amounts of food, mostly protein, to pack on yet more muscle. By his senior year, his talent for manipulating opponents was matched by their inability to budge his hulking physique. He was both the irresistible force and the immovable body.

Michael joined the team at Jason's request, simply because the team lacked a 135-pounder. At every dual meet they'd have to forfeit the weight class. True, Michael had little skill and none of Jason's passion for the sport, but he did manage to win a few matches on points. Though he failed to qualify on his individual merits, Michael attended the State Tournament as a member of the team and thought of himself more as cheerleader for Jason than likely to contribute in the overall team standings.

"I'm telling you, she ain't comin'," Michael said. They were seated on the far end of the row of chairs. Their distracted coach was at the other end by the judges' table. Jason was scanning the crowd for any sign of Amy. "Dude, she hasn't seen you wrestle in four years."

"She's comin' this year, I'm telling ya," Jason said. "I left a note on her locker after fifth period."

"Oh, that sounds familiar. No chocolates this time? That was a sure bet for the last dual meet of the season."

"Shut it, Michael, or I'll crush you with my earlobe."

"The teddy bear for the League Meet was a nice touch."

"I'm warning you…" Jason said with a smile. Off the mat, Jason himself was more teddy bear than Grizzly. Their friendship could survive any amount of playful teasing.

"Maybe you should…" Michael started, then thought better. He almost mentioned the unthinkable—that Jason would likely do better to just go up to her and introduce himself. In the five years since they'd all hit puberty, Jason was still attempting to impress her from afar, the peacock version of *Homo sapiens*. He figured with the right resume she'd come to him. Last year he won the State Championship easily, but it failed to bridge the gap. With his natural talent and undefeated record, anything less than total domination would have been considered failure. There was nothing to overcome, no great struggle to demonstrate his devotion. Of course, no one saw the hours in the weight room, the miles on the road, the manual labor on the farm, building up his stamina.

One incident had made its way from truth, to legend, then to Amy's ears. At preseason workouts, Coach Rice was evaluating the returning talent. He was checking to see which freshmen had hit their growth spurts, mentally sizing up who could fit where on the roster. His mind was a living calculator of weight classes. Like a circus barker he could size up any scrawny kid in a pair of loose sweats and determine whether he was a 112- or a 119-pounder.

That Jason would make the team wasn't even a consideration. He'd been a captain since his Sophomore year and was coming off a Championship season. With his growing knowledge of technique, he could have coached the team. He'd spent the summer as he had every year, at his uncle's farm, working endless days of manual labor; throwing hay bales, lifting and planting fence posts, wrestling with the animals. He stood off to the side of the weight room with a giant barbell at his feet, penned by a fence of graduated dumbbells on their racks. The rest of the prospective teammates were taking turns at the various stations on a universal machine, going through leg presses, military presses, bench presses, working the large muscle groups. The man at the front of the line would enter at the bench press. Coach Rice blew the whistle every thirty seconds or so and the young men changed stations clockwise around the machine to work a new body part, then went back in line to rest.

Jason stayed in the same spot and continued doing reps, working only his biceps and adding more and more weight with each whistle. After a few rounds of additional weight, the bar began to show a noticeable bend at the middle. As the stacks on each end grew thicker, the other wrestlers started to ignore their own workouts to watch.

Coach Rice blew the whistle but no one entered the bench press station. He looked to the front of the line where a tiny tow-headed kid was staring with his mouth open. Coach consulted his clipboard and bellowed, "Roger! Hit that bench press or hit the road!"

Roger responded by raising a skinny arm to point at Jason, who was adding twenty kilo plates to each end of the barbell. Coach looked over to his star athlete. "Very impressive, Jason. But you're not going to pin anybody with your biceps." Jason responded by lifting the barbell and curling it thirty times.

"Look kid, I appreciate your strength, but you're just gonna pull a back muscle and ruin your season."

Jason set the heavy bar down like it was a baby in a crib. "Coach Rice. How much does my average opponent weigh?" It was a rhetorical question, so the coach just crossed his arms and waited for the explanation. "Two twenty-five? Two forty? The biggest guy I faced last year was two sixty-five and he was soft as chewed bubble gum."

"Yeah? So? You won the match. You won every match."

"I couldn't pin him. He just flopped there like a beached whale. I killed him on points in the first period. Escape, reversal, takedown and it was over. I kept racking up points and then it came to me. He wasn't wrestling to win, he considered it a victory to avoid the pin. If he tries that on me this year, he's going flying." The room was silent but for the clank of the bar as Jason bent over to add two more plates. They all knew what he meant: The Karelin Lift.

Alexander Karelin, the Russian Bear, was the greatest Greco-Roman wrestler who ever squeezed his bulk into a leotard. His international, unbeaten streak spanned an incredible thirteen years, including three Olympic gold medals. In the last 6 years of his career, his opponents were unable to score a single point. Lifts and throws are common at all levels of wrestling but rare in the heavyweight division, for obvious reasons. If an opponent were lying prone, a defensive position, Karelin would lock his long arms around the man's waist, lift him into the air and slam the helpless wrestler violently into the mat. He used the technique with such success hoisting and tossing wrestlers weighing as much as two hundred and eighty-five pounds, that the move became known simply as "The Karelin Lift."

Now here was a 17-year old farm boy in the middle of Kansas, already at the top level of his sport, training to become even more dominant. He added a fourth plate to each side and did a set of twenty. With a fifth plate on each side, Jason showed signs of stress on his tenth rep. "How much is that?" Coach Rice said to no one.

"That's ten plates, Coach," Roger said. "He's over two twenty." The rest of the team huddled around the mat to cheer and marvel. The gym had no more large plates. Jason put a pair of ten kilo plates on each side and replaced the safety collars. He took five deep breaths through pursed lips. He grabbed the bar palms up and made the dead lift with ease. The bar came to rest against his massive thighs. Jason had to cheat his back into an arch but managed to get the bar to his shoulders, not once, but three times. Lowering the bar back to his waist each time doubled the strain and he let out a feral groan on the last rep and dropped the bar to the mat.

"That's two sixty-four, Coach," Roger said. "Not many guys bigger than that."

"You forgot the bar, son," Coach Rice said shaking his head in disbelief. "Those extra forty pounds put him way over the upper weight limit. I stand corrected, Jason, maybe you will beat someone with your biceps."

The Kansas State Wrestling Championships took place in a coliseum which held nearly seven thousand fans. It was normally used for basketball at the college level. The large space was needed to accommodate not only the athletes, but their family and friends from all over the state. Even if Amy came to watch, it was unlikely Jason would be able to find her in the crowd.

The basketball nets were removed for the event and the hardwood floor was cushioned with four regulation mats, each with a twenty-eight foot diameter circle. Around and between the mats was a constantly buzzing procession of wrestlers and coaches. With hundreds of athletes from four or five dozen schools represented in fourteen weight classes, the event spanned two days, even with four matches running simultaneously in the early rounds. It was possible that Amy would assume last year's Champion would make it through the first day and compete again on the second day. There was no need to make the drive twice or assume he'd lose in the early rounds.

Still, Jason's head was on a constant swivel, scanning the rows from top to bottom, then back again for any sign of Amy. "Dude, you gotta pay attention. You can't risk a disqualification on some stupid technicality,"

"You're up before I am," Jason said still squinting into the darkest upper reaches of the coliseum. "I'll start watching when you have your first match."

"And how long do you think I'm gonna last? One round? Two would be a near miracle."

The early rounds were a constant din of seemingly random cheering and eerie silence between matches. With all four mats going at once, cheering came from different sections of the crowd with each throw, escape, pin and victory. Announcements weren't made in the early rounds as no one in the crowd could hear anyway and the turnover would have necessitated a constant jabbering over the public address system.

Michael's first opponent had the unfortunate name Danny. Moreover, he was built much like his namesake from the movie, *The Karate Kid*. Danny was spindly thin, dark-haired with a permanently sheepish expression on his face. That is, until after they shook hands to start the match. The referee arranged them, both standing, facing each other and blew the whistle to begin the first round. Michael assumed the famous Crane position for a brief second. The referee didn't understand the move, so no penalty point was awarded. Danny became furious. Apparently, he'd heard and seen the joke before. Michael meant nothing malicious, he just didn't take the tournament or wrestling in general as seriously as any of the other competitors. As a result, he wrestled fast and loose with nothing to lose. Avoiding a pin was his only goal. Taking his first round opponent through three rounds and losing on points would be a major triumph. Advancing to the second round wasn't even a consideration.

Danny charged, grabbed Michael by his right arm and attempted to roll him to the mat. Danny put a bit too much enthusiasm into the throw and their combined momentum caused Michael to end up in the superior position with his arms around Danny's neck. The referee must have been in a generous mood and awarded Michael four points for a near fall. Danny was able to push Michael off after five seconds, gaining back a point, but Michael ended up outside the ring. They resumed the neutral position and spent much of the remainder of the period on their feet, trying to get hold of one another's heads and shoulders. Danny made a dive and managed to grab Michael's right leg and raise it up, but was unable to bring Michael to the mat. An awkward three-legged hop commenced ending with Michael outside the ring again and no points were awarded.

"Way to go, Shortbread!" Jason shouted when the first round was over. Michael looked to his friend with an embarrassed grin and rolled his eyes. He couldn't believe his luck. He had a commanding lead and Danny was visibly flustered. For the second period, Michael chose to assume the defensive position. He figured he was unlikely to pin his opponent, but neither could Danny likely do the same. Allowing Danny to start on his hands and knees was like giving him a free point for an easy escape.

Michael assumed the referee's position, hands spread wide on the far side of the forward starting line, with his knees behind the rear line. At the whistle, Danny tried to dive forward and take Michael in a headlock with his entire body weight. Michael sat on his heels and Danny flew clean over landing on his stomach, like a clumsy slide into second base. Michael was awarded another point for the escape and spent the rest of the period on his feet, avoiding a takedown, but not risking a near fall or pin.

As far behind as he was on points, Danny needed a pin in the third period, so he chose the dominant position, willing to risk the point for escape, knowing he needed to maintain control to win the match. Thinking Michael would sit back again, he tried a bear hug and throw from the starting position. Instead of sitting back, Michael stepped his left foot forward and tried to rise to a standing position. Danny was left kneeling on the floor with his arms sliding down Michael's scrawny, hairless thighs. Michael stepped out of Danny's arms like a toddler taking off his father's pants. A quick spin and sweep of the arms put Michael in control behind Danny, locking up his arms from behind. While he was unable to complete a fall, he did maintain control and won easily on points. When time was called, Danny graciously accepted a shake from Michael at the center of the mat. After the referee raised his arm, Michael bounced back to his team on the sidelines. Coach Rice gave him a high five and a swat on the butt, sending him down the line to high five each of his teammates. Jason stood up to receive his friend with an expression that said nearly everything. "That was the worst display of wrestling technique I've ever seen," Jason said. "The ref should have penalized you for being so weak and boring."

"Hey, man, where's the love? I think I did pretty well not to pee my pants. That gets my record for the year up to about even, wins and losses. I think. Anyway, let's not forget the points I just scored for the team."

"Have a seat and let me show you how it's done. Don't go to the bathroom, I'll be right back."

Jason pinned his first opponent in less than thirty seconds. From the neutral position, they locked hands and necks face to face for a few moments. In an instant, Jason dropped out of the hold, grabbed his startled opponent between the legs and lifted him overhead in a fireman's carry. Rather than slam him to the mat, however, Jason wrapped him in a fetal position and set his two hundred and fifty pounds gently on the mat, shoulders down with his legs in the air, pedaling like a helpless cockroach. The referee called the match, they shook hands, and Jason waltzed over to give the team a low five, starting with Coach Rice. "Any questions?" he said to Michael, then went back to the more important task of searching the crowd for Amy.

The only drawback of winning his first match was that Michael had to keep wrestling. "Tough draw, kid," Coach Rice said of his next opponent, Tyler Kane, last year's Champion at one hundred and thirty pounds. This year Tyler decided to put on five pounds of muscle and grapple at the heavier weight. Michael saw the challenge as a gift. He wasn't expected to last a minute, let alone win, so he had nothing to lose but the match. Tyler was a head shorter than Michael, yet built like a beer keg, all muscle, no neck. Michael gave it his best effort, even scoring a point for an escape. He was so sweaty with nerves and exertion that Tyler lost his grip allowing Michael to get to his feet to end the first period. Exhausted, he assumed the defensive position to start the second period, and Tyler pinned him mercifully inside ten seconds. Since Tyler went on to win the tournament, Michael still likes to tell the story of how he "came in second" at the State Championships by losing to the winner. He just neglects to tell how it happened in the second bracket pairing.

Jason's second match ended with something of an embarrassment. He failed to pin the wrestler, not for lack of skill or effort, but due to disqualification. The terrified opponent kept fleeing from the ring, afraid of being injured by a violent throw to the mat. After a rather generous warning and ignoring the constant stalling, the referee was finally forced to award Jason the match.

The third match was at least more entertaining for the average spectator, since Jason's opponent, Lauaki Tanumafili, actually survived until early in the second period. Lauaki was pure Samoan from his name, to his impressive physique, to his honorable disposition. Despite the family's move to the geographical center of the country, the Tanumafili's retained their strong sense of family, community, and culture. One of his teammates, ignorant of both Samoan culture and Mexican liqueur, gave him the nickname Kahlua and it stuck. Lauaki didn't seem to mind or at least never complained about it. Then again, he never complained about anything. Most of the team wrongly supposed he preferred it to the uninspired "LT," but he would have been most flattered to be called by either of his given names, which he didn't feel were all that exotic nor difficult to pronounce. Perhaps this mild injustice was the reason he switched to the football team after his junior year. He was good at wrestling, but preferred the tighter sense of community he got from the more popular team sport. His running backs set rushing records for yards and touchdowns. He didn't allow a single sack all season.

Lauaki gave a good effort in his match with the over-powering Jason, never fleeing, always attacking. He even assumed the dominant position to start the second period. He avoided a devastating throw, but to the well-trained eye, it was clear he never had control of Jason.

The match ended when Jason executed a no-hands pin by locking up his opponent and rolling himself over. The final position gave the impression Jason wasn't wrestling but lying on the carpet in his bedroom watching television. There just happened to be two hundred and sixty-five pounds of flailing wrestler locked up and staring at the rafters from between his own legs. Back at the bench, Michael couldn't help but ask, "You were just practicing, weren't you? In case you need some new moves in the later rounds, right? You know the other teams are scouting you. Not to mention all the colleges."

Jason gave him a studied look and one half of a smile. "You know, for someone who can't wrestle for shit, you're pretty observant. Yeah, I didn't just want any pin. I wanted to see if I could do it with a specific leg lock. Kahlua's pretty good and smart, too. So it was a nice challenge for me to manipulate him by letting him think he was getting a point for escape or to see if he'd go for a move he couldn't really pull off, you know, just 'cause I gave him the opening. I had the third period left, in case he got ahead in points. I had time to go back to brute force, less finesse, if I had to. Let's get some lunch." The consolation matches were held in the afternoon leaving Jason free until the Championship rounds on day two.

The wrestlers put on the team sweat suits over their leotards and walked out to the concourse. The coliseum sold standard fan fare, none of it appropriate for Jason; french fries, hot dogs, nachos, and the like, all carbs, fat and little protein. It wasn't that he was worried about making weight for his quarterfinal match the following day. Rather, he'd been eating like a pro athlete for so long, such rich foods did terrible things to his digestion. The friends found an empty table with molded plastic chairs attached and sat down to eat. From their backpacks they both extracted a dull, brown bag lunch. Jason ate half a dozen hard boiled eggs. He discarded the yolks and ate them without salt to avoid retaining any water. He took sips from a quart of a lukewarm protein shake and rinsed his teeth with cold water from a screw top bottle.

More out of habit than respect or need, Michael had a similar lunch. He could have had an all grease meal for all Jason cared, but instead he slowly munched celery sticks with low fat peanut butter. Tuna fish on dry crackers was his only concession to carbohydrates. He figured with all the chewing, he burned about as many calories as he was eating. They ate in comfortable silence like an old married couple, chewing slowly, not to protect their dentures but to savor every morsel. Fans and students strolled by ignoring the diners, seeking restrooms and snacks. Cheers came from the center of the coliseum at random intervals and washed over the two friends, content in the habit of their shared meal.

When it came to his lunches, Michael's mother still treated him like a third grader but understood his nutritional needs during the training season. As she often did for his away meets, she'd snuck in a treat for the boys—tiny meringue cookies. Instead of sugar, she used aspartame for the sweetener and whipped them to an airy consistency. Michael called them packing peanuts. They weren't quite Styrofoam, but if you had something to mail cross-country, they'd keep it from any harm dealt by the United States Postal Service. Her good luck charm was a single semi-sweet chocolate bit she'd slip into one of the cookies before baking. The boys divided them on the table like fortune cookies. Jason scored the treat on his second bite and stuck out his tongue to show Michael the smeared brown mess. "See dude? Nothing can go wrong," he said.

"Yeah, you're gonna kick ass tomorrow," Michael said.

"No, I mean with Amy. She's gotta show. And after the tournament I'm taking her out to Antonio's." The Italian restaurant was easily the most popular hangout in their hometown. The food was delicious, cheap, and came in huge portions. The owners had cleverly divided it down the middle with the kitchen and host stand at the center. On one side it resembled a college cafeteria, with large community harvest tables and the option of endless pizza choices on a buffet. On the other side, it was strictly upscale, jacket and dress only. College students on break who had previously downed endless pitchers of light beer while playing darts, were known to end up proposing to their long-time girlfriends on the fancy side over meals like eggplant ragout, bucatini, and tagliatelle.

"Don't you think it's a little early to be taking her to Antonio's? You can't even pronounce the stuff on that menu."

Jason gave him the disappointed father look. "Dude, it's all pasta. Besides, I was talking about the pizza side. It'll be our first official date. I'll wear my medal from finals tomorrow and ask her to prom. She'll swoon." Jason had countless medals from league meets, regionals, and invitationals. There were so many on his varsity jacket at one point that he decided to remove them all, including his State Champion medal from the previous year. There was no one left to impress. Even Amy was aware of his accomplishments on the mat.

"Yeah, sprinkle in lots of fancy words, like 'swoon.' I'm sure she'll go ape shit for you. Probably jump you right there in the buffet line." Michael realized he'd gone too far. He didn't mean to insult his best and only friend, but it seemed the courtship had been an eternity with nothing to show for it. Most couples of high school age could fall in love, date, get married, have children, and break up all before sixth period English class.

"I noticed you're constantly surrounded by cheerleaders and gorgeous runway models," Jason said. "What's your secret, Dr. Johnson? How can I be easy with the ladies like you? Can you toss me some extras?"

"Now you're talkin' sense. We'll start with your celebrity makeover. New hair, new clothes, and lots of plastic surgery. I'll arrange the final reveal at Antonio's. We'll have someone tell Amy to show up for a surprise birthday party or something. You'll be there on the long table surrounded by pepperoni pizzas. Or maybe you could pose as a waiter." The two friends had a good laugh and went through a few more renditions of the reality show dating scene until the joke ran out of steam. There were roses, desert islands, helicopters, diamonds, and bended-knee proposal versions. The more they joked, the more serious Jason's situation began to appear. He was in love with Amy, a girl he hardly knew and no gesture seemed too grandiose. They stopped talking and laughing and met each other's eyes. Guys, real men, even best friends for years don't look at each other that way.

"Dude," Jason said. "What am I gonna do? I gotta get her to notice me." Michael tried to switch his mental gears from smart-ass teenager to concerned and helpful friend. This territory was new to both of them.

"What do we know about this girl," Michael said, not really a question. "Let's start at the beginning." Michael pulled a spiral notebook and pen from his backpack. He opened it to the back page, flipped it upside down and wrote "AMY" in large capital letters. In the margin he placed a numeral one. When nothing came to him, he underlined her name. Then he did it again. Then, he put quotation marks around her name. "Dude. Help me out here. You're the stalker."

"You're serious," the Champion wrestler said.

"Sure. Why not?"

"Uh, okay. Number one, she's hot." Michael wrote it down. In the history of beautiful women, Amy and others of her type, would not be on anybody's Hot List. At best she was merely forgettable. She had no warts or disfiguring scars, it was just that she was bland. One could meet Amy in her high school incarnation, have a twenty minute conversation, and leave completely underwhelmed. It wasn't that she was in any way offensive, quite the contrary. She was undeniably pleasant. Her only fault might be that she was too nice. A dose of bitchiness might have served her well in high school, but it wasn't in her nature. The perfect word to describe her would be mousy. She had hair of a neutral brown sheen. The word "color" wasn't quite accurate as her hair didn't have the distinct features of what most people call brunette. She wore it all one length, sometimes parted in the center, usually in a ponytail. At seventeen, Amy had a mature figure, but not one that would stop traffic. With average height and the lack of a brand name wardrobe, it was hard to remember Amy or distinguish her from a dozen similar girls in the high school. Michael thought better than to argue the point. Any of the seniors on the cheerleading and dance squads would easily eclipse Amy in the category of physical attributes.

"She's super smart," Jason continued after a pause. Michael wrote it down. Truth be told, Amy was in the upper half of the class, but held an unremarkable B-minus grade point average. Maybe Jason was comparing her to himself, a C student only because his gym and shop classes brought up the low marks in math and English.

As the list grew, Jason picked up steam. She was devoted to her family, an attribute he found admirable. She'd been working at her parents diner since she was old enough to hold a coffee pot safely. They opened for breakfast on the weekends at what Michael called "farmer's time," hours before sunrise. During the school year, Amy got something of a break, in that she didn't have to report to work until after school. Jason was wracking the tiny thesaurus in his brain to come up with more adjectives. Somehow the word "durable" failed to seem like a compliment. It was more the way you'd describe your favorite farm tool than the love of your life. "And that's about all I can think of," Jason said.

"Dude. It's not exactly a Miss America resume."

"Hey, it wasn't my idea to dissect her like a frog. You're the one with the list. I just know she's the one for me. So there." Trump card played, end of discussion.

Michael had to admit, it wasn't like deciding which used car to buy. Maybe love really did just come to you. After that, the rest is all talk. Just because he didn't have an Amy of his own yet, he shouldn't deny Jason the pleasure and the pain. In our childhood and teenage years we're unaware of the vast spectrum of adult relationships. Some appear more successful than others, but it's only in hindsight that we realize the variety of human connection. We all think of our own family as the normal one, our caregivers as the standard of adult behavior. If anyone should have known that fact, it was Michael, but he was just a teenager at a state wrestling meet.

There was that weird Mr. Terrier down the block. Or was it Tennyson? No one seemed to know his last name, but he and his wife had lived in the same house longer than anyone could remember. They never seemed to vacation or socialize. The Turners—that was it—weren't shut-ins. They sat on the porch, tended the flowers, adjusted the sprinkler. They were kind enough to wave and say hi when someone walked down the sidewalk. They gave out decent candy come Hallowe'en. But they never had any visitors, no children or grandchildren sullied the pristine front lawn. One rumor had it that a daughter was grown, married off and estranged. Another rumor was that they were heartbroken over the loss of their only son in Vietnam. Maybe she was barren, or he was impotent. Whatever the situation, their marriage was of long duration and by any yardstick, a success. Maybe Mr. Turner had pursued his wife as avidly as Jason now pursued Amy.

As for the origin of Jason's devotion, Michael could only surmise it came from the negative example of Jason's own father. Mr. Williams was the antithesis of the family man. He openly despised child raising and wanted nothing to do with them after they were conceived. In the Christian attitude of charity, outside observers blamed the stress of work for his uncaring attitude. Less forgiving neighbors accused him of having affairs in the many cities he visited on his mysterious business trips. There were countless times when he was gone much longer than any convention or sales meeting would have required.

In the lives of his children it didn't matter what he sold. Was it plumbing supplies or farm equipment? Jason and his siblings didn't honestly know. They did know that one trip their father didn't return. Then, some months later, the checks stopped coming. Jason's mother never complained, she just got herself a job and a pre-teen Jason helped raise his younger siblings. Did Mrs. Williams somehow drive him away? What did she lack that he found elsewhere? How did they go from "until death do us part" to parting ways? Michael had heard Jason say it once only once, "he'd never be like his father." Amy was to be the beneficiary of his knight-like devotion, despite the fact that she'd done nothing to deserve it. She just was.

"But we've still got to get her to notice you, man. Maybe that's the list we should be working on. What's she interested in?" Michael said.

"Nah. No more lists. If she doesn't show, maybe I'll have you talk to her for me. She's probably gonna open the diner for breakfast tomorrow. Get there before the church crowd fills the place. Tell her to come see my medal. Or something."

"No way. I'm not missing your match. Plus, you said yourself I'm no better at talking to girls. As much as I'd like to help you, dude, I'd probably say something wrong." Michael stared at the list again. Number four said how she was a good worker. "Hey, doesn't she have her driver's license yet? She walks, like, three miles to that stupid diner. In the dark, no less. Why don't you pick her up and drive her there? But not tomorrow, of course. You've got the finals."

"Or better yet, I'll buy her a new truck with all the winnings from my wrestling matches," Jason said with sarcasm as thick as his biceps.

"I'm just trying to help, man. Everybody's gotta have wheels."

"I don't think that's it, dude. Her dad's got like, ten cars and trucks up on blocks around back of that old barn." The seed of an idea began to germinate in Jason's love-addled brain. It wasn't fully formed but with time he knew the power of his love was undeniable and would supply him with the answer. Amy's dad had plenty of old beaters around the property. Most without tires, but they probably ran just fine. Even if they looked a bit like Frankenstein's monster with mismatched doors, missing bumpers and broken windshields, maybe Jason could help get one running. He didn't have the guts to talk to Amy, but according to the logic of love, it seemed reasonable to approach her dad, whom he'd never met, and have a man-to-man talk about setting Amy up with a truck.

"Wow, you really are a stalker."

"It's not a big deal, Michael. Her house is on my way home from school."

"Yeah, if you go two country roads out of your way."

"Okay, it's a little far, but everyone knows the Addison's farm. It's public knowledge. It's not like I'm hiding in the bushes waiting for her to undress for bed."

"Let's not even go there," Michael said. "C'mon, let's head back in and watch some wrestling. The rest of the team still has some matches."

"Yeah, good thinkin'. She might have come since we started lunch."

"Dude, you're sick. Really, you need an intervention."

"But, in a good way, right?"

The friends returned to the coliseum to mingle with their teammates, console the losers, congratulate the winners, and of course, continue to search the stands for Amy. They watched a few of the consolation matches without interest. The first day of the Tournament ended with the feeling of unfinished business. Crowds departed in silence. Some to nearby hotels. Even the wrestlers who didn't make the finals intended to stay and see how the brackets resolved. Many had hotel rooms and were committed to the event regardless of outcome. They were fans of the sport, first and foremost.

Michael and Jason decided not to stay in town, but rather make the drive back to Bellaire and sleep in their own beds. It was only about one hundred miles, less than two hours in Jason's truck. He dropped Michael off at home, then swung by Amy's house to see, he wasn't sure what. Would she be home? Was her light on? At the top of his personal cauldron of love, his heart was bubbling and boiling over with more excitement than he'd ever had during a wrestling match. Deep in the stew, two ingredients were vying for his conscious attention. What would it take to make Amy love him as much as he loved her? How could he let her know, for once and for all, how much they belonged together? His love was boundless, his power to solve the problem had its practical limits.

The next morning, Jason swung by Michael's house in his Chevy S-10 to give him a ride to the Coliseum. Michael bounded out of the house before the truck even rolled to a stop. He was wearing the team sweats over his street clothes. He jumped up into the cab. "Hey Champ, how you doin'? Ready to kick some ass?"

"Nice outfit. You recall you lost yesterday, right?"

"Hey, I'm here to cheer on my bro', State Champ, Jason Williams, soon to dominate the college circuit."

"Let's not get ahead of ourselves." Jason pulled away from the house and started the long drive back to Hays, Kansas. On the way, they were mostly silent, listening to country music when the stations would come in clearly, and making small talk about the weather. Both men avoided the obvious question of the day: Would Amy make an appearance?

At the Coliseum, Jason took his first look at the remaining wrestlers in the bracket. His first match was against Jackson Keener, whom he'd beaten both during the dual meet match-up and at the League Meet to end the season. On the other semi-final, there was his nemesis Bubble Gum Boy, the wrestler he'd failed to pin in last year's Tournament. It was the only time he'd actually hoped the tubby guy would win a match. Jared Huffman wasn't the most physically gifted heavyweight, but it was clear he had cunning. One doesn't make it to the Quarter-finals without having at least a little bit of skill. Whatever the match, Jason was confident he'd succeed. What had shaken his confidence was his lack of ability to get even the time of day from Amy.

With fewer matches to finish the Tournament, the layout of the gym had been altered, with one central mat replacing the four from the previous day. Additional bleachers were installed in order to fit even more fans into the Coliseum. Athletes who were in sweats the day before, were now in street clothes and cheering on their remaining teammates across all of the weight classes. The end result was that Jason's first match against Jackson wouldn't take place until almost noon.

After parking and signing in at the scorer's table, Jason suggested they look for Amy. "Let's do a lap around the concourse before we go in. Maybe she's getting some food."

"You're sure she eats, Lover Boy?" Michael said. "Maybe she gets all her energy from the sun. You know, the one that shines out of her ass."

Jason stopped to face Michael. "I'd pound you right here, Shortbread, but I need you to help me find Amy." Jason grabbed Michael's head in one hand the same way he'd palm a basketball. He lifted his friend to eye level while Michael pedaled an invisible bicycle, arms wrapped around Jason's tree branch of an arm. Nose to nose and in a menacing growl, Jason said to his best friend, "I'll give you a chance to take that back before I pop you like a zit."

"Okay! Okay, okay, I'm sorry! I didn't mean anything by it!" Michael begged to be let down. Back on the ground he continued his apologies and rubbed the sore spots on his skull. At that moment it was clear to both men that their friendship would never be the same. The exchange underlined the obvious fact that no love between friends would ever measure up to the infinite affection Jason had for Amy. Jason had never shown an ounce of aggression to his smart-ass friend and never would again. But if there came a time in the future where circumstances demanded it, Jason would choose Amy over Michael every time. All the shared jokes, the common interest in sports and music, the dozens of road trips for wrestling meets and summer concerts, Jason would give it all up for a single moment with Amy. Jason didn't say anything but turned away and continued his circuit around the concourse. Michael trotted to keep up, determined to find Amy and make it up to his best friend.

After a loop, they went inside the main entrance and Jason suggested they split up, search one level at a time and meet on the other side of the coliseum. They worked out a plan to move from the top level, then crisscross down a section at a time and end up at floor level. That way they'd be sure to cover the entire crowd. Once she was located, Jason would know where to signal the crowd during his final match. He'd be Babe Ruth calling his shot over the outfield wall. He'd be Joe Namath guaranteeing a victory in Super Bowl III. Heck, future trash talkers would claim to whoop their opponents like Jason Williams dominated the finals at the Kansas State High School Wrestling Championships, two years in a row. The only problem was, they never located Amy or even a friend who had seen her.

Dejected, Jason changed into his leotard and took his place at the end of the team bench. Waiting through the first rounds should have been torture, but his mind was elsewhere. He didn't even watch the other semi-final match to see his old nemesis, Bubble Gum Boy, Jared Huffman win on points in the third period.

Jason's match was more like sumo than high school wrestling. When his time came, he sauntered to the center of the mat and shook hands with Jackson Keener. The referee blew the whistle and Jason stood up from his crouch. He walked towards Jackson with slow, deliberate steps and engaged him in a crushing bear hug. Jackson's expression went from confused to surprised to terrified in the space of two seconds. With his arms pinned to his sides, Jackson was helpless as Jason lifted him off his feet and threw him to the mat, crushing the breath out of him in a single flying takedown. Jackson's wide eyes were all white in the exploding flashes from the surrounding photographers. In the paper the next day was a picture of the two men, horizontal, four feet off the mat, Jackson hidden from view behind Jason's bulk. Unable to breathe after the fall, he had no defense and was tapped out by the referee for his own safety.

Jason helped him to his feet and asked if he was okay. Jackson responded by waddling to the edge of the mat where he heaved his lunch before he could find a bucket or towel. In future conversations about the match the estimates of the number of his rib fractures ranged from two to eight. The better versions had multiple fractures of individual ribs, putting the total of breaks well into the teens. Jason walked over and put a hand on his back and asked if he was okay. The referee joined the pair for a post-match caucus and the three of them decided not to return to the ring for the final arm raising.

The throngs in the coliseum were eerily quiet, as if they'd just been surprise witness to an execution rather than a sporting event. Jason returned to his usual chair and returned to the obsessive chore of scanning the stands for any sign of Amy. The announcer broke the silence by announcing a brief intermission before the finals of the lower weight classes. A white noise of fans eagerly exiting for the concourse made no register in Jason's brain. With the entire crowd shuffling at once, Jason gave up his search and only then noticed Michael staring at him open-mouthed. "What?"

"Dude. You could have killed him," Michael said.

"Nah, he's bigger than you think."

"Jason. You tossed him like a wet cat. It's a miracle he got up off the mat. They should give Jackson an award for still being alive."

"Whatever."

For Jason, the rest of the Tournament was a blur of frustration and anger, flavored with the bile taste of doubt. He didn't even bother watching the other weight classes. If Amy didn't care enough to attend, what was the point? The peak emotions of being in love are matched only in mirror fashion by the depths of despair.

When it came time to meet his opponent in the finals, Jason barely registered the name or face of Jared, the Bubble Gum Boy. They slapped palms at the center of the mat, but Jason failed to make eye contact. His eyes were still busy scanning the crowd. Jared took his indifference as a sign of weakness, a lack of confidence. He couldn't have been more wrong. To Jason, Jared was a speed bump, a mosquito, an insignificant trifle to be eliminated in the more important quest of obtaining the favor of his beloved Amy. Jason actually wished Jared was a more worthy rival, so that his inevitable triumph would register. As it was, why bother? A more significant and memorable gesture would be to forfeit the match, let the Bubble Gum Boy have the victory, then he could let the rumor spread that he'd been more concerned all along with getting the attention of Amy. Wouldn't that prove his point more efficiently than another title?

As the referee blew the whistle, Jason was still scanning the crowd. And then, the years of prayers were answered. A lone, slender figure stood up from the upper reaches of the stands. The face was obscured by the shadows, but the figure could only have been Amy. The slouching posture, the bland, loosely hanging outfit, the shy demeanor must have belonged to his future wife, the mother of his children, Amy. The woman raised a finger and wagged it back and forth. Jason smiled from ear to ear and raised a single hand to return the wave. At the same instant, Jared charged and tackled Jason with an attack to his legs. The wrestlers ended up on the mat, Jared sprawled across Jason's legs, the Champion seated unexpectedly on his rear, still staring up into the stands.

Jason watched as the woman of his dreams grabbed her toddler by the arm and dragged him into the aisle and began swatting him in a demonstration of parental skills straight out of the manual from five decades ago. A brief moment of confusion gave way to new waves of anger. Did Amy have a younger brother, or a nephew perhaps? Was that the reason she'd missed his earlier matches, because she'd been forced to watch someone else's snotty kids? The woman's behavior made no sense given what Jason knew of the gentle nature of his beloved. The cliche was true, she wouldn't hurt a fly. Squinting his eyes to see into the upper reaches of the Coliseum, Jason received his answer and reprieve when the woman stepped under a canned light and revealed herself to be old enough to be his grandmother.

The Champion wrestler shook his head like a cartoon character struck with a cast iron frying pan. Awakened from his delirium, Jason saw Jared was still working on his legs in some silly attempt to get Jason on his back. Jason laughed out loud, his palms back on the mat behind him as if waiting for the fireworks to start on the 4th of July. Even if Amy wasn't there to see it, Jason had some pride as the defending Champion. He slid his arms under Jared like a forklift, one arm under the chest, the other under the hips. Jared performed his own version of the Karelin lift, flinging Jared over his head and out of the ring like tossing a bag of garbage into a Dumpster.

The rest of the match was strictly for Jason's amusement. He had no intention of throwing the match, nor did he want it to end too quickly. Jared was flung about like an overcooked piece of Angel Hair pasta. Moe and Larry were never so cruel to Curly or Shemp. At one point, Jason held Jared by the ankle, and swung the heavyweight's entire bulk like a figure skater until releasing him in a humiliating slide out of the circle. The referee didn't know how to score the throw so awarded Jared a point for an escape. Jason stood with his hands on his hips and laughed a maniacal laugh which silenced the crowd. As the two wrestlers returned to their starting positions, the only noise above the referee's whistle was the buzzing of the fluorescent lights of the Coliseum. Jason kept one eye on the clock during his complete thrashing of Bubble Gum Boy. He let the poseur enjoy the rare treat of taking Jason to the third round which was when the real punishment started.

Jared took the dominant position to start the third period only to find himself flying repeatedly out of the circle. Lift after lift and throw after throw ended with Jared on his back, two hundred and seventy pounds of chewed bubble gum landing heavily on his chest, his back, his arms and legs flailing, over and over. He could barely stand on his own, but Jason refused to pin him before time expired. Nearing the end of the third period, the referee placed the men on the mat, Jared on his hands and knees, Jason with one hand around the defender's waist, the other on his left wrist. At the whistle, Jared expected to be thrown again, and he crouched as low as he possibly could to avoid another devastating throw. When nothing happened he chanced a look over his shoulder and was met with the grinning pumpkin face of Jason, Man In Love. "This one's for Amy," he said.

A single droplet of sweat fell from the tip of Jason's nose as he hoisted Jared over his head with one hand, like a sack of groceries. Reaching up with the other hand to steady his load, Jason did a complete circle scanning the audience a final time for his beloved Amy. There was no sound but that of Jason's feet making ballerina moves on the vinyl mat. At the pinnacle of his high school career, Jason realized he was alone with no one to share his glory, no one to admire his accomplishment, no one to admire his strength and skill. Amy was not in the crowd. With time expiring, Jason folded Jared into a comfortable taco, knees to his forehead and lowered him gently to the mat. The referee called the pin to end the match and the crowd continued to stare silently, seven thousand open mouths directed to the lights at the center of the coliseum.

What should have been his greatest triumph was but another of Jason's ongoing defeats in love. At the bench, Michael knew better than to congratulate his best friend. Instead, he handed him a towel, his duffel bag, and the two men exited the building. Coach Rice would later collect the medal, but rather than present it to Jason, he simply put it in the high school display case next to the team photograph for future generations to admire. Without a word, Jason took the passenger seat of his own truck, letting Michael find the keys to the Chevy S-10 and navigate the trip back to Bellaire.

Still ten miles out of town, Michael risked a question to his two-time State Champion wrestler friend. "You hungry?" was all he could muster.

"Yeah," came the tortured response. "Let's go to Antonio's. I owe you a pizza. Let's get some pizza, the greasier the better. See if we can steal some leftover pitchers of beer." Neither of the athletes drank beer, even in the off-season. Michael took Jason's comments as a sign of unusual desperation.

It was a busy Saturday night at Antonio's. Michael parked Jason's truck at the fringe of the lot and walked in silence to the entrance. At the host stand, Jason gave a quick glance to the fancy dining room side of the restaurant, half expecting to see Amy there with some guy on a proposal date. They nodded to the hostess and proceeded to the party side of Antonio's. Dressed in jeans and varsity jackets, it was clear they weren't there for a fancy meal.

Like every weekend night, the place was packed. They paid for the buffet, grabbed a tray each and gathered food and drinks. With no empty tables in sight they took the end benches on a table set with a birthday cake. Strewn pizza crusts, half empty plastic soda cups and loose wrapping paper indicated this party was nearing its end. The kids were all off using up the last of their video game tokens. A pair of soccer moms was seated at the opposite end. Michael gestured to the empty seats with his tray and one of the mothers stretched out a hand offering them seats.

Jason sat down heavily and started on his salad, no dressing, without even taking off his coat. Michael peeled the cheese off a single piece of thin crust pizza and replaced the pepperoni on top of the sauce. Two bites in, he stopped and raised his diet soda. "To Jason! Dude, you did it!" but the toast fell flat as the drink.

"Yeah, thanks Shortbread. You were pretty good yourself in that first match." They made some more small talk about the tournament. Between bites Michael asked about Jason's plans for college, did he see any recruiters he knew, where did he think he might go. Jason returned the favor of ignoring the obvious by mentioning that a lot of the good wrestling schools had strong programs in pre-med. They could be roommates, maybe join a fraternity together. It didn't have to end just because the wrestling season was over. "Sorry about squeezing your head. Before. I mean, I just...I didn't mean anything by it."

"You meant to tear my head off, is what you mean," Michael said. They both laughed and continued their sarcastic apologies as only best friends can do. It opened up the conversation to the topic most on Jason's mind. "Look. Here's the way I see it," Michael said. "You're not one of the Knights of the Round Table. Killing a dragon isn't going to get the job done. She's not a prize you win at a fair. Sooner or later, you're gonna have to talk to her."

"I'm listening," Jason said. "So what's the next step?"

"Well. Amy might be a modern, independent, liberated woman, but she's still a farm girl at heart. She's not going to make the first move. Here's what you do. Get home early tonight. Get a good night's rest. Show up at the diner tomorrow before the church crowd. You'll have the place to yourself and her undivided attention. Order the lumberjack special and leave a reasonable tip. Not too much or she'll think you're trying to buy her."

Jason drained the last of his water and looked around the restaurant, thinking. The place was total chaos, but he didn't hear a sound. Video games were ringing and pinging, kids were chasing each other trailing streamers of tickets to redeem for plastic trinkets. Someone from the Antonio's staff was dressed like a giant slice of pepperoni pizza. He was posing with toddlers for pictures, shaking their hands with his giant three-fingered gloves. The absurdity of it all came crashing down on Jason like Bubble Gum Boy knocking him to the mat. It wasn't that long ago that Jason and Michael were coming to Antonio's for their own birthday parties. He'd just won back-to-back State Wrestling Championships and not a single person other than Michael even knew about it, let alone cared. He needed someone with whom to share his life's accomplishments. There were big things ahead for Jason; College titles, probably the Olympics, maybe even a gold medal and a Wheaties box. Maybe that's why Amy hadn't made her move. Jason loved her for who he thought she was right now. Amy needed to see some evidence of Jason in the future. She needed more evidence of his potential. Who was the man she'd be marrying going to be in ten, twenty or even fifty years? Was he a good provider? Would he be a good father? Did his scary size mean she'd live all her days in fear of his temper? Or would the combination of his infinite love and nearly infinite size ensure her physical and emotional safety all her days?

"Yeah. You're right," Jason said, not showing anything of the deeper currents roiling through his mind. "I'll talk to her tomorrow and let you know how it goes."

The men stood, waved to the soccer moms at the other end of the table and mouthed a "thank you" since there was no way they'd be heard over the din of the partying crowd. Michael left two dollars on the table even though he bussed the trays and wiped up the few stray crumbs they'd scattered. At the front door of Antonio's, Jason held out his hand to Michael who grabbed it, shook it vigorously, then leaned in for a hug. "Whatever happens, I love you man," Michael said, choking back a lump in his throat. "I'm proud of you, too."

"Shut up, fag. Gimme my truck keys." It wasn't an insult for Jason to call Michael a name. On the contrary, Jason's use of the word was just as meaningful as if he'd told Michael he loved him, too. If anyone else called his best friend a name, you can bet they'd be in for a serious beating.

"Oh, yeah, sorry," Michael said handing over the keys to the truck. "And you're still a big dumb-ass, by the way. I was just seeing if you'd fall for it." Jason put Michael in a headlock and walked him to the far side of the parking lot, opened the passenger side door, then walked around and climbed in to drive.

They drove to Michael's house by way of the scenic route—Amy's farm. "Dude, you missed the turn," Michael said. Then the light went on in his head. "Oh. Yeah. It's early, let's go for a drive."

The farm was dark and quiet, with only a single light visible in the kitchen through the front windows. Jason cut the lights and rolled down his window to take in the scene. They drove past the old barn idling in first gear. Jason made a mental note of the auto graveyard with dozens of cars and trucks from different decades and in various stages of disrepair. Many were up on blocks, missing only their tires, but otherwise looking to be in decent condition. Why Amy walked to work was a mystery he couldn't divine.

He inched the truck past the property, one foot on the brake. At the corner of the property line, Jason swung around and pointed the truck in the other direction and repeated the devotion. Pilgrims climbing Mount Fuji don't have this much dedication. After the second lap, Jason came to his senses and remembered he had a passenger. "Okay. That about does it." Michael refrained from asking what "it" was but he figured it must include the plan to find Amy early in the diner the following morning. Jason eased the Chevy S-10 from the farm's dirt access road and back onto the main county road, this time taking Michael straight home. They exchanged pleasantries at Michael's house, Jason thanking his sidekick for the advice regarding Amy and Michael once again congratulating the Champion on his victory.

After dropping off his friend, Jason drove home fully intending to get straight to bed. His brain was clouded by a fog of physical exhaustion and his active mind ignored the road. In his mind's eye he played different versions of how he would woo Amy from his seat in a booth at the diner. Some of the versions started with him casually ordering breakfast. She'd giggle at a playful joke of his and cover her thin lips with the hand holding her pen. In other versions, she'd approach him first, ask him what took him so long. She'd yell to her mom behind the counter, "This is the guy I was telling you about!" Amy would take off her apron, throw it over the counter to her mother and they'd spend the day together getting better acquainted.

Like an afternoon commuter driving home on autopilot, Jason found he'd driven right to Amy's house. He was on the access road, heading straight to the barn and the auto graveyard. Instead of turning around to exit, he decided to make a loop around the entire farm. Only one half of the property was used for farming, the rest was never cleared. Jason estimated the portion left as wild forest to be at least forty acres, probably closer to eighty. Dividing the two halves was a dead-end two-track road which ended at a gate. He figured it was used as access for the larger farm equipment since it was out of sight of the more picturesque front entrance and led behind the barn and the auto graveyard. As he passed the working portion of the farm, Jason glanced up the two-track and saw the reflected brake lights of a truck parked with one set of wheels in the road, the other in a ditch. The way it was positioned looked as if the owner was trying to hide it rather than just keep it out of traffic.

He backed up slowly, then turned down the two-track and parked behind the truck to investigate. He left his own truck lights on to illuminate the scene. The first thing he noticed was the Nebraska license plate. The truck was a late model GMC Sonoma; clean, steel gray, with a generous cab and a standard six-foot box. Aside from a touch of road grime, the truck was gleaming from the shiny grill to the polished cast aluminum wheels. The presence of the truck made no sense for Jason. The owner must be trespassing at the least, or worse, off in the woods poaching. If someone were visiting from out of town, they would have parked at the house. He felt a strong need to vandalize the truck just to teach this asshole a lesson.

Jason went back to his Chevy S-10 and retrieved a large hunting knife from the glove box. A couple of slashed tires would send the right message. He knelt down and prepared to deliver the blow when a new and better idea occurred to him. Dazed by the logic of love it made better sense to Jason to steal the tires. The moron poachers would get the point for sure. Guilty as they were they couldn't approach Amy's father about why their tires were missing. They'd have to be towed and the thought of them dragging a deer out of the woods to find their truck in the ditch made Jason laugh out loud. He'd stow the tires somewhere and at a later date present them to Amy's father as a way to help fix up a vehicle for Amy. The pieces had finally coalesced to make a complete picture. In one grand gesture he'd be able to demonstrate his complete and utter devotion to Amy, defend the family's farm, and educate the idiots from Nebraska.

Jason stowed the knife back in the glove box and retrieved the jack and wrench off his own truck. He loosened the bolts on all four tires, then raised the car from the driver's side to remove the tires in the ditch. He figured with the bushes in the way he'd get the messier side done first. When the tires were freed he tossed them in the back of his own truck. Then he realized there was nothing to lower the truck onto and remove the jack. He looked in the immediate area for a log or rock but none was to be found. Without a flashlight and not wanting to delay his plan any further, Jason treated the truck like an opposing wrestler. He braced his hands on the side of the truck, one on the cab and one on the bed. With a move only a champion heavyweight could have pulled off, he simultaneously heaved the truck and performed a leg sweep to free the jack. The four-ton truck groaned as it hit the ground in the ditch, bounced once, then settled onto its empty wheel wells.

The passenger side wheels were even easier to remove without the bushes in the way. The truck slid an inch more in the ditch as he raised the jack, but that wasn't his problem. A tow truck could easily pull it out later, once the poachers realized they'd been schooled. He tossed the tires into his truck and went back to free the jack once again. Bracing his hands once on the cab and truck bed he heaved it up to perform the leg sweep. With much of the weight of the truck in the ditch he was able to shove it more than he needed and the truck lurched out of his hands. Jason lost his balance before he could sweep the jack. His legs slid into the ditch and the truck came down with a crash landing across his thighs.

"AAARRrrgggh!" Jason screamed as the full weight of the truck snapped both his femurs mid-shaft. In an instant his love-addled brain traced the arc of his new fate with equally faulty logic. His wrestling career was over before it had even started. When he got out of the hospital, if he could even still walk, he'd go straight to prison. When he got out of prison, Amy would be long gone and he'd be engaged to a guy named Bruno who ate two hundred and eighty-five pounds for breakfast. Jason lamely tried to lift the truck knowing full well it wouldn't budge. This obstacle was no fat wrestler he could heave with a simple curling maneuver. No, this new fate was brought to fruition by the combined weights of his enormous hubris, ego, and blinding love for Amy.

"What are you doing under my truck?" Amy said. Jason looked up, startled to see a slight and shadowy figure standing on the grassy center line of the two-track road. It must be shock, he thought, not a good sign. Jason rubbed his eyes and laid back on the ground in order to allow more blood to get to his brain. The apparition spoke again. "I said, what are you doing?"

"Huh?"

"For the last time, Jason Williams, what are you doing with my truck?" Amy said, arms crossed and foot tapping.

"You know my name?"

"Yes, Mr. Champion Wrestler, I know who you are. I got your note last week."

"I love you?" Jason said. It was at once a question and an explanation for his involvement with her truck.

"Sorry I didn't make it to your match. I really did mean to come, but me and my dad were up in Grand Island."

"What?" It wasn't the answer Jason was expecting.

"He helped me find the truck in the want ads and we drove to Nebraska yesterday to pick it up. The guy only used it around his farm, so it's got really low miles. I've been saving my tips for six years to buy it. Now it looks like I need some new tires." Jason just stared at her, his confusion strong enough to mask the blinding pain. There were no poachers. "Are you hurt? Sorry. Stupid question." She looked into the bed of Jason's truck and saw her tires in a tumbled pile. "Care to explain?" she said, pointing to the stolen tires.

Jason went through his entire story trying to rationalize the twisted logic, realizing how incredible it sounded. The pain had a clarifying effect on his thought process, pushing the logic of love to the background. Guilty and caught he was no less determined to sway Amy into his good graces. Amy was having none of it and resumed her defiant position, arms crossed, scowl on her face. "So you see. I did it for you. I couldn't imagine you walking to work another day. Not with all those trucks your dad has behind the barn."

"Tell me about it," Amy said. "But he wants me to know the value of a dollar and buy it for myself. He thinks I'll take care of it better. If he could only see the truck now." Then ensued a conversation which could only happen at the beginning of a relationship, two people about to fall deeply in love with each other.

"Speaking of which," Jason said. "Isn't this a little bit much truck for a girl? One hundred and eighty-five horse power of trailer-pulling manliness? I'll bet it's an automatic, 4-speed, right?"

"That, my felonious friend is a GMC Sonoma, regular cab with six foot box and one hundred sixty horses. You only get the extra fifteen horsepower on the extended cab model. Besides I could use the gas mileage. Until recently it had four brand new, seventeen-inch polished cast aluminum wheels with sticky new Bridgestones. Formerly Firestone until 1988, but you knew that."

"V-6?"

"Duh." Amy frowned at the crushed wrestler as if he'd just said Abraham Lincoln was the *first* President of the United States. "Vortec High Output 4.3L V-6. What year is the S-10? A 1990? I appreciate your buying a Chevy, but seriously, I could drag your silly 2.5L inline-4 around the block like a dog on a leash. Ninety-two horsepower. Gimme a break."

Jason giggled through the pain. He couldn't possibly have been more smitten with this delightful young woman. "So does that mean you'll take me for a ride in it?"

"When you get out of jail, you mean? Or to the hospital?" She was serious. "Look. I might be able to get the jack under the rear bumper, but speaking of liters, you've probably got a liter of blood leakin' out of each of those broken legs. Probably best not to move you. Didn't you pay attention in health class? Boy Scouts or something? Never move an injured person."

"Yeah. Could you at least get me a blanket or something? I'm kinda cold."

"No. You'll be fine. I'll call 9-1-1 when I get to work. It's gonna take me a bit longer than I planned, though, since now I have to walk."

"Take my truck!" Jason said as if he'd finally stumbled onto something he could do for Amy.

"Nope. This conversation never happened. And we're not going out in my truck or anywhere else."

"What? You said you would have come to the finals if you weren't busy."

"I was just sayin' that. I got everythin' I need right here in town. I'm not heading off to some fancy college. I'm not gonna be second fiddle to some famous wrestler. I'm staying with my family and workin' in the diner. And if a man comes along and it all works out, then that'll be just fine. I'm not leaving everything I know and love for the likes of you."

"So you *have* thought about me," Jason said. He was giddy with the thought that all he'd need to do in order to win Amy would be to give up wrestling. There was a moment when he thought he could bounce back after the broken legs. But what college would want him with a police record on his resume? The question may have answered itself. Maybe stealing the tires was a good idea after all. "Well, what if I don't need all that stuff either? Would you consider dating me then? Just get to know me better. With this"—he gestured to the truck across his lap—"I think my wrestling career may be over."

Amy uncrossed her arms and moved her hands to her hips. While softening a bit, she was hardly doing back-flips for Jason's amusement. Her silence lasted longer than the hours he was alone in the freezing cold. It was everything he could do not to break the mood by blurting out how much he loved her, admired her, cared for her. She stared off into the woods. She crossed her arms again. She looked up at the stars shook her head and let out a heavy sigh. Finally, Amy dropped her chin and looked down at Jason. She snorted and giggled, showing her bright, even teeth. She took two steps and knelt down next to Jason's head as if preparing to perform CPR. What she did was equally life-saving. She kissed him gently, first on the forehead, then seeing his pleading look, she kissed him again, full on the lips. "I've got three miles to walk to work. If an ambulance comes in about forty-five minutes, you'll know I'm willing to give you a second chance. Make that a first chance. This hasn't exactly been dinner at Antonio's."

The ambulance and tow truck took almost an hour to find him despite specific directions from Amy. Jason was beginning to give up hope.

5

ROSE IS A ROSE IS A ROSE IS A ROSE

The coach pulled Hannah and put the first string players back into the game. Neither team was able to score in the first quarter. Michael's example of Jason giving up everything for Amy had not altered Jennifer's resolve to end the marriage. The only thing in his favor was that James had yet to appear with the divorce papers. She continued her barrage of complaints. "We have nothing in common," Jennifer said as the players took the field to start the next quarter. "You spend more time with your fantasy football buddies than you do with me."

"We're married," Michael said. "What more could we have in common? Of the six billion people on earth, we're in an exclusive club of two. No one else can say that about their relationship with either of us."

"We used to go dancing."

"Well, I'll be off the night shift soon. It'd be worse if I were a doctor, you know." Like many courting couples, they had spent much of their time at concerts, bars, and sporting events. Since Hannah was born it had been harder and harder to find baby sitters. Family members who pledged so much support when she was in diapers, babbling and cooing and adorable, had mysteriously found more pressing obligations after her second birthday. Michael's irregular schedule made their time off increasingly precious. It was rare that the three of them had a weekend together without some conflict. Michael would have to work both Saturday and Sunday, or worse, he'd get off a night shift and need to spend the day in bed exhausted, recovering. If Michael were free, Jennifer would have a big presentation for parent teacher conferences, or endless mounds of paperwork to prepare the budget for the school district. Hannah seemed to have countless sleepover birthday parties. One girl or another from her class was forever inviting her for the day and night, bowling, roller skating, and laser tag. The end result was a home full of vagrants who never saw one another.

"I don't like country music," Jennifer said.

"Now you're just being silly. If you want to talk seriously, then let's talk about children. I want to have more—even if we have to adopt."

Jennifer's jaw hit the grass. She turned from the game to address Michael face-to-face. "You're not listening," she said through clenched teeth. "It's over."

"Look at David and Kimberly. They're perfectly happy with eight kids. And a set of twins in the middle, to top it off. You can't tell me he's making more money than we are."

"Bad example, they're Mormon. Or something. And she's a stay-at-home mom. Just 'cause he does your taxes doesn't mean he's got the secret to a happy marriage." Jennifer leaned forward with her hands in her pockets and scanned the row of parents. She spotted David and Kimberly and gave a silent wave, then turned back to the game.

"What? I'm just saying, maybe the focus is more on their family and less on whether they still go dancing anymore. A few more kids would be great for us. At the least Hannah would be old enough to babysit."

"Yeah? How about your football buddy? Christopher and his wife Heather. I heard they just got back from a lovely trip to Mexico and you don't hear them making noise about wanting a dozen children. Ashley is on the Honor Roll every quarter."

Michael's face caved and he stood in silence. He couldn't even bear to watch the game. With effort and a cracking voice he was finally able to mutter under his breath, "You don't know them. It's not fair."

"What's not fair? That Chris married the best girl in town and you got stuck with me? I'll bet Heather weighs ten pounds less than she did in high school. And those are not the boobs she was born with…"

"Shut up, Jennifer. You don't know them. It's not about the kids. Ashley's great, but they wanted more and…" Michael stopped because of the lump in his throat. The mental and emotional fatigue were becoming too much and he turned away from Jennifer to wipe away a tear and swallow hard. Jennifer turned back to the game, satisfied that she'd won the "Number of Children" argument as well.

It was after the draft for their fantasy football teams that Michael and Chris found themselves together at Antonio's. They were seated at the bar on the casual side with an untouched pitcher of beer and three hours until closing time. Chris was a firefighter and like Michael his schedule was irregular. They both had the following day off work. The other members of the league had begged off one at a time after the draft was completed, citing "early mornings" and "diapers to change" as excuses for heading to bed early. "Hey, man, this beer's not gonna drink itself," was all Chris had to say to convince Michael to remain behind the others.

Jason was the last to leave saying, "Don't stay up too late you two. It's a school night." He threw a fifty dollar bill on the table and gave Michael a bear hug. "I love you, man." For Chris he threw a salute, "G'nite, Chief."

"Later, dude," Chris said. "Oh. And sorry you didn't get a running back. I'm sure you'll make up for it with that sweet kicker you picked up in the third round. That's all I'm sayin'."

"Hey, Chris. Remember. It is what it is," Jason said. He waved his hand in dismissal and walked out of the bar.

"Ooh, I'd like to strangle the first athlete who barfed that up in an interview," Chris said.

"Go easy on him," Michael said. "Don't forget, he used to wrestle, never played football. He doesn't even know how to pronounce 'Favre.' Although I agree with him that the whole idea of having cheerleaders at professional games is pointless."

The two men compared their rosters, a procedure which involved numerous high fives. As the pitcher filled with air and the bellies filled with beer, the number and volume of the shouts increased. Both teams were made of durable players, known for never missing a game. They shared an affinity for the workmanlike running backs and eschewed the flashier quarterbacks and receivers. "Hey, look what else we have in common," Chris said, pointing to an imaginary entry on his roster. "Hot wives!" They looked at each other with goofy grins, then burst out laughing and exchanged another double overhead high five. The hands swiped past each other and the total was more like seven or eight. They almost ended up in an awkward hug which resulted in more giggling.

The waitress came over to remove the other league members' empty glasses. "You guys doin' okay?" she said. "Where'd your girlfriends go?"

"Very funny, Alyssa. I'm sure you know," Chris slurred, "that Mr. Michael and I here, we've got the hottest wives in Smith County."

"Well, that's not sayin' much. You want another pitcher?"

"Oh, you're all business, aren't you?" Michael said. "Sure, but let's have some chips and salsa to wash it down. And a couple of fresh mugs. Thanks."

"Make this one last a little longer, guys. If you're slurring your words at closing time I'm taking your keys and calling you a cab. You know Miller loves to nail you on the week nights." They both watched the waitress sashay back to the bar. Officer Robert Miller was the law in town and a friend to both men. He'd known Michael for years, and unknown to Alyssa, was a member of the fantasy football league as well. He was currently on duty and thus unable to attend, but had e-mailed his picks for the season. Michael and Robert met at St. Bernadette's while both attended to injured or drunk criminals in the emergency room. Robert supplied the handcuffs while Michael cleaned the knife wounds or stabilized the C-spine. Since Chris was the fire chief they found themselves responding to the same emergency calls, fire or not. Alyssa returned with the mugs and pitcher in one hand, and a tray with tri-color corn chips and salsa balanced on her other arm.

"Enjoy responsibly," Alyssa said without waiting for the men to respond. She wiggled back to the bar with a cackle as if she'd said the most clever thing imaginable.

"Get a load of her," Chris said. "Lecturing us. She's barely a few years older than Ashley and Hannah."

"It's cute the way you say Ashley, like your dentures are slipping."

"Shut up and eat your salsa," Chris said with an exaggerated lisp. They both cracked up again.

"Hey, you know what else we have in common?" Michael said. Chris shook his head. "We've both got a little girl who's growing up too fast."

Chris raised his fresh mug for a toast. "To little girls who grow up too fast!" They clinked mugs, drank, then both stared at the colorful chips.

"I think that was the worst toast I've ever heard. You make it sound like Ashley and Hannah are pregnant and ready to move out of the house."

"I only meant to say…you know, you try to treasure each moment, 'cause then it's gone. You're makin' breakfast one day and you notice your daughter is taller than your wife. You fold the laundry and you don't know which pile to put the shirts in. She hasn't even gotten her period and they're wearing the same clothes. That's all I'm sayin'."

"Personally, I'd be good for six or eight," Michael said. "It's Jennifer who only wanted one. She's all about her career, giving Hannah, the 'best of everything,' the clothes, tutors, vacations, saving for retirement. When I get home from work and Hannah's there to give me a hug, that's all the vacation I need. Retirement for what? The house already feels empty. I've always wanted more kids. She's gone on so many sleepovers, it's like we're retired already. Empty nest and all that. I need a pet turtle or something." Michael was staring into his beer during the entire monologue and didn't notice the wetness on Chris's cheeks. "I guess you got it made, though. Heather's flower business is really taking off. Ashley's on the Honor Roll every quarter. Vacation condo in Cancun. You're livin' the dream, dude."

Chris made no attempt to wipe the tears from his cheeks. He took another sip and clutched at his mug with both hands. "Those damn flowers ARE her babies," the chief managed with a cracking voice.

Michael then noticed his friend's anguish. "What? Too much time on the business? Don't tell me there's trouble on the home front. You guys are great."

"Yeah, you might say that. I mean, sure the money was good at first, but it's become like, an obsession, with Heather. Don't get me wrong, she's really good at it. I mean, you've seen the bouquets." Michael nodded and took a sip. "So, like, it started with a few standards, you know, Hybrid Tea, Floribunda. Then you got your Grandiflora, your climbers and miniatures."

"Florida, what? That ain't a real word. Maybe you should switch to water. I'll finish this pitcher."

"Dude. Floribunda. 1909. Cross between a Polyantha and a Hybrid Tea Rose. Dense clusters, big simultaneous blossoms. Hardy. You see 'em in public parks all the time. Bushy. Makes a nice, low-maintenance border."

"I promise not to tell anyone at the station, chief. Your secret is safe with me."

"Yeah, but that's it. No more kids. Those are the kids, now."

"You wanted more, too?" Michael said. "That is SO unfair. How come the women get to make the decision?"

"No, no, no. Heather wants more kids, too. You're not hearing me, man. The doctors…" and his voice trailed off. Chris took another sip of his beer. "I thought you knew. I figured everybody knew." Michael shook his head. "Something went wrong. After Ashley was born, I mean. Scar tissue, something. I don't think the doctors even know for sure. That's all I'm sayin'."

"I'm sorry, man. I didn't know. So, she's put her life into the business? Is that the problem?"

Chris looked up from his beer to Michael. His eyes were clear. "Her life in the business? You have no idea."

The first moment Chris realized there was something wrong, he was making love to Heather. She began to cry, first in quiet whimpers, then in heaving sobs. Like all men, he thought things were going particularly well. Nothing groundbreaking, but he figured she was enjoying it as much as he was.

He'd gotten off another forty-eight hour shift for the fire department, a rare one during which he was able to get some quality sleep. Instead of crashing to bed, he'd been able to work on the house all day. Heather was at work, shopping, visiting her mother, having lunch, it didn't matter. He had time to clean the house from top to bottom. He did laundry, folded and put away all of Ashley's tiny clothes. She was only a year or two old at the time. He cleaned the entire kitchen, including those hidden areas for which no one ever gets proper credit; under the stove, inside and behind the refrigerator, and the utensil drawers. He even swapped out a box of Arm & Hammer to freshen up the garbage disposal. He attacked the bedrooms, cleaning Ashley's so thoroughly, wiping each and every surface, that it no longer smelled as though it were occupied by someone who wore diapers.

When Heather came to the door he'd already picked Ashley up from day care, given her an early bath and put her in her Sunday best. Dinner was ready, nothing fancy, just his specialty; fajitas with spicy beef, fresh vegetables, guacamole, and white corn tortilla chips with his homemade salsa. It was heavy on the cilantro, but he made no apologies for his preferences. The house smelled like a Mexican restaurant on Cinco de Mayo. He handed Heather a Corona at the door and kissed her on the cheek. "Hi honey. How was your day?"

"Oh, you made dinner! I'm famished." She grabbed the beer without drinking it and sat down at the dinner table. Ashley was beaming from her booster seat and looking like an angelic squirrel rotating a soft flour tortilla between her tiny front teeth. "They made me fast for the doctor's appointment, then they bumped me to the afternoon. Dr. Clark had some emergency with a patient at the hospital. Had to reschedule all his patients." Dr. Clark was one of the last of a vanishing breed. He still practiced full-spectrum general practice including in-patient medicine, prenatal care and obstetrics.

Chris stared at her, still holding the front door handle. "What's this all about? You tell me you're at the doctors office?" He closed the door and walked to his seat, eyes on Heather the whole time. "Go on. I'm waiting. Is everything okay?"

"Sure. No problem, just the usual stuff. You know, my annual. Periods have been a little off, but no biggee. Could have been the birth control."

"So, everything's okay for tonight? You know. Bedtime? That's all I'm sayin'."

"Oh, yeah, sure. I may need my sunglasses though. The kitchen is blinding. Thanks for cleaning, hon'. I'll make it up to you. Then I've got a surprise to tell you about."

The rest of the evening was spent with intense flirting. Ashley commanded most of their attention on the surface. In a few years they would no longer be able to get away with such overt foreplay. To any adult observer their interplay was PG-13, borderline rated R. Heather had her hands in Chris's shirt, hugging him from behind while he did the dishes. Chris returned the favor—or was it vice versa?—when Heather wiped down the stove top. He unbuttoned her jeans to run his fingers across the top elastic of her frilly underpants. He nibbled her neck while she replaced the grates over the gas burners. Turning to face him, Heather put her arms around his neck, kissed him chastely, lips only, then whispered in his ear to move the action upstairs. Ashley just giggled from her booster seat, licking powdered sugar from the sopaipillas. The amount of honey smeared across her cheeks and in her hair would necessitate another bath before bedtime. "To the bathroom it is, then," Heather said.

The teasing continued during all of bath time. "As usual, you've overfilled the tub," Heather said. She came from the laundry room with a large towel. Ashley sat with warm water to her shoulders and soap suds to her ears. She was filling a souvenir plastic cup from Chris and Heather's honeymoon to Cancun and dumping it over her own head.

"What? She's having fun. I'm right here. She's not in any danger."

"No, you're going to get water everywhere."

"Huh?"

"Yeah, look over there," Heather pointed to the corner behind Ashley. Some old caulking showed signs of peeling along the lower row of tiles. Chris, already on his knees, leaned over the tub for a closer look. Heather grabbed Chris's buttocks in both hands and shoved him into the tub with Ashley, clothes and all. Water splashed everywhere, including the floor outside the tub. Chris came up with soap suds all over his face looking like the Grinch dressed as Santa except his ear-to-ear grin gave him away. "See? There's water all over the place."

Ashley stood with a full cup of Senor Frog's water and waddled over to her grinning father. He crouched in the corner with his legs hanging out of the tub. She dumped it over his head washing away the soap suds mustache and beard. "Thank you, Ashley. At least someone appreciates me."

"Come here, Peanut." Heather wrapped her daughter like a burrito from head to toe with three plush towels. To her husband she scolded, "I expect you to have your clothes off by the time I get back."

Heather returned soon after wearing only her short silk robe. It's color was the same delicate pink as the blush on her cheeks. She made a pretense of cleaning the bathroom as if Chris weren't watching her every curve. She bent over to wipe up the water letting the front of her robe fall open to his full gaze. She stood to hang a towel but dropped it. "Oops," Heather said as she bent over from the waist to retrieve it and show her husband what she was hiding under the hem. She left the bathroom again with no explanation. She turned out the light, leaving Chris in the dark. She returned carrying only a single candle.

"You've lost your robe."

"Oh, I didn't see you there, honey," she said coyly. "Is there room for two?" She placed the candle on the closed lid of the toilet.

"Probably." Chris slid back to make room so she could drive from the front seat of the liquid toboggan. "How's Ashley?"

"She didn't even make it half way through *Goodnight Moon*. Sugar crash after dessert, I guess. I think we're on our own."

They talked some more about nothing, lazily caressing each other's bodies above and below the waterline. Heather washed her hair and Chris helped her rinse with the cup from Cancun. She stood, turned and let him see her full length, dripping into the tub. Careful not to step on anything important she shuffled forward until her slender thighs were right at his face. "Are you moving, or what?"

"Oh." Chris slid forward, letting Heather sit behind him. She washed and rinsed his hair, then washed some parts that didn't need washing. "I'm getting pruned. What say we take this party to the bedroom?"

"I don't feel any wrinkles," Heather teased. Chris got out first, dried himself, then handed Heather a towel without using his hands. "Ooh, clever boy. I'll bet you could teach Edward Scissorhands a few tricks." Heather got out, grabbed the towel, then Chris, and led him to the bed like she was trailing a wagon. Chris brought the candle. Heather threw back the duvet to find the sheets had been freshly cleaned by Chris. The movement of her arm set free a cloud of perfume that Heather had worn on their wedding night. She released Chris and crawled into bed, letting him see her from every angle again. She finished her tease by reclining in a full sprawl, prepared to make a sexual snow angel. When Chris joined her she covered them both by flinging the duvet back in one deft throw and enveloping them in the flowery scent of their honeymoon.

At one point in their lovemaking, the normally reserved Heather let out a tiny squeak. Encouraged, Chris doubled his efforts. He misinterpreted a quick inhalation of breath as more reason to go on. She then made a sound that could only be read as a sniffle. Chris began to sense something was wrong, both in his mind and his loins. He pushed himself up to see her face and a new, metallic scent mixed with their lust. He could also see by the candlelight a tear was rolling out of each eye down her temples to the pillow. Heather's face was a contorted mess as she tried to keep from crying out loud. "Heather? Am I hurting you?"

"No, just the opposite. You feel so good. Let's have another baby."

Chris returned to his duties even though the mood was broken. He was able to finish, but it suddenly felt like a chore. They exchanged vows of love and he gave her a tender kiss. He held her with his full weight resting along her length like a human afghan. After a while, he rose up to go to the bathroom. When Chris turned on the light to find a towel he was shocked to see himself covered in blood from navel to knees. He ran to the bedroom to find Heather crying as before. Even in the pale candlelight he could see a spreading stain of dark red under her hips on the mattress. She was crying more softly now, not from the pain of the bleeding, but from the pain of loss.

"Geez man, I was into the story until that last part," Michael said. He sat there in Antonio's with his mouth open, a warming mug of beer in one hand and a soggy, uneaten corn chip in the other.

"And that was her first miscarriage."

"Aw, dude," was all Michael could say.

"She'd just found out she was pregnant at the doctor's office, too. That was her big surprise for me. Ashley was going to get a little baby brother or sister. That's why she didn't drink the Corona. I don't know what's worse, losing the baby when you have a couple of months to plan or losing what you didn't even know you had." Chris poured himself another beer and topped off Michael's mug as well. "That didn't make much sense, did it?"

Michael tried to eat his chip but it stuck in his dry throat. "Wait," he coughed. "Her *first* miscarriage? How many has she had?"

"Dozens, now. We stopped counting. That was eight years ago."

"Shit, dude. I thought you just wanted one, like Jennifer. I don't know what to say."

"It's alright, neither does anyone else. We wanted them close together, so we kept trying, but it never stuck. As Ashley got older we didn't care about the timing, we just wanted another baby. Boy, girl, didn't matter."

Michael downed his entire mug in one breath, then filled it again from the pitcher. "I'll tell you what I can't figure. If it's worse to try and try, but lose the babies or to have a wife like mine who won't even consider another kid."

"I'll tell you what I think is worst, but you may not agree," Chris countered. "Try having sex knowing that this could be the one, and if it is, you'll likely just lose it again. Have your hopes raised and crushed over and over."

"Yeah, but at least you've got Ashley and you're on the same team about it. You've got hope. Jennifer slammed that door shut on me years ago. What did the doctor say?"

Heather and Chris quickly exhausted the expertise of Dr. Clark. He'd done a terrific job with Ashley, from prenatal care through delivery. But Heather's problem was beyond his skill and they admired him for admitting as much. When Heather starting having miscarriages he educated himself beyond his level of skill to intervene. He explained the few known risk factors. They tried every trick from the medical literature, but nothing helped. Chris went through the humiliation of a sperm count, but it was obvious to all that his side of the equation was not the problem. Heather was getting pregnant, she just wasn't staying in the family way.

They suffered the added confusion of not understanding why Ashley was such a breeze. They'd conceived right there in Cancun on their Honeymoon. They joked that she was a beach baby and despite growing up in Kansas, she craved the ocean. When she was old enough to ask for it, they painted a mural to make her bedroom look like a lanai. Every bedtime was a constant reminder of how easy it was the first time. A palm tree arched over the head of her bed. Tucking her in was like picking at the scab on a wound that refused to heal. They even planned vacations back to the same resort. Neither of them was superstitious, but they also didn't speak out loud the real reason they requested the same room, year after year.

Chris was reluctant to tell even Michael about the time she asked for a divorce. The stress of her miscarriages, both emotional and physical, caused her to break down on a weekly basis. He rationalized and with some good evidence, that her behaviors were mostly a side effect of the wildly swinging hormones. There was a time when parenting and chores took a backseat to her reproductive issues. Chris confessed that in a weak moment, he even entertained the idea of leaving Heather. She was a shell of her former vibrant self. Then, it was her turn to save the marriage and beg for another chance. They spoke of adoption, but in the end, agreed it felt more like giving up. Not as bad as divorce, but nearly so.

The trip to a subspecialist in Kansas City was both educational and dumbfounding. Dr. Robinson was personally recommended by Dr. Clark. They'd known each other in school and still consulted one another. Dr. Clark would answer questions about primary care and Dr. Robinson would help with his friend's obstetric and gynecological queries. They shared an easygoing bedside manner that helped patients through the tougher times.

"All we're saying is that Dr. Clark already told us that." Chris was frustrated early on in the interview process. He'd been forced to pace in the waiting room while Heather went through the usual history and physical exam nonsense. Waiting to meet the doctor had been more nerve-wracking for him than attending Heather during Ashley's delivery. When he was finally allowed into the exam room, he was both delighted and angered that no new information was forthcoming regarding Heather's condition. Of course she was healthy. Dr. Clark had been very thorough. Now Dr. Robinson had nothing to add.

"I'm simply stating how common miscarriages are. Of women ages thirty to forty, one-fourth of the pregnancies don't make it." Dr. Robinson sat forward putting his elbows on his large desk. His fingers were laced in a double fist under his chin. He was wearing baby blue scrubs. The overall impression was that he was a man of action. He had a genuine investment in helping them solve their problem, beyond the fact that they were friends of Dr. Clark.

"But I was in my early twenties when this all started," Heather said.

"She never smoked. She hasn't had a drink in a decade," Chris added. "We've been through all that with Dr. Clark."

"Were you always so thin?"

"Sure, I guess. I weigh about what I did when we had Ashley. My periods are regular. I've cut out caffeine."

"There's an association with low Body Mass Index. That's all." Dr. Robinson sounded as defeated as his clients. "Well, how many miscarriages have you had?"

"We stopped counting," they said together. The question had been asked so many times it had become a reflex answer for Heather and Chris. Dr. Robinson's face fell another level.

"Oh. Oh, that's not favorable. Even after four losses, the odds drop to less than half that any subsequent pregnancies will make it."

"What about a cerclage?" Chris suggested. He was referring to the stitch doctors will sometimes place around the opening of the cervix to help prevent early deliveries.

"You really have done your research, Chris. But that only helps women in the second trimester. Heather's not even getting out of the first two months. I'm afraid it wouldn't make any difference." The couple looked at each other. It was becoming clear that no solution would be found, surgical or otherwise. "Look. I don't want to overwhelm you with numbers. But that's it, they're just statistics. Even if ninety-nine out of a hundred don't make it, there's one that will. You guys are doing everything right. Just keep loving Ashley, keep loving each other and if it happens, it happens. Rose is a rose is a rose is a rose…"

"What's that supposed to mean?"

"It's Gertrude Stein. It is what it is. We don't have all the answers."

"You don't have ANY of the answers," Chris said.

"Touche. But what I mean is…" and he stopped. Dr. Robinson looked from Heather to Chris for permission to proceed. "I don't want to get too deep here. But I see it over and over. A lovely couple like you all who deserve to have ten kids, is stuck with no explanation why things aren't working out. They spend their savings on in vitro fertilization and nothing happens. Then they spend their retirement just so they can adopt. A homeless teenager downtown turns a few tricks for meth and is carrying her fourth child. Drinking the whole pregnancy, not taking her prenatal vitamins and she comes in to the ER fully dilated to deliver a perfect baby she hasn't got the capacity to love for a minute, let alone the resources to care for the child. I can't explain it. There is no justice. Sorry for ramblin' on and on, here."

"Well, what do we do?" Heather and Chris were on the edges of their seats, holding hands across the armrests of their chairs.

"Just live your lives. Do what you do. Start a new hobby. Take up gardening. I don't know. But try not to let the issue define who you are, or worse, come between you. Have sex, but don't let it become a chore as if every time could be the one. Remember Ashley. She's more important than this problem."

Heather and Chris thanked Dr. Robinson for his time and left the office holding hands. The four hour drive from Kansas City was like a second honeymoon, a surprise vacation gift from Dr. Robinson. They both realized how desperate they were for another child that they had forgotten how fortunate they were to have Ashley. Conceiving and its efforts had taken over their lives. The future robbed them of the present. They reminisced, they celebrated their new life, they felt buoyant, they made a vow to never talk about divorce again. Not having a reason for their misfortune was freeing in a way they hadn't expected. Their guilt for doing something wrong was removed. Their plans for having a big family gave way to enjoying the beautiful gift of the one they already had.

Ashley thrived under the constant attention of both her parents. When Chris was away on his long shifts for the fire department, Ashley would spend the day with Heather. They would run the house together, cleaning, cooking, and sharing every moment. In the early years, Ashley was more of a passenger and a tourist. She'd nap in her car seat while Heather turned the garden soil. As she got older she'd help fold the clothes, plan the meals or even position a new plant. On his days off, the three of them would enact scenes most families only see on Hallmark birthday cards. They'd picnic, go to the zoo, take drives to one of the nearby reservoirs and go for a swim.

As Ashley grew, so did the garden. Heather started with a simple plot in the corner of their small suburban yard. She started with the easy standards; carrots, tomatoes, lettuce, and corn. Then, recalling Dr. Robinson's comment, she tried a rose bush, an American Beauty with giant blossoms. Finding it easier than pumpkins, she put in another. As plants grew larger, or she acquired new varieties, the rose garden grew exponentially. The first casualty was the small vegetable garden they started when Ashley was in first grade. The food it produced was substandard and of such small quantity, that no one was sad to see it go. Ashley learned what she could about how a kernel of corn could produce an entire plant, or a flat pumpkin seed could turn into a fruit the size of her head. After those early lessons, they began the more complicated science of attempting new hybrids for the expanding rose garden.

Soon, Heather was taking over small sections of their modest back lawn. The idea of making her hobby into a business came with no effort. Heather brought a fistful of blooms to every event to which they were invited. If a friend moved into a new house, she'd bring over a dozen roses, each of a different breed, to admire over a bottle of wine. Birthday parties were an excuse to show off a single, blood-red bloom the size of an outstretched hand. Baby showers were the most difficult of all for her emotionally, but the perfect occasion for her miniature roses. If the sex of the baby were known, you can bet she'd have an overflowing vase of pink or blue exotics on hand to go with her gift of a stroller or car seat.

Many of her friends began to ask for a few blooms to decorate the tables at other events as well. While Heather's presence wouldn't be appropriate at a family reunion, a wake, or a wedding, her roses were always welcome. Of course, her friends insisted she take some money for her efforts. The excuse they gave was how much money they'd saved by not having to order them off the Internet or drive all the way to Hays, which had the only good flower shop for miles around. Besides, Heather's flowers emitted a heady aroma which the commercial roses somehow lacked. On Mother's Day, she'd clean the garden of her yellow, pink and white varieties. For summer weddings she had a dozen varieties of red. The entire graduating class was wearing her flowers at the senior prom. Chris had to beg for a small patch of grass, just enough room to put down a pair of Adirondack chairs. The backyard became an English garden with only enough space to walk between the varieties and tend to their nutritional needs. Heather opened a bank account to track her modest expenses and her impressive profits. She quietly saved for years, never letting her hobby become a drain on the family expenses. In fact, without the extra income, they could never have afforded the annual pilgrimage to Cancun. When she had enough money saved she was going to surprise him by suggesting they pursue a formal adoption. A boy and a girl, maybe even twins. If there was any left over, they'd start a college fund.

"Oh, so that explains the lifestyle," Michael said. "Sure, it all makes sense."

"But then things started to get a little strange."

"Uh, oh." Michael hoisted the pitcher and divided the remaining beer between their mugs.

"She started to get very defensive about the garden. People would ask questions about how come her roses were so nice. She'd give the usual answers. You know, manure, egg shells, and then brush it off. If they pressed, she'd get a little snippy. They'd figure it was a business secret and let it go. One night at dinner I asked her what the real secret was. No way it was that simple or everyone would grow their own, you know? Who am I gonna tell? That's all I'm sayin'."

"So, what did she say?"

"That's just it. She bursts into tears, runs from the table and locks herself in our bedroom. Not another word out of her the whole night."

Chris knew after ten years of marriage when it was time to back off. Rather than bring it up again when she was in a better mood, he attempted the romance angle. The last thing she needed was a dozen roses. With Ashley in school and Heather off to lunch with her mother the next day, he had time to deep clean the entire house. The laundry was done, kitchen cleaned, the frames dusted. To really impress Heather, Chris started on the closets. First, he organized the linens. He knew better than to discard any of the bed clothes from Ashley's crib or toddler bed. He refolded them and placed them on a top shelf, freeing up two shelves on the bottom of the closet. Digging deeper, he came across three large boxes he didn't recognize. Inspection of the first revealed a wide selection of women's hygiene products; tampons, maxipads, and panty liners. He knew Ashley wasn't using them yet, but it made sense to save money by buying in bulk. The second box was more of a mystery. It contained two gross bottles, twenty-four dozen containers of generic prenatal vitamins. Each bottle contained one hundred pills and bragged about having extra iron. The third box was like the second, except half the bottles were gone.

Maybe she was selling them on the side to augment her flower business. But any markup she could get from buying them in bulk would be more than eaten up by the cost of shipping them to any buyers. Plus, by the time most women found out they were pregnant, they'd only go through at most, one or two bottles before they delivered. Even starting on them prior to conception, it would be unusual to use three full bottles before having your baby. Chris replaced the boxes in the same order and stuffed the baby clothes and linens along the floor to hide the fact that he had seen Heather's stash.

A week later, Heather's distress was becoming more apparent to Chris. She was ignoring the most basic housework, but worse, she was beginning to argue with Ashley, something she'd never done. They had a brief discussion over dinner that perhaps she needed a break from her responsibilities. Rather than go away herself, they agreed that sending Ashley to her grandmother's would be a better solution. Heather could recover mentally without the added stress of trying to make do in a motel or imposing upon the good graces of one of her friends. The two adults could reconnect and perhaps share some intimacy without threat of interruption. Heather's mother was more than happy to help and their wedding anniversary was the perfect excuse to give without arousing suspicion that Heather was one breakdown away from in-patient therapy.

The first two days went well. Heather seemed to be relaxing. The color had returned to her face and she even smiled when he left for work. She wished him well on the third day, kissing him passionately at the door in her nightgown. Chris had secretly traded a shift with a friend in order to surprise Heather with a night at a bed and breakfast hotel. He left the house with his briefcase and even waved as he drove down the street in his truck. Rather than heading to work, he was driving to the local grocery to pick up some treats for their special night. Having candles, strawberries and whipped cream lying around would have spoiled the surprise.

After his surreptitious shopping trip, Chris circled back around to the house. He put the truck in neutral and cut the engine for the last block. He rolled to a stop by the curb and stepped out of the cab, closing the door as quietly as he could manage. Once inside the front door he let out a yell, cheesy as a sit-com actor, "Honey! I'm home!" Chris listened for an answer but all he heard in the house was the sound of running water from the upstairs bathroom. Hoping to catch his bride in the shower, he bounded up the stairs two at a time. He knocked on the door but still no answer came. "It's Big Surprise Time!" He tried the handle and the door swung open. The bathroom resembled a murder scene. The water was running into the tub and down the drain, raising a thick cloud of steam. He turned off the tap, then noticed there was a puddle of dark, thick blood, almost black in and around the toilet bowl. Chris noticed the footprints in blood leading out the bathroom door behind him.

He followed the steps down the first few carpeted stairs where they faded to nothing. He called out for Heather again but got no answer. He checked every room on the first floor, saving the bathroom for last. Terrified, he opened the door to the garage, sick with images of what he might find. The light was off and her car was parked quietly in its spot. He found no blood and no Heather. In the kitchen he noticed a few drops of blood on the beige Mexican tile. They led out the sliding door which was still ajar. Heather was in the center of the garden, kneeling with her back to the house. A shocking red stain had spread across the bottom of her nightgown, which Chris could see clearly from the darkness of the kitchen.

Under any other circumstances the view would have been worthy of a postcard. The entire yard was a brilliant fireworks display. Every color of the rainbow was represented in stunning array. The deep green background of the stems and leaves would rival the fairways of Augusta National Golf Club. At the center of this artist's palette was the artist herself. Heather in shocking white, with a horrifying bloodstain at her back side, was tearing at the ground with her bare hands. Chris ran from the kitchen screaming her name, "Heather!" As a firefighter, he'd seen his share of tragedy and gore, but nothing literally this close to home. He crashed in a heap at her side with one hand on her shoulder.

"What happened? Are you all right?"

"…slow-feeding organics…" was all she mumbled.

"What?"

"…trace elements, fast-acting chemicals…"

"What are you talking about?" Heather's calm demeanor had the opposite effect on Chris. He became more hysterical. "How can you be so calm? There's blood everywhere!"

"...nitrogen, phosphorous, potash. Iron, manganese, copper, zinc, boron..."

Heather looked up from the shallow hole she was digging and met his concerned gaze. Her eyes were bloodshot, but no tears were flowing. "Would you hand me that pot?" She pointed to a one-gallon, plastic container with a medium-sized polyantha rose bush in it. Heather took the pot gently, as one would accept a baby for a feeding. She grabbed the thorny stem in her bare left hand and inverted the bush. A single, sharp rap with her right hand and the plant was free. She teased the roots out with her dirty fingernails. She set the rose bush aside and stood. Reaching under her nightgown, Heather removed her underpants and a single, large and clearly inadequate, feminine napkin. She knelt back down and presented it to Chris. In the pad was a tangled mess of blood clots and unidentifiable tissues. She knelt down and proceeded to invert the pad over the hole.

Chris stopped her by placing a hand tenderly on her arm. "Please. Can I do it?" Heather nodded and he took the pad from her. His hands were shaking, but for new reasons. He no longer worried for his wife's safety, but the blood had taken on a new meaning. He cradled the products of conception in his hands. None of the tissue was identifiable. He rubbed his fingers around the pad and felt the heavy, grainy texture. He thought of Ashley and the day she was born.

Heather roused him from his daydream by placing a hand on his shoulder. Their eyes met but no words were needed or spoken. Together they placed another future in the hole. On top went the polyantha with its pure white, tiny blossoms. They spread the roots of the bush and sprinkled moist dirt into the hole. When the rose bush was secured they turned their attention to one another. The couple held hands and shared another moment of silence.

After a moment, Heather said, "It never gets any easier."

"What?"

Heather looked around them at the roses. Climbing varieties covered the fences in all directions, blocking the views of the neighbors' houses. On their knees at the center of the garden, all they could see was a forest of color and a dome of blue sky. The only unobstructed view was a stripe of grass, leading back to the house. Chris looked left and right, then back to his wife. "Every single one?"

Heather nodded. "I love you."

"Not as much as I love you," Chris said, meaning it more than on their wedding day, more than Ashley's birthday. They rose to their feet and walked back to the house and the rest of their lives.

6

IRRECONCILABLE DIFFERENCES

For Michael, the game plodded forth like a cricket match. Days turned into weeks. Would halftime never come? In his sleep-deprived state the game looked like an endless mix of the Chinese fire drill and an interminable Monty Python skit. "I need a break," Michael said.

"That's just another way of saying divorce."

"I don't mean a separation. I'm just tired. Remember? I worked all night. And all night every night last week."

"Saying you want a separation is just for people who don't have the balls to admit it's over."

"Listen to me." He turned to face Jennifer, shoulder-to-shoulder. He spoke slowly. "I'm just tired. I need to sleep. Can't we talk about this when we've both had a good night's rest? I feel…out of my skull. Let's have an even playing field."

"You got another ticket."

"What? I haven't had a ticket in years."

"No," Jennifer said. "Look." She pointed to his Ford F150. Under the driver's side wiper blade was a rectangular piece of pink paper that could only be a parking ticket. "Isn't that Officer Miller's Harley?"

When Michael looked he saw that Officer Robert Miller had already parked his motorcycle, written the ticket and was on his way to the sideline where Michael and Jennifer stood. He wore his full highway patrol uniform; leather motorcycle jacket with diagonal Sam Browne belt, tapered breeches tucked neatly into knee-high riding boots. Under his arm he carried his two-tone motorcycle helmet. He scanned the sideline for his wife Michelle, who was somewhere in the crowd. Their daughter Alexis was on the team, but like Hannah's other teammates, Michael couldn't have picked her out of a police lineup. "Oh, that. Geez, Jennifer, you had me worried there for a minute."

"Great. Now you've not even got any concern for the law. Common decency."

Michael almost laughed out loud. When Robert approached he held out a hand in greeting. "How's it going, Robert?"

"Eh. About the same," Officer Miller replied in his thick Brooklyn accent.

"Oh, sorry to hear it. That bad, huh?"

"Well, you know me. I can't complain." They both had a hearty laugh, leaving Jennifer bewildered and more than a little perturbed. It was part of their usual friendly banter and started when Robert told Michael about his Uncle Louie. Didn't every Catholic Italian family from New York have an Uncle Louie? He was the one who was perpetually listing everything wrong with his life and the world, from the weather to the price of gasoline, concluding that the world was going straight to hell, only to finish by saying, "But you know me. I can't complain."

"Thanks for the ticket. I wasn't sure if the 'No Parking' zone was just for weekdays or what. You understand."

"Sure," Robert said. "It's the least I could do for an old friend." The two men had a chuckle which elicited from Jennifer another theatrical sigh. Robert couldn't help but notice and comment. "What's with the ball and chain, Michael? Forget to put the toilet seat down?"

"Um, maybe we should talk another time." Michael waved his hand low to signal an end to any further discussion.

"Oh, sorry, did I just step in something? Sorry. Again. My bad." Robert had responded to his share of domestic disputes. Even in a small town in Kansas, an officer developed a skill not found in other disciplines. He sensed the tension from their body language but didn't think much of any real importance could be happening on a beautiful Saturday morning. Soccer games were supposed to be family time.

"Don't worry, Jennifer," Michael said, "Robert gives me blank tickets to keep any of the new officers from writing me up when I happen to commit a victimless crime. Don't you Robert?" It wasn't a question.

"It'll cost you a running back, you know."

"Sure, something in the third round?"

"Yeah, right. I'm thinking we swap first round picks and I get a second. Plus, your wide receiver."

"Why not take my wife, too? Do you need a Golden Retriever to keep Alexis company? Forget it. You'll take my second round running back and be happy. Or no deal."

"Fine, fine, don't get your panties in a bunch. Jennifer, your man drives a hard bargain."

"Hmpph," was all she could muster. Their fantasy football league banter was more than she could stand. "There you go again, ignoring the obvious."

"What? That Robert has no quarterback? He's hoping to get one in the third round, for a song. Good luck with that."

"No. Our irreconcilable differences."

There was a sudden and awkward silence amongst the three friends. They were aware of the noises from the field, the shouts of the other cheering parents. Michael continued to be stunned she was persisting with the divorce talk. He was even more shocked she would air their dirty laundry in front of an old friend. They cast uncomfortable glances at the field, then back at their feet. "Uh," Michael stammered. "Honey, shouldn't we discuss this later? At home? When I've had time to catch up on some sleep? I'm sure Robert has other things he needs to take care of."

"What's the difference?"

"That's what I'm saying," Michael said. "Whatever is on your mind, we'll figure it out. Now's not the time."

"Yes, it is. I've got my reasons."

"Have I ever told you how I met Michelle?" Robert said. He felt the need to diffuse some of the tension, even if it was none of his business. He'd stood by such disputes early in his career and regretted it later. Now, and especially when in uniform, he felt this authority and experience gave him the right to intervene in domestic disputes. He'd helped load enough ambulances in his career to know that family violence was not only common but could be brutal in ways the movies didn't even begin to address. True, he didn't think either Michael or Jennifer was the type to get violent, but that's what everyone says, in hindsight and when it's too late. Like a reflex, he couldn't help but offer advice. "We've got as much stress in our marriage as anybody, but we manage to keep it together. You want irreconcilable differences? I'll give you Middle East peace talks. Makes Northern Ireland look like, like...well, worse than China and Tibet. "

"Clearly, politics isn't your strong suit," Jennifer snapped.

"Well, I know people and you guys got no reason to be fightin'. Did I ever tell you how we met?"

"Only a million times," Jennifer said. "You know, we all have our own version of 9/11, Robert. You're not the only one with tragedy in his life. Just because it doesn't involve planes flying into buildings doesn't mean it's any less important."

"Uh," Michael stammered. He didn't know what to say, he only knew he didn't want to get into a comparison of their lists of marital strife.

"Just hear me out. You don't know the whole story. It's not even halftime, right?" Robert looked at his watch, then began without waiting for permission.

When the South Tower fell, Robert and his partner, Mark were shielded from the initial blast by the North Tower. Their eyes met across the sidewalk to the sound of a thousand steam locomotives crashing. As part of the motorcycle highway patrol, they were called to the scene of an emergency at One World Trade Center. No details were given so they assumed it was something similar to the bombing by terrorists in 1993. The streets were clogged with an impassable jam of Tuesday morning rush hour traffic, throngs of gawkers with cameras and some tourists, hysterical with fear. Using mostly the sidewalks, they were able to approach the North Tower on their Harley Road Kings when other emergency vehicles were stopped miles away. Mark led their mini-parade weaving around pedestrians, parked cars and oblivious onlookers. Their emergency lights and sirens seemed to have no effect on the crowds.

Just getting the last couple of blocks to the scene required all their skills of navigation and diplomacy. It seemed every driver within a mile of the World Trade Center had rear-ended the car in front of him while staring at the top of the Tower. Black smoke was billowing out of the higher floors and streaming away over the South end of the island. On their arrival to the complex, it was clear that no one was in charge. Their radios were awash with meaningless messages and distress calls. Robert stopped his bike across Vesey Street by the Verizon building to write a ticket. Some moron had double-parked his van, probably just to make a delivery, but rules are rules and they apply to everyone.

Mark proceeded to the walk between buildings One and Six. Debris from the initial plane crash had rained down on the top of Six WTC, prompting an efficient evacuation that took only twelve minutes for the eight-story government building. He parked his bike by the exit and killed the siren, but left the lights flashing. Panicked men and women in business suits were streaming out of the glass doors of the North Tower. He implored them to remain calm for fear that someone would end up trampled, but the situation was beyond the stage of reasoning.

Robert finished with his duty of keeping the peace and drove his Harley onto the plaza. He made a lap around *The Sphere*, a 25-foot bronze sculpture surrounded by fountains. The normally busy Plaza was occupied not with tourists and workers on coffee and lunch breaks but all manner of emergency vehicles and their occupants, streaming into One WTC to assist victims of the fire. Robert found his partner on the northwest side of the North Tower trying to assist a woman with a twisted ankle. He parked his bike by West Street and killed the lights and siren. She was babbling about leaving something in the building and wanting to go back in and get it. She'd turned to go back, ran into someone leaving and now her ankle was turning purple as it swelled over the top of her black pump. New to the scene and with an air of authority, Robert convinced her whatever it was, she'd have plenty of time to get it later, after the fire was out. They just needed her to cooperate for now and convinced her to take a seat at the back of an idle ambulance.

The partners walked back to their bikes by the bank of glass doors. Fewer people were coming out and those who did seemed oddly calm. Some firemen were making their way into the building heading for the stairwells. The motorcycle cops craned their necks up the side of the Tower. "Nice job with that lady back there," Mark said. "She'll thank you later."

"Just doing my job to keep the peace. Nothing any lesser officer couldn't have done. That's a pretty big fire. Think they'll get it put out?"

"I don't see how they're gonna get up that high. That's gotta be eighty, ninety stories. Even if they can get up there, then what? They'll be too exhausted to help anyone down."

At that moment, the South Tower was hit from the side opposite the officers. Debris flew north in a fireball high over the Plaza, building Five WTC, and the Post Office. "I've got a bad feeling about this," Robert said.

"Yeah, brother. Something tells me this is no ordinary fire."

For the next hour, the partners tried to assist with people exiting the North Tower. Those unconvinced by reports of the first fire were now certain it was time to leave. The men directed those with minor wounds to clear the area. When tourists arrived to loiter and take pictures they were given a firm reprimand to leave the area or risk arrest. Most of them listened. Awhile later, when bodies started falling like rain, it took less effort for the men to clear gawkers from the area. Robert didn't have the fortitude to inspect any of the bodies that hit the pavement. The sound was sickening enough, but the splattered remains were barely recognizable as human. He could tell that some were women by their clothing, which only made the horror more inconceivable. There was no way anyone could have survived the fall from above the 90th floor.

When the South Tower fell, Robert and Mark were standing near their motorcycles. The sound was deafening. The ground heaved like an earthquake. In moments they made the decision to leave the complex. "There's no more we can do here, Robert," Mark said. He mounted the bike nearest him, then realized it was Robert's. "Oh, sorry brother," he said. They started to put on their helmets to leave, but before either officer could start his machine, they were enveloped in a cloud of dust and debris so thick they couldn't see their own feet, let alone find a path to safety on their motorcycles.

Robert bolted. He headed up what he thought was West and past the Verizon building. He became disoriented and ended up near WTC 7. A break in the dust cloud allowed him to see the tangled mess of WTC 2, illuminated in ghostly fashion by the early morning sun. The decorative spines of the lower portion of the tower were sticking up from the pile of debris at the center of the Plaza. He turned and ran away from the wreckage up Greenwich Street. The dust burned his lungs but he sprinted without thought or purpose, only to escape the confusion, as if running would answer all of his questions.

He passed other people, all of them in the same shroud of clay-colored dust. Some seemed to have the same thought as he, that physical distance from the damage would also afford some emotional distance. The thought of his partner Mark entered his brain for a brief moment. The last he remembered was Mark smiling his goofy, Chiclet-toothed grin after getting on Robert's machine by mistake. Then, winking and getting off to let Robert have the motorcycle.

Farther up the road, Robert passed a group of confused locals. They were a mix of generations, sexes and races. Covered head to toe in dust they made a new race of human where previous qualities of uniqueness were rendered moot. They now all belonged to the group of Americans, attacked by some unknown entity, yet with a new bond, that of victim.

At Hell's Kitchen Robert found himself surprised by how far he'd come. The air uptown had cleared somewhat and let him read a street sign indicating how far he'd run. He dared a glance downtown, but what he saw only disoriented him anew. The North Tower was still spewing a thick, black cloud of smoke to the South, but no tower existed there to block or disperse the smoke. The South Tower was gone, in its place was only empty air. As long as the North Tower stood, there was a chance that Mark would escape. They'd laugh about it later, complaining about the paperwork this silly bomb scare had generated. The mechanics would bitch about the dust in and on their motorcycles, but they'd get them running again and the partners would be back to managing post-game or post-concert crowds at the Garden or Radio City Music Hall. In weeks they'd be bitching about escorting some dignitary from a country the size of Rhode Island to the United Nations building, and it would all be a distant memory.

When the North Tower fell, Robert knew he'd never see his partner again. In slow motion, his past and his future both collapsed into a pile of rubble. He continued up 9th Avenue, again without purpose or direction. At 51st, he ran out of breath and fell to his knees, coughing, vomiting, and hoping to be run over by a car. Something large, like an old Checker Cab, or better yet, a giant truck, so there would be no doubt.

"Hey," a voice said. "Are you okay?"

"I just threw up a gallon of blood," Robert said. He looked up enough to see a name tag that said Michelle. It was pinned on the blouse of a pair of drab, green surgical scrubs which were filled to capacity by a woman with straight, black hair to her shoulders. "What do you think? You're the nurse."

She placed a grey blanket over his shoulders. "Phlebotomist."

"Hippopotamus?"

"No, I draw blood. Is that a fat joke? Never mind. Are you okay?" She pointed to some thin streaks of pink mucous. "Is that it?" Michelle looked at the pavement where Robert had emptied his stomach. There was a wet pile of plaster with some faint pink tinge to it, and maybe a thin streak of bright red blood. "Well, better out than in. But I don't think you'll need a transfusion. I'm Michelle by the way."

"I want to help. I should go back."

"Help who?"

"Isn't there something I can do? There must be lots of injured. Sick."

"We watched them fall."

"Huh?"

"On TV. Since the planes hit. It's been all over every station. Where have you been?"

"Mark. He needs me. I've got to go back."

"I doubt there's anything you could do at this point. He either made it or he didn't."

"That's a shitty thing to say. He was my partner. We worked together for years. I was closer to him than my own family." Robert looked up to his rescuer for the first time. Her raven black hair was lustrous bordering on iridescent, reflecting the sunlight where it curved around her head and cheeks. Her eyes were pale blue and had a caring and sympathetic look about them with little wrinkles at the corners. In the center of her face where a Barbie doll nose should have been was the fist of Chuck Norris, robbing her of an otherwise beautiful countenance. Robert couldn't help himself. He stared. Then he stared some more.

"What? Is there something on my face? Dust?" Michelle wiped her rosy cheeks with one hand.

"No. It's nothing, small, really. Tiny—actually."

"Oh, my nose. In my family we wear it with pride. It's a Silverman badge of honor. Great for the men, almost a calling card for the family jewelry business. Not so great for the single woman in the family."

"Surgery?"

"Unthinkable right now, but yeah, I'm saving up my money. You just get right to the point, don't you cowboy? All I have to do is get some insurance, then convince an ENT I have a deviated septum or some allergies. Or it'll help my imaginary migraines. Plus, this thing ain't gonna stay in until high school graduation." Michelle rose to her feet dragging Robert up as well. She stuck out her pregnant belly making it look like she was either fifteen months pregnant or having quintuplets.

"Oh. Congratulations." Robert started to say that the nose obviously wasn't a hindrance to finding a male partner, but he refrained. Something about her comments regarding the single Silverman woman put a halt to his tongue.

"Here. Help me carry these blankets inside." Michelle handed Robert a small pile of three grey blankets and led him back to the Emergency Room of St. Clare's Hospital. The bays were empty. People had better things to do this Tuesday morning than go to the hospital. She explained to him how the television kept showing the towers falling over and over again, but she couldn't believe it. So she came out to the street to look for herself, and there was nothing downtown but a pillar of smoke. Then, she saw Robert throwing up in the street. No one else seemed to need any help, so she went up to him.

They gave each other a little introduction. Robert explained how he'd been called to the scene of the fire to give some assistance to the rescue workers for crowd control. Michelle said she was dragged from her spot at the blood donation center to help out in the Emergency Room. Most of the patients were fine, they just had to be reminded they were okay. It was clear there was far more emotional shock than medical.

"Can I ask you something?" Robert said stacking the blankets on a counter by the nurses' station.

"Yes, the rear end keeps me from falling forward and landing on my giant nose." Michelle turned her back and showed off her bulging scrubs. It appeared as though she was trying to hide a pair of basketballs in her pants, each one perched solidly on thighs like tree trunks. "Afraid lipo is not gonna do much back here."

"Um, no." Robert was in no mood for jokes. "I was gonna ask why you nurses always hand out blankets. In every natural disaster you ever see, tornado, flood, tsunami, you got people wandering around in ugly grey blankets."

"It's the color you don't like?"

"No, here it is a beautiful day, not a hint of fall in the air, and you hand me a blanket."

"Well, I guess one reason is that if someone is in shock, it'll help keep you warm. But the real reason is that if someone at a mass casualty scene has got a blanket on, it lets everyone else on the team know that at least they've been triaged by one of the workers. Maybe the patient feels a little better too, like you're wrapped in Nana's afghan."

"Hmm. Guess you're right. I do feel a little better. Plus, it's nice to meet ya'. Really, I mean that, not just 'cause. Ya know."

There was nothing to be done in the Emergency Room, so Michelle was released back to her job at the blood donation center on the other side of the building. Robert found himself tagging along, not knowing what else to do. A line of donors was snaking out the door of the building and around the block. Aside from the usual shortage of blood city- and nation-wide, no calls for blood were coming from the area that would become known as Ground Zero. Robert wasn't the only one who felt a sudden need to want to help, to do something, anything in the wake of the tragedy. "Oh, my," Michelle said. "We're going to be sending people away."

"What? I thought you guys always needed blood."

"Well, sure we can always use Type O and Rh Negative, but those are pretty rare. What are you?"

"I'm A Positive."

"See? The most common type, which is great if you need some, we'll probably be able to find a pint or two. But it only lasts a couple of months. They can take out the platelets and plasma, but the red cells aren't as useful, strange to say."

Robert tailed Michelle the rest of the day. They made a strange pair. He the tall, blonde, and handsome motorcycle cop, still covered in white dust, she the short, waddling pregnant one, every part of her sticking out in bulbous round fertility with the exception of her giant pointy Jewish nose. Michelle enjoyed the company and Robert was helpless in emotional shock and didn't know what else to do, so he just followed her and passed out supplies or held clipboards while she interviewed donors, checked hemoglobin and drew blood. Thankful for the extra pair of hands she never thought to ask if he had anywhere else to be.

At the end of her shift, the absurdity of their situation was something neither could avoid. "Well, thanks for helping out today. I wish I could say I can return the favor, but I'm sure there's nothing I could do. Imagine this on the back of your motorcycle." She spread her hands wide and looked across her hips, first one, then the other. She turned sideways and slapped herself on the butt.

"I don't want to be alone," Robert blurted. "I'm scared. I should have stayed with my partner. I bolted. Ran. I'm scared." He collapsed in the nearest chair and continued his wicked self-assessment. "I can't face the guys. Mark is dead. I've got nothing. I am nothing."

Michelle didn't know what to say. She placed a hand on his shoulder which came up nearly to her own, despite him being seated. Robert leaned into her and buried his face in her huge pregnant belly, hugging her harder than was comfortable, both physically and emotionally. "Hey, hey, give a girl a break. You're gonna squeeze this kid right out of me."

"How can you make jokes?"

"What am I supposed to do? I don't know you, you don't know me. What do you expect me to say?"

Robert stood up from his chair. He collected himself as well as he could, wiping tears from his face and leaving smears of white which continued to fall from his hair. He dusted himself off more symbolically than effectively. He sniffled once, loudly, then picked up his helmet and left the blood donation center.

A month later, Robert returned to the center to donate blood. He was right in figuring the supplies would be dwindling again and they were happy to check him in for a pint. He requested and was given Michelle as his phlebotomist, a condition of his donation, he claimed. During the twenty minutes of his donation, he spilled everything to Michelle about his previous month. "It's like I buried Mark six times. First, I watched him die when the towers came down. Then, there was the searching for the bodies. We didn't even find anything that looked like a motorcycle. They held a ceremony, but they had nothing to put in a casket or cremate for an urn. Turns out a bunch of other cops lost their partners, too. Way more firemen, though. Now, every time someone brings up a memorial or talks about rebuilding the site or catching al-Qaeda, it's like going through his death all over again."

He finished his monologue without a single interruption or question from Michelle. He apologized for his previous behavior, the hug, the desperation, the begging, the crying, but she waved him off. "Keep squeezing the ball."

"Oh, right. Did the bag stop filling? Thanks for listening, I figured you'd understand. So, did you name your little guy after me? You're skinny as a rail. Ready for the runway."

"Sure did. Alexis," she joked. "My parents hate it. Not the baby, the name."

"Oh, a little girl. That's great. I'm sure she's a doll."

"Yep, full head of hair, one eyebrow, and a nose like a foot. Ugliest baby I've ever seen."

"Oh, come on. The father must be very proud."

"Wherever he is." Michelle picked up the clipboard and made a notation. She grabbed Robert's donation bag and tilted it gently back and forth as blood dripped down the tubing.

"Huh?" Robert dropped the ball and his mouth fell open. "He left you?"

"What? Is that so shocking? I wanted a baby. You think anyone wants this?" She spread her hands wide as she'd done when she was pregnant. Aside from a little more space in the front of her scrubs nine out of ten people would have guessed she was still pregnant. Her saddlebags hung over both sides of the chair she was abusing. She glanced around the room to be sure no one was watching. She leaned forward to show Robert her cleavage. Violent purple stretch marks were visible above the V of her scrubs where her milk-swollen breasts had exploded from the pregnancy. Michelle sat back in her chair and lifted a hefty leg to show him how she'd stuffed her swollen foot into her tennis shoe. "I swear my feet grew two sizes. It's not just water retention. I'm not wearing rings because I don't have any, not because they don't fit."

"I don't understand."

"Look, if I were a rich Jew, I would at least have a chance. Maybe dad would fix me up with one of his partner's kids. Too bad the days of selling the ugly one with a big dowry are over. Not that he could probably afford it."

Robert didn't know what to say. Michelle told him she was the surprise baby in a family of four strapping and virile Jewish men. They excelled in everything; academics, sports, art, and especially with the ladies. With a father who ran a chain of jewelry stores they were never at a loss for impressive gifts. When she came along five years after the youngest, one would have expected that she'd be treated as a precious doll. Instead, the entire family, including her mother treated her as if they wanted a Golden Retriever all along. At best she was raised as another boy, living in hand-me-down boys clothes until she was in sixth grade. The teasing was relentless. With puberty came the extra weight and her only defense was a vicious and mostly self-deprecating sense of humor. "Not to get too heavy here, but what would you do? I wanted a baby and the clock is ticking, as they say."

"Oh, you're not so bad."

"You're sweet, Robert, but also full of shit. I know I'm no catch. Men have been telling me to my face for years. So one night I went to the darkest bar I could find, drank as much as I possibly could and found the drunkest guy I could throw myself on. Sort of a date rape in reverse. He was passed out for the whole thing. No one even noticed when I followed him into the men's bathroom. I like to think he was pretty cute, but I don't really remember, so if anyone asks he's a grad student in Physics at NYU and captain of the sculling team. Sound good?"

"Let's get outta here."

"Oh, yeah, your bag is full. Sorry about that, I got sidetracked with my life story. Hope it doesn't hurt too much. Thanks for listening." Michelle tilted his blood donation bag back and forth a few times to be sure it was full, then deftly removed the needle and wrapped his arm in stretchy gauze. She lifted his arm and said, "Keep some pressure on that for a minute while I clean up."

"Let's get outta here," Robert said again.

"You said that. I've got six hours left on my shift." When Robert stared deeply into her eyes she had to look away. Robert didn't say anything and the tension grew with her confusion. "What? You're acting funny. Why are you staring at me? I know you're not asking me for a date. No one asks me for a date."

"You're right. I'm not asking you for a date." Robert continued his staring, all the while holding his free hand on the bandage on his donation arm.

"Then what? Don't tease me, I can't take it anymore. I won't."

"Come away with me. I'm sick of this city. Let's go somewhere, anywhere. I'm a cop, I can get a job. You're a phlebotomist…"

"Hippopotamus."

"…and I'll bet every hospital in every town in the nation needs good people like you."

"I've got a kid."

"I'm great with kids. Instant family "

"Are you prepared to make an honest woman out of me?"

"What—you want to get married? Are you proposing?"

"Are you offering?"

"I guess I am."

With that, Robert and Michelle left New York City with Alexis and never looked back. While the west coast might have made the most sense geographically in terms of getting away from New York, Robert was adamant about not trading one big city life for another. They chose Kansas in the middle of nowhere, as Michelle put it. Finding work was easy and the cost of living was so low they felt like a king and queen. Meeting new friends was a breeze with Alexis as the common link between them and the other breeders. No one ever thought to question whether Robert was the father or not.

"So. That's it?" Jennifer said. "That's your irreconcilable difference? She's a non-practicing Jew from uptown and you're a non-practicing dago Catholic from the Bronx? I think I'm gonna be sick."

"Hey, ease up Jennifer," Michael said. "We didn't know he lost his partner. And it takes a big man to raise another man's kid. Props to you, Robert." The men nodded to each other since no words were necessary.

"Oh, please, I can't stand it. All we've really learned is that Michelle is a woman of questionable morals who got a nose job at some point and lost a lot of weight. Hardly something to drive you apart. Hell, you said yourself that's how you met, not how you stayed together."

"But that's not the whole story," Robert said.

Rural life agreed with both Robert and Michelle. She found work in the laboratory department at St. Bernadette's drawing blood. She later took some classes to get her technician's certificate in order to run tests as well. Coincidentally, Robert's first assignment was security at the hospital. In the wake of 9/11, police forces nationwide seemed to have unlimited funding to hire new officers and install new programs in the name of National Security. As the months and years passed, the metal detectors were removed and staff were reduced by attrition. Retiring officers were not replaced with new hires and the hospital bean counters were happy to wipe the expense from the books. Even the zealots had to admit that a tiny community hospital in the middle of Kansas was not and would never be, a major terrorist target.

Robert was transferred to the motor pool which he found deliciously dull compared to the Saturday night knife and gun show he had to oversee in Manhattan. He volunteered for what he considered to be the most entertaining duties. None of the other officers seemed to want to babysit at the high school football games, wrestling matches or give up a holiday weekend to ticket drunks at a parade. The overtime pay was welcome and he and Michelle lived a life of comfort. Robert never pushed her to have additional children and she had her hands comfortably full with her work, which she enjoyed and her daughter which she enjoyed even more.

Officer Steven joined the force a few years later and was placed under Robert's tutelage. The two men hit it off like long lost fraternity brothers. Budget cuts came around and Robert couldn't have been more delighted when Steven suggested to the department that they start a motorcycle patrol. Two bikes for he and Robert would cost less than half of a single cruiser and they argued successfully that they could cover twice the area on patrol. When told that the shop didn't have a motorcycle mechanic Steven said he'd be happy to maintain the bikes on his own time, in fact, he was a Harley rider since he could stand. He grew up around motorcycles of all kinds, riding dirt bikes around the farm where he was born, street bikes in college, and always wanted a Harley like his father's. Robert swooned. Riding was the one part of his life in Manhattan that he missed and he was happy to get back on the bike.

One day on patrol, Robert got a call from Steven. "Hey partner, I'm at the hospital."

"I thought they scrapped that duty. Who put you on security detail? You want me to talk to the boss?"

"No, I'm on the other side. I'm the patient this time. No big deal, maybe a sprained ankle. Or two. They're checking the x-rays right now."

"Okay, hang in there. Call me when you find out. I'll let the lieutenant know you might need a few days off."

When Steven failed to call in a reasonable time frame, Robert decided to stop by the hospital on his way home from work. He'd check in with Michelle and see what she had in mind for dinner. Maybe he'd get started on some pasta when he picked Alexis up from day care. At the admissions desk he was informed by the clerk that Officer Steven had been taken to surgery four hours prior and may or may not be in the recovery room.

Robert ran to the surgical floor and rounded the corner to the post-op ward. Why did it always seem so calm and quiet compared to the other floors? Lives were hanging in the balance and these people were so blase it was infuriating. He questioned the only person sitting at the nursing station and was directed through the double doors to the recovery room. The lights were low and aside from the rare beeping of a machine or two attached to some of the patients, you would have thought it was a morgue rather than a hospital ward. He scanned the row of sleeping patients, over-looking his wife the first time, then seeing her drawing some post-op labs on a patient. "Where's Steven?"

Michelle finished drawing the blood, removed her gloves and turned to face her husband. "He's right here."

Robert's stomach dropped to the basement of the hospital. This creature wasn't his friend and partner Steven, this beast was Frankenstein's monster. Tubes came from every important orifice and his arms were tethered by them, either removing or restoring precious bodily fluids, Robert didn't know. At the far end of the bed was a medieval torture rack from which protruded two giant purple eggplants which resembled human feet. Metal rods poked through bandages from his left leg and were attached by adjustable screws to a device which encircled the limb like the rings around Saturn. The right leg was merely encased in fiberglass and attached by weights to a traction device.

As bad as the legs appeared, Steven's face was more horrifying to Robert. There were no bruises, but the eyelids were swollen beneath moisturizing gel held on by clear tape. His tongue lolled to the side nearly touching his shoulder. A tube protruded from his mouth, held in place by thick gauze making him look more like a prisoner of war during interrogation than a modern medical miracle. Every time the ventilator triggered a breath, his body jerked. The filling of his lungs and the expirations appeared more like an internal fight, than a life-giving breath. Robert imagined the Hulk would spring forth any moment, or he'd awake to find the lovely Dr. Jeckyll had transformed into the hideous Mr. Hyde.

A tear formed and he wiped it away before Michelle could see. "Is he gonna be alright?"

"Oh, yeah. And they were able to save both the legs. They're just letting him rest. He's comfortable. Makes me wish I could get some morphine every once in awhile. Look at him. Sleeping like a baby, not gonna remember a thing."

Robert was overcome and he ran from the hospital without any explanation. When Michelle came home from her second shift duties, she explained that they'd since let him wake up, removed the ventilator and by the time *The Late Show With David Letterman* had started, he'd eaten dinner and been laughing along with the monologue. Rehabilitation would start immediately. The sooner he got up and moving, the better his muscles could maintain their strength and the fluid and blood would be recycled and the swelling would come down. The Millers visited as a couple the next day.

"I did it, but good, didn't I?" Steven said when they entered his private room with a gentle knock.

"I don't think Mrs. Vickers is going to be doing any more driving," Michelle said.

"What? Who's Mrs. Vickers?" Robert said.

"Nice lady, rich old widow, possibly demented but certainly a few decades past her prime and ten years past the time she should have given up driving. Word around the hospital is she didn't just get her Rolls Royce across the yellow line, she cleaned you right off the road and into the ditch. Says she didn't even see you."

Robert's eyes went wide as saucers. That explained the left leg. If Steven tried to swerve out of the way, her grill would have crushed the left leg right into the engine of the Harley. He suppressed the urge to leave the hospital immediately and put the woman behind bars.

"Typical. It's never the driver's fault, is it, Robert?" Michael Johnson, the newest addition to the nursing staff, entered with a lunch tray. "How's your pain, Officer? Need anything?"

"I'm good for now. Only hurts when I breathe."

"Toughest guy I've ever met. Hasn't asked for a Tylenol. Next thing you know he'll be up and walking out of here." Michael made his exit as swiftly as he'd entered with a promise to return if Steven changed his mind, just hit the call button.

"I've got a favor to ask you guys," Steven said. "When they spring me from this joint, I'm gonna need a ride to my mother's house in Kansas City. She can put me up until I'm back on my feet, ha, no pun intended. I'll be back on the bike before you know it."

"No," Robert said.

"No? You're serious?" Steven looked to Michelle. "Is his sense of humor always this keen?"

"We've talked it over, Steven. We're not taking you to Kansas City, because we want you to stay with us. You're the closest thing we've got to family and we wouldn't think of letting you get out of our sight."

Robert added, "We've got a spare bedroom, but for the first few weeks you'll probably be more comfortable on the first floor. We've got it all worked out. Alexis can't wait to spend more time with Uncle Steven."

With no reason to protest, Steven moved to the couch at the Miller household, conveniently located equidistant from the kitchen and the main bathroom. Alexis, now preschool-aged, was as much help to Steven as he was to the Millers. She delighted in fetching him the newspaper, the remote control, or a snack. In turn, he was a captive, willing, and ever-present babysitter. They played games, read stories, and watched Disney movies in a perpetual rotation.

Robert continued his usual duties in the motor pool. One evening about sunset and just before his shift was about to end, he was summoned to the scene of an accident that tore him from his suburban idyll and thrust him right back to the emotions he'd left unresolved in his escape from New York. Early reports were that a trucker on I-70 had fallen asleep at the wheel in broad daylight, rolled straight through a curve across the grassy median and hit another truck, grill-to-grill. Both of the 18-wheelers were carrying a mix of industrial and construction materials weighing tens of thousands of pounds. They were wearing their seatbelts and might have survived had not the combined weight of their cargo crushed them in their cabs at a cumulative speed of one hundred and sixty miles an hour.

Robert arrived at the scene before any rescue vehicles. On his Harley Road King he was able to skirt the shoulder without tipping into the ditch. He set up a perimeter with flares but cars were already backed up for miles behind the scene of the accident which blocked both lanes of the eastbound traffic. Aside from the burning tires, there was nothing to indicate that the pile of debris used to be two trucks. A load of drain pipe had broken loose from its straps on one of the trucks and was now wedged in the cab of the other truck like uncooked spaghetti sticking out of a sauce pan. Robert had the sickening thought that the load of pipe had to pass through the cab of the first truck, in order to end up in the second truck. Bags of concrete mix had burst and covered the scene in a cloud of grey dust that was all too familiar. Adding to the cloud was a load of drywall which had been pulverized at impact. Mixed with the black smoke from the burning tires and backlit by the sun, the wreckage was identical to the view Robert had to endure after the South Tower fell. He sat on the grass upwind of the devastation, put his face in his hands and wept uncontrollably.

Some time later he heard sirens and was roused from his memories by the hand of a fireman on his shoulder. "Hey, you okay? Can you walk?"

Robert rose to his feet in answer and gave the man a hug and wouldn't let go. "Okay, okay Officer. Good to know you're okay. I'm Christopher and we gotta get this fire out before it spreads to the field. So let me help you get out of the way." The two men walked a safe distance from the wreckage and another fireman presented Robert with a grey blanket. Robert started laughing out loud to the confusion of Christopher and his colleague. "I think he's okay," Christopher said and the two men ran over to help with the hoses.

Robert shook his head as he watched them unloading the Jaws of Life. What a silly name it was. Great marketing, but hardly an accurate description of the tool's purpose. He had the sense to call to the station and report that he was clear of the scene, nothing to be done, and he'd be in to work the next day to finish up the reams of paperwork. He activated the lights and sirens and drove straight home, leaving his personal vehicle at the station and pulling up to the family home with a fresh set of tears streaming down his face.

He dragged himself through the front door, took off his gloves and helmet and put them on the hall table. He sniffled loudly and wiped his nose, then saw Steven on the couch with a surprised look on his face. Robert rushed to the couch and took his friend in a firm bear hug. "It was horrible, you wouldn't believe," he mumbled into Steven's shoulder. "There was wreckage everywhere. Bodies. I ran and ran. I can't believe you made it out, Mark. We're so lucky to be alive."

"Mark? Who's Mark?" Steven said. His legs were up on the divan and his arms were pinned to his sides by Robert. He was able to find the remote control and turn off the television.

Robert sniffled loudly and broke their awkward embrace. He shook his head and seemed to clear his mind in an instant. He stood up off the couch and corrected himself too quickly. "Steven. I meant Steven."

"What's this all about? I only broke my leg. It was a month ago. What's going on?" Steven patted the couch next to himself, inviting Robert to take a seat, which he did.

Robert told him about the truck accident and how it reminded him of 9/11, the smoke, the tangled wreckage, the concrete dust, the way the sun shone through like the end of the world on fire. "Listen to me. I sound like a Vietnam veteran with all my war stories. Sorry for unloading on you."

"It must have been horrible for you. Not just tonight, I mean, but back in New York, too. So who's Mark?"

"He was my last partner, before you, in New York. He died that day."

"I'm so sorry. I can see why you and Michelle would want to leave. You wanna tell me about it?"

"It's not something I'm proud of, you know. It's hard to talk about. I haven't even told Michelle."

"I'm here for you," Steven said.

"Everybody knows it from television, but it's not the same. Those pictures were from miles away. We were there, on the ground, right in the thick of it. They called us when the first building was hit. We were helping people get out and trying to keep the peace, you know, protect the gawkers and tourists from becoming another statistic. For their own good. Then the South Tower was hit. We never thought they'd collapse, but there was no way to put out those fires. Then the bodies started falling. People were jumping from the top floors. It must have been horrible. Were they being burned alive up there? Were they just trying to get away from the smoke so they could breathe?"

Robert was staring across the family room at the silent television. In his mind the screen replayed the events he was describing. Without saying a word, Steven took Robert's hand, like a therapist helping a client with a breakthrough.

"When the South Tower fell we knew we only had one chance to get out of there. The bodies kept falling and we were about to leave, but Mark got on the wrong bike. It was my fault. I should have just told him to go. It should have been me."

Steven didn't know what to say. He just squeezed Robert's hand to let him know he was there, that anything he said would be alright.

"We swapped back to our own bikes and Mark got on his. That's when he was hit. A jumper landed right on him. The force of the impact must have killed him instantly. The windshield and handlebars acted like razors. Hands and feet were severed through the joints. He didn't have time to put his helmet on and his head got crushed right into the gas tank. The pile of limbs and machinery was so jumbled I couldn't tell if it was a man or a woman, where the jumper ended and Mark began. I panicked. I ran. I couldn't even look back. I'm so ashamed."

This time it was Steven who hugged Robert. They would later argue over who kissed whom. Robert said it was Steven who kissed him, while Steven insisted it was Robert who made the first move. Regardless of who made the first advances, there was no argument that the other man didn't resist, but rather welcomed the attention. Kissing was soon abandoned for heavier groping and explorations. In his hobbled state, Steven was far from mobile, so things progressed at a leisurely pace. Clothing was left in place, for the most part.

Michelle burst in the door with Chinese takeout for dinner. "Robert Steven Alexis I'm home and I've got your favorite I slaved and slaved over a hot stove. I hope you're hungry." She stopped short at the entrance to the family room and took in the scene. Robert was still wearing his boots but his normally crisp uniform was in a state of complete disarray. The shirt was unbuttoned to the waist and untucked from his pants which were in place, but similarly loosened. Steven was still wearing his pajama bottoms but the drawstring would need to be retied at some later moment. His t-shirt was crumpled in a pile beside the divan. "Oh. Sorry guys. I'll just put this in the kitchen."

"Wait, Michelle. It's not what you think," Robert said.

Michelle peeked her head back around the door jamb. "Oh? What do I think?"

"We're not…"

"It's just…" Neither man could finish a sentence.

"Shall I make up a few plates? I'm assuming Alexis is down for a nap?" When neither man had an answer she continued. "Oh, c'mon now, Robert. You didn't think I knew you were gay from the day I met you? I'm a Jewish princess from New Yawk. I got gaydar like a pimp has gold chains." Still no response came from the men. "Look, Steven. You've got—what?—twelve pairs of biker boots, all polished to a mirror shine. And you, Robert. Who marries a fat, pregnant woman who's carrying someone else's baby? Call me a fag hag, I've been called worse."

"I don't know what to say. I'm sorry," Robert said.

"There's nothing to say and there's nothing to be sorry about. I'm just happy to have a good father for Alexis. You're actually employed and not on drugs. Although I'll tell ya. If you're gonna play that bisexual angle, we've got some work to do. I appreciate you sleeping with me once in awhile, but you've gotta learn what a girl likes. I'm going through batteries like potato chips. And Steven, I'd trust you to drive cross-country with Alexis before I'd let her spend ten minutes with any of my lousy brothers. You're welcome here any time. Just don't try to take Robert from me. I'll fight you and I don't plan on letting him get away. So. What's it gonna be, the garlic chicken or the sesame?"

Michelle went to the kitchen and made up three plates of Chinese food.

7

CRUISING

After Robert's confession, he told them to not give up on the marriage. He knew his situation was unique, but where there's even a little love, there's a reason to stay together. He excused himself and went off to find Michelle in the row of parents.

Michael scanned the crowd, looking for marriages that appeared to be working, but with struggles that made Jennifer's complaints irrelevant. Set back from the line of parents a gaggle of kids was playing their own soccer game. They were all ages like the Von Trapp Family Singers had decided to have a pickup game. There was no competition, only passing the ball around and the occasional breakaway, the successful athlete then stopping to kick the ball back into the fray. The older kids stopped and cheered every time the ball ricocheted off a leg of the youngest who couldn't have been more than two. Her bulging pants suggested she was still working on her potty training. She rolled onto the ball and somersaulted more often than she made contact with her foot. Michael recognized the kids of his fantasy football friend and accountant, David Wilson. He'd been married to Kimberly for only eight years but they had a child for every year. David never tired of the Mormon jokes, mostly because they weren't, but also, he was quick to point out, because they had two sets of twins.

One pair was identical and looked so much alike they were dressed by their mother in different clothes in order to tell them apart. The hand-me-downs from the older siblings helped in this regard. Kimberly received a severe scolding the day David came home from work and found them wearing name tags. The other pair was fraternal and could have been adopted from different parents for their shocking dissimilarity. In addition to being different sexes, the girl looked East Indian, with gorgeous straight hair and glowing olive skin tone. Her brother was a classic carrot-top, complete with adorable freckles. Michael gave up trying to keep all their names straight after the fourth or fifth Wilson child was born. Now there were eight and by the looks of Kimberly's waddle, they'd been having sex again.

"C'mon, Jennifer. We've had some good times, you've got to admit. You can't just throw it all away."

"Yes. I can. And it's not about what I'm giving up. It's what I'll be gaining."

"What about the next time you go on a cruise? You'll be thinking of me the whole time. You loved that cruise."

"What?" She turned to face him, arms still crossed in defiance. "David only dragged us along because he made so much money off us that year and felt guilty. Worst. Accountant. Ever."

"Not just that—everything you do—you'll be thinking of me. Your next guy will make a comment about how you wear your socks to bed and you'll be reminded of me."

"That cruise was the worst. Put that on the list of things that make this the right decision. Sign the papers."

"David and Kimberly aren't so bad. Sarah's a great friend to Hannah, you have to admit."

"Here we go again." Jennifer turned her attention back to the game. "You don't even know what position she plays." After a beat, she added with emphasis, "Goalie. She plays goalie. A lot you know."

"It was just a misunderstanding," Michael said.

"And their twenty kids were all brought by the stork. That middle kid doesn't look like David at all."

"What are you saying? They seem happy enough."

Jennifer ended the discussion with a "humph."

For their fifth wedding anniversary, David and Kimberly Wilson went on a Caribbean cruise with the five children they had up to that time, including the first set of twins. David convinced Michael to join them for a family vacation—Hannah included. He countered Michael's protests with frequent-flier miles. Convincing Jennifer to agree was a more daunting task given it was her idea to skip their honeymoon. If she wouldn't spend money on a vacation to celebrate their wedding, she sure wasn't going to spend it to celebrate someone else's anniversary. In a further stretch, at the time Michael and Jennifer were between their sixth anniversary and their seventh, not exactly landmark occasions.

After the final series of compromises, the families agreed to schedule it over the summer vacation so as not to interfere with the demands of the school year. Hannah would be off and old enough to remember the extravagance, a major point for the frugal Jennifer. Michael hadn't taken vacation since starting his job at St. Bernadette's Hospital, six years prior. He was more than ready to take a break. Jennifer would be available after final exams and the school board had decided on the budget for the following school year. The Wilsons had cruised before in all seasons, averaging once a year since before they were married, even risking the hurricane season in order to get better rates on plane tickets and cabins. As an accountant, David's work was portable, most of his clients' information was kept in digital format and available from any location with Internet access.

"How well do we know these people?" Jennifer said over dinner one night.

"David's been our accountant for how many years? Since we were married, for sure. And don't forget, he's in my fantasy football league. Don't underestimate the power of fantasy football." Michael emphasized the point by waving a spear of asparagus on the end of his fork.

"Oh, well. You're practically brothers, then."

"What are you worried about? We'll be trapped in the same room for seven days? It's a big ship. They're bringing their nanny for goodness sakes. It's like built-in day care. We can go to shore in each port or get lost on the ship—if we find out we have nothing else in common besides taxes and our investments."

Jennifer acquiesced, making it clear that anything short of a perfect trip was Michael's responsibility. Prior to departure, Jennifer's fears were allayed by Kimberly who behaved like the best big sister ever. She worked from home as a part-time travel agent, the only occupation she could probably manage raising a brood of five. Telling people she was a day trader made her sound too risky. With their growing family, she didn't want to seem reckless with the family finances so only revealed her stock market skills as a hobby to those who seemed sympathetic. It seemed as though she was either pregnant, breast feeding, or both for the entire time they'd known the couple. Through email and phone calls in the months leading up to their departure she assured Jennifer she knew her way around the 110,000-ton, three thousand-passenger ship as sure as she did around her own kitchen.

Flights were booked, connections were made, passports were rendered. It all went off like a trip to the mall in two minivans. Getting eleven people from the middle of the country to the Caribbean was as smooth as any military operation under the guiding hand of Kimberly Wilson. They left Kansas City on a red eye flight and landed well-rested in Ft. Lauderdale. The ship would sail first to the Bahamas and over the course of the week, circle the Eastern Caribbean, a different island every day. Their first stop was Grand Bahama, a mere one hundred and five miles from port.

After the morning check-in and the tedious lifeboat drill, Kimberly sought out Jennifer at her cabin. When the door opened to her trademark "shave and a haircut, two bits" knock, Kimberly handed Jennifer a flute of champagne and grabbed her by the wrist. Kimberly leaned her head in the cabin door and made eye contact with Michael, still unpacking his suitcase. "Sorry, Michael, ship's rules. Mandatory girl date and ship orientation." To Jennifer she said, "Time for our mani-pedi."

"It's three hours before noon. Isn't it? What time zone are we in?" Jennifer said.

"Exactly. Not a minute to lose. We'll catch up to the boys at lunch." Kimberly waved a couple of coupons in the air. "Found these online for a song. Spa treatments. The whole works. All we have to do is bill a tip to the rooms. They're gonna pamper us like Cleopatra."

For two hours the women got better acquainted in their side-by-side recliners. Kimberly got acrylic nail extensions that stuck out a quarter inch from her fingertips. Jennifer had to be persuaded but finally relented to a shorter version they called Active Length. They ignored the foreign language whispers of the two women performing their pedicures. Choosing nail color for their toes was a task no less important and equally difficult as choosing their china patterns.

With fingernails freshly painted and their tongues loosened by the champagne, the women bonded in short order. They shared stories of child-raising, schooling and the predictable ups-and-downs of their respective marriages. The women complained about meal preparation, laundry and the cost of disposable diapers. They had similar tastes in music and an aversion to sports. In time, the conversation segued to the familiar topic of men, where the women had even more in common. Despite marrying men of admirable quality and dependability, they both admitted to favoring the more athletic type, tall and blonde, if you must know. "So how did we both end up with two short, dark-haired guys?" Jennifer said.

"Don't forget the receding hairline. David had a curly mullet in college. Used to love to run my fingers through it. Now he's barely got enough for a comb-over."

"Oh my gosh. What if it turns out we're not actually super models, ourselves? Tell me the truth, Kimberly. Am I short and hideous? Could my looks only be improved with a disfiguring car accident?" The alcohol kicked in like Manischewitz and took Jennifer back to her college speech patterns.

"Maybe it's my sexy legs." Kimberly raised her spare foot out of the pedicure tub and showed Jennifer her stubby, chubby leg. "Note the way the razor burn parallels the sexy varicose veins. Talk about war wounds. I'm not even thirty." A long, thin scab extended from her outside ankle up to mid-calf. A spot of blood oozed from the lower end where the water had splashed. She raised the hem of her fluffy robe up to expose a sturdy thigh. "Most guys can't resist this flabby, pale cellulite."

"Do you shave with garden shears? How do you get a gash like that?"

"New razors are low on my priority list, what with the five kids and all. You should see the grocery budget. David shaves with an electric."

"Geez, that's wife abuse."

"Naw. He'll be a terrific ex-husband. Very dutiful to the kids. Probably won't miss a single alimony or child-support payment."

"That's terrible! Don't say that! Don't even joke."

"Well, you know what they say. The first time, you marry for love. The second time for money. I'm planning on getting my trophy husband the third time around. Did you see that Fabio model at the breakfast buffet line?" Kimberly said in a whisper. She leaned towards Jennifer as if sharing state secrets.

"No, what was he wearing?"

"Those European-type trunks and nothing else. You know, like boxer briefs. I swear I could tell he wasn't circumcised."

"Oh, Kimberly, you're terrible."

"And the muscles. I would have eaten him up right there next to the bacon and eggs."

"I repeat, you're terrible."

"Well, let's hope he's one of the cruise ship employees." Jennifer gave her a look. "I swear, if I see him again, I'm totally gonna flirt with him."

"What?" Jennifer said sitting up straight in her chair. The two pedicurists ignored the exchange.

"Hey—what happens on the ship, stays on the ship, right?"

"Uh, yeah. Except for STD's and pregnancy. Duh."

"No, really they're clean, trust me. I'd totally have his baby."

"Now I know you're joking," Jennifer said and sat back in her chair.

"Have you noticed those people dancing around to the piped-in music? Or that free welcome drink, how it seemed like everyone started to do the Electric Slide at the first note of a country song?" Jennifer nodded. There were a handful of people who seemed to be having just too good a time. There were young couples who looked a little too glamorous to be slumming with the breeders in steerage. "Well, I have a theory," Kimberly continued. "I think they're paid by the company to act like tourists, literally showing the other folks how to play. You're much more inclined to let yourself go a little if you're not the first one out of your chair. A little free booze and you become part of the show. At the end of the trip you didn't know you had it in you to act like a teenager again."

"Yeah, fine, dancing in the buffet line. But flirting with a total stranger. You're a married woman. With children!"

"But, but, but. You've got a rule for everything. By the end of this week, I'll have you out of your shell. You'll thank me later. Promise."

At lunch, the nanny seated the Wilson children and Hannah at a long picnic table and promised to bring their favorites if only they'd stay seated for ten minutes. Vanessa wore a backpack stuffed with essentials; baby wipes, sunscreen, diapers, and emergency snacks. She put Hannah, the oldest of the group, in charge to make sure no one got up and wandered around. Carrying the infant Wilson in a front carrier, she made a quick trip to the pizza station and another to the grill where there was a constant stream of hot dogs and hamburgers flowing over the counter. Neither station had a line and she carried two platters of fast food with piles of french fries back to the picnic table to the cheers of the kids. They dug in while she made another trip to the soft drink station, also without a line, for a pitcher of water and another of lemonade. She monitored their meal from the salad bar and returned with her own lunch, then made a bottle from her backpack supplies to feed the youngest, who wasn't yet taking solid food.

The adults took their places in two different lines opposite the wading pool, to see which might move faster. The men took the port side arguing that people instinctively turned right when they entered a new area of the ship, therefore the left line would be shorter. The ladies looked over the crowd and agreed to the challenge noticing a distinct age difference and suspecting the older population in the starboard line would move faster. The theory was that they were familiar with the buffet concept, perhaps had even cruised before and would therefore make their choices more quickly.

"Michael," David whispered. "Don't look now, but check out the leggy blonde in the other line." Michael looked immediately but saw only a typical crowd of tourists in various states of casual dress. "You don't follow directions very well, do you?"

"What? I don't see her. What's she wearing?"

"Red bikini, cork wedge sandals, white sun hat. How can you not see her?" Michael scanned the line again from where it ended to where the plates and trays were stacked. He made eye contact with Jennifer and Kimberly and gave them a little wave. Kimberly was wearing a red one-piece, a sarong wrapped at the waist to better cover her stretch marks and post-partum thigh fat, flip-flops, and a white baseball cap. Jennifer still had on her clothes from the lifeboat drill; Bermuda shorts, a loose Hawai'ian shirt tied at the waist over her sports bra. Her hair was in a single, functional ponytail. Michael scanned the line a second time and said he still couldn't see the leggy blonde. "You're blind. Try my sunglasses," David said, handing his Ray Bans to Michael.

"Nope. Still don't see her."

"Well, I'm gonna meet her this afternoon at the pool. While you were unpacking, I saw her at the bar. I've never in my life wished I was a chair, but the way she was sitting…you know."

"No, I don't know. Enlighten me."

"You gotta lighten up Michael. Meet some new people."

"I'm not like you. I can't just walk up to someone and start talking. What would I say? Plus, I'm here with you right now. We're having a fine time."

"Watch and learn," David said. He left the buffet line, walked around the wading pool, which was full of mothers and kids in sagging diaper pants. He ruffled the hair of one child who was repeatedly dumping water from a plastic cup into an ice bucket. He pointed to the attending mother and smiled, giving a thumbs up. Michael thought David was going to approach the mystery blonde. Instead he walked past the other buffet line and straight to a table with two elderly diners already enjoying their lunch. David bowed to the gentleman and said something that made the older woman blush and cover her mouth. Soon, the three of them were laughing and shaking hands all around like old friends. The man at the table wrote something on a napkin and handed it to David who did the same. He bowed again and returned to the line where Michael was waiting. "See? Easy as losing money in Vegas."

"What did you say?"

"I introduced myself and apologized for interrupting their lunch on such a beautiful day. Then I asked Burt if I could have his daughter's hand in marriage. He saw my ring and laughed. Bernice and he are celebrating their fortieth anniversary on this cruise. Their six kids and twenty grandchildren are scattered all over the ship. I told him he left me no other choice. Pistols at dawn tomorrow on the stern, Lido deck. I told him after I put a bullet between his eyes, I'd throw him overboard and ravage his wife until she forgot he ever existed."

"How do you come up with this shit?"

"Turns out he needs a little help with his retirement planning, which I told him I could handle in my sleep. We exchanged email addresses. I'll probably get some work from his kids, too. Some of the grandkids are even reaching college age. There's always something coming up that a good accountant can help you with."

"You're amazing. How do you do it? Do they teach you that in accounting school?"

"Aw, c'mon, Michael. We all have our talents. I'm a people person. I don't think about it. It just happens and it's not about getting work or making money or getting laid. That's just secondary to meeting interesting people and doing fun things. The stuff you do in the hospital with patients? I could never do that."

The men made more small talk, collected their heaping plates of food from the buffet when it was their turn and joined the women and kids at the picnic table. The women refrained from rubbing in the fact that they'd chosen the faster line. In either case, the kids were done eating before any of the parents arrived and they started migrating to the wading pool for soaking and splashing. Always working, Vanessa bussed their leftovers and joined the kids for their safety and entertainment.

Plans were made for the afternoon. Not wanting to ruin their fresh pedicures, the women decided to hang out by the pool with Vanessa and the kids and maybe tour the rest of the ship, see the art gallery, and check out the casino. They held up twenty fingers to show off their French manicures as if clear nail polish settled any and all arguments. "Nassau's got better beaches, anyway," Kimberly said. The men decided to go ashore, window-shop Freeport and take in a little snorkeling. Trays were cleared, cheeks were kissed and they all agreed to see each other at dinner, if not sooner.

David and Michael went to their respective cabins to prepare for their impromptu shore excursion. Michael wanted to bring his camera and David said something about taking a shower and brushing his teeth. "I'll meet you at the dock, just off the gangplank. Don't forget your room key, you'll need it to get back on," David said.

"Have you got any gear?"

"We'll rent it on shore—it's cheaper."

"Oh, okay. Hey, wait a minute. You're going to your room to shower before we jump in the ocean?"

David ignored the point. "Plus, we can haggle. You gotta stretch those American dollars. It's hard to tell the IRS you've been talking business all day with a snorkel in your mouth."

"Right. Always thinking money, aren't you?"

"Always."

An hour later, the two men met as planned on the dock and Michael spoke first. "You always bring your laptop to the beach?" Michael was dressed for the excursion like he shopped at Tourists "R" Us; sandals with tube socks, shorts over his bathing suit, a Hawai'ian shirt bought from a department store, and a Jayhawks baseball cap. In his hands he held his point-and-shoot camera, an airline-legal tube of sunscreen and his beach towel.

David looked like he was on his way to a meeting with Donald Trump wearing a freshly dry-cleaned, linen shirt tucked smartly into his navy slacks. The black leather belt and shoes matched his briefcase. Michael could have sworn he'd grown three inches taller since lunch. In the other hand, David held a canvas gym bag which presumably had his beach attire.

"Got a little banking to do—you know—work, work, work."

"Well, let's grab a shuttle. The vans to the beach are filling up."

"Nope, got a taxi waiting. Trust me, it'll be cheaper in the end. We've got a couple of stops to make. And they'll never let you in the van if you didn't pay for a reservation."

At the end of the dock a thin man with jet-black skin was standing with his hands folded behind his back, attending the passenger-side door of his sparkling yellow, 1979 Lincoln Town Car. Despite the Bahama heat, he was wearing a full suit with jacket and vest. His 8-point chauffeur cap made it clear that he would be servicing clients of great importance. As the men approached he tipped his cap with a white-gloved hand and said, "Good day, Mr. Wilson. Will the ladies be joining us then?" He moved to get the rear door for the men and took David's briefcase and gym bag, putting them in the front seat.

"Hubert Christie, please allow me introduce my good friend Michael Johnson." The two men shook hands and exchanged pleasantries. "No ladies today, my friend. They're nursing their manicures at the pool."

When the men were seated, Hubert went around to the driver's seat and fastened his belt. "What time will we need to be back to port, sir?"

"We have the early dinner seating—so, let's say just after tea time."

"Very good, sir."

Hubert drove away from the dock on Queen's Highway and navigated the narrow streets of his hometown with a sure hand and a steady foot. The devastation from Hurricane Frances two years prior was evident at every turn. Some stands of Australian pine looked like burnt matchsticks. Being non-native they had little chance when the saltwater storm surge swept over the island. Downed trees were stacked in messy piles. A few homes were missing walls. The contents inside suggested a zoo display with captive humans. At one house a couch sat opposite a television on its side, a refrigerator stood on a front lawn with its door ajar, and a motorboat sat on blocks across a dirt driveway where a car should have been. Other piles of rubble and cinder blocks gave the impression of a war zone, with the suburbs of Freeport on the losing side.

David answered the question on Michael's mind. "Yeah. I know. You'd think a tourist town could recover more quickly, but where do you start? The airport was underwater. Caskets were uplifted. Imagine 400,000 dead birds at the chicken farm. Most of the money is in the hotels down in Port Lucaya. Of course, they spent whatever it took to fix up their own grounds but thought nothing of helping their workers. Some of the cruise ships stopped coming. They skip right to Nassau, but we felt that choosing a ship that still stopped here would be a way to do our part, however small."

"Thank you Mr. Wilson."

"It's hardly a drop in the bucket, Hubert. You've been so good to us over the years we wish we could do more." To Michael he said, "The entire banana crop was lost that year. All they have left is tourism."

Past the airport, Hubert began working his way south to the seaside suburb of Lucaya. He wound around private homes and resorts, past empty fields and low lying swamps. As they neared the main tourist area the private homes gave way to larger hotels and condominiums, the fields becoming finely manicured golf courses. When they turned onto Sea Horse Road, Michael couldn't resist pointing out the name. The road soon ended at a left turn and the entrance to the Port Lucaya Marketplace, a collection of shops with tourist trap written all over them. Hubert drove past the parking lot and straight to the Yacht Club which stood on a manmade peninsula across from the Marketplace. He did one lap, showing Michael the boats moored at their piers, then parked the Lincoln in a roundabout across from a fifty-foot catamaran. "You're welcome to come along, but I shouldn't be more than fifteen minutes. Boring banker stuff, sorry. Grab a beer and check out the boats if you want." David pointed to the center console of the Town Car. What Michael thought was a drive shaft or transmission bump, turned out to be a cooler filled with ice and a twelve pack of Kalik, the Bahamian beer.

"Uh, sure. Maybe after we snorkel?"

"Suit yourself. Back in two shakes." David took both the duffel and the briefcase. Before he could open the door, Hubert was there to assist him out of the car, first taking his bundles, then handing them back to David with a tip of his cap. David wheeled around the front of the car with a jaunty hop and into a pale green building with a sign over the door reading "Columbian Emeralds International."

Still at the door, Hubert said, "Would you care to take a stroll, sir? I'd be happy to escort you around the marina, give you a tour of the boats."

The two men did a lap of the peninsula in reverse and in ten minutes were back at the Town Car. David soon appeared and the three resumed their seats for a ride to Hubert's favorite beach towards the west end. "Emeralds? I thought you had banking to do," Michael said as they pulled out of the marina.

"Oh, that's just a short cut."

"To what? All I see is a food court."

"Scotiabank." When the name didn't register with Michael, David continued. "Scotiabank, as in Nova Scotia. It's a Canadian company with branches all over the world. They do a brisk business in offshore accounts and they treat little companies like mine as if I've actually got some assets. Hubert works for the bank, don't you friend?"

"That's right, Mr. Wilson. Are we heading to Bootle Bay?"

"I think that would be a nice treat for our guest, don't you?"

"A capital idea, as always, sir."

Hubert made for Queen's Highway by a more direct route and they were soon circling the bay past the cruise ship and around the container port. Huge ships towered above the road, blocking the view of the ocean and most of the sky. It seemed only minutes before they were away from civilization and Michael saw only beaches and ocean between the sparse trees out his window. They turned down a dirt road with no name which ended after a quarter mile at a deserted beach. "Nicely done, Hubert," David said.

The men both grabbed a beer each from the built-in cooler and tried to open their doors but Hubert was already holding them open. How he got to both sides of the car so quickly they didn't know. The trunk lid was also open revealing a stash of snorkeling and scuba equipment and a bathing suit in David's size with the tags still on it. David put his beer on the roof of the Town Car and began to undress. Hubert took David's clothing as it came, put it on a solid oak hanger and hung it inside the car. "Don't really need a dressing room when you've got Hubert, huh Michael?"

"Did you fall down a flight of stairs? Attacked by a wolverine?" Michael pointed to David's flanks where eight parallel scratches, four on each side, extended from his hip bones up to his shoulder blades. On his left side one of the middle lines stopped halfway as if the attacking animal had changed its mind. The wounds oozed a pinkish liquid just short of bleeding, from where the skin was missing.

"Perhaps some aloe before you enter the saltwater, sir?" Hubert held a pump bottle of green gel he retrieved from a box in the trunk.

"Yeah. Good idea. She was a little rough, eh?" Hubert spread a generous helping of aloe from David's shoulders down the length of the scratches. Over that layer he spread another of sunscreen heavy with zinc.

"No. Not the leggy blonde," Michael said.

"You said it, I didn't."

"Be careful in the surf, gentlemen," Hubert said. "That coral has a nasty bite and those rocks can be slippery with algae. Before you know it you're tossed by the waves and scraped from head to toe."

"Right. Safety first."

The beach was every cliche of the island paradise. The white sugar sand was warm to the foot, but not too hot. A shell collector could have spent a lifetime of bliss. Fluffy cumulus clouds dotted the horizon and overhead the sky was a deep royal blue. The color of the water was transparent where gentle waves caressed the beach, then grew steadily darker from a lime green hue to the deepest indigo at the horizon. To the east and west the bay curved gently until the view was interrupted by stands of lazy palm trees. Not another soul was in sight. The men drank their chilled beers while taking in the scene. "Shall we?" David said when the beers were empty.

"After you."

"Let's just go together," David said. Then to Hubert he said, "I hate to ask but I forgot my camera. Any chance…?" Before he could finish his question, Hubert produced two disposable, waterproof, point-and-shoot cameras complete with wrist straps.

"Once requested, always carried, sir."

"Hubert, they don't pay you enough."

"It's my pleasure just to serve and share our beautiful island. You honor me with your friendship."

"Be sure and tell your brother thanks and send our regards."

"The Christie's own this?" Michael said.

"Only the dirt road and an acre or three on both sides, right Hubert?"

"Nobody owns the beach, since we are all stewards of nature, but yes. The two acres from the sand to the road is ours."

The men waded seaward and put on their masks and fins when the water reached their navels. Shadows in the azure water suggested isolated coral heads and curious fish came to investigate even before the men were submerged. They made laps along the shore gesturing left and right, outdoing each other by pointing to ever more colorful and exotic fish, coral and invertebrates. The variety of sponges alone covered the visible spectrum of colors. Each passing fish was more vibrant than the last. An hour passed in a blink and the men found themselves on shore struck dumb by the beauty. They could speak only in one-word exclamations.

Hubert met them at the waterline with thick, white beach towels, taking their cameras, masks, snorkels, and fins. When they walked back to the car they found he'd spread out a picnic on the hood; warm ham and cheese sandwiches, fried plantains, and of course, more Kalik beer. For dessert he'd set out chocolate chip cookies and let them warm in the sun. "I can't thank you enough for bringing me here," Michael said. "I ran out of film in the first five minutes."

"It's my pleasure," David said. "As much as I enjoy Hubert's company, it's more fun to show it to someone who's never been here. You notice Kimberly didn't bother to come. Can you believe she prefers Nassau? Look at this "

"Which brings me to something I have to get off my chest. I'm a little shocked at the whole leggy blonde thing. We're not swingers, you know, Jennifer and me."

"I wouldn't think of holding it against you," David said with a laugh. "As long as you're satisfied with your sex life, then who's to argue? We're pretty happy, too, I assure you."

The men finished their lunch and sat on their beach towels leaning against the Lincoln Town Car, finishing another beer, admiring the view in silence. When Hubert was certain they'd had their fill, he joined them on the ground and finished the remains of the picnic. After a time, Hubert spoke. His comments revealed he was listening to their conversation. The boldness of his statement also underlined the fact that to David, he was more friend than servant. "The shoe knows if the stocking has a hole."

"What?" Michael said.

"Old Bahamian proverb," David said but didn't explain further. "Well said, my man, well said. Shall we make our way back to the ship, then?"

Hubert wouldn't let the men load their things or help him clean up the picnic. They noticed he'd placed towels on their seats to keep the leather from getting too hot in the sun. They took their seats and waited for Hubert, taking in the gorgeous view as the sun began to sink. Hubert started the car and drove back to the cruise ship berth at leisurely speed with time to spare. At the dock the men shook hands, but David would have none of that and gave Hubert a firm, long hug. "May you always have sand in your shoes and a dollar in your pocket," David said.

"May you get to heaven a half hour before the devil knows you're dead," Hubert answered.

As Hubert drove away with a wave out his window, David said, "I swear I'm gonna name my next kid Hubert. Even if it's a girl." The friends walked up the gangplank and onto the ship.

After lunch, Jennifer found herself alone in the gallery and getting more perturbed as the minutes turned to an hour. The gallery was full of pretty paintings, if repetitious, but the prices were preposterous, she thought. At first glance, she thought about surprising Michael with an impulse buy, a large landscape of an anonymous desert isle complete with an endless beach framed in slanting palm trees. It could be had in lithograph, unframed for one-tenth the price of the original and she figured the difference between the extra checked baggage fees and having it shipped home would be a wash. The more she waited the more common sense took hold. There wasn't a single wall in a single room in their Kansas, ranch-style home where it wouldn't look like wings on a rat. In the end, she decided it was a total waste of money. Never mind that Michael would probably love it more than that stupid pottery he bought.

"You know how people always say they're sorry to keep you waiting?" Jennifer turned to see Kimberly beaming at the entrance to the gallery. "Well, I for one, am going to be honest. Maybe what I have to tell you will make up for it, but I don't really care. C'mon, let's hit the slots." She grabbed Jennifer by the arm and dragged her out of the gallery. Then laughed hysterically and said, "Oh, my gosh! That's awesome! Hit the slots! That's just what I did, in a perverted way, so to speak."

"Don't you want to see the art?"

"Sorry. Can't go in there without David. I'm not allowed. I want to buy everything I see and my day trading doesn't quite cover the costs. Our first cruise I wanted to buy a massive oil painting of a beach scene. David said, quite rightly, that it didn't match anything in our house. I told him I didn't care if we tore down the house, hung the painting in a tree, then built a new house around it. Wrong thing to say. I guess I seemed a little crazy."

"So, what happened?"

"I got a little print of it in the gift shop and hung it in the guest bathroom. I swear I beat off to it when I'm in the tub." If Jennifer had been drinking milk, it would have come out of her nose. "Oh, please. Like you don't help yourself along when Michael's on a double weekend shift at the hospital." Seeing her expression, Kimberly continued, "Oh, you poor thing. I'll give you some tips. Just between you and me, we have to keep buying new toys, 'cause the old ones get worn down to the size of pencil erasers."

"Have you ever heard of the expression 'over-share'? Well, that was one."

Kimberly gave Jennifer a hug. "Sorry, just trying to have a little fun here. And was that a roll of quarters in your pocket, or are you just happy to see me?" Jennifer gave another confused look. Kimberly reached into her pocket and pulled out two rolls of quarters. "See? The most fun you can have for ten bucks!"

With a stop at the nearest bar for margaritas they made their way to the casino and a bank of slot machines by a window overlooking the Atlantic Ocean. Just steps from the gallery, where it was so quiet, the casino was like stepping through a space-time warp. The jangling machines and blinking lights made it feel to Jennifer liked they'd docked in Monte Carlo. Every three minutes a huge roar erupted from the craps tables, the winners and losers giving the same shouts. Lights flashed on winning slot machines and coins clanked into payoff trays with loud rattles. "It's not like Vegas. You've got to buy your own drinks, but with any luck we'll break even and these eighty quarters will last until we have to get ready for dinner. I like the video blackjack. Look at the little dealer," she said pointing to the monitor. "He's invisible except for his top hat and wears these cute little white gloves, like Mickey Mouse. You should try the video poker, it's a hoot. The dealer wears a cowboy hat. Get it?"

"I'm not sure."

"Texas Hold 'Em, dummy. You gotta get out more."

A few minutes into their play, Kimberly could no longer hold back. "I'm sorry, I gotta tell someone and you're here, so bear with me. I'm so horny I feel like I got antlers growing out of my ass."

"Horns are permanent, antlers are shed."

"What?"

"Like on a rhino or an elephant. Deer shed their antlers every year. It's the males that grow them, not the does. Then again, female caribou and reindeer grow them, so you could have a point." Jennifer took another sip of her drink. "This margarita's like rocket fuel."

"I thought an elephant tusk was a tooth," Kimberly countered.

"Yeah, you're right. And the rhinoceros horn doesn't have a bony core, like say a goat or a cow, so you could make a point there, too."

"Is this how you talk to Michael? It's a wonder you ever had Hannah. No offense."

"What?" Jennifer continued to look at her video poker monitor. She had just won a small bet with three-of-a-kind and missed the dig at her sex life.

"Anyway, remember Fabio?"

"Sort of. I didn't really see him."

"After lunch I stalked him like a hyena," Kimberly said.

"Who's the hyena in this scenario? You or him? You realize hyena are scavengers, right?" Jennifer took a sip of her margarita never taking her eyes from the screen.

"No, I'm pretty sure they hunt in packs, like, say wolves. Anyway, that's all beside the point. Sorry, forgot you're a teacher, you probably can't help it. It must be genetic. I'm trying to tell you I had the best sex since I was a camp counselor and you're talking about grade school biology."

"What?" Jennifer just made even money on two pair. Between the margarita, the noise of the casino and the math required to make her bets, she was having trouble following Kimberly's story.

"So, after lunch, I saw Fabio get into an elevator and I ran up to get in with him. I figured he'd go to the lower levels where the crew are berthed. Nope. He not only held the door for me he went up to the Lido deck. Can you imagine?"

"Nope. But try me."

"He waited for me to exit and I had to act like I knew where I was but I wanted to see which way he went so, I gave a snort and looked at my watch like I was waiting for someone. When he went left, I went right. And then you know, I gave it the three count."

"Huh?"

"Yeah, you know, after you pass someone, you count to three and turn around. If he's looking too, you know you're good to go."

"Sorry, never heard that one. Money!" Jennifer screamed scoring a full house. "I think I'm up a few bucks here."

"So I turn around," Kimberly continued, "and I swear, Fabio is staring right at my ass. He didn't even know I saw him looking. I told him, hey buddy, my eyes are up here, but he didn't even stop walking, just turned around and went to his room."

"Maybe he doesn't speak English."

"That's what I thought, especially with the noises he was making later. He could be Italian, but that'd be weird for a guy with blonde hair."

"So then what happened?"

"I loitered. I figured he'd come out, but it must have been twenty minutes and he never showed. The housekeeper was making progress down the hall and when she got to his room she keyed in and then turned right around. He didn't put up the 'Do Not Disturb' sign. So when she came back out I told her I needed to get in and I forgot my key. I guess she believed me 'cause she opened the door for me. If I was there to rob the place, the guy inside would put a stop to it, right?" Jennifer nodded. "So I walk in and guess what?"

"I can't imagine. He's brushing his teeth after lunch?"

"Oh, you. How did you guess? But picture this: Tall, blonde god standing on the balcony, wearing the outfit he was born in. I can see him through the glass door. The muscles, the hair to his shoulder blades, blowing in the breeze. His butt looked like a pair of happy cantaloupes."

"Ooh, all wrinkly and rough?"

"No, silly, round and firm. I was thinking size more than texture. Why do you have to be so literal?"

"Oh, sorry. Then what?"

"What do you think? I slammed the door to get his attention. He spun around and covered himself with the towel, but not before a few other fruits and vegetables came to mind if you know what I mean. I put the chain latch on the door and jumped him right there on the balcony. You've never had a mouthful of Crest that tasted so good, let me tell you. I was glad he didn't resist, since I was sure I didn't have the language skills to start over."

"You're kidding me."

"Nope. I started him off right there on the balcony, but then we moved to the bed. Why waste perfectly good furniture, right? He was so tall I got a sore neck looking up at his beautiful face. He didn't even mind it when I scratched the hell out of his back with my new nails. That's when he made those funny Latin noises."

"You slut "

"Tell me about it. I feel like I'm sixteen again. Check this out." Kimberly held up her right hand and showed the broken nail on her middle finger. "Totally ruined my manicure. If we have a baby, I'm naming it Fabio."

Jennifer stopped her video poker. "What would David think?"

"Oh, he'd kill me. He hates it when I waste money on acrylics and hair color, that sort of stuff. But hey, I'll tell him I used a coupon. I'm sure they'll fix it for free, it's just one nail."

"No. I'm talking about the sleeping around. Aren't you worried about diseases? How would you feel if David was screwing some bartender right now?"

"I don't know, is he? It's never come up. Maybe we should talk about it."

"How can you be so…so…Ugh!" Jennifer slammed down the syrupy remains of her drink and stormed out of the casino leaving her tray and cup full of quarters.

"See you at dinner, then?" Kimberly said to Jennifer's back.

When Jennifer arrived back at her cabin, she found Michael reading the ship's daily newspaper. It served mostly as advertising for the onboard shops but also detailed the plethora of activities that could be had should one venture to go ashore. "Did you see this honey? Let's take Hannah onshore tomorrow and get in the water. Maybe this Glass Bottom Boat tour? I swear it was like being in a giant aquarium today."

"I don't want to talk about it." Jennifer's tone made it clear that there would be no discussion about any frivolity.

"Okay, sorry. It's just that we've only been on the ship a day and I feel like I haven't spent any time with you guys."

"I said I don't want to talk about it."

They dressed for dinner in silence. A low frequency rumbling suggested the ship was underway and a glance out the window confirmed they were heading for the next island. Jennifer wore the only fancy outfit she'd packed, a standard little black dress with black pumps. Michael put on a pair of pants with creases that revealed they'd been on a hanger for months if not years. "There's no way you're going to dinner wearing those in that condition," Jennifer said when she saw the wrinkles. Give me those. Michael dutifully removed his slacks and stood in his dress shirt, tie, and black socks while she ironed them on the small board provided in the tiny closet of the cabin.

Their walk to dinner was a funeral march. Michael felt romantic and tried to grab her hand, but Jennifer pulled it away without making eye contact. "Hey, let's get our picture taken. You look so nice, I'd like one."

"Forget it. Look at that line, I don't want to be late for dinner."

The couple proceeded to their assigned table but the Wilsons had yet to arrive. Michael held her chair and Jennifer sat down with a heavy sigh. It was a small table for four on the port side and had a gorgeous view of Grand Bahama Island slipping by as they headed for Nassau. The children were assigned a separate table for dinner, under the careful watch of Vanessa. A less fussy menu allowed a more efficient delivery of food to the hungry offspring. The main dining hall seated thousands but was tastefully designed to give the impression of an intimate and fancy restaurant. Potted tropical plants, vaguely sexual statues and Romanesque columns supporting nothing, served to divide the massive space into manageable rooms, yet allowed the staff to serve quickly from hidden kitchens. Jennifer and Michael had entered on the lower level, but could now see a wide staircase which allowed entry from a higher floor. It emptied into an atrium that was three stories tall. A lone musician was tinkling the ivories of a massive Steinway grand piano.

As the sun went down, the couple stared in silence out the window. The angled light made the island glow like the paradise it was. Michael was thinking it was views like this that made people quit their mainland jobs and take work on a fishing boat, in a souvenir shop, or in the kitchen of a restaurant—anything to be able to live on a beach. "I miss the prairie," was all Jennifer could say.

"Well, it's a good thing we live in Kansas."

Michael knew better than to ask her what was on her mind. After even a few years of marriage, he knew if pressed, she'd only become more defensive and silent. He wracked his brain trying to think of something he might have done wrong that he could apologize for at great length and therefore save the rest of the week. "I can't spend another minute with Kimberly."

"What? I thought you guys had a great time at the spa."

"I think I'll grab a slice of pizza and go back to the cabin."

"Please don't. Tell me what happened. Let's just try not to make a scene. We are sort of their guests, you know. The plane tickets weren't cheap."

Jennifer told Michael what happened at the casino, how Kimberly seemed so casual about her careless encounter with Fabio. Michael then related his identical concerns regarding David and the mysterious leggy blonde. They agreed to let it be and try to keep to themselves for the remainder of the cruise. It was none of their business, after all. "Like Jean-Paul Sartre said, 'Hell is other people,'" Jennifer said. "Present company excluded, of course. No offense."

"None taken. They'll be their own punishment," Michael added.

Feeling superior, both Jennifer and Michael were prepared when their fellow diners came down the grand staircase. Kimberly wore a simple peasant dress with flats. Around her shoulders was a sheer wrap. The only thing remarkable about it was the fire engine red color. David looked very dapper in his black slacks, black shirt, and a tie that matched his wife's dress. They were all smiles and positively beamed when they spotted Jennifer and Michael at their table by the window. Kimberly had a flush to her cheeks that wasn't from any makeup. "Can you believe this view? Sorry if we kept you guys waiting, but I insisted we get our picture taken. I feel like I'm at the prom again."

"Oh, listen Buttercup. He's playing our song!" The pianist was tinkling out a simple tune with endless arpeggios.

"That's not our song, silly. That's Pachelbel."

"Yeah, well I for one happen to love it. So it's our song for tonight. Can you believe this spread?" David gestured to the china, the silverware, the crystal glassware. "I'm suddenly so hungry I could eat my knife and fork." He picked up his water glass and proposed a toast.

"I can't wait until the drinks arrive. I just want to say, you guys are the best friends a guy could ask for. To friends and memories!"

Kimberly raised her glass as well. "Ditto. We've been so much about the children these last five years, that it's such a treat to spend some time with other adults." They clinked glasses and Michael looked at Jennifer to check her reaction. She remained neutral, and didn't say anything back, so he followed her lead and remained silent.

Any awkwardness was avoided when a sudden hush came over the room. It was as if the National Anthem were about to be sung. Murmured conversations could still be heard throughout the dining room, but all eyes were on the grand staircase. Descending to the music was a couple from the cover of a modern romance novel. She was easily over six feet tall with legs that appeared to grow straight down from her shoulders. Her body was packed into a sheath dress the color of a cooked lobster. It was too high at the thigh, too low at the bust, and so tight there couldn't have been any room for underclothes. Parts of her were threatening to burst forth with every step of her matching four-inch heels. Her hair was shoulder-length, pin-straight and platinum blonde, bordering on white.

Guarding her every tenuous step was Fabio. He wore a black silk suit with shiny lapels, a red bow tie and matching handkerchief. Even in her heels the tall blonde came only up to his chin which looked like it was designed for breaking open coconuts. His hair was the perfect blonde which comes only from being conceived, born, and raised on a surfboard. It cascaded down his shoulders and fluttered gently with every step they took.

David took a sip of his water, made eye contact with Michael and nodded his head sideways in their direction, as if to say, "Are you checking this out?"

Kimberly nudged Jennifer under the table, cupped her hand and whispered, "That's Fabio. The guy I was telling you about. Isn't he incredible? It's like he was carved out of marble. Oh, my god, they're coming this way." A couple of empty tables were still available nearby. To the rest of the table, Jennifer said, "You don't think they're in our section, do you?"

Michael spoke in a high falsetto. "Awkward!" Jennifer kicked him under the table. "Ow!"

Fabio and the Leggy Blonde came right to the table where Jennifer Smith, Michael Johnson and the Wilsons sat holding their breath. When they were close enough, Fabio made eye contact with David and nodded. He came over and placed his hand on David's shoulder. He towered over the them but didn't lean down to speak. In a booming, bass voice with the most charming English accent he said, "All apologies for interrupting your meal, but may I be so bold as to compliment you on your fine fashion sense?"

David looked straight up to the towering oak of a man beside him. He glanced at his wife, then at Leggy Blonde. Compared to them, David and Kimberly looked like their squat, fun house mirror reflection. The only similarity was the color of their outfits. "Uh, thanks. Thanks a lot." Fabio nodded to Jennifer and Michael, then led his date to a table for two, also overlooking the ocean, just steps away.

Like a miracle from the shadows, five servers appeared, presenting meals that the couples had ordered online when they made their reservations months prior. In an instant the table was heavy with appetizers, five kinds of bread with a full pound of fresh butter molded in the shape of a swan, four different soups, and a magnum of champagne. Each entree was served on a platter and could have easily fed the entire table. There was food for sixteen. David looked down at his twin lobster tails and steak. The baked potato was the size of a football. The asparagus could have been painted by Monet, only he wouldn't have put so much butter melting on top. "I think I'm gonna cry," David said. "I don't know whether to eat it or have sex with it." To Michael and Jennifer he said, "I hope you guys don't mind I ordered the champagne."

"Then perhaps we should give thanks?" Kimberly said as she reached for David's hand. They bowed their heads and were silent for a full minute, then Kimberly spoke again. "…and thank you Lord for making my husband prematurely bald so I don't have to constantly clean his sexy, flowing, long, blonde hair out of the sinks and drains."

With his eyes still closed, David added, "And thank you Lord, for making my wife so short that we can save money on clothes by shopping in the kids' department. Ah-men." Opening his eyes he spoke across the table where Jennifer and Michael were staring back with their mouths open. "Anything you'd care to give thanks for?"

"No," Jennifer said. "We're good."

"Yeah, let's eat," Michael said.

Throughout the meal, the Wilsons flirted continuously. When Kimberly went to the butter dish, David came after her with his knife and knocked off the pat that she'd picked up. Then, he did it again. She retreated and let him get his butter first, tapping the fingers of her right hand on the table, while he buttered his sourdough bread. With the missing acrylic nail, her fingers made a distinct rhythm; tap-tap-bump-tap, tap-tap-bump-tap, tap-tap-bump-tap. David wriggled in his seat, like a cockroach was crawling somewhere inside his shirt. "Everything okay, honey?"

"Oh, fine. The aloe's just sticking to my t-shirt a little. Got some scratches on the coral today."

"Uh-huh. Well, perhaps next time you should wear a rash guard like I always tell you." Kimberly reached for David's potato. "I've got to try this giant tuber of yours." She scooped out a bite, then brushed the back of his hand with her fork leaving a large dollop of sour cream. "Oh, sorry I'll get that," and she bent her head over and stuck her tongue right to the back of his hand like a bug on a windshield.

"Thanks, Buttercup.'"

A crouton jumped from Kimberly's Caesar salad. David flicked it back with his steak knife. A tabletop game of hockey ensued and ended only when Kimberly loaded the crouton on her soup spoon, balanced over her butter knife. She brought down the palm of her hand and the crouton flew over David's water glass. "Oh, wide right! Care to try again, sweetie?"

"That's it. I can't take it any more!" Jennifer shouted.

"Sorry, I know, I know, we're like kids at the lunch table. I just get so happy when I get David all to myself." Kimberly put her arm around her husband, squeezed him tightly and put a kiss on his neck.

"That's it?" David said. "I thought I rated at least a kiss on the lips. Maybe some tongue."

"Stop it! Stop it! Stop it!" Jennifer wailed. "How can you two be so, so…such…?"

"So, what?" Kimberly said.

"Hypocrites," Michael said, looking at his hands. "Look, we're all very uncomfortable with…" and his voice trailed off. "I don't know what to say."

"Exactly what are you implying, Michael?" David said.

"Is there something I should know about?" Kimberly said to David.

"You know perfectly well what I mean. Scratched your back on some coral? I was with you the whole time. You had those scratches before we left the dock with Hubert. And I don't remember seeing them at lunch. The leggy blonde?"

"And what about you, Kimberly, the stalking hyena?" Jennifer said. "Forgot your room key and that whole nonsense with housekeeping? How'd you break your fingernail? Does David know about Fabio?"

David turned to Jennifer with a laugh. "You called me Fabio? That's so cute. Sorry I'm so short. I know you like tall, blonde guys."

"You're the only guy for me. Sorry about your back. Couldn't help myself."

"It's okay. You can get a new nail tomorrow when the spa opens. Before we hit the beach. They'll come in handy for sand castle building. If you liked Grand Bahama, Michael, you guys are gonna love New Providence."

"What? Wait. She's the leggy blonde?" Michael pointed at Kimberly with an asparagus tip on his fork. "What about you guys being swingers and all?"

"Sure, who else would she be," David said. "And you're the one who said you weren't swingers. I never said a thing."

Jennifer finally put two and two together. "David's the reason you were late to the gallery?" Kimberly nodded.

"Aww, you told Michael I was leggy? That's so sweet. You know I wish I had legs like a stork, but these hips are way better for making babies."

"Don't I know it," David said. "Wear your bikini tomorrow?"

"Sure, why?"

"I love to see your stretch marks. They're so sexy and our kids are so wonderful. I want to get you pregnant again as soon as possible."

"Well, what are you waiting for?"

"Dessert. I'm going to bag it and eat the chocolate cake off your double-wide rear once the kids are asleep in their cabin."

"Promise?"

"You know you're the only one for me."

Michael was relieved to hear that all was right with the Wilsons, if a little over-the-top with puppy love. Jennifer stopped shaking and was able to calm down enough to finish and enjoy the rest of her dinner and dessert. The rest of the cruise went smoothly and a fine time was had by all, including Jennifer, Michael, and Hannah. Inspired by the Wilsons, they even had a little more sex than usual, agreeing it was a fine honeymoon, even if it was a half dozen years late.

8

Deal Breaker

As the game wore on, Jennifer showed signs of increasing distress. She began to watch the game less and scan the park more. Every car that drove by caused her to jump and move a few steps more away from Michael. "I don't know what the hell is taking James so long," she muttered.

"How come you never tell me you love me?"

"Not this discussion again." Jennifer rubbed her temples like the question itself gave her a migraine.

"Is it because you never did?"

"Just because I don't feel it every day, doesn't mean I don't. Or didn't. Stuff gets in the way. You can't explain love, it's ineffable."

"But you don't have to explain it every time you say it. Just say it once in awhile."

"Water under the bridge. Your being so needy isn't exactly making me change my mind. In a few days it'll all make sense when you realize life will go on without me. You'll be fine. Trust me on this, don't make me list my complaints in alphabetical order."

"We're having such a delightful time, spending the day with our daughter in the park. What's there to complain about?"

"Just sign the papers when James gets here. If you really love me, you'll do that much. I know it doesn't make sense. But trust me. This'll work. Think of Hannah." Then she added, almost pleading, "…please."

"No. It doesn't make any sense. And I *am* thinking of Hannah."

A black Cadillac Escalade with deeply, illegally tinted windows pulled into the service drive behind Michael's truck. Jennifer's anxiety reached its peak and she slowly sidled away from him, keeping her eyes on the soccer game. She edged back until they were twenty feet apart and different rows from the sideline. With the growing distance between them, any casual observer would not have suspected they were a couple. She whispered in Michael's direction, "Don't say anything to me. Don't look at the black truck. When James gets here, be sure to sign the papers."

By reflex Michael couldn't help but look over at the giant Escalade hemming in his Ford F150. It didn't look like anything special, so he looked back to the game and tried to find Hannah on the opposite sideline. "You're beyond nutty. You just dove straight into the deep end of Paranoia Pool." Michael thought he'd made a clever joke, but when he looked back to see Jennifer's reaction, she was gone. A short man was escorting her rather roughly into the passenger seat of the Escalade. He had the diminutive build of a prepubescent boy, certainly not Jennifer's type, so Michael didn't suspect any infidelity. His grip on her arm, the dark blue designer suit, his dark sunglasses, the wire in his ear; none of these suggested she was headed to Antonio's to save seats for a soccer team pizza party. The short man slammed the door, scanned the field as if looking for someone else, then went back around to the driver's side. Michael was determined not to rise to the bait. Clearly, this wild behavior was designed to goad him into making a mistake. If there really was to be a divorce, he wanted to be sure Hannah was his first priority. He returned his attention to the game and waited for James to show.

A few exchanges of the ball between the ineffectual teams was more than Michael could stand to watch. During what seemed like a decade of a third quarter, James finally arrived. He parked his Chrysler K-car in the spot vacated by the Escalade. Michael turned his gaze from the game to the spectacle of James getting out of his car. He spun each leg out of the driver's side door individually. Leaning back for momentum he hauled himself out with both arms to a standing position. He tripped around the open door and slammed it shut by heaving his hip into the panel near the handle.

Michael had seen plenty of patients with a limp. There were those with cerebral palsy who had a consistent wiggle. There were those with multiple sclerosis who had a variety of techniques to lift their legs and pivot. The career nurse had seen patients on crutches who supported their weight primarily on their forearms and swung their legs in a graceful dance. James had a limp that was painful to watch and must have been equally painful to perform. His gait had the awkward asymmetry of severe injury. This walk was in no way associated with a birth defect or neurological disease. James walked like both his legs had two knees, one of which was attached at ninety degrees to the other.

He lurched around the car to the passenger side. He opened the door and pulled out a large soft-sided leather briefcase. The walk towards Michael was a modern version of the Bataan Death March. James stepped heavily onto his left leg and swung his right limb around like he was attempting a sixty yard field goal. When the right leg landed it gave the impression of stability at first, then the torque caused a mysterious bone to protrude sideways, bending his khakis at an angle that suggested something the scarecrow from the *Wizard of Oz* would find uncomfortable. It took James two minutes to cover the few yards from their cars to where Michael was standing. "I guess you know why I'm here," James said. Sweat was beading up on his temples.

"Madison has been playing brilliantly, but you haven't missed a goal or anything."

James dropped his briefcase heavily to the grass. He bent over with one leg straight, the other one thrown behind like a donkey. From his briefcase he retrieved a thick wad of papers and presented them to Michael. "Sorry. Maybe you should get a lawyer."

"Dude. You *are* my lawyer. Did you forget that? You helped me update my will when Hannah was born. You helped me close on that stupid rental property we owned. Then you helped me sell it. If you don't remember, maybe you could check your bank account for the commissions."

James bent over again and retrieved a Mont Blanc Meisterstuck pen and held it out to Michael. "Just sign the papers, Michael." It was jet black with three gold rings and an embossed individual serial number on the gold-plated clip. Michael had no idea that it would retail at over three hundred dollars. He only knew that it didn't fit with the man's physical appearance or the fact that he drove a twenty-five year old car from the brief glory days of Lee Iacocca.

"This doesn't make any sense."

"That's what everyone says. Believe me." James practiced general law but by sheer volume, he handled more family law than criminal. He'd seen his share of divorces, custody battles and knockdown, drag out fights over estates and wills.

"Hey, you've been divorced, are you kidding me? Does this make any sense to you?"

"I'm not at liberty to say."

"Great. TV, cop show, lawyer-speak. Thanks a lot."

"I guess there comes a time in a marriage when it's better for everyone involved to just let go. Quit with the mind games and control issues and realize a separation is best." James gave Michael a wink and leaned in to give his forearm a squeeze. Michael couldn't have been more confused by the gesture.

"That's just it. We're doing fine. That's why it doesn't make any sense."

"I wasn't talking about you two." Michael gave him a look.

"Is there something you're not telling me?"

"Maybe. Lawyer-client confidentiality and all that," James winked again. "Did Jennifer happen to mention that it's in your best interest to sign the papers? Hannah's too?"

"Go on."

"Sorry. I'm not at liberty to say. Just sign the papers."

"Yeah, you said that. You lawyers are always sorry, but you don't do a damn thing to make it right. You have no idea what it's like…" Michael stopped himself, remembering that in fact, James did know what it was like. "I'm not signing without a good explanation."

"We've got no reason to be enemies, Michael. Trust me. And yes, I know about the pain that leads up to divorce, the mental anguish, too. You think I got these legs in Vietnam? I was three when the war ended. You really should sign the papers."

"Right. I've known you a long time, James. What would you do? Put yourself in my shoes. Think about it from what I know. Does it make any sense?"

James shifted from one crooked leg to the other. He held out the pile of papers on a clipboard with the pen. "Trust me, I've been in your shoes. It's for the best. Think of Hannah."

"Why does everyone keep saying that?"

"Because it's true. My first marriage was murder. Well, almost."

"Yeah? What's your story?"

"How much time is left in the game?" James looked down the line of parents to see Melissa. She was shaking her cowbell in the direction of Madison who must have come within a sand wedge of the soccer ball.

"I don't know, half an hour? And dude, I've got to ask you, what's with the cowbell?"

"Nothing. Melissa, uh, injured her hands once and it hurts if she claps. So she does the cowbell thing. You heard about Laura?"

"Not really. Seemed nice enough. What happened?"

"Ha. Things were going well for the first few years, until I realized she was already married." Michael gave him a look. "Yeah. Bride of Satan. No exaggeration."

"I've got to admire your sense of humor, considering. It's gotta be tough, start to finish."

"There's no finish. Love and marriage may not last, but divorce is forever. Visitation, alimony, child support, carting Madison around like so much property. It's ridiculous." James explained to Michael that all was not as it appeared. Plenty of marriages were ended because of the typical financial differences, infidelity, or illness. James and Laura's marriage must have had some unique complications. "You want the long version?"

Michael nodded. "Sure. Why not? My day can't get any more weird."

James kicked over his briefcase and sat down heavily. Michael remained standing, looking at the soccer game without watching. "It didn't occur to me there was a problem until my third trip to the ER," James said. "Look at this." He put a hand to his forehead and raised a thin, flopped Donald Trump comb-over. Michael took a quick glance. Under the wispy hair was an angled scar as thick and long as his finger.

"You fall on a chainsaw?"

"You might say that." James smoothed the light brown hair back over his scar. He drew up his knees and hugged them, still sitting on the briefcase. He looked across the field not really focusing. "Denial, wishful thinking. You don't believe it at first, then you start to think it's just a one-time deal. Then you think you'll be the one who can help, make it all better. Finally, it comes down to self-preservation."

The first accidental injury was from a knife. It was early in their marriage. James and Laura had just moved into a darling three-bedroom in the new development outside town. He was a junior lawyer at the only practice in town with a brilliant future ahead of him. Laura was the model wife. Organized, frugal, loving and optimistic. The newlyweds were in their kitchen making Mexican food. James was on duty chopping vegetables for the homemade salsa. "Nobody can screw up salsa," Laura had said. The precise ingredients didn't matter because everybody has their favorite. Some people like a touch of cilantro, others like it heavy on the garlic or balanced more to the onion. No, the only universal truth to salsa was that every ingredient had to be freshly chopped.

Laura had a "secret recipe" for spicing the ground beef which she claims was taught to her by her grandmother who had some equally secret amount of Mexican blood in her. By extension, that fact qualified Laura as some percentage Mexican and therefore, she could do no wrong when it came to preparing Mexican food. She refused to write down the recipe, swore she could remember every step and ingredient in her sleep, and even removed the labels from their spice jars, in case James tried to figure it out on his own. While they arranged the meal for two, James sipped a margarita. Laura did tequila shots.

James lined up all the ingredients on the granite counter top like the numbers at the top of a typewriter, all fresh: tomato, avocado, red onion, a clove of garlic, parsley, cilantro, and a jalapeno pepper. He reached under to retrieve their cutting board from its cabinet. It was a thick and heavy board of some exotic hardwood with not a scratch on it. "Aw, look honey. It's the first time we're using our special cutting board." He leaned over to give her a peck on the cheek.

She pulled away before his lips could land. "No you're not. That has to be conditioned first."

"What?"

"It's real wood. It's got to be oiled. You'll ruin it. It'll get stains, not to mention the drying and cracking."

"What?"

Laura stopped stirring her ground beef and gave James a beatific look of infinite patience. Her words and tone of voice let him know just how much of an idiot he really was. "That's a handmade cutting board. Maple, walnut and birch." James picked it up and tilted it under a canned kitchen light to admire the grain.

"So?"

"So? So, you'll ruin it. And I'll be the one to have to explain to Nana why we had to throw it away after only a month. You've got to condition it, at least overnight with mineral oil, or wood salad bowl oil."

"I've never heard of such a thing. You're telling me we can't use the salad bowls either?"

"And don't cut on the granite."

"Don't tell me, I'll ruin the counter top."

"No, you'll dull that professional chef knife." James held up his chopping knife, another wedding gift. It seemed like any other knife to him. He looked to Laura for an explanation. "That's a Chicago Cutlery knife. Only the finest blade money can buy." She reached under the counter on her side of the stove and retrieved a small, poly cutting board, then handed it to James. "Here. Use this."

James took the board in silence and began his cutting. Laura corrected his technique until she was satisfied that he could be trusted to cut the third tomato by himself. The first two had to be discarded. The onion took another lesson and five more minutes. After each ingredient was diced, he swept them into a glass bowl. "Don't drag the knife across the board, James. I don't like plastic shavings in my salsa."

When the salsa was finished, James reached for an avocado and began slicing it across the equator to make guacamole. "You better wipe that cutting board, pal. I don't want my guacamole tasting like jalapeno." Laura thought she was being cute. James went to the sink, wiped the board down with hot soapy water, rinsed it, and dried it with a new hand towel from the folded pile in the towel drawer. Looking at the stack of towels he was reminded how she'd forced him to wash the brand new towels before he could use one. He argued they came from the factory, ready to use. She claimed they had chemicals on them and needed to be washed. When the board was clean, he held it up for Laura's inspection. "Better."

James grabbed the avocado again and started across its waist with his knife. He felt Laura's eyes on him again. Before he touched the fruit he looked up to meet her eyes. "What?" When she didn't answer he looked back to the knife which was still moist with juice from the other vegetables. He went back to the sink and repeated the procedure with the knife, wiping it dry and showing it to Laura for her approval.

"You're not really going to cut that avocado sideways, are you?"

"What's it matter?"

"It's just wrong. Maybe we'll want slices for a salad or a hamburger. You don't cut it that way."

"I'm about to mash it up in a bowl and you're worried about which direction I cut the skin off? Oh, and before you start in about how I get out the pit, maybe I should just go do this in the dining room and show it to you when I'm done."

Laura felt control of her kitchen slipping away. This meal was supposed to be perfect, but all of her expertise was going to waste. She'd spent a lifetime learning how to cook Mexican from her grandmother, just so she could one day make a perfect meal for her future husband. Now the very man for whom she was making her special meal was ruining it. She stopped stirring the beef, threw the wooden spoon into the pan and slammed it to the back of the stove top. A spray of orange-brown sauce splattered on the wall and up into the vent of the microwave. James stood frozen, the knife still poised above the center of the avocado. Laura's eyes were wide with fury. "*Now* look what you've made me do!" she screamed at him. "Give me that knife!"

She reached across the stove and grabbed the handle of the knife while James stood frozen in shock at the intensity of her anger. Laura pulled the knife from her husband's hand with the force one would use to start a lawnmower. Another spray went up against the wall, this time the shocking bright red of James's blood. There was no pain at first. James looked down to his hand where a surgically straight slice extended from the tip of his index finger down to the base of his pinky. At his palm, a filet of skin was drooping like a worm on a hook, not dripping, but pouring blood onto the kitchen floor. He grabbed the new hand towel which must have had pain woven into the fabric because as soon as he squeezed it to his injury to staunch the flow, a flood of agony rushed to his brain. James fainted, hitting his chin on the granite counter on the way to the floor. He bit his tongue causing another laceration.

Laura stared at James lying in a crumpled pile on the floor. "Oh, come on, now. It couldn't be that bad." She rinsed the knife in the sink and dried it with another towel. When she turned and saw James was still immobile, she gave him a kick in the ribs that was harder than necessary. He still didn't budge, so she rolled him over to investigate further. Seeing the blood coming from his mouth, she screamed and started shaking him harder. "I'm sorry! I'm sorry! I'm so sorry!" she wailed. Laura shook James harder as a puddle of blood formed under his hip.

James finally awoke in a daze. Through thick lips and a bleeding tongue he mumbled, "What happened?"

"You cut yourself. Then you fainted. We've got to get you to a doctor."

She re-wrapped his maimed hand in the bloody towel, since it was ruined anyway, and escorted him to the passenger side of her car. At St. Bernadette's emergency room, they were able to bypass the tedious check-in procedure and were shown to a bay without a word of explanation. There was so much blood on his shirt, the triage nurse—her name tag said Nancy—made the decision to throw it away. She gave him a hospital gown and told him he could look through the lost and found for a sweatshirt or hoodie to wear home. While he was undressing she noticed a large bruise on his flank. "That happen tonight?"

"What?"

She touched the right side of his chest where a softball-sized bruise was forming. "You fall on a chair or something?"

"I don't remember."

"Little too much to drink, sailor?"

They all gave out uncomfortable laughs and James explained that he barely got through half of his margarita. Dr. Wright threw back the curtain and without a word went to his cart of suture supplies. He peeled off the blood-soaked towel and numbed the hand with lidocaine. He put a topical gel on the tongue and told James he'd do his best to be gentle, but there was just no way around the pain of having a needle stuck in your mouth. "So. You must be left-handed, right?"

"Humph?" James mumbled.

"You cut your right hand off at the elbow, so I'm guessing you're left-handed," Dr. Wright said.

"No, I'm a righty. I'm not quite sure what happened, since I fainted and fell."

"You made that drink way too strong, James. I've told you about drinking liquor on an empty stomach. Plus, the kitchen was hot. I guess it was too much for you." Laura was more than happy to fill in the details for the doctor. She said she couldn't explain the bruise, but he must have landed on the step stool or hit the handle on the oven door, on the way to the floor.

Dr. Wright was too busy to bother searching for other explanations. He did his best to sew the fingers back into a usable position and replace the flap of skin on the palm. "You're lucky you didn't catch a tendon. I'm not sure if all this skin will reattach so well, but if it peels you'll make more. Like a starfish," and he laughed at his own joke. "But I doubt you'll grow an extra finger."

As Dr. Wright sewed James's tongue back together at the edge, he explained that the ribs were probably broken by the looks of things, but there wasn't much point in doing X-rays. "They'll heal fine and the treatment is the same if it's just a bad bruise. Lots of ice and ibuprofen, got it?"

The drive home was silent, since Laura was hiding her guilt and James couldn't move his numb tongue. Things were fine between the newlyweds for another month, despite the fact that James couldn't eat any spicy Mexican foods for awhile.

James drove himself to the emergency room the second time. He told Dr. Wright that he just bumped it on the corner of a cabinet door that swung open when he wasn't looking. James had come home late from work at the law firm. It was an increasing source of stress for the newlyweds and Laura didn't hesitate to let him know how she felt about it. He'd called from work and explained that a deposition was taking longer than expected and he had to stay late working on the summary. Another client was late for an appointment, but he couldn't reschedule since the case was pending in three days. By way of consolation, James stopped by the video store and picked up Chinese food, Laura's favorite take-out. He'd picked out a documentary, a romantic comedy, an action flick—just in case Laura was in the mood to let him choose—and the most recent Best Picture film. "Got a favorite?"

"You never want to watch what I like," she whined.

"That's why I got you four choices, honey." James set the selections on the coffee table for his wife's perusal and turned to the kitchen. The next thing he knew, he'd been struck in the head with the remote control. Shards of plastic vaulted over his head and landed in the sink. The batteries clattered to the floor and bounced off the refrigerator. James turned back to his wife, still holding the Chinese food, his mouth open in shock and surprise. A warm trickle of liquid flowed from behind his right ear. He felt it gather at the collar of his shirt. James placed the food on the dining room table and reached up to the sore spot above his ear. The tip of his finger disappeared inside the bleeding dent in his scalp. Without a word, he grabbed a hand towel, wrapped four pieces of ice and put it to his wound. "Enjoy your dinner."

"A kitchen cabinet, huh?" Dr. Wright said as he put the needle into James's scalp.

"Yeah, it swung open when I turned around. I dropped a fork. Or a knife." The lie wasn't going well.

"It's just that most cabinet injuries tend to get folks in the forehead or on the top. Yours is way back behind your ear. That's all."

In the ensuing months, Laura was apologetic to a fault. James told her repeatedly it was okay and he meant it. She was his wife and it was easy to forgive a mistake or two. He still loved her and their life together was just beginning, getting better all the time. Her irritability returned after awhile, faintly at first, then in full force. The verbal abuse was the easiest to handle, or so he thought. Every conversation, no matter how trivial, ended with her reminding him that he was wrong in so many ways. Just because he was a lawyer, didn't mean he knew everything. The jet stream was *not* the cause of global warming. Her mother *would* be coming for the holidays, including the two weeks before and after Christmas. Yes, they'd have to give up their bed and sleep in the guest room as her mother could not sleep in anything smaller than a king-sized bed.

The physical abuse was nothing a real man couldn't handle. At least that's what Laura assured him. The bruises healed in rapid succession. When he got in her way on the stairwell as he was carrying a laundry basket of freshly folded clothes, it was reason enough for her to check him into the wall, to get him out of the way. A dirty pair of socks was reason to drag him by the arm from his home office where he was busy with a case preparation. She didn't let go until they were up the stairs and standing in front of the bed where she pointed to his offending footwear. He bent over to pick them up and she swatted him on the back of the head. In the shower the next day he noted five bruises—one for each finger—on his upper biceps.

One day in their second year of marriage, after a brutal tongue lashing over his inability to fold the towels correctly, James could stand it no more and confronted her behavior. She explained that she was trying to make the house more than just livable and needed his help. All was forgiven when James found out she was pregnant with Madison. They had a tearful hug and became a team again in planning for their little girl's arrival. The guest room became a princess's boudoir. James spent every hour after work and on weekends making the bedroom live up to his wife's every demand for perfection. They picked out paint, furniture, and even shopped antique stores to find the best deal on a classic rocking chair for feedings. Laura convinced James of the importance of spending more on a changing table than he'd spent on their home entertainment system, big screen TV included.

After Madison was born, he could do no right. His typing was too loud. He chewed with his mouth open. He smelled when he came home from his morning jogs. The screen door was too loud when he let it slam. James started parking his car in the street so as not to have to raise the garage door or start his car under Madison's bedroom, never mind that she was sleeping through the night from the age of six weeks. It was imperative that he return the baby wipes he'd purchased and this time, buy the correct brand.

On his third trip to the emergency room, James told Dr. Wright the truth. He came home late from work. It was his fault, he said. He'd forgotten his own birthday in the days leading up to a big case. If he impressed the boss with his work, he'd be on the fast track to partner. It was a products liability case with the complication of deep pockets all around. The other team brought in an entire team of high-powered lawyers from New York. The injured party claimed the ladder manufacturer was at fault for failing to advise of the dangers of pruning a tree near electrical wires while standing on an aluminum ladder. The insurance company didn't feel like their policy should cover mind-boggling stupidity. James had spent the afternoon researching precedents, building an ironclad case and lost track of time. Laura had emailed and texted to remind him of the special meal she was preparing, his favorite, linguine alfredo with homemade sauce, real garlic and for dessert a special Death By Chocolate cake with ice cream.

James came in the front door after dark to see the table set with their wedding china, white roses, and candles burnt down to puny stubs. An empty bottle of wine rested on its side at the head of the table. A messy highchair showed that Madison had enjoyed her meal and he heard her snoring through the baby monitor resting on the buffet table. Laura was asleep with her head on her left arm, her right hand still holding an empty wine glass. In the candlelight, James could see lipstick smudges at the rim. He put his briefcase next to the monitor and went over to his wife to rest a hand on her shoulder. Laura came up groggy with hair stuck to her cheek and drool down her chin. James grabbed the plate from in front of his chair. Orphans in the musical *Oliver!* wish they could be as humble. "It looks delicious, honey. So sorry I'm late, I totally forgot. It's a really important case and we made some good progress on the defense."

"You want some dinner?"

"Sure, it smells terrific."

Laura rose to her feet as James sat in his chair. She rounded the table with the giant ceramic bowl of linguine. Instead of spooning out a helping for James she slammed the ladle on the table causing James to jump in surprise. When he looked up to her all he saw was the bottom of the bowl coming for his head. The blow knocked him off his chair and he suffered another bump to the back of his head when he hit the buffet table. His hand went to his forehead and he looked in shock at the blood on his fingers, black in the faint candlelight. "Why?" was all he could muster. Laura turned to the table and grabbed the ladle. She flung it at him and returned to the table for anything else that was in reach. James covered his face while she pummeled him with plates, cutlery, the empty wine bottle and finally, the roses in their vase. Injured and humiliated, he rose to his feet covered in noodles and sauce. "Why?"

"You were with that slutty secretary of yours, weren't you!" she shouted. "Go ahead, deny it!"

James took a napkin off the table and put it to his bleeding forehead. Laura was screaming at him and making more wild accusations. He left the house without saying a word and drove himself to the emergency room.

"You should leave her," Dr. Wright said when James told him the story. "That's crossing a line. Even Dr. Phil says that's a deal breaker." He checked James's pupils and felt his neck for bony injuries. "You know the drill. Here comes a poke and a burn," and he put the lidocaine into the wound.

"Oh, don't think I haven't thought of it. Where am I gonna go? The Home for Battered Husbands?"

"Uh. Yeah. I see your point."

"Can I stay here tonight? I've got a really important case tomorrow."

"Well, I really don't have a good reason to admit you."

"Understood, but you know I can't go home tonight. Just give me a bed off in a side room so I can get some rest."

Michael stopped watching the soccer game and stared at James. The lawyer was still seated on his briefcase like a bird, knees bent at impossible angles. "How did you stick it out?"

"You know. The same way you would have, Michael."

"Madison."

"Yep. What was I supposed to do? Could you imagine the damage that beast could have done if I left her alone with my daughter?"

"So, what happened?"

"Just what you'd expect. The doctor had to report it. I wasn't going to press charges, you know, it'd just make it worse. But it was too late, the wheels were in motion. It was State of Kansas vs. Laura. The evidence was a bit too much, especially when Dr. Wright brought my medical records and said the story didn't match my wounds from the previous visits. The judge put her in jail for a few nights to cool her down. He ordered her to take anger management classes, mandatory counseling, the whole phony bit. Plus, I had to attend marriage counseling, like it was partly my fault she was abusing me. Can you believe it? Talk about humiliating."

Michael shook his head. He'd seen enough cases at the hospital where the woman was the victim. He'd heard the excuses for staying, seen the denial firsthand. In some cases it was too late and the wife paid the ultimate price for her love and forgiveness. There was no mechanism in place for a man who needed protection and it struck Michael as the worst kind of dilemma. Even if you could get someone to believe you were being abused by your wife, there was no help to be had. The situation filled him with equal parts sadness and anger.

"That's not the worst of it," James said.

The summer Madison turned four, Laura decided it was time for a prolonged visit with her mother. Due to his busy caseload, James was unable to join them for the trip. The firm was doing well enough that they needed more space, both for the new associates' offices and a conference room for meetings and depositions. Their lease was up in the old location but the new building hadn't yet been renovated. Still striving to make partner, James volunteered their house for storage of records and as a temporary law office. Madison would be gone with her mother for most of the summer, so the situation was best for all concerned.

Friday morning, on the last day of the lease, James kissed his wife and child goodbye and drove to work. Between preparing for his upcoming cases he packed box after box full of old, current, and future case files. All afternoon the partners loaded their things into a twenty-five foot rental truck in preparation for the move to the temporary office. When all the offices were packed, James volunteered to drive the truck to his house. The shared secretary, Melissa drove James's K-Car and their boss, Scott King followed in his Chevy Impala. The caravan pulled up to the dark house. James backed up the truck and the three of them silently hauled box after box into the living room. Files for upcoming cases were stacked in the dining room. The two men returned to the office to collect the furniture while Melissa arranged an office, converting the domestic space into a usable war room.

The men returned to unload the office furniture, storing it in the garage until it could be transferred to the new office. They worked late into the night and collapsed exhausted. Melissa slept upstairs on Madison's bed while the men fell asleep across the couch and love seat of the living room.

At first light, Melissa was up, showered and ready to get to work. She'd planned for the weekend and had packed a carry-on suitcase with her personals and her work clothes. She put on her usual navy business suit with a skirt that went past the knee. She tied up her deep, brown hair in a severe bun. Melissa slipped out without waking the men, let the K-Car roll down the driveway in neutral before starting the engine and returned with breakfast: a dozen bagels, two flavors of cream cheese, assorted donuts, and a gallon of fully-caffeinated coffee. The men were soon awakened by the smell of fresh coffee and the gentle rustling of papers from the dining room. Melissa set up her work station using a short end table. She used a towel of her own as a tablecloth so as not to cause any scratches. On it she placed a jar of pens and highlighters in various colors, a stack of legal pads, and her main tool, a nine pound, Stentura 8000LX stenograph machine. Even used, the machine had cost the firm thousands and she treated it with the respect it deserved. In its digital memory were the extensive notes from all their pending cases. They used it for dictation as well as the all-important depositions from witnesses they'd interviewed. She kept a file of back-up cards under lock and key.

James ambled from the living room with his eyes half open, rubbing his heavy beard and yawning. His dress shirt was as deeply wrinkled as his face. He wandered to the fridge by memory, opened the door and took out a pitcher of filtered water. Eyes still closed he went to the cupboard and retrieved a tumbler. He poured out a full glass and downed it in one breath. "Ugh. I feel like I ate the worm last night, but I don't remember having any fun."

"No rest for the wicked."

"Oh, coffee. Melissa, you're an angel from heaven," James said. She'd set out two coffee mugs for the men. "Remind me to give you a raise when I'm the boss."

"Hey, I heard that," said a groggy voice from the other room. "Win this case and I'll give you both a raise."

The trio worked throughout the day, arranging files, tidying up the new workspace, and then plunging into the most recent case. Melissa took dictation from both men throughout the day, depending on the case. They had some shared files and some more minor cases on which to put the finishing touches. At one point in the early afternoon, James realized it was hours after lunch and none of them had had a break to eat or otherwise. He asked Scott if he wanted to order Chinese takeout and James would pick up the tab. Melissa continued to tap away on her Stentura 8000LX oblivious to the fact that the conversation had taken a less noteworthy turn. "Sure, Michael, I'm crazy about their orange chicken."

"You think Melissa ever gets hungry?"

"Nah. Robots don't eat. You just have to make sure the battery doesn't get too low. Then they don't take the charge as well."

"Oh. So that's why you leave her plugged in most of the time, huh?"

Melissa transcribed it all without a blink. She looked up from her legal pads only when the men stopped talking. "Will that be all for the Simpson case, gentlemen?"

"Uh, sure," James said. "Read back that last page, though."

Melissa scrolled back a page with the touch of a button. On the electronic screen she read out loud to the men, a smile coming to her face as she got to the part about lunch. "Oh, no. I'm so sorry. May I have permission to take a fifteen minute break?"

The men burst out laughing. "No, you may not," Scott said. "You're taking at least an hour. I changed my mind about takeout. Let's go to Antonio's and get a nice lunch. On me. I'm sure David can put it down as a business expense."

James assisted Melissa into the passenger side of Scott's Impala. They used the excuse of lunch to return the rental truck. Scott followed James to the depot and waited with Melissa while paperwork was finalized. At Antonio's James and Melissa started towards the more economical buffet side of the restaurant. They both looked back when they heard Scott say to the hostess, "Table for three, please."

Melissa, feeling guilty enough about eating on the company dime, picked at her enormous twenty dollar chicken salad, the cheapest item she could find on the appetizer side of the lunch menu. She had the rest packed in a doggy bag. The men ate with gusto, replacing calories lost the previous night in their sideline job as furniture movers. Between them, they split an appetizer of mussels, two enormous platters of seafood and linguine, and a piece of chocolate cake the size of a basketball.

Back at the house and with renewed energy, the trio resumed their industrious positions in the makeshift office. Melissa did some more filing and arranging of the remaining boxes for a few of the other partners. Scott piled law books and legal references along a wall till he could no longer reach the top of the stacks. Standing back to admire his handiwork, he considered the precarious nature of the leaning towers and decided to stack them three rows deep instead. James read and took notes at the coffee table. He sifted through a dozen depositions and wrote drafts for as many briefs and proposals for strategy. None of the three noticed the sky was darkening until James's stomach let out a loud growl. "Oh, wow. Look at the time. Is anyone else hungry?"

"I've got my salad."

"After that cake, I may never have to eat again, James."

"Well, suit yourselves. I think I'm still craving Chinese, since a certain party who shall remain nameless, ruined my plans for a tasty boxed lunch."

James went to the phone and hit speed-dial to the Imperial Palace Chinese Restaurant for delivery. From memory of the extensive dinner menu, he order an egg roll and six fried won tons for an appetizer. As was his custom, he planned to wash it down with a small bowl of hot and sour soup. For an entree he ordered a double serving of the

Four Seasons platter: shrimp, beef, chicken, and pork sauteed with vegetables in brown sauce. "Just how many people are coming to this party?" Scott said.

"Did you guys know that fortune cookies aren't even Chinese?"

They all had a laugh and James offered them a drink from the basement refrigerator. Even though only three persons lived in the house, the kitchen fridge was for water and milk only. Laura had a strict and specific nutritional plan for her little girl. She complained that Madison should never have juice or soda pop, but admitted that exposure about once a month, on special occasions, would do little harm. As for James's desire for a Lite beer after a long day at work, Laura relented but only if he store it in the basement in a separate ice chest. Out of sight and out of mind, she always said. While Michael was in the basement the front door bell rang. He bounded up the steps two at a time with a cola in each hand. "That had to be the fastest delivery in the history of Chinese food."

"I didn't hear the helicopter land," Scott said.

James set the colas on the counter and went to the front door. He opened it with his wallet in hand. Instead of dinner in a bag, James was met with the pinched face and narrowed eyes of Laura. "Honey. What a surprise."

Instead of answering, Laura shoved James in the chest with both hands, knocking him to the floor. She stormed into the living room and shouted, "Where is that slut?" Oblivious to the stacks of legal files, she marched to the fireplace and wrestled the poker from its stand. It had a pointed tip, a hook for positioning logs, and was charred black from use. She swung it backhand at the stand sending the tongs, brush and dustpan flying. She turned to James and pointed the weapon at his chest. "Where is she?"

James scrambled to his feet. "I don't know what you're talking about."

"Whose car is that? I knew I'd catch you, you dirty bastard."

James backed into the kitchen keeping his eye on Laura. When he got to the threshold of the dining room he pointed through the door at his boss and their secretary. "It's just a misunderstanding, honey. Remember? We're moving offices. You said last week I could use the house for storage while the workers are painting."

"Oh. You are sick! A woman I could almost understand. But a three-way? And with a man?"

"What?" Scott said.

"Hey, you're being rude. That's my boss and his secretary Melissa. There's no need to speak to them that way."

Melissa sat frozen, her hands poised over the stenography machine. Scott stared with his mouth open. He shook himself awake and stood up. "Uh, maybe we should go. We can pick up tomorrow, it's been a long day for everyone."

"You shut up, asshole!" Laura took out her anger by whacking James across the left shin with the head of the poker. The blow made an audible crack and everyone in the room heard the bone break. James didn't fall but managed to catch himself on the door jamb to the dining room. Laura took another full swing, this time catching James mid-thigh on the same leg. The hook caught in his muscle and she was unable to retrieve the blow. Using both hands she pulled with all her weight and tore it loose of the muscle, ripping the quadriceps tendon in the process. Hugging the door frame and standing on one leg, James looked down in anguish at his torn pants. The muscle was hanging loose and he could see the back of the kneecap where it flopped over the broken tibia.

Laura poked him in the chest. "Anything to say for yourself? Huh? Huh? Any last words before I carry out sentence, counselor?"

James began to cry, mumbling how it wasn't right, that he was faithful, it was just a work meeting, she said they could use the house, why was she doing this? She poked him in the chest and he began to retreat, one-legged, hopping along the wall into the kitchen to avoid her prodding. James ran out of wall at the door to the basement, but Laura kept prodding. She pushed him harder until the poker drew blood from a cut to his chest. James looked down at the spreading blob of red on his chest and then up to his wife, pleading for mercy and understanding. His weakness enraged her further and she butted him square in the forehead with the handle of the poker. James went tumbling down the stairs in a cartwheel, breaking more bones the entire way.

Laura raised the poker overhead, preparing to heave it like a spear when she heard a sniffle from the dining room. She ran to the dining room tripping over boxes and scattering papers in all directions. At Melissa's tiny end table desk she renewed her screaming. "You whore! Look at me when I'm talking to you!" The secretary raised her face to her attacker keeping her hands poised over the stenography machine. A single track of tears was streaming down each side of her face. "He's a married man, you slutty home wrecker. You're not good enough for him!"

"You're right."

"What?"

"I said, you're right. James is the best man in the firm, about to make partner. I'm not good enough for him, even if he were single.

He's a great father to Madison and he adores you. You're a lucky woman, Laura."

At the mention of her name, Laura's anger returned two-fold. She raised the poker overhead with both hands and prepared to deliver the blow. Melissa didn't move, flinch or take her eyes from Laura as the shaft of the poker came down across both her hands, crushing the bones into the keyboard and shattering the digital display on the screen. The light went blank signaling that all of the partners work from the day was lost. Laura hurled the poker in the direction of a stunned Scott who ducked out of the way as it whirled past his head. It lodged in the drywall making a great tear and rattling the glass in the picture window. Laura tore the machine from under Melissa's mangled hands and wrenched the cord from the wall. She stomped back into the kitchen with the machine raised overhead. At the basement steps she heaved it down onto James with all her might and fury, cursing and swearing at him the entire time. The nine pound machine hit him flush in the stomach rupturing his spleen.

The doorbell rang and shook Laura from her trance of anger. She composed herself and went to the door to open it. It wouldn't fully open and when she looked down to see why, there was James's wallet. She picked it up and opened the door to see an Oriental man dressed in white from head to toe, including a paper cap. "Yes? May I help you?"

"Seventeen, ninety-five," he said in a singsong heavily accented voice.

Laura reached into the wallet, pulled out a twenty dollar bill and told him to keep the change. She closed the door, returned to the kitchen and set the bag down on the table. She removed the contents of the bag and lined the little boxes up on the table in a neat row, Chinese characters facing outwards. From the cupboard she retrieved a plate and a glass. She filled the glass with water and set it and the plate down in front of the food. Laura got out a knife, a fork, and one napkin, set them on the table in order, then sat down and ate Chinese food for dinner.

9

FOURTH TIME'S A CHARM

The soccer game came to its merciful conclusion and the girls gathered around their coach in a giggling mass of bouncing adolescence. They joined hands in a crowd and cheered for the other team with more gusto than they'd played the game. The Bees cheered for the Sallys. The Sallys cheered for the Bees. It seemed the team who won was not the one who scored the most goals but the one who screeched loudest after time was called. The adults on both sides made a pair of human tunnels, standing in two rows with their fingers interlaced overhead. The teams ran under the arches back and forth in a figure eight until some mysterious signal caused a break in the pattern. By their behavior it was impossible to tell for either team if the game had ended in a win, loss, or tie.

The girls huddled on the ground cross-legged and tore into their commercially packaged Rice Krispie treats and Capri Sun juice pouches. The parents waited patiently as impromptu plans were made for play dates and sleepovers. Melissa packed up her cowbell and sidled over to James for a peck on the cheek. He grabbed her arm for support as they joined in a group hug with Madison. Michael noticed the lumps on the backs of her hands, the deformity from her previous fractures. He felt a moment's guilt for his unkind and shallow appraisal of her as a rebound trophy wife. Her meticulous French manicure took on a whole new meaning for Michael. James gave a wave as they walked to their car and tapped his briefcase as if to offer one more time for Michael to sign the divorce papers. Michael waved him off and started looking for Hannah.

Instead of looking for her father, Hannah bounced up when her juice and treat were done and put the wrappers in the trash. She walked with purpose to the opposite end of the field and directly into the arms of Judy and Hank Smith—Jennifer's parents. Michael hadn't even known they were at the game. The thought that Jennifer was already cutting him out of Hannah's life enraged and confused Michael even more. He walked over to where they were standing. Judy was congratulating Hannah on what a wonderful game she'd played.

"So," Michael said, "What's this party all about?"

"Hey, Mike," Hank said. His father-in-law was the only person who didn't call him Michael. He hit Michael in the shoulder with a punch that was sure to leave a bruise.

"Daddy!" Hannah said as she hugged her father around the waist.

"Jennifer asked us to pick up Hannah," Judy said by way of explanation. "Didn't you work last night? You must be bushed. Poor thing."

It was not unusual for the grandparents to have Hannah for extended visits. She was their only grandchild and they lived up to their stated desire to be a large part of her life. They spoiled her like the only child she was, as if it was their duty to do so. Jennifer and Michael were happy for the help. Due to his irregular schedule, Michael was often unavailable or at best, finishing a long shift. Jennifer was busy with administrative duties that kept her long after the last school bell rang. "That's the funny thing. She asked me to be here, too."

"Well, we've got plans for Hannah for the week. Did you want to come over after you sleep a spell?" Judy said.

"No thanks, but can I speak to you, Hank?"

"You know, I had two jobs when I was your age. Worked seventy, eighty hours a week. No one ever asked me if I needed to sleep. Your generation is soft as pudding."

"Yeah. You've told us," Michael said. He refrained from pointing out the fact that studies showed modern fathers spent more time with their kids and housework than previous generations did, by far. "Hannah, why don't you go with Gramma Judy and I'll bring Grandpa Hank along later. Guy talk, you know."

Hank handed his keys to Judy. The two pairs went off to their separate vehicles. Hank walked straight to the driver's side of Michael's Ford F150. Hank always drove, no matter the owner of the car. They joked he wouldn't get on a commercial airliner unless the pilot moved over to the navigator's seat. "No way you're driving, Mike. You'd probably get lost before we're even out of the neighborhood." Michael gave him a look as if to say such a thing couldn't possibly happen, not in a million years. "What? That GPS gonna help you? Don't make me laugh!"

"Hey. It's works pretty good."

"Man up, pussy willow. Know where you're going at all times. No excuses, no whining." Michael had known for a long time where Jennifer inherited her direct style of communication. "What's this all about, anyway? Bangin' my daughter for ten years, you never come over, and *now* we need to talk?"

He ignored the crude remark as it was always game on with Hank. Rise to the bait and he'd argue just for the sake of getting a rise, even if he agreed with you. "Has Jennifer said or done anything unusual? Lately, I mean," Michael said.

"No. Why?"

"James presented me with divorce papers today. In the middle of Hannah's game, no less."

"The cripple? His ass ain't worth kicking. Don't now what that hottie sees in him to begin with." Michael bit his tongue and tried to steer Hank back to the subject at hand. Knowing what he now knew about James and Melissa, he knew they were a couple worth defending against such crude judgements.

"I just wondered if she said anything about it to you."

"Nope. Sorry. Sometimes that shit don't make no sense. Sometimes it's long overdue."

"Yeah? Maybe for other people. Not for us. What's your secret?"

"Got no secrets. Maybe that's what kills a marriage, all the pussyfootin' around and little white lies. I say, tell it like it is."

"I mean, you and Judy. What's the secret to staying together for—what is it now?—twenty-five years?"

Hank didn't answer but guided the truck deftly around a few curves and straight to the main road back to town. "Judy? She's my fourth wife. Best one, too. Always wanted a half-blind old bag with saggy tits—just didn't know it. Fourth time's a charm."

"What? I thought she was Jennifer's mother."

"Of course she is. Also my first wife. Tits like big oranges when I nailed her the first time. Just as firm, too. Now they're more like deflated trout nailed to a barn door."

"Okay, you're gonna have to explain that to me."

"It happens when they have kids, you see. Blow up with helium when they're breast-feeding, then—poof. They collapse like week-old party balloons."

"That's not what I mean. Your fourth wife? Your first?"

Hank looked over at Michael. He stepped on the brake and brought the truck to a dead stop in the middle of the road. Ignoring the horns blaring behind he said, "You're serious? You really want to know?" Michael confirmed that he did. "Okay, here it is: Nobody knows what they really want. Even the people who think they know, they don't know. 'Cause the worst thing you can get is that thing you ask for."

"Do you ever talk sense?"

"I'll give you an example from your own life. You're what, thirty-five years old?" Michael nodded. "Same age as Jennifer. Fine. Got a nice daughter, nine years old. You're a male nurse, work your ass off nights in the hospital, she works her fingers to the bone makin' that school system run, teaching on the side. Like one full-time job's not enough. Between you both, you somehow manage to raise Hannah in your spare time. Riddle me this. If you met Jennifer now, as a single guy, considering what your lives are like, would you be thinking you're perfect for each other? That she's the one you'd want to spend the rest of your time with? Imagine you'll only get to see her after work for a few hours. She's more devoted to her daughter and her work than she'll ever be to you. She's got a life of her own. Still think she'd make the perfect wife?"

"But that's not how it worked. I didn't meet her now. She's not some divorcee with a bratty kid. Hannah's ours. We had her together. We got *here* together."

Cars started pulling around the Ford F150 and flipping off Hank as they got back on the road in a dusty cloud. Hank raised his hand to return the gesture to each driver.

"Who gets married thinking, 'Gee, you know, I'd like a kid with cancer. Sure hope one of my twin daughters dies before fifth grade.' No, we say we want kids, we don't know what it means. I ain't talkin' about the money to raise them and I ain't talkin' about the feedings in the middle of the night or the skinned knees on the playground. We just choose the best-lookin' guy or gal who will have us and hope they never change. Stupid. It's beyond stupid, it's a form of insanity. Kids change you, then you change each other. Life changes you. If you can't deal with it, you get divorced, thinking the next one will be better."

Hank put the truck back in gear and started driving. Michael's mind was reeling and he sat in silence. He tried to think of all the mistakes he'd made, the times he'd taken Jennifer for granted, or worse. He didn't beat her, he was supportive of her career, he didn't overspend. "I don't get it," he said. "We're all healthy. We do okay financially. Jennifer's great. Great at work, great with Hannah."

"Great in the sack?"

"Not that it's any of your business, but yeah. She's, uh, talented, keeps herself in fine shape. So why's she wanting a divorce?"

"When's the last time you told her all that shit?"

"Huh?"

"Women need the words, Mike. Trust me. More than flowers or orgasms. Fact is, they don't seem to need that last one much at all."

The men drove in silence for awhile, each lost in his own thoughts. "I guess my point is this, Mike. I wanted—needed—a different woman in my life at each stage. It just so happens that numbers one and four were the same woman."

"That's the most ridiculous thing I've ever heard. Do you listen to the sewage that comes out of your mouth?"

"Shut it, Nancy. I'm giving you the truth for free, here, so listen up. You'll thank me one day. We want kids, we don't want to watch 'em leave. We don't want to be grandparents, getting a card twice a year. It's lonely. You met Jennifer at a party, it was exciting, she was brilliant. When's the last time you took her to a party?"

"It might be the truth to you, Hank, but it's not for me."

"You asked me why people get divorced and I'm tellin' ya. If you asked me why they stay married, I'll tell ya that, too."

"Here it comes," Michael mumbled, rolling his eyes.

"The secret to staying married is to *not* get divorced."

Michael stared at Hank with his lips pursed and pondered the obvious for a moment. "Brilliant. Thanks, Yoda. Why hadn't I thought of that? Let's co-author a book and go on *Oprah*. The world will be such a happy place. Then we'll fix that silly little conflict in the Middle East."

"You're not listening. If two people are committed to the marriage, they shouldn't get divorced. The rest is just window dressing. If you got a mind to, you could find reasons to get divorced on your wedding day. You wouldn't be the first, either."

"So, what's your story?"

"When Janie died the marriage fell apart. Judy couldn't handle it."

"Who's Janie?"

"Jennifer's older sister. Well, older by half an hour."

"Huh? Jennifer's got a twin? Since when?"

"Had a twin. How can you not know this about your own wife?"

"It's not like it's tattooed on her forehead."

While Hank drove to his own house to meet Judy and Hannah, he gave Michael the background on his failed marriages. Jennifer and Janie were born thirty-five minutes apart at St. Bernadette's Hospital. "Just like The King," Hank said.

"Michael Jackson was a twin, too? I didn't know that."

"No dumb-ass. Elvis. The King of Rock & Roll, Elvis Aron Presley. Not the King of Pop, shit-for-brains. 'Cept his twin died at birth. Poor guy lived a lifetime not knowing his other half. Spent most all of his time with his mother. At least Jennifer got to know Janie a little."

"That's terrible. I think I'd rather not know."

"That's life. Pick yer poison. They had a few good years together. They probably don't remember sharing the changing table, but during grade school they were attached at the giggle."

Michael quoted the only poetry he knew. "So, you believe, *'Tis better to have loved and lost/Than never to have loved at all?'* You should talk to my lawyer friend James."

"If you quote Shakespeare all the time, it's no wonder Jennifer wants a divorce."

"It's Tennyson. And I was trying to make a point."

"The only point I got is that you're a stuffed-shirt, pretentious fag. I should just wring your chicken neck and save Jennifer the trouble."

"Okay, okay, back to Elvis. Did you know his first single, was also his first number one?"

"Lucky save, Mike. Now you're talking my language. 'Heartbreak Hotel.' Doubt there was a finer song ever written. Kind of fits our little theme here, doesn't it?"

"So. Judy left you?"

"In so many words."

Hank and Judy planned a sixth birthday party for the twins like it was Christmas, the Fourth of July, and the Invasion of Normandy, all wrapped up in one. Judy was the General MacArthur of birthday party planning. Although not a landmark birthday, Judy later claimed it was because she successfully argued that it was the first one the girls would remember. Hank made the more pragmatic point that it coincided with the first and last bonus he ever got at work. They decided to spend it on the girls, as any proud parents would.

Their quaint, suburban backyard was converted into a one-day carnival, the way the circus used to come to town. Janie and Jennifer were born on October 5th and Hank said it was the perfect time for a party, for a dozen reasons. Kansas summers can be brutally, dangerously hot for an outdoor party. Everyone's busy during the summer so it's impossible to plan a party. At that age the only friends you've got in the summer live next door. After school starts it's like making twenty new friends in a single month. The entire kindergarten class was invited and everyone was available to come whether they knew the Smith girls or not. At that age, a party is a party, and the kids hadn't segregated themselves into superficial cliques. Everyone can be included and really mean it.

There was a petting zoo with a donkey to ride. There were free carnival games and everyone who played got a cheap plastic toy prize whether they hit the target or not. By the end of the day, each child was wearing multiple stretchy bracelets and rings molded into the shape of a giant spider. Even the ring toss was popular, if only for the balsa glider that was given as a prize. If they couldn't loop the hard, plastic ring around a Coke bottle, well they got a glider anyway. In one corner of the yard, Hank set up a table with the twin birthday cakes. Each girl had her own custom, multilevel creation decorated with their favorite Disney characters on one tier and symbols of their favorite sports and hobbies on the other levels.

The highlight of the party was not the juggling clown or the strolling minstrel, but a two-story Bounce House with a soft ramp connecting the two levels, an extravagance not lost on the guests. It was the early 1980's before such things were commonplace at every backyard barbecue. The inflatable house was designed in a tropical theme with fat palm trees at the corners that wiggled in response to the slightest step of any occupant. The main platform was surrounded by netting and the rental price included a wrangler to keep the house optimally inflated, ensuring the maximum bounce for his forty-five pound clients. The supervisor was also in charge of limiting the number of kids bouncing at once, since most injuries happened when one kid bounced into another, not when they fell by themselves or landed in the netting.

Kids and their parents started arriving at noon. A table was set up for receiving presents. It was soon covered by showy packages, in every conceivable color, shape and size, all in duplicate, like Noah had planned the gift-giving and was filling his ark.

A row of classic carnival foods was available, the machines manned by volunteer parents of the kids attending the party. It was as much fun to make as it was to eat. There was a cotton candy machine, elephant ears, funnel cakes, Sno-cones, and of course, kettle corn being stirred in a giant vat. The kids were eating as fast as the parents to could make it.

Janie and Jennifer were the queens of their domain and went everywhere together. For the occasion, Judy gave them white t-shirts to decorate as they chose. The girls used paint and permanent markers to designate themselves as "Birthday Girl #1" and "Birthday Girl #2" based on their birth rank. Janie only rarely pulled the age card when it suited her, but Jennifer was happy to let her best friend take the first ride, the largest piece of pie, the hand of her favorite parent any given week.

During the party, as elsewhere in their life, they were inseparable. They rode the tethered donkey in a circle together. They ate phenomenal amounts of junk food together often stuffing it in each other's faces. They ran around the Bounce House for hours, taking breaks only to drain large cups of Kool-Aid. Hank took a turn in the dunk tank and when Janie missed the giant bulls-eye repeatedly, Jennifer ran up and pushed the lever releasing their father from his perch. The splash sent waves of water out of the tank onto the lawn and waves of adolescent laughter rippled around the yard.

Sensing everyone had sampled what the party had to offer at least once, Judy called them all together for the opening of presents. She set up two chairs by the gift tables and the guests sat around on the lawn in a semicircle. Janie, being the oldest, got to go first. She went to the gift table and chose a three-foot tall box that she could barely lift. Instead of opening the gift, she presented it to her sister, then returned to the table and retrieved the matching box for herself. "You go first, Jennifer."

Janie's permission was all the encouragement she needed. Jennifer tore into the wrapping and pieces flew in all directions, revealing a giant doll with features similar to the twins. She let loose an ear-piercing shriek and held up the box for the crowd to see. Her scream was soon echoed by Janie who performed the same maneuver with her gift. Holding up the dolls in their chairs the group looked like quadruplets. The girls faced each other and let out another glass-shattering scream which was again echoed by the guests as if the Beatles had just arrived for a concert. When the screaming was done, the twins looked at each other with smiles that said it would never get any better than this moment.

Blood dripped down Janie's nose and over her lip. "You're bleeding," Jennifer said.

Janie wiped her arm across her nose smearing the blood from cheek to ear. A fresh rivulet followed the first, replacing the one she'd just cleared. Looking at her bloodied arm, Janie cried, "Mommy!"

"Oh, honey. Come here. Too much excitement," Judy said. The crowd went silent as Judy picked up Janie from her chair. The older twin let her doll fall to the grass, still in the packaging. It tipped softly on its back and the eyes closed behind the cellophane. The tight-lipped smile remained as if the doll were having a most pleasant dream.

Janie hugged her mother around the neck with one arm and tried to staunch the flow with her other hand. Jennifer grabbed Hank by the hand to follow them, full of the kind of concern only a twin can have for its sibling. Judy carried Janie to the kitchen and sat her on the counter top. Blood was pouring generously from both sides of her nose down her chin. Much of it landed on her special T-shirt, dividing the words "Birthday" and "Girl" with an angry gash and soaking the "#1." She raised her arms overhead to allow Judy to pull off the ruined shirt. On Janie's chest was a bruise the size of a softball. "Janie, what happened?" Judy said, pointing at the purple insult.

"I don't know," she said looking down and touching the bruise. "It doesn't hurt." Janie tried to cover it with an open hand, but even with her fingers apart, the mark spread beyond her reach, from nipple to nipple.

"Did she get hit in the Bounce House?" Hank asked Jennifer.

"No, we were having fun," Jennifer said, then added with the logic only a child would understand, "the entire time."

Judy took a rag from under the sink, ran it under cold water and had Janie lean her head back and pinch her nose. In a few minutes the bleeding stopped. With her head righted, Janie coughed once into the sink, producing a large rubbery clot that Judy immediately washed down so neither of the girls would see it.

They walked to the bedroom and Janie picked out a new shirt. Jennifer changed as well so their outfits would match once again. The twins walked hand in hand back to the gift tables and received a round of applause. The girls returned to their booty and meticulously unwrapped each present, but with subdued enthusiasm. Hank wrote down who gave what, including the cash envelopes, in order to later write out the thank-you notes. When all the presents were opened, the guests dispersed to enjoy the various diversions. The bloody nose and its significance were a distant memory. The party continued to be a huge success.

As the sun set, Judy instructed Hank to set up the stereo. This was before karaoke, but Hank was a pioneer. He'd been in a band and figured out how to hook up his microphone to the hi-fi sound system. He started with a Beach Boys song and at the first mention of surfing in the lyrics, guests stopped what they were doing and joined him on the side of the yard. The more brave members took a turn at the microphone, squeaking out their favorite tunes from his extensive LP and 8-track library. The rest were content to dance in a congested lump under a disco ball that Hank had hung from a tree. He spun it on a thin length of fishing line and the momentum caused it to be self-winding, first one direction, then the other. To complete the party effect he aimed two garden lights at the orb which scattered gems of dancing color on the revelers.

The most unforgettable part of the evening was when Judy joined Hank in a duet to "Rock Lobster." The twins imitated each other using their hands like claws and swimming on dry land, holding their noses as they went down for imaginary dunks. Soon other kids were joining in to the Simon Says dance routine, mimicking the twins. At the bridge in the song, Hank groaned, "Down, down" and the kids all did a slow crouch to the grass. Janie flopped on the lawn and stared at the disco ball. In a moment she started shaking like a trout in a boat. All the guests fell to the lawn and started shaking their limbs. When the song ended a round of applause went up for Hank and Judy. The boys and girls got up and wiped the grass off their pants and skirts. Janie continued to shake after the music ended.

"Hey, Janie. The song's over," Jennifer said.

Janie answered with a gurgle. Her head shook up and down like a bobbing porpoise, her tongue hung out in a grotesque grimace as her eyes rolled back in her head. Fresh blood began streaming from both sides of her nose and the cut on her tongue. Not knowing what was going on, some of the kids started dancing or shaking on the ground, even though no music was playing.

Hank realized what was wrong and turned to Judy who was about to put on another platter for the dancers. "Judy! Call an ambulance!" He ran around the DJ table to his daughter's side not really knowing what to do. He saw that she'd bit her tongue and looked for something to put between her teeth. His keys were too narrow, but on the ring was a bottle opener than he was able to wedge between her shaking teeth. He rolled her on her side and rubbed her shoulders.

The other parents were frozen, feet nailed to the ground watching the spectacle. It was years before cell phones and none of them knew the Smiths well enough to feel comfortable entering the house to make the crucial call.

Judy looked to Janie, saw the shaking and the blood and froze. "Judy!" Hank said, "Janie needs to get to the hospital!" Judy answered by slumping to the grass behind the stereo system. She wept uncontrollably, shaking with her head in her hands.

Hank looked at Jennifer who was stroking her sister's shaking head, trying to keep the hair out of her eyes and the blood pouring from her nose. Their eyes met. Without a word, Jennifer ran to the house phone and dialed 9-1-1. "What is your emergency?" a voice said.

"My sister is sick."

"How old are you?"

"We were dancing, then she fell down."

"You can get in big trouble for making prank phone calls, little lady."

"She was shaking all over, now her nose is bleeding. Again." There was silence on the other end of the line. "Are you there? We need an ambulance."

The operator finally spoke, asking for the address and telling Jennifer to stay on the line.

"So? What happened next?" Michael said.

"Well, simple. We got divorced. You could say the cancer broke us up, but I think it was that second nosebleed. Judy couldn't handle it. It's like, when Jennifer stepped up, she knew she wasn't needed. Or something. Anyway, when Janie died, Jennifer took over running the house. Poor thing had to grow up way too fast, but someone had to pick up the slack when Judy flaked out."

Hank pulled Michael's Ford F150 into his own driveway next to Judy's Ford Taurus. He put the car in park. In the street was Jennifer's Honda Civic. "What the…?" Michael said. "Jennifer's here?"

"No, dumb-ass. She came over before the game with Hannah for breakfast. We all went together in the Taurus. Didn't know she had other plans, did you?" Michael shook his head. "Well, neither did we."

"So, what happened after the birthday party?"

Hank explained that Janie had leukemia and it had spread to her brain, causing the seizure. The doctors said her platelets were too low or not functioning or something, and that blood test explained the bloody nose and the bruises. Judy put on a good face during the endless doctor visits and even during the chemotherapy. But the second relapse and Janie's eventual death were more than she could bear. The prognosis was supposed to be good with a five-year survival rate over eighty percent. The problem with statistics, they learned, is that Janie wasn't ten thousand kids in a research study. She was one child with leukemia and her survival rate was going to be either one hundred percent or zero. Even that favorable cure rate leaves one out of five kids on the wrong side of the grass, or as Hank was fond of saying, in the marble orchard. Judy left Hank and Jennifer, moved into her mother's basement and didn't come out for a year.

"Why are you telling me this?" Michael said. "I mean, it's nice to know, but it was over twenty years ago. I mean, how does that help me with Jennifer today?"

"The truth shall set you free."

Hank met his second wife through an ad in the newspaper. Everything he thought he was building for their marriage suddenly felt like a sham. In the process of building furniture for the house he'd accumulated an impressive array of woodworking tools. One day in the garage he was staring at the accumulated mass of milled steel and realized the money he'd spent on the tools was enough to buy the furniture he'd made at retail costs. Add to that expense the time he'd spent away from his wife and his daughters to build the furniture and Hank realized he'd been robbed of the most precious thing he had to spend, his time. How much was a minute with Janie worth? What would he give for another bedtime story, a vacation, a moment after school, heck, even a diaper change when she was just an infant. He'd give anything to have another minute with her. It all had to go, simply for the reason that the machinery might rob from him even one more hour from his beloved Jennifer. Hank put an ad in the paper to sell all of his tools.

The only response to his advertisement was from his future second wife. She was as much interested in the actual tools as to why a man would be selling his entire collection. Ruby was the kind of woman who learns to change the oil on her father's tractor, because that's the way things are done. Ruby learned about sexuality from watching the farm animals. When it's time to have sex, that's what animals do. She learned as much from school as it could teach her, then she was independent from the time it suited her. Starting her own farm was a natural extension of her upbringing. Saving money from babysitting, waitress tips, and other jobs was all she needed to buy herself a small plot on the outskirts of town. She knew crops weren't as reliable or as profitable as animals, so she hedged her bets and starting raising sheep, goats, pigs and a few cattle. When she saw the ad for Hank's tools for sale, it was almost too much to believe. She could outfit her entire stable and start a handyman business on the side to supplement the cost of her feed.

Ruby called Hank to confirm that the deal wasn't a hoax. When he said it was for real, she agreed to drive her truck over for a look. Jennifer was in school at the time, so yes, he had the whole morning to show her the tools and machines for sale. Yes, it was for real, not some scam you hear about on TV these days. No, I'm not a con man, rapist, or murderer.

When she arrived in her early model Dodge Ram, Hank met her at the door before she could even ring the bell. Hank was unimpressed with the petite waif standing in heels on his porch. Her natural red hair was shocking, bordering on orange. The mini skirt and tube top did not give the impression she was serious about woodworking or auto mechanics. The bright, yellow-green color common for the decade didn't add anything to improve Hank's first impression. "Really, lady. This isn't a bake sale. If you're looking for Bingo, check the local church listings."

"Your ad said you had a dual-signal deflecting torque wrench. Don't tell me it's one of those shitty coil springs. I'll kick your ass right here." Although she was probably in her late twenties or early thirties, the woman's figure was no more intimidating than Jennifer's who was in her early teens at the time. The narrow hips and slender shoulders did not suggest an ass-kicking was in anyone's future. The only proof Hank had that she was an adult woman was the obvious fact she was not wearing a bra under her tube top, nor did she need one given her modest proportions.

Hank answered with raised eyebrows. Ruby responded with a jaw of steel. Without exchanging another word, and only the quick jerk of his head towards the garage, Hank motioned her to the display of his tools. They walked across the front lawn to his garage where he lifted the manual door to the pristine display of Hank's most prized possessions.

The Smithsonian Institution doesn't keep such meticulous care of its artifacts as Hank keeps of his tools and machines.

Hank and Ruby bonded in record time over the topic of his tools. The connection snuck up on him as unexpectedly as Janie's cancer. Ruby was knowledgeable without being pretentious. She had some specific needs for her house and farm, but was interested in the other tools and machines as a hobby. She deflected his sexist questions about whether she was shopping for her husband or a brother. Hank couldn't remember the last time he'd been with a woman. He knew it was with Judy, of that fact he was certain. He'd just lost track of the number of years. After Judy left, he didn't go looking and no women came calling. Raising an independent child like Jennifer was as easy and delightful as any single father could have wished. If he were so inclined, Hank had plenty of time to seek out companionship. The idea simply never crossed his mind. There was always the grief of losing Janie to fill any spare moments he might have had to think of himself. The last five or six years had slipped past him like sleep. It wouldn't have surprised him to see a calendar from the year of the twins' birthday party.

When it came to his tools, Hank was conflicted. Their sentimental value was substantial and far outpaced their resale value. It cost him nothing to store them, but to let them go would be nearly as costly as losing Janie. Rationalizations for keeping them were easy to list. Someday, he'd get back to his woodworking hobby, just as soon as Jennifer was older, moved out, or wasn't so much fun to be with on their various adventures. He might need them to repair a piece of furniture in the house. Maybe, he'd frame another picture one day.

The rational side of Hank knew the tools were a symbol of his old life, and therefore an anchor shackling him to the past. He'd never move on as long as they were in the garage. If another woman were ever to take Judy's place, he'd have to make room, in a word, get rid of the place in his past which Judy still occupied. But was that the correct analogy? Judy wasn't a piece of furniture he needed to move, in order to make room for a new entertainment system. There was no making rational sense of it.

A day would come when Jennifer would be too old to go to the movies, out for pizza and ice cream. He'd be left with a garage and shed full of tools with no purpose but to document his past like so many archaeological curiosities. Future scientists would piece together his life based on the meticulously ordered machines in his house, garage, shed and basement.

With a heavy heart and aching stomach, Hank gave Ruby the tour of his garage. He'd enjoyed arranging the tools, somehow divorcing himself from the idea that he was doing it for the sole purpose of getting them out of his life. Faced now with the distinct possibility that someone else would pay him for the privilege of putting his tools back into useful life filled him with an aching mix of nostalgia, guilt, ennui, and angst. He felt like he was selling one of his grandmother's kidneys.

Once inside the garage, Ruby walked to the back wall as if she owned the place. "What's the story with the lathe?"

Hank took a moment to answer. He'd been insulted when she rudely tore away the custom dust cover he'd fashioned for the lathe and threw it to the garage floor. "Uh, that's a Jet. Obviously. Fine American product, got a horse and a half. Plenty of power for whatever you want to spin. The stock rotates of course, in case you're into turning bowls."

"Uh-huh. American *import* company, anyway."

Before Hank could stop himself, the litany of logistical features had devolved into a story about what the machine had meant to him personally. He'd turned countless toys on the lathe, mostly Christmas gifts for the twins but also for friends and family; dozens of yo-yo's, a brilliant custom mash-up of hardwoods for Chinese checkers, tops, walking sticks, and even a baseball bat for a distant nephew. Before Hank knew it, Ruby was already looking at the next tool along the back wall while he was waxing wistfully about the toddler bed he'd made after the twins outgrew the swinging crib he'd made.

Ruby ignored his blubbering and asked about the table saw. Yes, it had excessive horsepower, yes, the out-feed rollers were included, but did she happen to see the love seat swing he'd made for Judy in the front yard? He could also show her the play set he'd made in the back yard for the twins. Pure redwood, mortise and tenon joinery like the finest Japanese handmade classics, it was something to play on for generations. He'd planned on keeping it until the girls had children of their own, then he'd help them move it to their own yards.

Ruby, couldn't have been less interested in the stories. For her, it was an opportunity to outfit her entire shop in one stop and likely at a steep discount.

The pattern was repeated with each tool. Hank had salvaged the original, old-growth hardwood from a barn using his planer and jointer. You can't buy wood like that anymore, and those trees don't exist anywhere in the world. He'd sold enough to cover the cost of acquisition and turned other boards into frames for pictures of the twins. He'd had enough left over after building himself a shed to make a custom night stand for Judy.

He'd used the band saw to prepare veneers from the gnarled roots of an old juniper. Not just any scraggly bush, but the one the twins used to decorate for Christmas in the yard like it was their own personal tree, until the year they'd burned it down by accident by putting real candles on the boughs. He used the drill press to make ornaments, the multiple sanders, with belt and oscillating cylinders to make all manner of gifts, both practical and extravagant, ball point pens, three pairs of matching earrings for "his girls."

"You say all this stuff is really for sale?"

"Yeah, it's gotta go. Got no time for woodworking. Plus, with just the two of us, nothing much needs repairing. Jennifer is too old for classic toys. She's already sleeping on a queen and you can't make a video game on a lathe."

"I just meant that you seem a little attached to them. Beyond their obvious quality. You said yourself you don't need the money. There's a way you can have your cake and eat it too, you know."

"You don't say. How do you figure?"

"I'd love to be able to take it all off your hands today. But even at a price I can afford, I don't have a place right now to store it all. I need to build a shed and workshop first. I'll make you a deal. I'll pay you to store the stuff while I come use it when I need to. Sort of a rent-to-own deal. I can't use everything you've got. Not right away, if you know what I mean. I hate to see you lose it all to some cheap bastard, considering your investment. Or worse, let it sit here and waste away unused."

Hank crossed and uncrossed his arms. He shifted his weight from one foot to the other looking around the shop at all his tools, his babies. The details of the arrangement didn't matter. He'd get a little rental money and just in case, be able to use the tools himself in a pinch. "Alright," he said holding out his hand. "You got yourself a deal."

Ruby took his hand and shook it but didn't let go. Instead she led him across the garage to the cream-colored Jet table saw. She removed the fence, blade guard, and miter gauge. She placed them carefully on the workbench and then returned to crank down the 10-inch saw blade. She instructed Hank to sit on the table saw while she retrieved two wood clamps from their rack on the peg board. "It's plenty sturdy. The sucker weighs three hundred pounds and that's not even including the cast iron wings." Hank hopped up and sat on the table, rocking back and forth and kicking his legs. The table didn't move. "See? Solid as a rock."

"I'm counting on it."

Ruby took Hank's hand again, but instead of shaking it, this time she clamped it palm down to the edge of the table. "Hey! What are you doing?" Hank tried to reach the quick release handle but couldn't twist his arm far enough to reach the trigger. Ruby ran around to the other side of the table with the other clamp. Hank made an ill-advised lunge in her direction. "Come back here! Let me go!" When Hank reached out to her she grabbed his left hand and just as deftly clamped it to the other side of the table. The woman knew her way around a workbench.

"Hank. You got some serious learnin' to do, starting with this table saw. It was made in Malaysia, by the way." While she spoke, she lifted his left leg, then his right, clamping them tightly by the pants to the end of the cast iron wings. "It's just a saw. Sure, it's got a decent 3-horsepower motor and you've kept it in great condition. But listen close, 'cause here's the lesson: It's a saw. It just cuts wood."

From his spread-eagled position, Hank gave her a look of confusion mixed with a generous portion of terror. "What?"

"It's not your failed married or your lost daughter. You gotta start thinking of this hunk of metal in a different way. It can't love and it can't make someone love you, no matter how many wonderful things you build with it and give as presents."

Ruby started the motor and the saw blade kicked into motion below the level of the table. The perfectly balanced blade barely made a sound inside the cabinet, but Hank could feel the wind it generated cooling the sweat which poured down the small of his back. "What the…you crazy…" He pulled against his restraints but the clamps were designed to generate hundreds of pounds of pressure per square inch and they weren't moving. The rubber clamps that kept him from marring his precious hardwoods, now kept him from being injured as he thrashed lamely on the table. After a moment, Hank stopped himself, knowing he wasn't in a position to intimidate or bargain, only beg.

"I'll forget that you almost called me a bitch. I could raise this blade and cut you right in half, Hank. Solve all your troubles."

"Please, what are you doing? You've got to stop." Hank tried to call on his anger, to keep from crying, but only managed to think of losing the one person left in his life. "Jennifer," he finished with a whimper.

"I told you. You need some mental restructuring. You ain't got it so bad, so quit your whining about the past. Before I'm done with you, you'll never look at these tools the same way again." Ruby cut the power to the saw and it came to a quick stop, due to the built-in brake mechanism. She disappeared from Hank's view and all he could hear for a moment was the sound of his own heart thumping. He was angry at himself for getting in such a stupid predicament. He thought of Judy, Janie and Jennifer in a jumble of fond memories. The click-clack of her high heels on the concrete floor brought Hank back to the present. When she returned, Ruby was carrying a large pair of razor sharp pruning shears, the kind with long handles and maximum leverage for cutting thick branches in one snap. "I see by the sweat rolling down your face that you think I'm going to continue the torture. Cut off a finger? Don't worry, it won't be that kind of torture. I'm not crazy, just lonely and we can help each other."

Ruby climbed up on the table and stood between Hank's legs. He could see from her black pumps all the way up her slender legs to the simple, cotton panties she wore under her tiny miniskirt. Embarrassed and shamed by his base thoughts, Hank turned his head and looked to the work bench across the garage. "Hey. You're gonna miss the show." Ruby slipped the jaws of the shears under her tube top and rubbed the handles across her flat chest. She nudged Hank gently on his inner thigh with the toe of her high-heeled shoe. When he looked back from the work bench she continued her dance of seduction. She hooked the curved tip of the shears across the top margin of her top and slowly pulled down the handles. Hank was transfixed as each nipple popped free in turn and the tube top hung loosely at her narrow waist. She flipped over the shears and nudged Hank in the crotch. He was still terrified from the neck up, but his body was responding without his permission from the waist down. She might not have been his type—did he have a type?—but any man who was alone for as long as Hank, would have responded in the same way. "Sorry about before. I see from the looks of things that I may be forgiven. Oh, and you need a new belt, too."

"Huh? What's wrong with my belt? It's perfectly fine."

"It's at *least* twenty years old. Plus, it's falling apart." Ruby crouched down, knees askew, giving Hank an unobstructed view between her thighs. She inserted the jaws of the pruning shears under the buckle of his belt and slid the handles back and forth, gently rubbing his privates. With a snap and a flourish, she cut the belt, pulled the strips of leather free from their loops and gave Hank a wicked grin. "Don't worry, I'm not going to whip you, although, that's a good idea." She flipped the belt onto the floor where the buckle landed with a clank. She set aside the pruning shears and explained her method to Hank. "No matter what brand of tools you buy, made in America or not, new or used, electric or manual, your best tools are right there at the ends of your arms." She held up her soft, pink hands for his inspection. "But they're not worth a damn if this thing ain't in top condition," she said putting a finger to her temple. "Got it?" Ruby kept her eyes on Hank and undid his zipper reaching inside with one hand.

"Whoa, whoa. Hold it right there," Michael said. "I'm sure I don't want to hear every last detail of Ruby's expertise. You forgot your audience."

"Oh sure, but you were plenty quiet when Ruby was taking her top off."

"Never mind that. You were still married to Judy at the time, right?"

"Technically. Funny story about that. You know how, if you're dating or living together for years, people start to call you married?"

"Yeah, Hank, they call it common law marriage."

"Right. So, how come if you're married, but don't live together, they don't start to call it common law divorce?" Michael shrugged. Hank took the keys from the ignition and tossed them to Michael. "C'mon. I'm not done with my story."

The two men left the truck and went to the garage. Hank hoisted the door, flipped a single switch on the wall, and swept his arm across the room, obviously proud of his immaculate workshop. It looked like the display room for a specialty woodworking boutique. Every Delta tool was gleaming under a pristine coat of blue enamel paint. Overhead was an intricate system of paired fluorescent lights illuminating each work station. Ducts for sawdust removal ran from each tool to a common port at the back of the garage, like an octopus with too many arms. Hank explained the collection vacuum took up too much space so he built a dedicated shed attached to the back of the garage to keep the area pristine. Nothing worse when putting on your fifth coat of polyurethane than a cloud of stray dust particles landing on the work.

Michael walked to the center of the room where the table saw waited patiently for Hank's next project. "So this is the scene of the crime, huh?"

"No, dumb-ass. Can't you read? This is a Delta, that was a Jet."

"Ruby bought it all, then?"

"You might say that. After that first time, Ruby came over once in awhile to make a payment, get a lesson on a tool she'd never used and uh, you know, act like we were married. One day she came by in her overalls and nothing else. I won't go into details but let's just say it involved the band saw and a bunch of bungee cords. She's got me tied down and the doorbell rings. Without a word she goes to answer it and comes back with a single page divorce declaration. Tells me it was some guy named James. She puts a pen in my free hand and has me sign it, then gives it back to James. Can you beat that? After seven or eight years of non-divorce, she has me served in my own house by that lousy lawyer."

"Same guy?"

"Same guy. Shit, that bastard gets around. That was before Melissa, though. Did you know he was married before?"

"As a matter of fact, I did."

"Well, this was way before he even met that weirdo, Laura. Anyway, me and Ruby went on like that for a couple of years. I bugged her to make an honest man out of me, but she always said she'd think about it. She never came around when Jennifer was home, so there weren't any awkward times. We didn't go to movies or out in public, but we sure acted like newlyweds, if you know what I mean. So the way I see it, we were married. Shit, some marriages don't last as long as I was with Ruby."

"I thought common law had to be seven years."

"Common misconception. I said the same thing to Ruby, so we looked into it. The bottom line is, if a judge thinks you're acting like you're married, then he's gonna divide your shit in half when you break up."

"Is that how you lost the workshop?" Michael looked around the garage at all the machines and tools. He couldn't imagine having to replace the row of pipe clamps, let alone the thousands of dollars it must have cost Hank to get a new set of power tools.

Hank explained how he finally convinced Ruby to marry him. He didn't need or want a big ceremony and neither did she. He argued successfully that since they were enjoying each other's company and looked to be making it a long-term thing, he'd appreciate the piece of paper. Might even want to introduce Ruby to Jennifer. They could combine their assets or keep them separate, he didn't care, but it didn't seem to make much sense paying two different mortgages and only using one house.

Ruby agreed to meet Hank at the County Clerk's office where they'd sign the papers and make it official. He debated putting on his best suit, then decided since it was the one he wore to marry Judy, a new suit might be more appropriate. He donated the old suit to the

Goodwill and bought himself an outfit in order to surprise Ruby. On the big day he showed up freshly showered and shaved and took a seat in the waiting room. Ruby was late. Then, she was two hours late. The staff at the Clerk's office went to lunch and came back. At closing time, Hank was forced to decide that Ruby had stood him up.

Dejected, he drove his truck home with a pit in his stomach. True, he hadn't eaten all day, but the gnawing at his gut told him something was wrong. An envelope was taped to the door of the garage. Inside was a wad of cash and a note from Ruby, thanking him for the tools and the lessons, and his other attentions. She claimed to be flattered by his proposal of marriage, but had to decline as her husband was back from his two-year tour of duty overseas and they were relocating to his next assignment. Hank opened the garage door to find nothing but pegboard and a few stray piles of sawdust. She'd taken everything. A quick mental calculation, adding up her rent and the stack of hundred dollar bills in the envelope confirmed for Hank that she'd satisfied their agreement as stated. In the end, he had to admit he had no complaint with Ruby, other than disappointment with himself that he'd inflated his own future with false expectations. Ruby was nothing but fair.

"That stinks. She says she'll marry you but cleans out your garage, then tells you she's already married."

"I don't think of it that way. At least not any more. Sure, I was pissed at first, more for losing Ruby than the tools. But she did compensate me well enough to buy all this. Plus, she was right, I can't look at a table saw now without reminding myself, it's just a tool. It's a bit kinky to have all the sex memories, but it helped to switch brands. I like Delta better anyway. Besides, if I married Ruby, I never would have met Soo-Min."

"Oh, Number Three, huh?"

"You're not such a dumb-ass after all, are you? Follow me." Hank led Michael through the back door of the garage and past the shed where his vacuum unit was stored. For the second time, Hank presented the vista with a wave of his arm.

"You're kidding me," was all Michael could mutter.

An absurd expanse of bamboo flooring extended the full width of the back yard. It was covered with a combination pergola and latticework supported by large beams and attached to the house. There were accents from different Polynesian and Far Eastern cultures. What should have been a boring and sedate suburban lawn was instead a Japanese garden that looked like it was tended with care for hundreds of years. The delicate sounds of a babbling stream emanated from some hidden corner. The central feature was a large koi pond that must have been thousands of gallons. At one end Michael could see gold and white shapes moving lazily near a small waterfall, its source out of view behind a proud rhododendron bush. Pathways led in and around the mature trees and bushes. A stone bridge spanned a dry streambed that led around a large decorative boulder. Everywhere Michael looked was another fascinating detail, accent, or interesting plant. "How many acres is it?"

"None. Just a standard lot, same as the rest of the neighborhood."

"Sun did this? Is she Japanese?"

"Soo-Min. Everyone just called her Minnie. She helped me with some landscaping, it was her design. But mostly, it was her inspiration that mattered. A journey of a thousand miles and all that. I would have never thought to do this myself." The two men set themselves down on a pair of bamboo chairs to continue their conversation. Hannah came out to play and explore all the nooks and crannies of the yard.

Judy came out with a lemonade for the men and heard a snippet of their exchange. She left, then returned with a bowl of peanuts. "You telling him about Minnie?" Hank nodded. "Such a shame. Lovely girl." She set down the drinks and returned to the kitchen without waiting for an answer.

After Hank sold his tools to Ruby, he found himself lonelier than ever. Jennifer was entering high school with all of its attendant distractions. He made himself available when she needed him, but between her sports, after school activities, and homework, those needs were limited to food, clothing, shelter and the occasional ride to the movies. When she went away to college, his isolation became complete. He vowed not to lose the one remaining person who meant the most to him. When Jennifer graduated from college he planned to follow her wherever she might land. That place happened to be Michael's hometown, where they were both able to find their first jobs after graduation. Hank sold the home and acreage where the twins were born and his first marriage had ended. He found and purchased the bungalow he was currently living in with Judy—close enough to Jennifer to visit on a whim, but far enough away so as not to be intrusive.

Not long after that time, Hank decided to get his workshop going again. He didn't have any projects in mind, so the shop itself became the project. He chose only the best tools available and selected those a contractor would use, not the inferior tools of the home hobbyist. It was rare the local hardware actually carried the items he was seeking and invariably the salesmen would send him to the service desk for a special order. That's where Hank met Minnie.

"What you need big saw for?"

"Nothing, yet. I'll think of something. Maybe I just like fine tools."

For every tool in his shop, Hank had to see Minnie to have it ordered, then delivered, then settle his account. He could have outfitted the entire garage in a single season, but it seemed every third order was incorrect. Hank would have to return to the store and correct the mistake, have his money refunded, then reorder the correct part or tool. It became a weekly chore on his Saturday mornings to fix some minor clerical mistake on his credit card. Sundays were his returns days. Nights after work, he'd peruse catalogs at Minnie's desk. It started innocently enough, but Hank soon began to wonder if some of her errors weren't done on purpose to bring him back to the hardware store. "But I told you Minnie, I don't buy DeWalt, I only buy Delta."

"Of course, mister. That yellow color ugly, too."

"It's not about the color. I've been waiting a month for that planer."

"What for?"

"Just because."

"Still no wood, yet?"

"Look, here's the layout," Hank said grabbing her pencil and order pad. He flipped it over and started drawing the layout of his home shop. "The main stock starts here by the door. That way I can back up my truck and put the heavy stuff here." He pointed to an out-of-square box on the pad which was supposed to represent a storage bin with overhead racks for stock up to sixteen feet long. "I rough it out on the table saw here," he drew another box, "then it gets glued up and clamped on this bench. Paint or stain go on here by the vent and then, it's done."

"But what is it?"

"Whatever I happen to be working on."

They both looked at the pad. The workshop appeared to have been drawn while riding on horseback. In his eagerness to show her his plan, Hank realized he'd violated not only her space at the service desk but her personal space a well. His evidence for this intrusion was the fact that his nostrils were full of her delightful scent of lavender soap. Their eyes met. "Uh. Maybe I should just show you once, so you'll understand why I need what I need and where it's all going."

"Okay."

"Okay?"

"Yeah. Sure. You hungry? I bring dinner."

Hank hung around until her shift ended and followed Minnie in her Hyundai with his GMC truck. At her house Minnie disappeared through the front door. No lights came on in the house but Hank could see the glow of her refrigerator through the kitchen window. She soon emerged with four shopping bags and got back into her car. Minnie followed Hank to his house. Their first date was a smashing success. "You're sure these are leftovers?"

"You never had kimchi stew?"

"No, 'course not," Hank said through a cheek bulging with fermented cabbage and pork. "What's in it?"

"You like?"

"Yeah. It's amazing. I like it strong."

"Ha, ha, ha. For you, I make mild. Medium too much. Hot, you not ready."

"That sounds like a challenge. You should know something about me, I never back down from a challenge. Pick the date and time." Just like that, Minnie and Hank set up their second date before their first date had barely begun. They never did get to the workshop that night. Minnie educated Hank, who proved to be a good student. The conversation flowed naturally from the food, to Korean culture to the obvious question of how a nice girl like Soo-Min found herself being called Minnie in the middle of Kansas. She met her husband during the Korean War and like so many young girls was more than happy to leave the country when troops were withdrawn. She moved with him on his assignments and kept the house while he did his six tours of Vietnam. They never had any children and in the end, she was widowed. He died happily in retirement of "natural causes" being much older than Soo-Min.

"How much older? Wait. How old were you when you left Korea?"

"I'm not sure exactly, but you should know never to ask a lady. And I promise never tell."

Minnie destroyed Hank on their second date by serving him the hottest meal she could create. She was impressed that he managed to finish his appetizer, but also apologized for making him sweat so much. On their third date, back at Hank's house, Minnie finally got her tour of the workshop. It was then she proposed "something for the yard." It started with the lanai and the bamboo deck. From there she helped him design and create the entire garden. They were married by the koi pond. In two years she was dead from stomach cancer. Judy heard all about it through friends at the hospital and showed up to the funeral and wake. She and Hank got to talking and the rest is history. They ended up back together and remarried. Judy was Hank's fourth wife.

"What? Wait. That's terrible. There's got to be more."

"You're telling me. That woman could eat anything. Ironic, isn't it? Stomach cancer?"

"No, I mean, how many years were you together? How come I've never heard any of this? What else don't I know about you and Jennifer?"

"Hey, you're the one who wanted to know. You can't complain 'cause you don't like the story. What more do you want to hear?"

"You were telling me why people get divorced, why they stay married. I'm supposed to be trying to figure out why Jennifer wants a divorce."

"Well, I can only give you my story. Ruby had the feminine side, and the wild side, that Judy never had. Maybe we seek out what we're missing. She just didn't have Judy's good qualities, like that simple thing about her being married before. Would have been nice to know. But she woke me up, made me start living and enjoying life again. Minnie taught me everything about being at peace. Funny, she grew up knowing so much about war, married a professional soldier. In the end, it made complete sense to her that with all the countries in conflict, no two people should ever be fighting. When you're calm on the inside, when you know what really matters, differences between husband and wife don't matter. Inner peace allows you to be peaceful on the outside. This garden is her legacy to that teaching."

"Hank, I don't understand. You treat me like a dog. Maybe you're the Zen Master with Judy, but you don't practice what you preach. Not with everyone."

"Sorry. I'm not so great with guys."

"That's a lame excuse for being an ass. And as for your philosophy of marriage, all I can see is that a few women were willing to give you the time of day and you took whatever they gave you. Hardly a romantic world view. It's more like proximity. If someone's nearby, there's your next wife."

"Best not to insult me in my own backyard."

"I'm not afraid of you Hank. I just see a sad, old man who's another cancer away from being very lonely again. Nice garden. If you see my wife, tell her to call me. Thanks for the lemonade." He caught Hannah in the yard and gave her the usual instructions about staying with her grandparents. They hugged goodbye and Michael got in his truck and drove home.

10

THE PASSWORD IS

After his disappointing visit with Hank, Michael had only a day to rest up and regain his bearings before starting a stint of day shifts at St. Bernadette's. All he'd learned from Hank was a likely reason why Jennifer had never wanted to change her name to Johnson. Sure, she'd earned her degrees as a Smith, but with a father like Hank, one would think she'd be happy to change it to anything else. With such close proximity to Hank's example, it's a wonder she agreed to get married at all. Michael had to conclude that her divorce threat was no reflection on him and their relationship, rather a symbol of her disillusionment with the entire institution of marriage.

Knowing what he knew about Jennifer's lost sister Janie, helped him understand why she didn't bother celebrating birthdays. Hank and Judy never again celebrated the birth of their twins and the family tradition, or lack thereof, was set. Michael always chalked up her aversion to her penny-pinching ways and never thought to ask if there was more to it. But neither of those revelations explained why she was pursuing a divorce. It was no idle bluff, either. James had presented him with the actual papers.

By Monday morning, two days later, Jennifer had still not materialized, nor had she left an e-mail, text or phone message. Despite the silent treatment, Michael was determined to continue with life as they knew it. Jennifer was never one to ignore a problem. Like Hank, she lived for confrontation. If there was a scab to be picked, she was sure to make it bleed. No argument could be left unresolved. They used to joke the next best thing to Jennifer winning an argument was her losing one. If she was serious about the divorce, she'd have to come around and convince him it was real. If she meant to send a message by cutting off all communication, then Michael would call her bluff.

Hannah was in safe, if despicable hands, and there were bills to be paid. Life continued. If her lawyer James showed up to his home or work with papers he already knew what he was going to say. He always slept poorly in the transition from night to day shifts, but showed up at work with more than an hour to spare. Security had relaxed since the days of post-9/11, but the local police still maintained a dwindling and irregular presence at the hospital in addition to the regular security staff. Keeping the handicapped parking unsullied and the entrance ramps to the emergency room clear seemed to be their only concerns.

When he arrived at the hospital, Michael flashed his name badge but was surprised to see a new face seated behind the desk. The guard was poorly groomed as if he'd been working the night shift for twelve hours rather than having just arrived for the day shift. His uniform was at least two sizes too big for his welterweight frame. His hair was a disheveled, curly dark mop. His face held a few days of dark stubble.

Michael failed to receive a friendly wave or any other acknowledgment that he would have gotten from Steven or Robert. He walked to the elevators and joined the group waiting to go up to the regular patient floors. He glanced from his place in line at the elevator bank and saw the officer looking after him and punching a number, not into his desk phone but the cell phone he removed from his shirt pocket.

Once on the floor he checked with Shirley for his daily assignment. "Hey Shirley, how was the weekend? Anybody interesting get admitted?"

"Fine, no and what are you doing here?"

"I start my month of days today, right?"

"Not by my schedule. Check the computer. Kathy isn't here yet, but my posting says you're not on at all." She threw a thumb over her shoulder to the bulletin board without looking up from the charts she was organizing.

Michael walked behind the station to the cork board and ran a finger down the schedule. Next to his name for the week was a row of shaded days and the word "VACATION" in large block letters. "Hey, wait a minute. That's not right. I'm supposed to be on days. We're not going anywhere." He tried to remember when he last looked at the schedule but it was pretty easy to memorize, a month of nights, a month of days. They had no vacation plans and he hadn't made any changes. The system was computerized and accessible from his home computer, but he'd had no reason to change it. Shirley didn't know and had no opinion, happy only that the schedule, as posted, accounted for every shift with adequate staff. She'd made the schedule two months prior and only checked it when she printed the weekly version. Her policy was that if you made a switch, just be sure you remember and show up as planned. "You mind if I wait to be sure Kathy shows? There's gotta be some kind of a mistake."

"Suit yourself. You can check stock and count the narcs if you want, but don't bother meeting any patients yet, they won't be here when you get back from vacation. Ha, ha," Shirley chuckled at her own joke and walked off with five charts under her arm. Michael arranged some items on the drug cart, restocked the supply room with paper goods, then went to the Broom Closet to wait for Kathy.

At ten minutes to the hour Kathy arrived and when she saw Michael in the break room, her eyebrows went up. "Hey, Michael. I didn't expect to see you here."

"Apparently the schedule changed, but I was never told."

"Weird. I got a call over the weekend that you were sick, or gone, or—oh, I remember—'personal problem' was the way they worded it. And could I cover. For you, I said sure. I didn't ask why. I know you'd do the same for me." She gave him a wink.

"Well, thanks for covering, but who are 'they?' Shirley seems to think I had vacation planned all along."

"Don't know." Kathy put her helmet on a locker and her motorcycle coat over a hook. Then she had a thought. "Did you see the new security guy? He asked me if I knew a male nurse. He got your name wrong, called you Smith. I told him everyone knew you, but that I hadn't seen you since last week."

Michael got up from his chair. He pushed open the door just enough so he could see ten rooms down the hallway through the crack by the hinge. The scrawny new guard was there talking to Shirley. She had a look on her face that said she was too busy for this nonsense and can't you see I've got work to do, patients to care for? Something about him wasn't right. It went beyond the ill-fitting uniform and the two-day stubble. He had scuffed shoes but they'd pass for regulation black. He had a ring of keys that would be the envy of any janitor. Then he saw it. On his utility belt where a flashlight should have been was a gun that could take down an elephant. It was holstered, snapped in place, but looked absurd against his diminutive thigh. If Michael knew about guns he would have recognized it as a Mark XIX Desert Eagle holding enough .50 caliber Action Express rounds to take down a herd of bison. The barrel was an impressive ten inches. Any civilian knew that such a gun was excessive even for his friends Robert and Steven on the legitimate police force, and unthinkable for a hospital security guard. "Kathy. Do me a favor."

"Sure. For you? Anything."

"Distract that guy until I can get to the emergency exit."

"Okay, I'll think of something. He's new. I'll introduce myself and ask him to show me his stamp collection."

"Thanks, I owe you."

She pushed open the door with her hip and reached up to put her blonde hair in a ponytail. "I'll remind you if you forget." She winked again, then rolled her eyes as if she were about to perpetrate the most lame practical joke in history.

Michael counted to thirty, then pushed the door open enough to peek down the hall. Kathy was twirling her ponytail with one finger and giggling at something the guard had said that couldn't possibly have been as funny as her reaction would suggest. When she saw the door to the break room ajar, Kathy grabbed the guard by the elbow, spun him away and starting walking down the hall in the other direction. She stood half a head taller than him. Michael laughed to himself. Men are so easily manipulated. Kathy was two classes out of this bozo's league, but he probably thought he had a chance with her. Just as likely, if he found out from Shirley that the schedule had been changed, he'd look elsewhere for Michael. But Michael Smith?

Michael slipped down a seldom-used stairwell at the end of the hallway, then made his way through a door used only by smokers taking their breaks. Someone had disconnected the alarm long ago but it had never been fixed. He took the long way around the hospital to his parking spot, never once turning back to see if he'd been followed.

With time on his hands and Hannah at his in-laws he decided to try to get some answers. He called Jennifer's cell phone for the fortieth time, but it went straight to voice mail. He called James's office. Melissa answered and told Michael that James was in court all week, but she'd take a message. He contemplated calling Hank, then thought twice about it. Maybe the guard was somehow tracing his calls and would then be able to find Hannah at the Smith's house. Best to be careful. No need to bring Hank or Judy into this confusion. School was still out for the summer, but Jennifer was always working on budgets, planning and furthering her career. He could possibly catch her at work, cell phone be damned.

Not wanting to attract any attention, Michael drove as inconspicuously as he could when exiting the St. Bernadette's Hospital parking lot. He dared not look to see if he was being followed, but took the most direct route to James Buchanan Elementary School. His routine disrupted, Michael began to regret some of his previous thoughts and feelings about his marriage, the work of raising Hannah, and the tenuous life balance they'd struck. Jennifer hated when he called it "work" or worse if he told anyone he was "babysitting" his own daughter, as if Jennifer was paying him ten dollars an hour so she could have a drink with friends or see a chick flick. What he wouldn't give now to suffer the predictable morning routine. His mind wandered as he drove the familiar route to the school.

Mondays for Hannah were usually a struggle during the school year. Jennifer was up so early to prepare for her own classes and administrative duties that she was gone long before Hannah needed to be awake. The morning childcare duties often fell to Michael and half the time after he'd been up all night caring for the most ill patients on the ward. Michael let her sleep late on weekends and play all the video games she could stand. The sleep deprivation was compounded if she'd had a birthday party or sleepover to attend. It made waking up for school on Mondays that much harder. After Sunday dinner he'd ask if she had any homework and invariably she'd reply that there was a math page to finish or an Internet research topic to be summarized. Procrastination became part of their bonding process and something Jennifer despised. He'd keep Hannah up late finishing a project, then slip quietly out the door to work, while Jennifer headed to bed alone. It was something else to add to the list of a thousand tiny cuts.

In the mornings, Michael would wake Hannah as gently as possible and help her dress with eyes closed. Waiting for her to choose an outfit would have been fruitless, so he helped her into the standard pre-teen uniform, regardless of the change in seasons; low hip hugger jeans, her two favorite contrasting color tank tops and a pair of flip flops. Jennifer would object to the choice of footwear, but where was she to complain? Already at work, no doubt, bettering life for every child but her own.

Michael would make himself a bagel with schmear, for Hannah, the usual. He mused that for breakfast anyway, it was best to treat her like a puppy; same food, same time, same plate. A frozen waffle with maple syrup served on a Disney Princess plate. They had a series of eight heroines, none of whom he could remember by name. He was sure to fill every waffle square with an even level of syrup.

It was fortunate that Hannah was staying with her grandparents this week. The politics of separation could get ugly and his daughter was sure to ask after her mother. Truth was he didn't have any idea where Jennifer was, probably a friend's house. Was she really going to divorce him? How could he explain it to Hannah? He didn't know why himself. Best not to disparage the wife to Hannah, especially if it was all a simple misunderstanding, something that would blow over with time. Arguing about the argument becomes the new complaint, then something about which to continue arguing. Apologizing for not apologizing becomes the new thing for which one has to apologize. Good luck if the apology is inadequate in some way. The failed apology becomes one more problem. In that vicious cycle of complaints a couple could easily spiral so far from their shared reality that it could seem their love never existed. The levels of metaphysical relationship negotiation could be mind-boggling. How could he and Jennifer get back to the porch at the Sigma house?

The pair would put their dishes in the sink and head for school. Michael would help Hannah into the high seat of his truck cab, then walk around to buckle her in from the driver's side. "Safety first," Hannah would say. It was a line she remembered her father saying from the time he was strapping her into an infant car seat.

They invariably drove to James Buchanan Elementary School in sleepy silence. Michael always parked instead of just dropping her off at the circle drive like the other parents. He usually didn't have to rush to work and made a point of treating her like the little princess she was. He would open Hannah's door, help her down from her perch, carry her twenty-pound backpack, and hold her hand across the lot.

At the entrance to the school, a gaggle of Hannah's friends would be chirping into cell phones, texting and screeching. Why a nine-year old needed a four hundred dollar phone with Internet access he could never divine. The girls acknowledged her with further screams as if they hadn't seen one another for years. Michael would let go of her hand, give her the pack and lean in to say goodbye. Hannah always rolled her eyes but would finally relent, despite the sniggers from her friends and kiss Michael on the cheek. A little girl is never too old to kiss her daddy goodbye.

This morning, Michael parked in the first non-handicapped spot by the entrance and replayed the scene in his mind. The visitor's parking lot was empty. Jennifer's Honda Civic was nowhere to be seen. If she was staying with a friend, it was possible that she'd been dropped off to do some work. He'd head to her office and try to make some sense of it all. Then he remembered her car was parked at Hank and Judy's house. How did she get to and from the mystery friend's house? The more he thought about it, the more questions he raised. One path of inquiry started with a false premise and led to another maze of contradictory speculations. Of course, if she were here, she'd have parked in the faculty lot on the other side of the building and the Civic would be in her reserved space. Even if Judy or a friend had dropped her off, she'd have likely entered through the staff entrance with her name tag.

With summer heat shimmering off the pavement he was filled with nostalgia. Certain places should never be empty. An animal habitat at a zoo was particularly tragic without a large mammal. No playground, at a school or otherwise, should want for screeching children. And then there was the question of queen-sized beds. Yes, that was the worst. A bed for two should never have just one person in it. It was like the old Police song when Sting sings, "The bed's too big without you" over and over. The more he thought about it, the more the previous night was unlike any of the others. Sure, with his night shifts they often slept apart, but Saturday and Sunday night this weekend were the first nights he'd spent alone where Jennifer had made the choice that they should be apart. That choice changed everything about the idea of sleeping alone.

Michael shook his head clear and brought himself to the present with a force of will. He had work to do, a problem to solve. Summer school might be in session, he thought, or at least some teachers would be there for summer sports programs or counseling. He sauntered into the security office and gave his driver's license to the obese and sedentary security guard. "Hey Sam, how's it going?" Michael tried to act nonchalant.

"Okay. Just checking in with Jennifer?" Sam was on a first name basis with all of the staff. He put down half a chocolate donut and wiped his greasy hands across his black polyester pant legs. "I haven't seen her. Must have arrived before the rooster was awake. Ha."

"Uh, yeah. We've got to arrange rides for soccer practice," he lied. Sam gave a ritual nod, his mind on the scanner, and didn't ask why Michael didn't just call or e-mail so the deception was maintained. If the school were under siege, Michael mused, Sam would be the second and most expendable casualty. The first casualty would be either the buttons on the front of his undersized shirt, or the overstressed seams on his pants as Sam attempted to rise from his chair and defend the school. On the other hand, Girl Scout cookie sales were no doubt enhanced greatly by his presence. Then there was the fall popcorn drive and the pasta dinner fund-raiser. Yes, Sam with his enormous beer belly and his all-important driver's license scanner, served an invaluable role in the quality of education his daughter was receiving, not to mention her enduring safety while in the building and on the grounds.

"There you go," Sam said, handing Michael a sticker with a grainy and unrecognizable rendering of his driver's license picture on it. Michael put the sticker on his shirt, walked through the metal detector and down the hall to Jennifer's office.

Her office door was closed and locked, but Michael had a key, given to him by Jennifer. Given her ruthless efficiency he was never called upon to retrieve any forgotten item, but she insisted he carry it "just in case." The nameplate said "Jennifer Smith, Ed. B., M.B.A.," a nod to her hardworking days in academia. How her Master of Business Administration degree augmented her Bachelor of Education, she had yet to explain. All her degrees were acquired under her maiden name. She retained the surname she said for professional reasons, which Michael found irksome. Was she his wife first and foremost, or a school administrator? Shouldn't a woman take a man's name? "We're not losing a daughter, we're gaining a son" and all that? Maybe he was just oversensitive since the divorce talk. Truth be told, it never bothered him before this weekend. Her independent streak was one reason he was attracted to her in the first place. Who cares about surnames? "A rose by any other name…"

Michael scanned the hallway to be sure no one above four-feet tall saw him enter the office. Inside, he locked the door behind him and surveyed the room. Not a Post It note was out of place. Her modest book case was pristine, the desktop sterile as an operating table. There was no evidence that Jennifer intended to teach her classes that day or any other day. It looked like the way a curator might represent a typical "School Administrator's Office" in some future museum. There was no telling it was an actual working space in regular usage. The way model homes were set up to impress buyers, this space could have been a centerpiece at Office Depot. The blinds were drawn, the computer off.

He sat in Jennifer's leather armchair and turned on the desktop computer. At the prompt for her password, Michael paused to contemplate how much he loved his wife. He knew he had only a few chances before the computer locked him out for good. Their tenth wedding anniversary was coming. "Hannah" would be too obvious, same with "teacher" or "Michael." Did he have to add a number? If the divorce threat was real did he have a chance to guess her password? She trusted him with the key to her office. What could she possibly have to hide?

On Jennifer's desk was a picture of Hannah as an infant, asleep, smiling with her eyes closed. Michael remembered the night well, though it was nine years ago. He and Jennifer were so surprised when Hannah slept through the night, that they couldn't sleep themselves. They checked the baby monitor which turned out to be working fine, no new batteries needed. They padded into her room to check on her and found Hannah asleep and cooing, her angelic face set in a blissful smile. The proud parents stood holding hands and staring at their daughter a full ten minutes. When Michael insisted they commemorate the event with a photo Jennifer relented only when Michael promised to spend the night rocking her if she happened to be awakened by the camera. Hannah slept through the flash and Jennifer rewarded Michael with his first physical contact since the delivery. It was a memorable night for more than just Hannah sleeping through it all. The fact that Jennifer had the picture on her desk gave him hope.

Tucked under the transparent blotter next to the calendar was an 8x10 photo of Michael and Jennifer with a tiny Hannah, all of them sunburnt, bathing-suited, and vacationing blissfully in the Bahamas. Michael wasn't even aware she'd had that particular photo enlarged. It must have been taken by David or Kimberly and at their friends' insistence. How many times did their documentary pictures include either parent with Hannah, yet almost never the entire family? It made choosing Christmas card photographs particularly difficult. The picture was so big he could read the cruise ship name and logo inscribed on the souvenir glassware. He typed in "Hannah" and their wedding date. "Have you forgotten your password?" the computer prompted. He tried another version of the same information and received the same warning. Michael was running out of chances.

Then he remembered the vacation had nothing to do with their wedding as the honeymoon never happened. Obviously, Hannah came later. It was only due to the generosity and insistent prodding by their accountant David and his ever-pregnant wife, Kimberly, that they made the trip at all. What was most important to Jennifer that she'd use it as a password and never forget it? Where did she spend her mental and emotional currency? Michael typed in his next guess and her desktop pinged a happy welcome note.

Michael felt a surge of vindication and satisfaction. His wife's password was tied to a meaningful event in their shared life. If the divorce business were serious, wouldn't she change her password to maintain her privacy and perhaps more importantly to force him out? He felt validated that he knew her well enough to guess it. How many husbands could pull off that trick, he wondered? Moreover, he knew he was snooping in her business and would be privy to a severe tongue-lashing when she found out he'd hacked her computer.

He almost cried when her desktop background picture appeared. It was a close-up photograph of Michael and Hannah making goofy faces for the camera. Both had pizza sauce across their upper lips in the manner of the "got milk?" magazine ads. Hannah was balancing a sliced, black olive on her nose and Michael's head was tilted back to do the same with a large slice of pepperoni. He remembered the dinner well as it was his spontaneous idea to go to Anthony's in the middle of the week, and "celebrate" for no good reason at all. For once, Jennifer agreed and thought the made-up event was important enough to document for posterity. The photo was taken five nights prior to its appearance on Jennifer's computer, three days before the fateful soccer game. She'd not only taken the time to download the photo from her camera's memory card, but had thought to make it her background picture.

Michael scanned the shortcut icons to see if there was anything that might help him make sense of Jennifer's unusual behavior. The picture under her blotter and the desktop background sure didn't make it look as though she was cutting Michael out of her life. There were the usual links to her favorites sites, stored pictures, Alumni of Kansas State, a virus scanner, email, and the recycle bin. He scrolled the pointer over a blank folder and double-clicked. A spreadsheet appeared announcing the district budget for the following school year. There were endless columns and rows with everything from salary estimates to phone bill contracts, to allowances for updating computer systems. He scanned through pages of numbers listing the janitorial service contract, the groundskeeping inventory and the cafeteria budget. He almost fell out of his chair when he came across the cost of lighting the parking lot for the year. The grand total for James Buchanan Elementary School, a mid-sized school in a tiny, rural district, came to over eight million dollars. He scrolled back up a page to see the budget allowance for retaining the incomparable services of the amazing security guard Sam and found himself getting angry.

There was an icon for the scheduling system for the staff at St. Bernadette's hospital. The link provided instant access to a website for complete control of one's work schedule. Given a simple username and password, one could not only find a schedule, but request vacation time, trade shifts with other workers and even examine the entire employment history of the worker. He'd always shared his passwords with Jennifer. Not intentionally, but by listing them on Post It notes on his computer monitors more as a memory aid to himself than to demonstrate some form of ultimate transparency.

In one instance of frivolity, Jennifer had arranged for him to have a day off work by electronically dropping a shift picked up by another worker who thought Michael had made the request himself. No call was made to Shirley and the rest of the staff were none the wiser. It was no trip to Europe, no *Pretty Woman* jet airplane ride to see *La traviata*, just a surprise day they got to spend together.

Jennifer took Michael to an art museum to see a traveling installation of Damien Hirst's *Saint Sebastian, Exquisite Pain*. The work consisted of a young bull, suspended vertically with cables by its neck in a vat of formaldehyde, and pierced with modern arrows. They would later refer to the event and the art on multiple levels. If their suburban married life was becoming dull, rote, and uninspiring, they could casually drop in conversation that they've seen a 10-foot high display of preserved beef worth almost six million dollars. Go ahead and top that. If issues of child-raising came up, the argument's trump card could be, "would you let your daughter see *Saint Sebastian?*"

The significance of the event was forever burned in Michael's memory. The bull wasn't Michael's cup of tea—when it came to serious art, he was more of a pottery guy—but what he took away from the afternoon was how much Jennifer loved him and wanted to share her interests and experiences with him, even if it meant stealing him away from work for a day. Michael didn't "get" the bull with arrows, but he saw what it meant to Jennifer to share it with him. The memory resonated with him for years. It was what made their marriage unique and valuable. Now Jennifer had changed his schedule again, not just for a day, but an entire week, one in which Hannah was away, yet his wife was nowhere to be found. Clearly, it wasn't because she wanted a divorce. The pictures on her desk confirmed that point to his satisfaction.

Michael opened her Internet homepage which happened to be the James Buchanan Elementary School portal. He opened the "Favorites" button and found nothing of interest. Then he had an idea. Michael opened the "History" tab and scrolled through all the Web sites she'd visited in the previous days, weeks, and months. If the link didn't have an obvious address, he'd click on the page and find out what it was. There were the usual e-mail addresses, their credit union account, and some travel pages. He figured at first that they must be junk mail or pop-ups, but decided to click on the links in order to be thorough. With nothing obviously out of the ordinary, he gathered his courage and hacked her e-mail account.

The same password allowed him access to her work account. There were pages of old memos from the principle, other teachers in her department, and a few from members of the board of education. He scanned the subject lines and opened a few, then found himself stifling a yawn. He knew she liked to keep a separate folder for personal e-mail, those from Hank and Judy, her college friends and Michael himself. He closed the work account and opened her personal folder.

The inbox was empty as was the "Deleted" folder. Who has an empty email account? He scrolled the menu items and found an option for those items she'd sent recently. It too was empty, so Michael opened the drafts folder. Jackpot. Over eighty items were present, all addressed to the same person, apparently a man by the name of Mario. Michael's heart sank. Could she be having an affair? Between work and home when would she have time? Maybe it was in the early stages and it was just harmless flirting. He scanned his mental Rolodex and failed to come up with a single person by the name of Mario.

With great trepidation, he double-clicked on the most recent entry and his confusion doubled. It was formatted as a formal business letter and riddled with legalese and pronouns. She must have mentioned "time frames," "schedules," and "deadlines" at least seven times. There were allusions to large numbers and reasonable time frames, but there was no tone of flirting. Perhaps it was just another aspect of her budget responsibilities for the school, but if so, why was it in her personal e-mail account? Why hadn't she deleted it as well? It would have been no problem to print a copy, then erase the memory, like she'd apparently done with the inbox, deleted, and sent folders. He chanced a peek at a few others but the information was equally cryptic, with no hint of a personal relationship. Satisfied that she wasn't having an affair, he closed the account, erased the history for the day and shut down the desktop. Michael took one last look around the office and decided his sleuthing skills weren't up to the task. He locked the office door and walked back down the hall. It was all a big misunderstanding. Jennifer would reappear as she always did and all would be revealed.

Michael gave Sam the best friendly wave he could muster as he left the building, stewing inside now that he'd seen the bottom line for the security budget. He sat in his car long enough to text Jennifer but no reply was forthcoming. He finally decided to call, hoping to just get her voice mail, not knowing what he'd say if she actually answered. The phone rang once, then a friendly voice informed him that her number was no longer in service. He started the truck, put it in gear and pulled out of the parking lot.

11

RELATIONAL EXCHANGE

Leaving the school parking lot, Michael had a horrible feeling. It felt like divorce. From the lump in the back of his throat it was a straight shot through the giant hole in his chest, through the empty pit of his stomach to the twisted knot in his bowels. Despite the positives he took from his visit to Jennifer's office, he was still no closer to solving the problem. He had to admit, the nice pictures and his clever deduction of the simple password didn't prove a thing. The last he'd heard from Jennifer was two days ago and she never wanted to see him again. He was driving his truck, alone, with no purpose in life. This was what it was going to be like from now forward. Sure, he'd work again and that was satisfying in its own way, but his time off had no reason. He'd no longer be building anything, working towards a common goal, for a vacation or their retirement. There would be time with Hannah, but never again with Jennifer. He might call or text his former wife, but she'd feel no obligation to answer.

Marriage had changed Michael in a way he'd not fully realized until the divorce threat. His days were filled with obligations he found fulfilling. His life had meaning in a way it didn't when he was training to be a nurse. What it lacked in originality it made up for in its totality. He liked it. He was built to care for his family in a way that was irreversible at this point in his life. It was like he'd gained a superpower that brought his loving demeanor to its ultimate expression. Now it was gone and he was back to being just another civilian. Michael was alone with a week off work and nothing to do. It wasn't yet 10:00am, his first official day in exile. He drove out of town to his mother's house.

If Hank's version of marriage was as disconcerting as divorce, he knew his mother would have a positive spin to put on it. He knew she'd be home, so he decided to pay her an impromptu visit. There was no reason to call, he would always be welcome. Plus, Mary Johnson didn't have a phone.

From the parking lot at James Buchanan Elementary school he made his way towards the interstate. Two crossroads later he was in the middle of farm country. As the crow flies, the distance wasn't more than a few miles, but it always felt like another world by the time he got to his parents' house. He left the highway, took a state road for three miles, a county road for five more, then an unmarked gravel road for another two. A flood of memories came when he passed the Bus Stop Ahead sign. It was installed when Michael moved to the house with his mother, twenty years prior, his house being the only stop on the road. It was faded, tilted and riddled like Swiss cheese with rifle and shotgun blasts. Before the road disappeared over a low rise, it swelled on both sides, evidence that frequent travelers were using the shoulders for a makeshift parking lot. There was no formal driveway to the Johnson household. The only evidence that anyone was inhabiting the ranch style house was a hand-painted plywood sign reading "Fresh and Canned Produce" and below, at a forty-five degree angle "Baked Goods" and an exclamation point.

There was a low fence with two rows of widely spaced barbed wire and a double gate, enough to keep in the few goats and chickens milling about the property. Michael pulled his F150 to the side of the road and hopped out. There was an alternate route around the fence, a two-track with no formal name that led to the back of the house, but Michael never used it. He knew his mother would be home. She was always home. She'd likely have visitors or customers despite the absence of other cars, but she'd be happy to see him. Mary always had visitors.

A dirt footpath led up to the covered porch where two rocking chairs sat empty. A grungy backpack was tipped over by the screen door. Ten steps before he reached the porch, Michael smelled the unmistakable scent of his home, an infallible reminder of his childhood: peaches and cinnamon incense, his mother's favorite. Sitar music was coming through the screen door. Michael shook his head and laughed, noting how some things never change. He opened the screen door and called, "Hello? Hi, Nana Mary, it's Michael!" Since Hannah was born his mother's name had mysteriously changed from mom to nana.

An alto voice from the kitchen shouted back, "I told you not to call me that. It makes me sound so old, especially in front of young Joshua here."

Michael walked the long hallway back to the kitchen where he found his mother in the process of canning. The term never made sense to him since she always put the fruit in jars.

"Mary is your name isn't it? And you are a grandmother?" He recited the script of their ongoing joke of familiarity and love.

"Call me Moonbeam. You know I love it when you call me Moonbeam. Makes me feel like I'm headed off to the Woodstock again." She always called it "the Woodstock" as if it were the circus and would soon be touring through town again. Mary wiped her hands on her apron and tossed her braid over her shoulder. Her hair was all one length, parted in the middle and the thick braid reached to the small of her back. She kissed Michael on the lips by way of hello. She introduced him to Joshua and then complained about his long absence from her life. "How come I never see you any more? It's been a month of Sundays since you came around."

"It was last week, mom remember? And I don't come around so much any more because I graduated from high school seventeen years ago."

Joshua sat on a stool at the counter eating a fresh peach. Next to the word "goofy" in the dictionary is a picture of Joshua and his smile. He was dressed in cargo shorts that extended well below his knees almost all the way to his dirty feet which were nearly done abusing a pair of cork-bottomed sandals. Michael could see where the sole at the toe was delaminating off the base and the gap smiled up at him much like Joshua. Despite the heat, he wore a threadbare hoodie with long sleeves that must have been purchased on spring break in Mexico. His blonde, white boy dreads looked to be about two years old. There was a week of peach fuzz on his chin reminiscent of the fruit he was enjoying.

"Joshua here is walking his way to college in California. Seems he took that Henry David Thoreau to heart. Where you from, son?" Then to Michael she said, "That's what we were getting to when you came in."

"I'm from Georgia, ma'am. And I do say, this fine produce rivals anything we grow in my fair state," he said, holding up the dripping peach.

"What brings you all the way out here? You're miles from the nearest highway," Michael said.

"Well, that's the idea. I've got plenty of time and I'm already halfway to California. One more ride and I could be there in a day. I figured I'd check out the local flavor here in the great Louisiana purchase."

"Isn't he a thrill?" Mary said. Michael remembered the speech pattern all too well from his own days in college. Far from impressing him as to Joshua's rapier wit and cleverness, it only made him think of and miss Jennifer all the more. "Would you mind showing Joshua how to peel the peaches? He's got to earn his keep somehow."

Michael surveyed the kitchen. Canning was as much a part of his summers in Kansas as the ever-present scent of cinnamon and the sound of sitar music. The layout was the same as always. Mary had her stations set up in the usual order. There were boxes of peaches in neat rows extending in the adjacent dining room and onto the harvest table. On the back burner of her vintage cast iron gas stove, Mary had the sugar syrup already boiling. Another large pot held water at a rolling boil which Michael knew was for sterilizing the jars. Most were in cupboards under the counter, but a few dozen were stacked on the harvest table and the counter by the stove. Piles of peaches were in the sink, already washed. Something was missing. "Where's the lemon juice?"

"Oh, I always forget something, don't I? Last year we tried that commercial stuff but it didn't work as well to prevent browning. Would you be a dear and squeeze us some fresh juice? The lemons are in the fruit drawer."

Michael gave his mother a look as if he were the parent, not the other way around. She knew it was his least favorite job and the most labor intensive. It wasn't anything malicious or sinister, she really was prone to forget such things. Maybe he'd show Joshua how to do it and he could pass off the chore while he did the easier peeling. It sounded worse to peel all those peaches but Michael knew even a boy from Georgia wasn't likely to know how easy it could be with the proper technique. "Jason, whaddya say I set you up with a few lemons? Either that or you can start peeling those bushels of peaches."

"Right on, braddah anything to help. Maybe I'll try the lemons." Michael noted his mix of fake accents. This joker couldn't decide if he was a Rastafarian or a surfer bro'. Spring break will only teach a trust fund baby so much about life and his place in it. It amused him since he'd grown up in the house and seen a similar parade of characters come through every year.

He set Joshua up with a few dozen lemons, a juicer, and a bowl to fill. He showed his student how to cut a lemon and extract the juice in a way that would maximize the juice, minimize the pulp, and then how to strain it into the collecting bowl. Michael made a show of how hard his job peeling all those peaches was going to be. To Joshua's surprise, rather than grabbing a potato peeler, knife or similar implement, Michael simply lifted a colander of washed peaches and settled it neatly into the pot of boiling water on the stove. He reached under the same counter and removed another large sauce pot. This one he filled half way with cold water, then topped it off with ice from the freezer and set it on the counter. While Joshua labored with the lemons Michael rested on a stool and engaged his mother in a conversation about the weather.

After a minute, Michael transferred the peaches from the boiling water to the ice bath and let them sit for another few minutes. He removed them one by one and the skins fell off like water from a duck. He placed the pristine peaches in a bowl by the cutting board and the skins into a smaller bowl he retrieved from an overhead cupboard. "You must have picked these all yourself this year. Not a single bruise. Are you going to make peach honey this year?"

"Oh, that's a great idea. Yes, dear, save the skins."

The three of them made more small talk while they went about the delightful and fragrant task of canning bushels and bushels of peaches. When Joshua saw the importance of the lemon juice to prevent browning, he returned to his chore with renewed energy and refused Michael's generous offer to switch stations. The boxes of empty jars and lids were slowly transformed into a uniform wall of yellow that extended down the length of the hallway. "Mary?"

"Yes, Michael."

"May I ask you a question?"

"Of course, Love."

"Do you ever listen to anything besides Ravi Shankar when you're canning?" The three of them had a good laugh and Mary offered to put on something else, but nothing recorded after 1975, the year Michael was born. They decided on some early Beatles and Joshua got a good education on the difference between psychedelic music and the later acid rock which Mary was quick to point out had nothing to do with what ended up being called Heavy Metal. More importantly, Joshua learned not to be a music snob. It would come in handy in his first semester at college.

To his surprise and delight, Michael saw a faded, red VW van swing past the kitchen window and come to a dusty halt by the back door. His mother Linda got out and jumped up all three of the wooden back steps in a single bound. She opened the screen door, ducked her 6-foot plus tall head under the header of the doorway and with no introduction started a monologue. "You would not believe the aura on my first customer today. It was the most brilliant shade of creamy yellow and gold, bordering on auburn. I felt like I should have tipped *him* when the massage was over. He was hairy, really hairy, the most beautiful dark, black, curly back hair you've ever seen. The more I rubbed it, the more the hair on his back started forming these swirls and shapes and mixed with the oil and his aura I started to get hypnotized. It swirled like the Milky Way Galaxy. I went way over time and I didn't come out of it until he snored. Dead asleep. Said it was the best massage he'd ever had. Two hours went by like a minute. I had to come tell you immediately."

Mary was standing with her mouth open like it was the most amazing story she'd ever heard. The moment Linda burst into the kitchen, Mary was in the process of removing a jar from the boiling water with her canning tongs. When she turned to face Linda the jar intercepted a shaft of morning sunlight coming through the kitchen window. Her eyes went from Linda to the jar, to Linda and back again. The peaches appeared to be glowing from the inside, generating their own light. "Was his aura anything like this?"

Linda took two giant strides and closed the distance in an instant. She held Mary's hands and guided the heavy jar to a safe spot on the counter. Linda took the tongs and put them on the counter next to the steaming jar of peaches. "I just knew today was a special day, I felt it even before I saw that aura."

"I felt it too," Mary said. Her head only came to the middle of Linda's chest and that's where she rested it when they hugged. Linda rested her head on top of Mary's. Then they kissed. "I really missed you. I'm so glad you came back to tell me about your morning."

"I missed you too."

Michael grew up with such moments and he just smiled and let it be. What could be more wonderful for a child than to see one's parents showing their affection for one another? Joshua couldn't contain himself. "Well, all right," he babbled. "Right on!" He couldn't quite match his cliches with the beauty of the moment.

After what seemed like an eternity, but was only a few moments, it was Linda who broke their embrace saying, "Thanks for being here for me. I love you."

"I love you. I hate it when you're gone. Minutes are like days."

"Can I help you with the canning? That last batch is probably done."

"Oh, that batch will be a little overcooked, but no worries. I'd let the house burn down around us if it meant we could never stop hugging," Mary said.

Linda removed the slightly over-boiled peaches from the pot to the cooling area. Finished with that chore, she came to the sudden realization that she and Mary were not alone. "Oh, Michael. It's so good to see you!" She said it and she meant it. Linda needed more sleeves upon which to wear her emotions. "And we have a new friend. Who might you be?"

"I might be the Pope, but I'm not. I'm Joshua. Old Testament." They exchanged names and nods. Joshua met Linda with a handshake.

"Names are such clumsy appendages, aren't they? It's like having a horn in the middle of your head. Totally useless. You can't wear a hat and your hair never parts right!" Linda laughed at her own silly joke, then closed in on Joshua for a hug that was too hard, too long, and too intense. He came away from the embrace with fire in his pale cheeks. "We're so lucky that the All Mother brought you to us."

"Actually, it was a Mack Truck hauling a load of onions from Georgia."

"You've already enriched our lives by being here. And present. Thank you, Joshua," Linda said.

"So. Um. Uh, what color is my aura?" Joshua asked trying to overcome his awkward feeling at this display of selfless affection. He wasn't used to such unconditional acceptance.

Linda made a show of examining Joshua as if she were inspecting a horse for sale. She stepped back. She crossed and uncrossed her arms. She walked around him and inspected him from behind. She stepped back again. Michael was certain she wouldn't call Joshua on his bullshit to his face, but she wanted to see how she'd handle the situation. "Green. Definitely green. Such a positive color. Fresh, clean, but also young. So much to learn, like the first new growth of spring. You're going to have such a wonderful growth in the next year at college. In a way I envy you. Oh, that's so funny. I'm green with envy!" Linda chirped.

Michael couldn't see auras. He'd never bothered to learn despite his mother's insistence that it was easy. He guessed what she saw was not the fresh green of spring growth, but rather the dark, nasty green of bile or the decay of gangrene. Michael never understood the seven chakras but he knew people. If there was a prevailing energy surrounding Joshua, it was not a positive one. If Kathy the nurse's energy was sometimes over-the-top and aggressive, it still came from a place of generosity. She wanted those around her to benefit from her presence.

Joshua didn't aggressively put those around him down to his own benefit, but he was more likely to take than give. If someone didn't elevate Joshua in some way, he had no use for them. He didn't use other people directly, like a parasite, but he'd ignore them if the relationship weren't somehow to advance whatever his cause of the moment might happen to be. Then the reason came to Michael in a moment of clarity. Joshua had never been in love.

At the moment, it appeared Joshua had been seeking some marijuana. Michael guessed he'd already gotten it in one form or another from Mary and had been looking for a socially acceptable way to exit the scene as gracefully as possible. The peach canning had been more than he bargained for, the diagnosis by aura a surprise, and the realignment of his reality regarding relationships was completely unexpected.

"Oh, that's wonderful!" Mary said in response to Linda's reading of Joshua. "I knew he was a special person."

"You guys are…I don't know what. I don't know where to start," Joshua said.

Linda, Mary, and Michael all looked at each other and then back to Joshua. "What do you mean, start?" Michael said. "Start with what?"

"I mean. These, they…Linda and Mary are *both* your mother? I have so many questions."

Mary and Linda answered him in quick succession with a barrage of hypothetical questions.

"What's more important: the answers or the questions?"

"What is your goal in seeking this knowledge?"

"Is it knowledge you seek, or wisdom?"

"Is knowledge your goal? But what is your intent?"

"If your curiosity is satisfied, will that be the end of your suffering?"

Michael smiled inside but he spoke with calmness and clarity. "Joshua. What is it you'd like to know?"

"I…how did you all end up here?" Joshua finally stammered. "I mean, you've got to admit. This is hardly your Beaver Cleaver-type arrangement, made-for-TV, traditional child-raising household. All due respect, no offense, and all of that. But how does one come to be raised by lesbians?"

Linda and Mary looked at each other, then back to Joshua. It was Mary who spoke first. "We're not lesbians. What silly notions you have in your darling little head. Michael wasn't delivered by the stork and Linda sure didn't get me pregnant."

"I lost my husband in the Vietnam war," Linda said.

"Oh, I get it," Michael said. "You saw the sign for baked goods. You thought you'd score a little pot, then be on your merry way. Listen up, maybe you'll learn more on your way to college than you learn in the next four years."

"I'm all ears," Joshua said.

"In that case, let's get the rest of these peaches canned and Linda can make her next massage appointment on time." Michael spoke to his two mothers. "Do you want to help me tell the story?" His two mothers nodded their approval for him to start. For them it was like reliving the most wonderful time in their lives and they were always game for positive emotional experiences, however familiar.

Michael recalled the story from the version he'd been told. It started with Mary, a shy, quiet girl from the east coast, city undisclosed. She was born in 1950 to a family that would have been comfortable in the television shows of the day, if not the actual Cleaver household. By the age of fifteen the most rebellious activity she was able to muster was extensive use of the words "goofy" and "gyp." Whenever her parents acted in a way that was the least bit conservative, Mary deemed it goofy. Whenever she was called upon to perform some act of heinous servitude such as cleaning her own room, it was a "gyp" as if all the other kids in her class were never treated so unfairly. Her parents were mildly amused by her vanilla forms of teenage rebellion. She wore makeup on the weekends, stayed up all night on sleepovers with her friends, and kissed a boy under the bleachers when she was supposed to be watching the Homecoming football game. They pretended to be shocked and threatened severe discipline at all points. That is, until Mary heard the song "Penny Lane" by the Beatles. That song got her thinking. "Hang on Sloopy" was no longer good enough after she'd had her first taste of psychedelic rock. Mary saved her babysitting money for weeks and bought the single on the sly. It was all over when curiosity got the best of her and she flipped the 45 rpm and listened to the alternate side: "Strawberry Fields Forever."

Mary was later vindicated when in 1985 "Hang On Sloopy" became the official rock song of the state of Ohio, the most square and uncool state in the nation.

Musical rebellion led to disagreements over everything from bed time to her sudden change in wardrobe and hairstyle. Mary stopped bathing, shaving, and walked barefoot at all times. Her mother longed for the days when she had to tell her to refrain from using so much eye shadow. Makeup was only for people who wanted to continue to fuel the capitalist machine and ignore their true nature as spiritual beings.

The screaming arguments about the utopia of San Francisco usually ended with a math lesson. "You're only sixteen years old!" her mother would yell, exasperated.

"I'll be seventeen this summer," Mary would shout back, as if her mother didn't know and only needed to be reminded of that fact. A bus or plane ticket would be forthcoming.

"Everybody is going!" Mary shouted one day after school.

"Name one person," her father challenged her over dinner that night.

"Well, anybody who is anybody is going. It's the most important event of the year. I already missed the Human Be-In! There were 100,000 people there."

"As long as you're living under my roof, no daughter of mine, you've got a lot of growing up to do, what makes you think you're so smart?" and so on and so forth. Mary's father might as well have been speaking in Latin to a chair.

She punished her parents for not letting her join the spring break pilgrimage to San Francisco. Mary spent the week in her bedroom listening to The Beatles on endless loop and at maximum volume on her little one-speaker record player. She woke up with it and went to sleep with it, all the while planning her escape.

Hippies gathered in most large cities that summer, but for Mary, there could be no other destination than San Francisco. She satisfied her high school graduation requirements but forgot to tell her parents she wouldn't be sticking around to collect her diploma. There had been enough conflict over her desire to travel west for spring break that it was clear her parents had lost all authority. Mary didn't officially consider it running away. After all, when a bird learns to fly, it's supposed to leave the nest. She was there at Golden Gate Park when Timothy Leary told the counterculture to "turn on, tune in, and drop out." She experimented with drugs, philosophy, and politics just like many of her contemporaries. LSD had its charms she admitted but marijuana ended up being her drug of choice, then and to the present day. After the Monterey Pop Festival in the fall, when things were winding down and college students went back to school, she attended "The Death of the Hippie" mock funeral. That's where she met John. Of course, he didn't call himself that at the time.

A group of "mourners" at the ceremony was lingering after the event when John approached Mary and struck up a conversation. "I'll bet you call yourself Moonbeam," John said by way of introduction.

"Why no, silly," she said blushing. "I'm Mary."

"If I believed in names, that's what yours would be. On account of your smile shining like a moonbeam."

"What's your name? Or what would it be?"

"Oh, I don't use a label. I find them so divisive. What happens is this. See, you start to label things, thinking you can understand this magical creation we call life, but its ineffable. It's such a square habit to think you can control the world. Own it. Once you've got this multidimensional universe catalogued, then you start to covet things. But that's a false god. You can own some things, but you can't own everything, so you get depressed and constipated. You're unable to give. We're all just an infinite piece of the consciousness."

"So there are different sizes of infinity?"

"Absolutely. The second I laid eyes on you I said to myself, 'Now there's an old soul, a smart one who's wise beyond her years.' Here you are proving me right. And you deserve to be just as happy as all of us. Come join our little group." Mary was helpless in the face of such logic. Especially when combined with flattery and a large bag of weed. The memory of her authoritarian father was distant and fading fast. Here was a father figure who handed out compliments with every breath.

John and his nameless friends were starting a commune somewhere up north along the coast of Oregon. Prior to meeting John, one of those friends was known as Linda. She gave Mary her real name when they were introduced and the two became fast friends.

Rumors were constantly circulating about such intentional communities where the members would live out their counterculture philosophies in the flesh. This was the first one that seemed to Mary to have any real plan. In typical hippie fashion, that plan was murky, but she was all in from the beginning. She decided then and there to drop out of the rat race for good. Other flower children attempted to educate those back in their home towns, but she knew her parents were not going to change. Oregon seemed as good a place as any to start her new life. Linda became her best friend in short order and John showed all the promise of romance she could imagine.

The property was alleged to have been acquired from a logging company, but no one seemed to know just how it was obtained. A thousand acres was an incomprehensible expanse to anyone who'd been sleeping eight to a studio apartment all summer. There was a single dirt road into the acreage that changed to a two track, then a footpath that ended abruptly at cliffs overlooking the ocean. It was too rocky for a large commercial farm, too steep and remote to develop into suburban housing, and while lightly forested, the old growth trees were gone. In short, what had no monetary value to developers was the perfect location to start a commune.

John's entourage of a dozen souls started walking with a hand-drawn map. Over the Golden Gate Bridge and north towards Napa their numbers stayed more or less constant with some stragglers falling behind and new members joining the group. If Gandhi could walk to the sea to make salt, surely they could walk to Oregon to redefine what it meant to be alive and part of a community. They were offered rides and sometimes accepted. Eventually they made their way to the property in small groups, the first arriving by car or truck. No one hitchhiked intentionally, but the kindness of strangers can sometimes be hard to refuse. In the logic of the hippie, they reasoned they were doing their drivers a favor by making them feel good about their generosity. A joint or two was enough thanks and covered gas money more often than not. There was good karma all around.

While not a strictly religious group, the parable of the loaves and the fishes was often at play. Word of mouth spread and with it came colonists who were often better prepared than the founding members. In exchange for being welcomed unconditionally, the newcomers brought many of the logistical means necessary to make the commune function. Strangers brought basic carpentry and gardening tools which were shared in turn. Downed lumber from the logging company's clear cutting was converted into livable structures. No one seemed to know where the goats and chickens came from but they provided some much needed protein during the lean winter months. The animals ate all the weeds and bugs and turned them into milk and eggs.

With the spring came bags of seeds and an area was cleared to plant vegetables. While not as lucrative as the extensive marijuana fields, the produce proved useful for a number of nutritional needs, including the avoidance of scurvy.

Life went along swimmingly for those early settlers and changes happened slowly and by osmosis if at all. A source of fresh water was the biggest drawback. Poaching it from a nearby property where a stream flowed more or less consistently, was labor intensive and time consuming. On return from a Grateful Dead tour one of the new members brought a truck and drilled a well. Life improved dramatically, especially with the addition of the skills needed to make soap.

John was the major philosophical driver of the community and by holding frequent court around a bong or a bonfire, became a figurehead of sorts. He didn't have any medical background or training but in his study of a multitude of world religions and belief systems he became the go-to person for everything from a deep splinter to a bad acid trip. Most of his advice was harmless and thankfully, many of the ailments were self-limited. Thus, he was given credit for certain skills at healing, which he didn't actually possess.

Free love reigned, but it was combined inconsistently with the practice of modern birth control. Children came in all seasons and were raised naked and by committee. While Mary agreed with the politics in principle, she was still slow to adopt the lifestyle. Part of her was still that conservative shy teenager from the east coast and it took years of convincing and wooing by John, who remained her only male partner. Once she warmed to the new role of lover and enjoyed and relished it, she began to see their relationship as exclusive and committed.

In contrast to her own isolated and oppressive upbringing she loved the way the children were given the freedom to be children until that time came when they were old enough to make a contribution. More importantly, it was their choice to become a part of the community. Nothing was forced upon the offspring of the commune. Michael was one of these children, the product of the frequent union of John and Mary. Family legend held that it was John's role as healer for the community that inspired young Michael to pursue formal schooling in the art of medicine.

John was also fond of pilgrimages for the acquisition of knowledge, experiences outside their little commune, and the next great high, be it chemical or experiential. He followed The Grateful Dead for years, then returned. He begged, borrowed, and charmed his way to India, Tibet, and China, then came back with that much more self-assurance and authority.

As Michael grew, the time came for him to begin formal schooling and Mary found herself longing for the traditional way of doing things. Lacking running water, Vitamin C, and birth control was one thing, but lacking textbooks was another. She wanted to offer Michael the chance to make his own choices, even if he chose to reject traditional values in the end, as she had. Mary wanted public school for Michael, for the predictability of the path that would allow her son to pursue his dream of becoming a "real doctor."

"And that's how a young man comes to be raised by two women," Michael said, as if that explained everything.

"Far out," Joshua said thinking of an exit strategy. "It's been great learning about canning and hearing all your stories. I hate to intrude any more on the little scene of domestic bliss you got here. I'll just grab my pack and head on up the road."

Linda wouldn't let him escape so easily, she grabbed him for another bear hug which Mary and Michael joined. The four of them began to rock back and forth in a silent and spontaneous stationary waltz. After a time Joshua began to feel uncomfortable. He'd overstayed his welcome, like he'd been there two days, rather than two hours. Michael's mothers made sure he had more supplies than he'd need for a month of backpacking and followed him out the front door to help him with his pack.

Back in the kitchen Michael sat on a stool feeling a letdown, a hangover of emotional ennui. On their return to the kitchen his mothers put a hand each on his shoulders but didn't say a word. Finally, it was Linda who broke the silence. "Tell me what's wrong Michael. Your aura looks sick. Normally it's such a peaceful sky blue, but today the blue looks…"

"Strangled," Mary said.

"Asphyxiated," Linda added.

"Drowned and bloated."

"Frozen."

"Entombed."

"Jennifer told me she wants a divorce."

Condolences, more hugs, and a few tears were shared. The women expressed their dismay and asked all the questions Michael had been asking himself for the last three days. He told them about his weekend, from the soccer game up to the mysterious shift change and his ransacking of her office computer. He even told them the new things he'd learned about his friends and their marital struggles. With nowhere else to turn he came to Mary and Linda to get their advice, guidance, and support. "You know," Linda said. "I like your version of commune living. But that's not the whole story."

"There's more?"

"Not so much more to tell. You've got the broad strokes right, but some details are missing. It's one thing to remember it through the romantic lenses of nostalgia. But commune life is unbelievably hard. Only marriage is harder."

Linda married young, right out of high school. She was a year or two older than Mary. Her parents were still under the spell of the Kennedy administration. They romanticized service to the country and Linda was raised a patriot. Her boyfriend's family was cut from much the same cloth and the marriage was approved on both sides, despite their young age. Nothing made the parents and in-laws more happy than when Lewis enlisted in the army to aid the troops in Vietnam, much as his father had done to serve in World War II. He didn't necessarily plan to make the military a career, but did sign up for more than his obligatory, one-year tour. Lewis did some field medic training at the Presidio Army base hospital a stone's throw from the Golden Gate Bridge. Linda took advantage of the on-base housing until she left with John and Mary for the commune.

It was understood by Linda that her new friends in San Francisco largely opposed the war, some because they understood the murkiness of those political times. Others were simply against war in all forms, being pacifists as part of their experimentation with eastern religions. Linda had trouble biting her tongue on more than one occasion when protestors unknowingly insulted her husband. But that's what a wife does, she sticks up for her man. That's not just a pretty cliche from the times before women had the right to vote, but Linda believed, a key to a good and lasting relationship.

Lewis spent most of the late sixties and early seventies in-country. He rose quickly in rank and experience, becoming a valuable asset to the army. The downside of his successful career was the physical and emotional distance it put between he and Linda. On his rare trips home he had a hard time assimilating and playing the role of good husband. Part of the reason might have been that he and Linda had to meet at the Presidio in temporary housing as the commune was impractical. He confessed to Linda that he was shocked at the reception he received and couldn't believe people who knew nothing about his sacrifice could protest him to his face. She supported him as best she could and promised to always be there when he was ready to give it up. Lewis was determined to see it to the end, then he'd consider his duty to have been served. When the war was over, he'd leave the army.

This was a time before cell phones, e-mail, and texting. A simple phone call from Vietnam was prohibitively expensive, not that either of the couple had access to a phone. When Linda moved from San Francisco to the commune, Lewis sent his letters to her mother's house in California, where they were kept until she came for her infrequent visits. If the Grateful Dead were playing nearby, she might stop in and catch up on her mail.

One day, on an afternoon like many others she came home unannounced. Instead of the usual scream, hug and tears of joy, Linda's mother broke down in grief. She slumped to the hallway floor in a heap, weeping into her apron. This was how Linda learned that her husband had been killed in action and she'd missed the funeral by four months. Having devoted all of her time and energy to the commune, she assumed like Lewis there would be plenty of time for them to come together and build a shared life. He had worked tirelessly on his career in service to the country, honoring his father and working towards a marriage partnership that was never realized.

Linda had performed in much the same manner, always thinking that Lewis would one day join her in the commune. She saved tirelessly for their future, using only a minimum of his military pay to install the well, buy the community new tools, and keep a fresh supply of staples flowing into the commune. The things we take for granted are never appreciated to the level of their importance. One doesn't think twice about running water and a toilet, until one is forced to dig a latrine by hand, either in the heat of war or the remote forests of Oregon. What we can never bank on is the future. That was Linda's lesson for Michael. She'd never fallen out of love with Lewis and had no interest in trying to recapture that emotion with another man. When the opportunity came to build a life with Mary, to help her raise her son, she was more than willing to help her best friend. She transferred both her savings and her love to her new family.

"That's why we took you away from that place," Linda said. "Most of the members of the commune who had children were children themselves. Their version of parenting was no parenting at all. Including your father."

"But why did John stay at the commune? Did he leave you? Is that why we've never been back to visit? And how does that apply to Jennifer and me?"

"Maybe Mary could answer that best."

Mary pulled a chair up to the table to join Linda and Michael. While Linda was telling her tale, Mary had been cleaning the kitchen and putting away unused jars. "It's true Michael. Your father was a child. And I don't mean that in the spiritual sense. He wasn't some student on the path to ultimate enlightenment, becoming a Buddha. He was emotionally immature. Never had a concrete goal. Do you know what I mean? It's like they say in the twelve step programs. It's one step to acknowledge a higher power, it's another to strive towards a higher purpose, your life's work. Your dharma."

They both nodded their heads politely. Michael didn't want to doubt his mother so he let the fuzzy hippie logic pass. He wasn't so sure about her use of the word dharma, either, which he couldn't somehow equate with child-raising responsibilities. "So you're saying Jennifer has some higher purpose in life that she's kept secret from me? Why? It doesn't make sense. All we do is for Hannah." In the space after his words, no one spoke. Michael realized how true it was. Since having a child, all their individual and combined effort was to benefit their daughter. The marriage had become an after-thought. He quickly added, "And for us. Everything we do is for our family. Our marriage." The words sounded hollow in the quiet house.

Mary spoke in a slow and serious tone. Michael had seldom seen her this way. She was always the flighty one, prone to smile so hard that tears came to her eyes. People who didn't know her well thought she was a little simple-minded, not the sharpest cheddar on the cheese plate, or worse, her mind had been ruined by a few bad LSD trips.

"True, at first I was just smitten with John. A school girl crush. If he said the commune was on a row boat in the middle of the Pacific I would have grabbed an oar. We were very lucky those first few years. Things always came easily to John and he had no idea that Linda and Lewis were subsidizing his experimental lifestyle. I'm sure if he'd known that the money responsible for drilling our well, building our house, and filling our bellies came from a soldier's contributions in the Vietnam War, well he would have had a lot to say about that. The irony was not lost on this pacifist, let me tell you."

Mary's version of events at the commune was a blend of the utopia of Michael's version and the dystopia of Linda's. Life was hard but there were benefits to be had as well. There was a freedom from want and a culture of acceptance. Some who came to partake of the lifestyle missed too many things about the outside world and only stayed a few months. Even the original founders of the commune found reasons to leave and enjoy the pleasures of air conditioning, indoor plumbing, or a grocery store. The excuse for leaving was that they were raising money for some necessity for the commune. The truth was it was more in line with their slacker lifestyles to not have to worry whether the corn would get enough water during the dry part of the summer. Some of those tourists never returned.

At the edge of the continent was Mary's favorite spot for meditation. High on a cliff over the Pacific Ocean the commune came to an abrupt end. The logging company had cleared the larger trees but left a few smaller specimens at the cliff which framed a view that could only be described as majestic. When the sun set on clear days most members of the commune would come to enjoy it, some as part of their religious observances but most because it was simply amazing. The only difficulty Mary had was trying to answer the question of which was her favorite time of day, month and year. When the moon was setting and the wind was howling up the cliff there were times she felt she could fly right off the planet. So far from the lights of any big town the Milky Way shone with a brilliance by which she could read her poetry.

One day after dinner, on a pleasant summer evening, she was walking to her favorite spot, yoga mat under her arm, up the winding dirt path. She heard sounds of lovemaking. It was not unusual given the free love culture to find people enjoying new partners right out in the open. As she approached the ridge, the grunts became more clear and sounded instead like someone winning the battle over severe constipation. She heard voices.

"Oh, oh, Oohh," someone moaned. "That's wonderful."

"It's the least I could do," came the reply.

Mary stayed back a dozen steps from the ridge to allow the couple their privacy. When it appeared they were finished she rounded a small grove of trees and was surprised to find her two best friends. John was prone and straddling a downed tree, using a hand-woven blanket for padding against the bark. Linda was standing over him with oil up to her elbows. John's shirt was hanging from a nearby branch but other than that they were fully clothed including hats. "Oh, I'm sorry to interrupt your massage," Mary said by way of sincere apology.

"Relational exchange," Linda said.

"It looks like a massage to me. He's laying there and you're rubbing his back. One plus one equals massage. You even have your massage oil out."

"John was having trouble connecting to the universal flow today. I'm just helping him expel some negative energy."

"Oh, I see. Sorry to interrupt your relational exchange." Mary said it without a drop of sarcasm, bitterness, or jealousy.

"Would you like to join us?" John said.

"I just came up to enjoy the view and do a little stretching." Mary blanched when people called her morning exercise yoga. She'd never studied yoga, didn't associate her stretching with any religious or spiritual practice and only did it when she felt a little stiffness after sleeping on the ground. She mostly left the labels to be supplied by others and they were generous to a fault in supplying them.

Linda offered, "That's terrific that you're doing such wonderful energy work. I sense in you a great power for magick. When you're communing with the flow you really experience the divine."

"I was thinking more about getting some fresh air after tending the goats and slopping the pig this morning."

"Ha, ha." John pushed himself up off the log to face his sometime lover. Linda rose as well and continued massaging his shoulders. "I love that you're so grounded, Mary. You're a real rock of the commune. Everyone benefits from you being here, just by you being here." Mary blushed a little but didn't say anything. John continued, "Look a group of us are going to be doing some divination later. I'd love it if you'd join us. If it goes well, we're predicting there's going to be some conscious creation."

"Uh, sure. Funny you should mention creation. Remember how I told you my period was late last month? Well, it never came. Skipped this month too. I've got a little creation of my own."

At this news, John rose from the log and gave her a big hug. Linda wiped her hands and then her eyes. Her husband was still in Vietnam at the time and children would be years away. John broke the embrace and with great enthusiasm bounded down the hill toward the main compound. He shouted back over his shoulder, "This is so great, I've got to tell the others. We'll have a party tonight in celebration!"

Mary stood with her mouth open, stunned, her mat still under her arm. Linda climbed over the log and gave Mary a hug as well. "John's the father, isn't he?" Mary didn't say anything. "And he doesn't know it's his, does he?" Mary's eyes started to water. "Do you want to talk about it?"

Mary walked to the edge of the cliff and threw her yoga mat as far as she could. She counted five and watched it fall all the way to the jagged rocks and pounding surf. She sat on the ground, put her face in her hands and started to cry.

Later in the week she screwed up the courage to talk to John. To break the ice she asked him to help her feed and milk the goats. John could barely tear himself away from welcoming a new group of refugees from the outside world. This group contained more than a few freshly scrubbed college co-eds.

At the first udder, John held the bucket and Mary started by explaining that she'd only ever been with him. The other guys were nice enough but she'd never been attracted to them sexually and so hadn't allowed their advances. John assumed she'd had multiple partners as he had all along. He tried to downplay the importance of sex for Mary and kept calling it "relational exchange" as if it were no more than a chat around the campfire. Other couples had set the precedent by raising kids as an extended family. Even in situations where inter-racial couples had a child and it was obvious who was the father, the children were seen as belonging to everyone. In the spirit of the commune, they'd all raise Mary's child as one, giant family. "That's what's so special about us, Moonbeam. We've evolved beyond that square, confining notion of one man, one woman."

"But if you have sex with everyone, then no one's special. And I thought we'd evolved beyond judging people for their choices. I live and let live. So I expect the same tolerance for my choice to want one man. Is that so terrible? I love you."

"But our parents have shown us that those ways don't work. Just look at Vietnam."

Mary paused her milking to look at John to see if he was really serious. His blank expression told her that he really thought there was a legitimate logical connection between his parents' monogamy and the Tet Offensive. "This isn't about war. It's about me loving you, wanting a life with you and you alone. I've always only wanted you. Is it so hard to be loved? All you have to do is just be, John."

"Why do you keep calling me John? You know labels are too restricting."

When the milking was done, John just stood up and left as if the discussion had ended in some sort of agreement. Subsequent conversations proceeded along similar lines—Mary expressing her love and devotion and John taking no responsibility whatsoever.

Months passed and Mary started to show. Her gait slowed, then changed to a tottering waddle. One morning after a poor night's sleep, she carried her new handmade mat up to the western ridge. As before, she heard noises of pleasure but rather than hold back she walked straight up to say hi to John and Linda. John was seated on the log facing the ocean, but it wasn't Linda naked and astride his lap. The woman's hair was jet black and formed a tent over John reaching to the small of his back. Mary unrolled her mat near the edge of the cliff and began her stretching routine. Introductions were made and Mary was asked if she wanted to join the two lovers on the log. Mary declined. Selu continued to grind up against John, who had apparently finished his side of the relational exchange prior to Mary's arrival.

Selu soon collapsed into a pile of colorful, wool blankets. John remained seated on the log, admiring the view. When Selu had recovered she addressed Mary and complimented her on her calm demeanor, her connection to the earth, and what Selu described as strong medicine.

"See, the tribe discourages boisterous behavior," John added. "Autonomy is respected, of course, but the harmony of the group is the focus."

"I see you are rich with child, a gift from Mother Earth and Father Sky, soon to be a mother yourself."

"Actually, this gift is from John."

"That's not my real name you know."

"Of course it is, that's what your parents call you. It's what they write on the letters they send you every month."

"But it is not my essence. And the Cherokee tell us that names change over time. Sure, I might have been John under my parent's regime, but now I'm a student of life. Selu is going to give me a name as soon as she understands my medicine better."

"This baby will probably want to call you 'daddy' or something similar." Mary lifted her blouse and patted her white belly. "That's all I know."

"True wisdom is having more questions than answers," Selu said.

"Well I've got a question for you, John. What are you going to do when this baby comes? Did you think we might have a partnership of sorts? Raise this baby together? Maybe even get a job? A little place of our own? What are you going to do?"

"I'm just going to be, Moonbeam. Selu has taught me that we're human beings, not human doings. Our purpose in life is to develop the inner self. Work is not our purpose in life."

"Really. Is that so? Who is Selu named for but the first woman to sow corn? She's the first farmer, right? Isn't that the story? If farming's not work, what is?"

"I saw this exchange in a vision at the sweat lodge," Selu said.

"Planting corn is a religious expression, babe."

"But that's what you said about hearing that King Crimson album."

"And it was. It is. It's all about the path to inner peace."

"Sure, that's all well and good, but this is going to turn into hard labor soon." Mary pointed to her belly again. "And this baby is going to want for some basic material goods in order to survive. He or she isn't going to get by on the mystical gifts of Grandfather Sun and Grandmother Moon."

"Well, of course he will. That's what the Circle of Life is all about, Moonbeam."

Mary rolled her mat and rose clumsily to her feet. "I hope you'll consider raising this child with me, not as work, but as part of your life's higher purpose. I'm not asking you to quit the commune and get a factory job. I'm saying I'd like some acknowledgment that you think I'm special, that our relationship is special, that our growing family means as much to you as your inner spiritual quest." She walked down the hill back to the main compound. There were animals to tend and chores to accomplish before the cold weather arrived.

In the spring, Mary's morning stretching sessions were replaced by morning feedings. For exercise she walked the hill carrying Michael Johnson, unrolled her mat, and took in the view while he suckled. She performed her version of meditation, reflection, and prayer. She chose the name as an ironic reaction to all the jumbled mysticism around her. In a sea of children named Leaf, Stream, Breeze, and Chipmunk, Michael had the most unique name of all. The surname was the pragmatic choice, and a sign that she wasn't letting John ignore the fact that he had a son.

One morning at the cliff, she came upon a familiar scene, John having sex with another woman. This time it was a woman dressed in a sari, performing an act of fellatio, while John was seated on his favorite downed tree in the whole wide world. As usual, introductions were made, invitations were declined, and Mary sat down at her usual spot. Since the woman had her mouth otherwise occupied, John did the honors. "This is Jyotsana. It's a Hindi name meaning moonlight. Isn't that pretty?"

"Of course it is. It's the name you gave me when we first met."

"Oh, I remember." John made some noises that led Mary to believe his mind wasn't entirely on their conversation, but rather his immediate spiritual satisfaction.

"Perhaps we should talk in a few minutes." Mary said.

When things had settled down to allow intelligent discourse, it was John who spoke first. He explained that Jyotsana was from Portland—Oregon, not Maine—and she was helping him with his latest exploration of the eastern religions. "We're exploring all of consciousness and our relationship to the entire multidimensional universe, plus both its manifest and unmanifest reality."

"Really," Mary said it like a statement, not a question.

"Really. She's helping me to open my chakras and explore the various kinds of vibrational energy of my soul."

"So that's why you had to combine your second chakra with the fifth chakra at the back of her throat?"

"We were mingling my red-orange energy with her blue sky energy."

"It looks like a blowjob to me. Why not call it what it is? No one's judging you, John."

"Because Jyotsana is helping me to facilitate healing, to escape the downward spiral caused by negative energy leftover from my past lives. See, she sensed my need to reconnect with the universal energy that connects all things."

Jyotsana remained suspiciously quiet through the entire exchange, leading Mary to believe she was either mute or didn't speak English. "Well John, what about your Fourth Chakra?" John's face took on a confused look, so Mary continued. "Your heart? Your green energy, sometimes also pink and gold like so many sunsets? Where is your love, compassion, and selflessness? Would you care to work on those things with me?"

"My journey is a solitary one."

"Except for every time a new woman comes to the commune with a new theory of spirituality. You're the first to jump on the bandwagon. Have you ever noticed you don't bother trying the path of any of the males who visit? You wanted nothing to do with the Mormons despite their polygamy. I thought that would be right up your alley. When the Hare Krishnas came you almost broke an ankle running from their tambourines."

"But this is different." John reached a hand to Jyotsana who was still in a subservient posture, on her knees at his feet. He lifted her to take a seat next to him on the log. John put his arm around her and announced his plan. "After tonight's Circle Fire, and when the full moon reaches the Twelfth House, we're leaving for Nepal. I'm going to continue my spiritual journey in the center of the religious world."

"So, which one?" Mary didn't bother to mention to John that tonight's moon would not be full, but rather, a third quarter, waxing.

"Which one, what?"

"Hinduism or Buddhism? In Nepal. Kathmandu, right? They're different, you know."

"Oh, you know I don't acknowledge such labels."

"Millions have died in defense and honor of those labels you so casually dismiss."

Mary had finished feeding Michael and burped him over her knee. He fell instantly to sleep and she propped him up away from the cliff for a nap. She rose from her cross-legged position and walked to where John still had his arm around Jyotsana. Mary looked him square in the eye and spoke in her most plain voice, devoid of accusing emotion. "John. I have never asked you for anything. But I'm going to ask you now. If not for me, then for your son. If not for your son, then for your future self. Use whatever rationalization you have to. Call it good karma, whatever you like, but I'm asking you not to go. Stay here and help me raise our son."

John looked to Jyotsana for direction. Except for her neutral mannequin smile, her face was an inscrutable blank. "We'll be back soon?" was his reply, voiced as a question.

"Then what, John? You head off to Mecca with your new Muslim friend? Climb Mount Fuji on your knees with your Japanese friend? Why not visit the Vatican with your Roman Catholic friend? Oh, I suppose that would be too much like a dream your parents might have had at one time."

Mary was so upset she nearly forgot Michael in her haste to storm away. John sat on the log with his arm around Jyotsana and stared across the water imagining he could almost see Nepal across the ocean.

By the time the evening Circle Fire came round, Mary had gathered her emotions and was able to approach John. She began by apologizing for letting her pent up frustrations get the better of her usually calm demeanor. She did not mean to entrap John or keep him from realizing his goal of reaching a higher plane of existence. In fact, to that end, she'd scored some LSD and invited him to take it with her later that night as the moon was setting. It was her parting gift to him with no strings attached. As the fire died down and the music came to an end, John shared all of his plans for the upcoming trip. Questions were answered, chants and prayers were shared, and handmade gifts were bestowed for a successful pilgrimage. The people dispersed to their cabins leaving John with no audience but the mother of his son. Mary put Michael down for the night and took John to the cliff.

The couple walked the familiar path that either of them could easily navigate in the dark. Mary reached for John's hand and he didn't resist when she walked beside him, hand in hand. At the cliff they sat first on the log, then decided to huddle down out of the wind front to back, bobsled style. The moon had not yet risen and John reminded Mary of his plans to leave with his fellow travelers when the moon was overhead. Mary presented John with two hits of LSD and took a button herself, making a joke about taking a trip before his trip. John smiled at the sight of the drugs. Mary wasn't sure he understood the silly pun. "Oh, Orange Sunshine. I haven't seen those in years."

"I've saved some from the first time I met you and we tripped in San Francisco."

"Are you sure they're still good?"

"Well, yeah, why wouldn't they be?"

While waiting for the drugs to take effect, Mary pleaded with John one final time to reconsider. "I'm worried you won't come back this time. It's not like you're just going to Woodstock again."

"You'll be with me in spirit."

"That's a copout John."

"Please, my child. Call me disciple. I must be worthy of a guru. Free from material attachments."

"I wouldn't equate your son with a sports car."

"But the desire for material things is just as dangerous as having them. Including the desire to have a son. Some sort of heir, a legacy. It's all bullshit."

Mary turned around to face John. "Are you feeling anything?" Mary was referring to his emotional state, trying to get him to open up about his son, probing to see if he had any sense of obligation for his offspring.

"I feel the wind. It's really picking up. You?" In his superficial way, John thought she was talking about the drugs and nothing else.

"Nothing yet. Maybe you're right, they lost some of their potency all these years. Here take another one." John took three more tablets. Just then, the first two doses began to take effect.

"I must be attached to nothing impermanent. Including a son, a wife, material goods." In a few short years a movie called *Star Wars* was going to be released. John was thus a pioneer of sorts when he experienced the rushing of the stars similar to the *Millennium Falcon* entering hyperspace.

Mary began to trip. The wind picked up but unlike John, she became scared of the stars, the wind, and especially the cliff. She started to feel as though her weight was increasing. She wasn't swelling or growing, but becoming more dense, collapsing, sinking into the spot where she was rooted to the log. Her body was becoming one with the earth, their gravitational force becoming more or less equivalent. She shared her fears with John. His response was to demonstrated the opposite sensation. He rose from his spot on the ground and stood up on the log. He started flapping his arms like wings, then decided even that feeble attempt wasn't necessary to fly. His confidence rose to the level of certainty. John stepped to the edge of the cliff and waited with arms outstretched, for the wind to take him aloft. No boat or plane was necessary. He'd decided to fly to Tibet on his own.

"I thought you were going to Nepal?"

"Far out."

Linda found Mary the next morning. She was carrying a wailing Michael who was long overdue for his morning feeding. The night had passed in a blink, her sense of time altered. She hadn't slept. Mary was still performing a bear hug on the downed tree, feeling like she'd been punched in the chest. Thinking it was just an excess of milk she was glad for the feeding. Michael latched on and the two friends walked back to the compound. No words were spoken as each woman had her own thoughts to occupy her. Mary was quietly fuming that John had left her without saying a proper goodbye.

Months later the rest of the pilgrims returned from their spiritual journey, but John was not among the enlightened. Questions were asked but no answers were forthcoming. It was understood in the commune that he'd left at midnight with the others but none of them could recall if he was actually among the group who hitchhiked to Portland. It was dark, he denied being their leader and so on. No one recalled seeing him on the boat, let alone in Asia. John was always somewhat of an enigma, difficult to get close to, so it was assumed he'd decided to make the trip in his solitary way. It would be like him to confuse Nepal and Tibet and end up in China. The optimists won out and a grand success was declared meaning it must have been he alone who found a guru, learned the sacred ways and achieved nirvana. Mary thinks he fell off the cliff and died, his body lost in the pounding surf.

"Was there a time you thought you might tell me my dad was dead?"

"Well, sorry Michael, it's not the sort of thing that you give for a birthday present. Son, here, I bought you these savings bonds when you were born." Mary wiped her eyes and took a deep, jagged breath. "Besides, he might still be alive. Maybe he'll come back some day."

"We're both widows? Why didn't you tell me?"

"I don't know, Linda. I don't know. It's all very foggy from that night. I can't remember. As far as I know John is still in Tibet. Or Nepal. Working his way towards complete spiritual awareness, becoming one with the Oversoul. Or something. At least that's better than what I think might have happened." Mary wiped at both her cheeks.

"Why didn't you tell me about the drugs before?" Linda said.

"My dad jumped off a cliff? Stoned out of his mind?"

"I'm sorry, Michael. Linda. I really don't know. Isn't it better to think he's still alive pursuing his dream of spiritual enlightenment than thinking of him as a deadbeat dad, another victim of the stupidity of the failed logic of the counterculture?"

Michael and Linda looked at each other. "Anyway, Michael. What I'm trying to say is, there might not be any reason for Jennifer's behavior. Not everything we do is thought out from start to finish. Maybe she doesn't love you as much as you love her. Maybe there's something in her life that's more important right now."

"What could be more important than Hannah and me? She got in a truck with a total stranger!"

"We can't choose to fall in and out of love, can we? It's not like ordering the steak, then changing to the lobster. I still love your father. Even if I got mixed up with the wrong guy."

"That's what Jennifer said."

"That I should have ordered the steak?" Mary's old thought processes were returning to form.

"No. That I married the wrong girl. And what do you mean by 'right now?' Do you think that she just wants to divorce me temporarily? Once that other thing's taken care of, we'll get married again? It doesn't make sense. She presented me with divorce papers. And knowing that about my dad is only making it worse."

"Well, Michael. Maybe John was right. It's not you or Jennifer that's the problem, it's that label you put on it. You can't get divorced if you're never married."

"Now you sound like Hank. Jennifer will be so pleased when I tell her."

The silly, circular logic caused a few gears in Michael's brain to collide and lock. He began to feel like he'd been taking drugs himself. Things made less and less sense the more he thought about them. The three of them sat quietly for a few minutes until Linda and Mary took Michael's hands across the table to form a triangle of love and support. After a while, his brain began to work again. What if the paper really was the problem? What if Jennifer kept her maiden name for some reason other than a symbol of her modern feminism? What if it only seemed like she was leaving him, yet her goal was that of protecting and enriching their relationship—not their marriage—so that they'd be closer than ever? Once her other business was squared away, they could put this nonsense behind them for good.

His two mothers sat at the table in silence and let Michael process all the information, new and old. One might think they had some specially trained or innate skill at child-raising, to remain so stoic in the midst of his anguish and confusion. But the real reason they remained silent was that they had nothing to say. They'd instilled in Michael his sense of optimism and complete lack of guile. People were basically good. When in love, they did things that didn't make sense, but they did them for the right reasons. Jennifer had her reasons but she still loved Michael, of that, he was certain. His mothers knew that love and life were anything but predictable. Circumstances either external, like a war, or internal, like a spiritual quest, could end up causing a separation of two people who nonetheless continued to be in love and devoted. That separation could only be temporary. And what was a year or a decade in comparison to something infinite?

Michael thanked his mothers for their support. Despite their constant reassurances that everything was going to be okay, he had his doubts. He left with a crate of canned peaches thinking it would take months for him to eat them by himself. Jennifer liked peaches more than he did.

12

BLOODLETTING

In a daze, Michael drove without the ability to link his thoughts. Jennifer had a lot of questions to answer. The incomprehensible divorce talk, the mysterious schedule change at work, and then the sinister security guard at the hospital all had his mind in a confused jumble. His guilt at hacking her computer diminished in the anger he felt at the position in which she'd put him. Michael had always defined himself by his work and home life, now both were out of sync. He was a rudderless ship. For the first time in his life, he had nothing to do. With no obligations, he was lost. Vacation time had its own set of rules, but this time off was a void. He wondered if this was what it felt like to be homeless, a veteran on the side of the road with a sign reading, "Anything helps." Like a salmon returning to its spawning grounds, he found himself home without reason, sitting in the driveway with the engine running. He turned off the truck and dragged his legs up the front steps. Once in the house his level of confusion lurched from dreamlike to sublime.

The living room was unrecognizable. Not a single piece of furniture was intact or standing on its legs. The leather couch, a wedding gift, was upended and gutted like a deer, spilling its innards onto the carpet. The houseplants were shredded and scattered, the dirt from their pots strewn about as if they'd been broken with sledgehammers. It took Michael a full five minutes to realize his home had been vandalized.

Michael had a single, prized possession. It was his one concession to luxury, a one-of-a-kind piece of luster pottery. Though diminutive in size at five inches tall, it possessed the regal nature of a much more substantial piece of art. Big things come in small packages, he always said. The layers of glaze held a galaxy of abstract patterns and colors. Its shape was in no way utilitarian with its long neck, what Michael called "masculine shoulders" and a military taper to the base. Depending on the weather, the light in the room would play off the smooth surface of the vessel with dazzling results. Jennifer joked during sunset one day that they should name it "Chips and Salsa." He reminded her that it was her idea to attend the antiques fair and his eye which gravitated towards the undervalued piece. She balked at the price tag, then later found out it was worth ten times the amount they paid. Michael spent months picking up extra shifts at the hospital to replenish their meager savings. He then built a special case in which to display the pot, complete with a dedicated light switch and a revolving pedestal. He wired the platform to a rheostat in order to adjust the speed of the revolutions, depending on his mood. At its lowest setting, the pot would spin with a subtle sensuality bordering on erotic, like the ultimate striptease, each degree of turn revealing a new and breathtaking vantage. The pot now consisted of obscene shards protruding rudely from the center of Michael's fifty-two inch plasma television.

His only thought while taking in the carnage was how glad he was that his wife and daughter weren't there when it happened. Everyone was safe. The material possessions were only meaningful when everything else in his life was in order. At present the damage meant nothing. After he got his family back together, he'd see about repairs and replacing his beloved pot.

Michael dialed Jason on his cell phone. His friend picked up on the first ring. "Dude, I've got a situation. You busy?"

"Oh, uh, I'm pretty sure I can get away. Nothing that can't wait. I could use an excuse to get some fresh air. Let me tie up some loose ends here at the office and I'll be right over."

"Is that all the cliches you've got, dude?"

"Hey, do you want me over or not?"

Jason arrived in Amy's old GMC Sonoma and parked in the driveway, next to the Ford F150. Michael met him at the storm door and showed him the living room without saying a word. Jason stared with mouth agape at the ruined television with fragments of the glorious pottery spilling to the carpet. The luminous blisters of fired clay fell like tears from the television to the carpet. "Oh, dude. Your pot."

"Never mind that. We need to talk." The two men went to the kitchen where Michael brought two beers from the fridge and put one in front of a chair at the dining table for Jason. "It's five o'clock somewhere." They cracked their beers and held them up for a silent toast. Before they exchanged a word, the door bell rang and the two men stopped, mid-sip.

Michael went to the door and looked through the peephole but saw no one. In the street was a black Cadillac Escalade parked by the curb. He opened the door a crack, blocking the view of the living room with his body. Standing there was Mr. Microphone Ear, from the soccer game, still sporting the crisp, blue suit and sunglasses. "Can I help you?"

"I'll say you can, shithead." The man said it like "sheet." Was that a Mexican accent? Spanish? Maybe Puerto Rico, but it certainly wasn't developed growing up in Kansas.

"Hey, there's no reason to be rude."

"Yes. Yes, there is. Do you have any idea who you're dealing with?"

"Well, no. I didn't know I was dealing at all. Are you sure you've got the right house?" Michael bluffed.

"I'm Mario Lopez, but you aren't gonna remember that." Mario peeled back his suit coat to reveal a shoulder holster and handgun of enormous proportions. The butt of the gun was under his armpit while the muzzle was tucked neatly into the waistband below his suspenders. "You're Mike Smith and your old lady is Jennifer Smith. You owe us money. Look, playin' stupid ain't gonna help you. I trashed this place myself. Got it?"

"Huh? My first name's Michael, you got that right. But nobody ever calls me Mike. And my last name is Johnson. Sorry. There must be some mistake."

Michael gave Mario a confused look and did his best to produce a laugh. It came out like someone was tickling his feet with a broken bottle. Keeping an eye on Mario he called to the kitchen in the most effeminate singsong voice he could muster. "Honey! Jason darling! There's someone at the door who wants to meet you!"

Jason rose from his chair but left the beer on the table. Instead of opening the door, he bent over to look under Michael's arm and keep his considerable bulk hidden. "Mr. Mario here thinks your name is Jennifer."

"Nope. He's cute and all, but I've never seen him before, darling," Jason said with an affected lisp, then closed the door.

Enraged, Mario Lopez drew his gun, opened the screen door and pounded with full force on the brass knocker causing it to rebound violently as if he were working the speed bag at a gym. Michael opened the door an inch and peeked through. "Really, Mr. Lopez. You've got the wrong house!"

"Bullshit, asshole," Mario said in his squeaky tenor. He pushed his way into the foyer and surveyed the damaged. "See? I told you this was the place." He pointed to the wreckage with the barrel of his giant handgun. His triumph turned to dismay as Jason grabbed him from behind in a brutal bear hug, trapping his arms against his sides. The gun fell impotently to the floor and Jason hoisted Mario off his feet by simply standing to his full height. It was a flawless Karelin lift without the throw. Michael picked up the gun for safety.

"What now?" Jason said to Michael.

"Break some ribs."

Jason squeezed Mario until the intruder was no longer able to breathe. The room was silent except for the sound of legs flailing, the silk material making a soft swishing sound. A muffled pop was followed by an anguished grunt from Mario. "That's one," Jason said. "And what's a little boy like you playing with a big boy gun like that for? You mess up my best friend's house, come in here waving your Desert Eagle around." Two more muffled snaps were heard as he squeezed harder.

"I think I'm going to need a couple of ribs for my luster pottery. And what do you know about guns, Jason?"

"You got it Michael." Jason tightened his grip until he could almost touch his own shoulders. Mario's legs stopped flailing. Jason inhaled deeply and gave a final massive squeeze. A sound like someone popping bubble wrap was followed by a bright snapping sound. "Hmm. That last one sounded a little funny."

"Check in his pockets," Michael said waving the gun and pointing it at their victim.

Jason dropped Mario Lopez to the carpet like a bag of wet leaves. They ignored his groans, which for Michael meant he was still alive, still breathing. In the right side vest pocket was a cell phone, now reduced to plastic rubble. The casing had cracked and caused a shallow laceration to Mario's chest. Drops of blood were oozing through his navy blue shirt. "Oops. Sorry, Michael. That phone could have come in handy. What now?"

Michael answered by going to the kitchen to retrieve a chair. "I've got an idea. We need some information and he needs to talk. Tie him up."

They propped Mario in the chair and Jason secured him around the chest with the cords from the three broken lamps. He used the cords from the DVD player and television to tie one leg to each leg of the chair. The blood stain on Mario's shirt stopped growing, but it gave Michael an idea. "Leave me an arm. I think I can use that." He handed Jason a broken leg from the coffee table. "Tie his arm to this, elbow straight. I'll be right back."

Michael waltzed out the front door, trying to appear nonchalant, and hoped no one else was waiting in the Escalade. He retrieved a large, plastic tackle box from the passenger seat of his Ford F150 and started back to the house. He made a theatrical gesture of noticing the Cadillac, spun around, then sauntered over to it as if he were about offer assistance. It had Florida license plates. He cupped his hands and looked in the passenger side window but couldn't make out anything or anyone. Looking through the windshield didn't reveal any occupants, so he tried the door handle. It was unlocked, so he opened the door for a quick peek inside. The interior had the look of a long road trip and the odor of a fast food joint Dumpster. The keys were in the ignition on a leather key ring with a hula girl charm. Hamburger wrappers were strewn about, empty cans of Pepsi and Jolt Cola littered the passenger side. Satisfied that Mario was working alone, he returned to the scene of the crime, towing his tackle box. Jason was still at the kitchen table, finishing his beer as calmly as if they were in the fifth round of the fantasy football draft. Michael joined him at the table and began sipping his own beer, deep in thought. Mario was still passed out in the chair from mild asphyxiation as much as pain.

The friends discussed the situation as best they could divine. Michael summarized the bizarre events starting with Jennifer's divorce threat, her mysterious—but seemingly willing—exit in the Escalade, and her failure to answer texts or phone calls. Jason said the website traffic on the school computer didn't seem like much of a lead. Nothing made sense. They were relieved from their ignorance by moaning and the sound of retching from the living room. The men rose to meet their attacker.

"So," Michael said. "Care to fill us in?"

"Fuck you. And your mother."

"Oh, not off to a good start, are you Mario? Care to try again?" Jason said. He poked Mario in the side figuring he'd find a broken rib sooner or later.

"Bullshit. You know the score, you owe us eight large."

"Pretend I forgot," Michael said.

"Yeah. And what's with the Desert Eagle .50 caliber semi-automatic? You going bear hunting?" Jason said.

Michael gave Jason a look of confusion. "What?" Jason said to Michael. "You don't watch movies? Every gangster has a Desert Eagle."

"You really are a pair of dumbshits. Behind the couch moron." Jason went over to the upended couch and lowered it to its former place opposite the television. In black Sharpie, a rude message was scrawled on the wall. There were plenty of four-letter words, an offer of amputation to Jennifer and some very disturbing references to a specific violation of Hannah's purity.

"Why would Jennifer need eight grand?" Jason asked Michael. Realizing he'd slipped up the ruse, he quickly added, "And who's Jennifer?"

"Okay," Michael said. "Assume we know who this Jennifer is, why did you have to trash my place? Heck, you could have stolen my stuff and sold it for that much."

"Eight large, moron. She owes us eight *million*. We can get a few grand for her organs, but we'd rather have the money back. *With* the interest she promised. As usual."

Michael was beyond dazed. He began to wonder if he really did know his wife. He decided to keep up the charade. "Sure. You've seen the place, Mr. Lopez. Does it look like I've got eight million dollars lying around?"

"Don't make us go after the girl. We normally leave the kids alone, but you see, Jennifer has put us in a difficult position." He paused to breathe twice through the pain. "We have interests, shall we say, on the East Coast and overseas which demand we be in a more liquid position."

Michael took Jason by the arm and led him to the kitchen for a whispered conversation. He announced their return to the living room by breaking his empty beer bottle across the back of Mario's head. "Let's cut the crap. Yeah, this is my place. Jennifer's my wife, and if you touch my daughter I'll make sure you'll be sorry you ever met me."

Mario laughed out loud, then stopped when the pain in his broken ribs reminded him he was in no position to argue. "Really, Mike. Don't make me laugh, it hurts too much."

"I've got a question for you, Mr. Lopez. You know how they say some people would die for love?" Mario gave him a look and a sigh like a teenager with a pending dentist appointment. "Well, how many people do you know who say they'd kill for love?" Mario's eyes grew wide as dinner plates. "How come you never hear about that, huh? I see by your expression, you've never met one. Well, you're meeting one today. And by the way. It's your *last* day."

Michael went to the kitchen to retrieve his tackle box. He returned and set it down in full view of Mario Lopez. He popped it open to reveal the tools of his nursing trade. There were countless needles, yards of tubing, syringes of all sizes, and three IV fluid bags of different sizes. Without a word he took out a tourniquet and put it around Mario's upper arm, squeezing it to the broken chair leg. In a few seconds, multiple veins stood out of his skinny arm, pale blue under the olive skin. Michael chose the largest IV needle he could find, a sixteen gauge, the kind they used for blood donations in the hospital and at the Red Cross. "Gimme that lamp."

Jason picked a broken floor lamp from behind the trashed television and righted it next to the tackle box. "Uh. What are you doing?" Jason said.

"I thought it was obvious. I'm going to bleed this pig until he dies. It won't even hurt. Well, the initial needle-stick will be like a pinch, but soon after, he'll just fall asleep."

"Aren't you going to ask him any questions?"

"Nope. Well, maybe one. You've got a brother don't, you? About your size, likes to play dress-up?" Michael was thinking of the sham security guard at the hospital. He was probably with Jennifer at this very moment. Mario spit on Michael. "I'll take that as a yes. Hope you've said your goodbyes."

Mario was sweating now. He flinched with the initial needle stick, then tried to act tough and stoic by not moving as Michael put in the catheter, attached the tubing, and hung the bag from the lamp. Michael reached into the tackle box and removed an ampule of some clear liquid. He snapped off the glass top and made a show of drawing the medicine up in full view of his victim. He flicked the syringe with the needle up as if clearing the bubbles would make any difference. Michael shoved the needle into a port along the length of the tubing and slowly pressed the syringe. Mario started shouting, screaming and shaking his immobilized arm in an attempt to escape the fluid. "What the fuck are you doing?" Every movement only caused him more pain as the broken rib fragments rubbed together in his chest.

"Just relax. You feel that warm sensation going up your arm? You feeling a little dizzy yet?"

"You're not serious. Stop it! I'll tell you anything you want to know!"

"Too late Mario. You had your chance to be nice. You might even have gotten your money back. Would have looked like a real hero. Now, you're just going to look like another anonymous overdose."

"My family knows I don't shoot up. You got one chance to let me go."

"I don't see you're in a position to bargain," Michael said. "When they find you next month in the reservoir with needle holes in your arm, what are they gonna think? Yeah, the money's gone, you wind up dead, full of drugs. How's that gonna look?"

"Dude," Jason said. "Is this really necessary? How are we going to find Jennifer? What if they go after Hannah?"

"Hannah's in good hands. Well, good enough. They'll never find her. Plus, this guy's useless. He's just a messenger. They'll send another stooge if we don't find them first. I've got a couple of ideas. We'll get rid of the body and clean this place up later. C'mon."

Michael led Jason out of the house and the two men hopped into Mario's Cadillac Escalade. "Wait a minute," Jason said. "Why don't we take my truck? Or yours? Aren't you worried about finger prints?"

"What for? I've got nothing to hide. The keys were in it. It's not like I'm stealing it. Geez, they've got Jennifer. When they see we've got the truck and Mario's not here, we've got something to bargain with. A hostage trade. I don't know, you're the crime show fan."

As they drove away, Jason gave Michael a look that asked all the questions at once. Michael felt his stare but kept his eyes on the road. "Oh, sure I'm pissed, but I'm not a killer. He'll need the IV fluids. No doubt those rib fractures are going to bleed plenty. I gave him enough pain meds to take the edge off, but not enough to kill him. I'd rather see his ass in prison a long time. Cute boy like that will be really popular, lots of friends. Plus, if they've touched so much as a hair on Jennifer's sweet head, I'll go back and kill him for real. He's probably useless as a hostage without the money, so we'd better get her back and find out what the hell is going on.'"

"Where we goin'?"

"First stop, we get Robert to figure out what he can from the card in that cell phone. It's gotta have numbers for Mario's boss, if not stuff like positioning information for roaming charges, that kind of thing. See what you can find in the glove box."

Instead, Jason touched the screen on the GPS and it came to life with a pleasing blue glow. "What are you doing? I know where I'm going," Michael said. "Plus, Mario's not working alone. I saw his clone at the hospital posing as a security guard. But I wouldn't put it past them to leave her tied up alone." Michael felt his breakfast rise, acid mixed with one gulp of beer, at the thought of Jennifer being held hostage for an amount of money with too many zeroes.

"I'll bet we can find out where this car has been every mile of the last month," Jason said.

Michael watched out of the corner of his eye as Jason worked the menus on the GPS. His giant fingers blocked most of the screen, but he drew it back when he found something of interest. "How stupid is this?" He pointed to a screen that said "POI" and a logo of the Statue of Liberty.

"What?"

"It stands for Point of Interest."

"Yeah, so? Who wouldn't be interested in the Statue of Liberty?"

"It's on an island, Michael. You can't drive there." He scrolled through a couple of lists with the names of gas stations, motels, and restaurants. "How depressing. Not a single point of interest in Kansas. Ha. Let's check the history."

Michael pulled out of the subdivision and onto the secondary road on his way to the police station. "What are you expecting to find?"

"Have you got any better ideas?"

"Well, yeah. I'm gonna have Robert run the numbers on this phone chip and we'll find out where Jennifer is. Then, we go get her."

"I doubt he's got the authority. Let's be honest, you haven't even reported her missing. You told me in the kitchen she went with these guys willingly during the soccer game. She said she wants a divorce. He'll need a search warrant. It could take months. Court orders and that sort of thing. I'd hate for a judge to ask us where we got the cell phone chip. Here, let me have it." Jason took the broken phone from Michael and cracked the case open like an oyster. "Looks like a standard memory card to me." He inserted it into his own phone, then had second thoughts. "If I call any of these numbers, then whoever answers will know that something's up with Mario, er, Lopez, whatever his name is."

"Hmm. Good thinking." Michael looked at his passenger. Jason was deftly maneuvering the tiny memory card into a plastic bag, into which he also put the broken phone. "GPS, gun models, search warrants, how do you know about all that stuff?"

"What? You don't watch TV? C'mon, man, it's Police Procedure 101. Real cops just eat donuts and get shot in the leg. It's the vigilante or the angry family member who gets things done. You know, revenge is great motivation, especially when you got nothing else to lose, right?" Jason opened the glove box and started rifling through the contents. Finding nothing of interest he opened the center console.

"Oh, thanks. Remember to remind me never to ask you for advice when I need a pep talk." Michael stopped the car in the middle of the road.

"What?"

"I just caught a whiff of Jennifer. Her conditioner. I know my own wife."

"You really are imagining things, now." Jason found an envelope in the center console and couldn't resist opening it. "All I smell is greasy hamburgers."

"Ah, never mind. I just remembered, she got in at the soccer game." Michael put the Escalade in gear and continued the drive to the police station.

"Uh, Michael. I think this is for you." Jason held up a lock of Jennifer's hair. It was wrapped in a ransom note made of block letters cut from magazines. "Maybe we should go back and talk to Mario."

"Or maybe I should just go back and finish the job. No, his partner, or brother, the fake cop from the hospital will know something is wrong if he doesn't hear from Mario soon. We don't have time. What's the note say?"

"It's not finished. It says they have Jennifer, they want the eight million, but there's no location or drop-off or exchange listed. They didn't even make a threat. They're supposed to always make a threat."

"I think that's written on my living room wall. Well, Mr. CSI: Kansas, what's our next move?"

Jason pointed to the GPS and started hitting buttons and scrolling screens. As Michael drove, Jason listed all the destinations in the recent memory. "Hmm. There's your house, St. Bernadette's, and the soccer field."

"You're kidding me. It took me an hour to find that place." Michael recalled with frustration his endless tour of the neighborhood two days prior. At this point, it seemed like another lifetime.

"Check this out. Can it be this easy?"

Michael pulled over to the side of the road and looked at the screen. Jason pointed to a line on the Previous Destination screen showing the location of the now-defunct Vickers's Company Headquarters. Jason was the first to speak. "You mind if I make a suggestion?"

"Shoot, bro'."

"I say we go get her," Jason said.

"Very noble, but did you see the size of that gun? I'll bet the other Mr. Lopez has one that's just as big and fully loaded."

"We've got one too!" Jason held up Mario's weapon and waved it around.

"Put that down! You wanna shoot my leg off?"

"Plus, we've got surprise on our side. You got a better plan, Michael?"

"We tell Robert what we've found, give him the cell phone chip like I said and let the professionals handle this."

"Oh, we'll tell Robert. Trust me, dude. We got this," Jason said. Michael drove in silence while Jason outlined his plan.

13

Until Death Do Us Part

 Every house is different. Michael drove the Cadillac Escalade and Jason rode shotgun. They hadn't been to the Vickers's Company Headquarters since they were in grade school on a field trip. What homes were out this far from town were built in all different decades by different builders and subcontractors. There were ranch style farm houses on ridiculous amounts of acreage. Most plots weren't large enough to raise commercial crops or animals, but they were much larger than needed to raise two and a half children and a Golden Retriever. Some houses were incomplete knock-offs of styles popular centuries ago on the East Coast; Cape Cod, Victorian, salt boxes, Colonials. Some had an acre of non-native lawn that stretched from the country roads leading up to their flower-draped front porches. At the property lines, a row of grass was allowed to grow wild, the acreage subdivided randomly, if it was no longer tilled for the planting of gardens or fenced for the grazing of animals.

 What stood out as most unique to Michael was not the architecture, but the ways in which the owners cared for and decorated their property. Some maintained ponds or fountains which he knew took a tremendous effort in this arid part of the country. Lawn decorations ranged from the pragmatic to the whimsical. How else to repurpose old farm tools? If it's metal, grows rust, and is no longer functional, then propping it up with a half barrel of petunias makes the perfect decorative statement to the world. If it was loved at one time, it was still loved, if only in a different manner.

At Jason's prompting, Michael had arranged for his team to meet at the intersection of two county roads, a quarter mile from the Vickers's building. He didn't know what to expect from the loan sharks so he invited everyone he knew. By the time he and Jason arrived they were already assembled. Fire Chief Chris and Officer Robert were both in uniform thinking their civic authority might hold some sway with these criminals. "Nice, Chris. Very subtle," Michael said out the window of the Escalade when they arrived at the rendevous point. Straddling the intersection was a full-sized fire truck, gleaming red, fifty feet long with a blinding white ladder and cherry picker hanging off the back end.

"Hey. You said to bring my tools."

"I meant, like an axe or something, maybe the Jaws of Life, in case we need to get through a door or something. Or your medical box, in case Jennifer's injured."

"That's all ready to go, bro'."

"I'm ready, too," Robert said. He poked a thumb towards the back seat of his police cruiser. Mario was planted in the back seat on his handcuffed hands. Blindfolded, he was craning his neck in a vain effort to hear what the men were saying. Officer Miller had swung by the house and picked him up on his way to the rendevous point. With sirens wailing he was able to make better time than if Michael had returned in the Escalade with Jason.

Michael went to the back seat to cap the IV. He threw the tubing and empty bag at Mario's feet, leaving the catheter in place as a precaution and a reminder as to just who was in charge.

"Alright, then. It's Plan A. Robert, you're up."

The officer gave a two-finger salute to the other men and returned to his cruiser. He drove the quarter mile to the Vickers's decrepit company headquarters at slow speed as if he were a meter maid looking for parking violators. The converted sorghum processing factory and its offices were all in the same building, a functional box on a small hill. The modest mound on which the Vickers's building sat was constructed from the dirt excavated to make room for the foundation and basement. A decorative pond on the east side had donated its dirt as well. It was a three-story concrete box with a small circle drive. There was a small employee parking lot on the south side near the entrance. Around the west side a service drive allowed access to the loading docks. It wound through a diminutive grove of pine trees designed to hide the trucks as they came and went, a nod to the architect's dabbling with Feng Shui.

A pathetic commercial real estate sign offered the building for sale or rent as if some passing farmer would decide to go into manufacturing, or for some reason, found himself in need of eighty thousand square feet of office space on three floors. The real estate sign was rusted, illegible, and leaning over on one broken leg. A pitch-black Cadillac Escalade was parked in the lone handicapped spot, identical in every way to Mario's. Robert pulled into the circle drive. Since the Escalade lacked the proper tags, Robert wrote out a ticket for the illegal parking and slid it under the wiper blade on the driver's side of the windshield. Besides doing his job to a fault, the ticket was also a permanent record of the license plate. He returned to his cruiser and hit his siren once to the let the kidnappers know they had a visitor. He got out his bullhorn and let whomever was inside know he had Mario and was ready to give him up for Jennifer. "We know you're in there, send out the girl and we'll let you have him. No questions."

A pane of glass burst from the window of a top floor meeting room. An office chair came crashing to the pavement and splintered into a constellation of plastic and fabric, followed by a hail of glass. A voice, thick with an Hispanic accent, shouted down, "Fuck that, Pig. Eight million. No deal."

"Where are you gonna go? Make the trade and forget this."

"How do we even know it's him?"

Robert opened the back door of the cruiser and pulled Mario out by his elbow. "Hey man, easy. I got broken ribs. This is police brutality, I got rights."

"Shut up. Tell 'em we want the girl. They cooperate and we'll see everyone benefits." Robert pushed Mario forward a few steps making sure to remind his prisoner that he wasn't in a position to bargain. Even if they didn't catch the whole gang, Mr. Lopez was looking at hard time.

"Don't deal with these assholes. They broke my ribs and drugged me," Mario yelled as best he could in the direction of the third story window.

The answer was a single gun shot. The bullet struck his leg and Mario hit the ground, arms still handcuffed behind him and blindfold in place. Robert ran around the trunk of the car for cover and drew his gun. Five more shots rang out in quick succession, then, nothing. Robert crawled around the cruiser, opened the passenger side door for cover and dragged Mario into the back seat. He crawled to the front seat, hit the sirens and pulled away from the building in a cloud of burnt tire smoke.

Back at the rendevous point, Robert came to a screeching halt by the fire truck. He cut the siren but kept the engine running. He rolled down the window. "What's Plan B?" he shouted at the men as they ran over to his window.

"I don't have a Plan B," Michael said. "What happened?"

Robert answered by jerking his thumb into the back seat. Michael looked through the window and saw Mario Lopez and a lot of blood. He sent Christopher for his medical kit. Mario was alive, but not talking. Robert gave a quick summary of events while Michael assessed the victim. "You say they shot him six times?"

Robert shook his head. "I counted six. From the third floor. Don't know how many hit him."

"Apparently you're not worth as much as my wife." Mario was in no condition to protest or lash back with an insult of his own.

Michael only saw three spots with blood. The leg looked bad but the exit wound suggested it was only a flesh wound. He'd walk. Same with the shoulder wound. The bullet went in at a steep angle at the biceps and up out the top of the deltoid. That bullet must have struck him while he was on the ground. The chest wound was another story. "Oh, nice." Michael said. "You hear about this stuff in school, but you never think you'll get a chance to see it." Jason and Christopher looked at each other. "Check it out, Chris." Michael pointed to Mario on the ground. His breathing was shallow, gurgling. There was an asymmetrical lump, rising out of his dress shirt collar, off-center.

"Cool," Christopher said. "You wanna do it?"

"Yeah," Michael said and held out his hand in the style of a surgeon. Christopher dug in the emergency tackle box and brought out a scalpel in its sterile packaging that looked like a carving knife. "I don't even need a stethoscope for this one. Beautiful. Textbook."

He felt for a rib under Mario's arm and plunged the scalpel into the gap. The chest made a sick farting noise as air escaped and his collapsed lung re-inflated. Michael snapped the blade off the scalpel and stuffed the handle into the gap to keep the wound open. "He'll be fine. As long as there's not too much internal bleeding." Michael instructed Robert to get him to St. Bernadette's. "Don't let him die. We might need him, yet."

Robert took off in another cloud of smoke, sirens wailing. Michael turned to Jason and Christopher. "I want my wife back. From the looks of Mr. Lopez, this might not…"

"I'm in," Jason said before Michael could finish his sentence.

"What are we waiting for?" Christopher said. Michael gave him a look and a shrug. "You really don't got a Plan B, do you?"

"Not, not as such, no. Not really. You?"

"Well, fuck. Let's smoke 'em out. Find out how many are in there."

"Huh?"

"Trust me. I'm a fireman. It doesn't matter how many there are. When I work my magic, they'll come running out that front door like so many Girl Scouts."

Christopher gave Michael and Jason his plan. He went to the fire truck and collected some supplies. "I'll be right back," he said and ran off on foot to the factory.

Michael turned to Jason. "I know how you feel about Amy. This isn't gonna be a walk in the park. You don't have to do this. If you want to back out, I'll understand. We'll figure something out."

"Is that all the cliches you've got, dude?"

"Oh. Very funny."

"Shut up," Jason said. "Besides, it's too late for second-guessing. Look at that." Over the treetops a faint, white wisp of smoke appeared on the breeze. It grew thicker, then darker until an evil-looking plume rivaling Mt. St. Helens's rose up from the factory.

"I think that's our cue." Michael took off running down the road.

"I'll bring the rig," Jason said and got into the driver's side cab of the fire truck.

Michael soon reached the circle drive on foot. Smoke was pouring out of the west end of the building. He waited in the overgrown landscaping bushes to see if Christopher would appear. Out of the glass front door flew a dead fern in a glazed pot, followed soon after by a skinny man in a security guard uniform that was two sizes too large. He had car keys in one hand and a handgun in the other. He jumped into the Escalade and peeled off down the circle drive. He threw a black box the size of a deck of cards out his window into the bush near Michael.

When the Escalade was out of sight, Michael ran straight into the hole in the door despite the black smoke billowing out. He ran to the east end of the building and up the staircase to the third floor, since that's the level where Robert said the shots had come from. He started checking office doors. If one was locked, he kicked it in without a thought. Love and determination had given him strength he'd not known he had. He'd deal with the broken ankle later. There was no stopping Michael on his mission to save his wife, even if it cost him his own life. What was life worth living without her? Sure, there was Hannah, but his daughter had a life of her own to lead. To Michael, Jennifer was everything, the alpha and omega.

At the eleventh door, Michael found Jennifer, his bride, his lover, the mother of his daughter. She was chained to an office chair with duct tape over her mouth. Dried blood was caked to the side of her head and down to her collar. He made a mental note that she was wearing the same outfit she had on at the soccer game which for him seemed like a decade ago. Behind her was a fifty gallon drum of fertilizer-based explosives. The digital timer over her shoulder said 3:20 and was counting down. "Oh, shit," Michael said.

He ran to Jennifer and tore the sweaty duct tape from her face.

"Ow! Fuck!"

"Sorry." Michael apologized.

"God. DAMN!"

"I said I was sorry."

"What are you doing here?"

"I love you."

"Who's going to take care of Hannah?"

"What? There's Hank and Judy."

"You idiot. *You're* supposed to take care of Hannah."

"Oh, so sorry for rescuing you." Michael had the strangest notion that nowhere in the history of marriage vows was it likely that anybody had promised to rescue the other from a giant explosive.

"Get out of here," Jennifer pleaded.

The view of the pond and the fields beyond would have been beautiful on any other day, through the expansive and impractical picture window. He guessed the room was used as an office by one of the high ranking members of Vickers's Manufacturing.

Michael examined his wife's predicament. It wasn't just the duct tape. There were bicycle chains around Jennifer's legs. It was clear from the blood that she'd been struggling for some time and with much effort. Most of the blood was fresh, but from the looks of her wounds, some of it had dried days ago. Angry gashes looped around her calves and ankles. Her wrists had similar stigmata. A loop draped across her breasts loosely, showing she'd made some progress. The bloodstains on her shoulders and upper arms suggested the precious few inches had come at a great cost. The chains wrapped in complicated figure eights around her ankles and made endless loops around the bomb at her back. In an instant Michael knew like never before what his wedding vows meant.

"In good times and in bad."

"In sickness and in health."

"Until death do us part."

Did any of their petty arguments ever matter? When he wanted blue and she wanted green? Was that paint or the color of a couch? He couldn't recall. When she wanted pepperoni and he wanted ham and pineapple. What does it take for us to realize what's really important? The clock on the bomb read 2:40.

"You're an asshole."

"Hannah will be fine."

"She *needs* you."

"I need *you*," Michael said. "I'm not going anywhere without you." He hugged her through her bonds. They cried. They shared a moment. They started to hallucinate.

"Honey?" Michael said.

"Yes, darling."

"Are we dead?"

"Not if you're seeing what I'm seeing."

"Is it a giant man floating by?"

"Yep, I got that too." A face peered into the window through cupped hands. The tinted window glass crashed into the room.

"What the..." they said in unison.

The vision of Jason was floating outside the windowsill. He hovered in space holding a giant pair of pliers, the Jaws of Life. "What's up, guys?"

There was only confusion. Jennifer was so sure she was already dead, she'd given up all hope. Michael would raise Hannah with the money from her generous insurance policy. He'd be a single widower, but a financially secure one, thanks to Jennifer's planning.

"Oh," Jason said after taking in the scene. He climbed from the basket on the fire truck ladder and into the third story window. He leaned back out through the broken glass and waved to Chris who drove the truck away. A quick survey of the room and he understood fully why there was so much hugging and crying. The clock on the bomb was down to 1:42 and counting. He got to work on the chains with the Jaws of Life. A well-placed snip and half the chains fell to the floor. Another swipe and Jennifer fell limp into Michael's waiting arms. "Uh, guys. There's a bomb here. Maybe you should run."

"Can't you cut the wires or something?" Jennifer said.

"Not a good idea. This is strictly amateur. No telling how it's wired."

"Dude, that's gonna bring down the whole building," Michael said.

Jason leaned into the drum with all his weight and managed to tip it partway over, then let it fall back to the floor with a thump. They all held their breath. The clock continued its countdown. Above one minute, it seemed like they had so much time. When the clock hit :59 and continued its crawl in double digits, the sense of urgency ramped up to toxic levels. Jason gave the barrel a giant bear hug. Michael had seen this demonstration a few times before—the Karelin lift. "C'mon Jason, you can do it."

Jason lifted with all his might, but was only able to get the barrel an inch off the floor. He gave Michael a pleading look. "Dude. Take Jennifer, maybe you can make it. Go to the west end and down. You can get out a window if you have to."

Michael answered by bending over and pushing the barrel onto its opposite rim. He locked his fingers under the rim and counted to three. The clock read 0:25, 0:24, 0:23. Together the men hoisted the barrel to waist-high and waddled over to the broken picture window. Jennifer counted herself, "One! Two! Three!" and threw her weight at the barrel as both men lifted it to the sill. The bomb tilted out the window, fell in slow motion to the ground, and landed on the edge of a berm of decrepit landscaping. It bounced once and started rolling down the hill towards the pond, where it sank, still visible through the murky water but rolling to the low point of the man-made hole.

"Maybe the water shorted out the timer. Or the detonator," Michael said.

"Not likely," Jason said. He grabbed his friends in a hug, forced them to the floor and covered them with his bulk. The explosion emptied the pond and blew the remaining windows out of the factory. Water showered the building, drenching the three friends cowering in a heap.

When they all realized they were still alive, Michael was the first to speak. "Jason?"

"Yes, Michael."

"Can I ask you something?"

"Yeah. Anything, buddy."

"Where did you learn to drive a fire truck?"

"Um. Have you ever heard that joke, I could tell you, but then, I'd have to kill you?" Michael and Jennifer both nodded. "Well, it's not a joke." Jason went on to explain to his two best friends that his job involved some intensively proprietary information. Jennifer was to be a key witness. He figured if she cooperated, they'd be able to dismiss the money laundering charges and make the conspiracy and fraud go away, too.

"Excuse me?" Michael said. "Is this the Jennifer that I know?"

"Uh, yeah," Jason said. "It's not every soccer mom who finances an entire school district from her personal checkbook. Let's just say you were on the radar."

They all stood up. Jennifer squeezed a pint of dirty pond water from her hair. Then she slumped to the floor in the fetal position. "Michael? My stomach really hurts." Michael put a hand to her belly. It was rock hard and her breath started coming in short pants.

Jason picked up Jennifer like he was lifting Hannah. "Let's roll." The men ran through the hallway, down the nearest set of stairs and out the front door. Chris was waiting with the rig, pointing out the circle drive. The two men loaded her in the front seat and piled in behind her.

"What's up? Sirens?" Christopher hit the emergency signals as he pulled away before waiting for an answer.

"Yeah, she may have some internal injuries," Jason said. "I don't think it was the explosion, we were all pretty well-protected on the third floor. Good thing the pond water put out the fire, huh?"

"Nah, it was just a smoke bomb. The building will be fine without us," Christopher said. He pointed the fire truck to St. Bernadette's and put the gas pedal to the floor.

14

INJURY TIME

Michael was at the bedside when Jennifer awoke in the recovery room. She opened her eyes, saw Michael, smiled warmly, and threw up on him. "Nice, hon'. Real nice."

"Oh, I'm so sorry."

"No, no. I like to start my day covered in burnt breakfast burrito. Geez, what did they feed you?" Michael stood up and looked around for a towel. As a nurse he was used to bodily fluids of all types, but he preferred not to wear them. He hit the call button and made his request.

Kathy arrived from the nurses' station with an emesis basis and a pile of towels. She dropped one on the floor over the brown mess and handed one to Michael so he could wipe off his jeans. She was there to transfer Jennifer to her room on the main floor. "Don't worry about it," she said. "Happens all the time after general anesthesia. From the looks of it, there was probably a little blood in it. Better out than in." She left with the dirty linen and put a clean, spare towel on the side of the bed for Michael.

"A defrosted, soggy frozen waffle, but that was…what day is it?" Jennifer said.

"Tuesday."

"Yesterday, then. What happened?"

"What do you remember?"

"I had the weirdest dream that Jason was flying by my window."

Michael wiped the corner of her mouth with a fresh towel and took her hand in his. "That wasn't a dream. What else?"

"Pain. A really bad stomach pain. C'mon, tell me what happened."

"As a parting gift, one of the brothers must have ruptured your spleen. They hit you, didn't they?"

"More like a dozen kicks or so. But I never told them about you or Hannah."

"You passed out right after we threw the bomb out the window. Jason helped me carry you to the fire truck and Chris drove us to the hospital. The surgeon said you were bleeding internally. It was pretty close. But, of course, don't they always say that? Especially when you need a transfusion. Or two. And everything came out okay. They always say that, too."

"Promise me, Michael."

"Anything, Jennifer."

"No matter where we go or what we do, let's take Jason with us."

Jennifer pushed the sheet down and looked at her stomach which was covered in a bandage the size of a diaper. She peeled back the tape under her rib cage to reveal the top of an angry gash and staples holding the skin together. A violet bruise marked the edges of the wound and a row of crusty blood clots had formed where the edges met. "They gave me blood?"

"Couple of pints. Four, maybe."

Kathy returned with some fresh linen for the bed. "Think you're ready to head to the floor? Or do you need a little more time to get your bearings?"

"Considering the surgery, I feel pretty good. Tired, but not too much pain."

"Nice, huh? A morphine pump will do that for you."

"I'm starving. When can I eat?"

"Like I said, if you're ready to go to the floor…otherwise, we can change those sheets and let you rest awhile."

"No. Thanks. I mean, yes, let's get out of here."

Kathy pushed the gurney and Michael followed, trailing the IV pole and the morphine pump. They rounded a corner, went through endless sets of double doors, and took two elevator rides. At each turn, conversations stopped and people pointed. When they reached the main medical floor Jennifer asked, "What is that smell? Did I have a concussion? It's intoxicating."

"No, I smell it too," Michael said. "Just a little something…you'll see. I figured you'd be more comfortable here on the main medical floor, rather than in surgery. It's quieter. Plus, we got you a private room."

"I thought hospitals were supposed to smell like pee and poop. And fear."

"Charming," Kathy said, looking at Michael.

"We pride ourselves on running a clean ship, honey."

Kathy hit a wall plate and double doors opened into the largest room on the floor. Inside was a riot of color and another wash of fragrance spilled over Jennifer. "Oh, my," she said. Every horizontal surface was covered in giant bouquets of roses. The entire length of the windowsill was ablaze with a rainbow of giant blooms. Vases lined the floor, hiding the baseboards around the entire room. A single mylar balloon reading "Get Well Soon!" was tied to the guard rail at the head of the bed. It bobbed and spun in the breeze created by the overhead ventilation system. "It's just a little something I worked out with Heather. When Chris told her the news, she worked all night. I hope you like it."

Michael helped Jennifer into bed and Kathy removed the soiled gurney to the hallway. "Give us a call if you need anything. You missed breakfast, but there's a lunch menu on the bedside table."

"Thanks, Kathy."

"No problem, I'm here for you both."

The couple recounted the events of the previous three days, starting with the soccer game, which now seemed like it was years ago. Michael assured Jennifer that Hannah was fine, enjoying her time with the grandparents. The three of them planned to stop by later in the day, when Jennifer was feeling better. She balked at Michael's choice of menu items, but then admitted he'd been right to keep it light. "I never knew chicken soup broth could taste so good."

"You're probably a little dehydrated."

"One question though. Why do hospitals include Jell-O with every meal?"

"Just keep that down and we'll see about something solid for dinner."

Their first visitor was Officer Robert Miller. He'd been assigned to guard the prisoner, Mr. Lopez on the day shift, since dropping him off at the Emergency Room after the failed kidnaping. Mario's leg and shoulder would heal fine after being shot by his brother, but he was still hysterical, convinced that Michael had put something in the IV at the house, which would kill him slowly and be impossible to trace. "Good," Michael said when told of Mario's condition. "I may pay him a visit later today. A little mental cruelty is the least I can do to pay him back for what they did to Jennifer."

"I'd like to be there for that," Robert said. "If he knew you saved his life from that collapsed lung, though, it might ruin the whole thing."

"He probably thinks I was trying to kill him right then and there."

"Then again, since his own brother shot him he'll likely sing like a bird when he finds out he's got you to thank."

"Until he goes to prison himself. Hopefully for a long time." The group made some more small talk about next week's soccer match, getting together for a barbecue or a sleepover for the girls, and finished by agreeing they'd try not to be such strangers to their friends.

Robert's departure was soon followed by Jason's dramatic entrance. He sidled in the door with a gentle knock looking like the newest member of the Men In Black, complete with dark sunglasses. He took them off when he entered the room, folded them and put them in his shirt pocket. The motion opened his suit coat enough to reveal a holster and pistol. Michael and Jennifer looked at each other. They couldn't have been more surprised if a dwarf, three-headed giraffe had come in quoting Shakespeare. "Hey kids, how's our star witness feeling? Oh, hey, nice flowers!"

"What are you, FBI or something?" Michael said.

"Ha, ha, no. You've got to have a clean record for that."

"Well, what then?"

"That time I tried to steal Amy's truck didn't go over so well during my application process."

"Yeah, so what's with the giant gun?"

"Oh, this little pea shooter? It's the standard issue, Glock 22 .40 caliber Smith & Wesson. Fifteen rounds but couldn't hurt a fly. It's mostly for show. Sure it's loaded, but I'd rather have something with a little more oomph, if you know what I mean."

"So you *are* FBI."

"No, but let's just say I wish Alcatraz was open for business again. I'd have a cell block filled all by myself. That'd be something for the tourists, huh. 'Step right this way and see Jason Hall, permanent home of the Cuban mafia.' That's my goal, anyway."

"Would you mind telling me what's going on?" Michael said. He looked to Jennifer but she was rolling her eyes, looking out the window, anything to avoid eye contact with either man.

"Mind if I sit down?" Jason said, then deposited his considerable bulk in a chair without waiting for an answer. "Do you remember that little thing a few years back called 9/11?" Michael gave his friend a look that said he was clearly not born yesterday. "Well, then you probably remember the USA PATRIOT Act."

"And? I'm waiting."

"When we—uh, I mean, they—starting tapping lines and following bank accounts, your wife's *activity*, shall we say, came up as *irregular*." He emphasized the words to show the jargon as industry euphemisms. Jennifer started to shrink into the bed, trying to hide herself.

"Jennifer? What's this all about?"

"Shall I tell him?" Jason said.

"Do I need a lawyer? Is this off the record? Are you wearing some kind of wire? A recording device?"

Jason laughed, looked at Michael, and jerked a thumb towards Jennifer. "Get a load of Ms. CSI Miami. Sorry to disappoint your romantic notions of law enforcement, but anything that I report you saying is as good as a tape recording. So, yeah, you're on record."

"So I need a lawyer."

"Well, that would make it look like you don't want to cooperate. I haven't read you your rights or anything, you're not under arrest. You haven't done anything wrong, have you?" Jason winked. Jennifer didn't answer. "Here. I'll tell Michael what you've been up to and you can shake your head if I get anything wrong. Okay?"

Jason's department—emphatically *not* the FBI, he was quick to add—was tracking Jennifer's personal and educational expenses since the time she overtook the budget at James Buchanan Elementary School. The first blip on the radar was a five-figure amount that was deposited and spent inside of a week. It happened about the same time they upgraded the computer system at the school, including brand new Apple desktops for the library, tutoring classrooms, and principal's office. The next noteworthy expense was in the high six figures and came about the time the new gymnasium was built. There were multiple smaller deposits and withdrawals throughout the school year which didn't seem to correlate with major upgrades. Then there was a shift in activity with small amounts of money going into an offshore account. It was registered under a Canadian bank with a branch in Freeport, Bahamas. The amounts were minuscule in comparison to the other heavy shopping, so attention turned back to the flow of money to the school upgrades. "What tipped me off was the timing of the last multi-million dollar upgrade, Jennifer. You see, the new buses are great and all, and we appreciate not having to drive Emily to school every day, but Proposition B didn't pass that year, did it? They didn't raise the millage, so you went elsewhere to get the funds, didn't you?"

"The people in this district are so cheap. It would have been fifteen cents for every hundred thousand dollars of assessed property value. Are you kidding me? These fools pay six dollars for a cup of coffee, hundreds of dollars a year on something they can make at home for pennies, and they can't vote for a couple of new buses for the kids?" Jennifer couldn't help herself, blurting out what amounted to a full confession. "Oops."

"So, it's true then," Michael said. "I don't know my own wife."

"You don't have to say anything, we're not after you, Jennifer," Jason said.

"Well, gee, isn't that a relief," Michael said.

"I'm guessing you just moved money around in the budget to get things done more quickly, rather than waiting for votes and Board approval. It's easy enough to do when you're shifting four or five grand at a time. But then you got greedy, right? Your suppliers—shall we call them?—offered to make it easier, you didn't even have to pay interest if it moved quickly, you could keep a little on the side, maybe save for Hannah's college or a nice family vacation. But did you know you were laundering drug money for the Cuban Mafia?"

"Hmmpf. If they didn't get it from me, they'd have gotten it from someone else. Plus, they said all the drugs were staying on the island and no one was getting hurt."

"Honey, they're going to lock you up forever." Michael's mind was already shifting back to the role of single dad, taking Hannah to the prison for visits once a month through six-inch glass, talking only by a telephone on the wall. Would there be conjugal visits?

"Oh, don't worry Michael, we're not after the little fish, here."

"Little fish? Eight million dollars is little fish?" Michael said.

"Well, of course. Why do you think they sent Beavis and Butt-head all the way from Miami to get it back? They didn't even fly them out. Made the poor suckers drive their own Escalades. Makes me laugh really. But that's one thing we haven't been able to track yet. Why the jump in cash? The previous flip was for only eight hundred thousand."

"The district is growing. We're going to need at least another wing to house all the new students, forty thousand square feet, give or take. If we don't have the capacity, they'll go elsewhere, or worse need to be bussed. Don't get me started on voucher programs. In the long run, building a new wing would be cheaper for the district *and* the state. I did the financial analysis and had subcontractors lined up. You know how that bus millage failed to pass? Well, let me tell you the Transportation budget is peanuts compared to trying to increase capacity for another thousand students. Do you realize how many tater tots these kids eat in a day? We needed to double the size of the cafeteria too, or rework the entire lunch schedule over four periods, splitting classes. But then, we've got to pay the cooks overtime. It just goes on and on. You can't imagine."

"Tater tots? You stole eight million dollars for tater tots?"

"He's not getting it, is he?" Jennifer said to Jason. "What I don't understand though, is why the Lopez brothers needed it back so soon. I had an excavator ready to break ground."

"Word is they had a deal lined up to get a container ship wholesale from the Chinese. We're building the case, but international law is tricky if you know what I mean. Of course, nothing's certain, but they were short on Compensated Gross Tons in their last shipment to Russia. Your money was part of a down payment. You're also their cheapest banker, taking only a few percent."

Jennifer gave a little giggle. Now it was her turn to be amused. Michael was still more confused than angry but the latter emotion was growing. He got up and started pacing the room but was penned in by the roses. "How much have you been skimming?"

"Not a lot, just enough for tuition for Hannah. It's safe. I'm not even sure Super Agent here knows where it all is." Jason held up his fingers as if he was counting for Jennifer's benefit. "Oh, so maybe you do know."

"What? Are we talking community college? DeVry?" Jennifer shook her head. "Kansas State? Can she afford to go where we went?"

"I was thinking more like Harvard," Jennifer said.

"Actually Michael, from our numbers, at about fifty grand a year for tuition, Hannah could go to Harvard for four years and take four of her friends with her."

Michael's head spun. He did the math and looked back and forth from Jason to Jennifer, then back again. "A million dollars? You've got a million dollars stashed away in a bank in the Bahamas?" A dim, fifteen watt lightbulb began to glow in Michael's stressed out skull. Two and two started walking towards each other. "Is David in on this?"

Jennifer shrugged and nodded. "Of course. More or less. How else are you gonna write off a cruise as a business expense? Once I saw the tuition thing was covered, I just figured I'd start on our retirement, then maybe surprise you one day by cancelling your schedule for good. I'd let Shirley know, of course."

"Then why all the divorce talk? You gave me a three-day heart attack."

"I knew the Lopez brothers were coming. But they didn't know I was married or that we had Hannah. We did it all by e-mail and direct deposit. I had James draw up the bogus papers. What do they call it on TV, Jason? Plausible deniability? I figured since you didn't know about the money and if you thought I was out of your life, they wouldn't bother trying to get at you to get to me."

"That's the stupidest thing I've ever heard."

"Well, they figured out the last name thing pretty quick, so I had to come up with something. It all just got out of hand so quick. I couldn't run off and hide in the Bahamas without you."

"Oh, gee, thanks for that. You torture me and leave me hanging? They trashed our house."

"Hey, I lost my spleen in the deal. I'll never be able to wear a bikini again."

"What is it with spleens, lately? Did you know James lost his in his first marriage, too?"

"What? You're not talking sense, Michael."

"I can see you two lovebirds have some things to sort out. I'll be back a little later. Right now I've got to see about the Lopez brothers. I'm pretty sure I can get Mario to talk. They found the other Escalade, but it was empty. Don't worry, we'll get up the chain of command."

Jason pulled the handle on the right-hand double door and Kathy fell into the room. It was clear she was eavesdropping. "Uh, hey y'all. I was just dropping by to see if you needed anything. The other patients are all taken care of for now. How was the soup? Any pain? Need another pillow? We have a nice library of movies on DVD."

Jason gave a wave and backed out of the room, letting the door close behind him.

"Give it a rest, Kathy. We know you were listening," Jennifer said.

"Well, can you blame me? It's so boring around here, nothing fun ever happens. You guys are like Brad and Angelina when they were cool. Before they got all old and creepy." Kathy walked over to the morphine pump and gave the impression she was inspecting it for fleas and termites. She turned her back to Michael and made some more small talk about the weather for a minute. "That ought to do it. And you know, the spleen is a very important part of the circulatory system. It recycles red blood cells and iron, it cleans out bacteria. It's amazing that we can live so comfortably without it."

"Was something wrong with the pump?" Michael said. "It was working fine since we moved from the recovery room. I'm pretty sure she hasn't even dosed herself, yet."

"And. Three. Two. One. Does Jennifer usually snore so loud?"

"Did you just knock out my wife?"

"I need to talk to you about something. Plus, there are some friends here to see you, too."

"Not Jennifer? Is she gonna keep breathing?"

"Sure, her too, but first, we have some business to discuss. The monitors will keep her safe. We'll be right down the hall. She'll probably only sleep for an hour anyway, which will give us just the time we need."

Kathy took Michael by the hand and dragged him from the room. Before he could protest he found himself being pushed through the door of the Broom Closet. With all that had gone on in the past three days he was supremely skeptical that anything Kathy might have to say would be favorable. Standing in the break room and pacing the small table were Jason, Christopher, and Heather. James was seated with his bad leg askew. "What's this all about?"

"Have a seat, Michael. We have a proposition for you," James said. "And I've got those other forms you wanted, too. Off the record, and if you want my opinion, I agree. Blood is thicker than water." Kathy and Jason remained standing by the sink. Heather and Christopher took seats opposite James and Michael at the tiny card table and laid out their proposal.

An hour later Michael had all of his questions answered, but one. "Jason? You mind if I ask you a question?"

"Sure, dude. Anything."

"You didn't really need my help to throw the bomb out the window, did you?"

"Nope. Anything else you want to know?"

"I'm good. Thanks, by the way. I appreciate everything you've done for me, for us."

"Just doing my job."

"Ha. Whatever *that* is."

"Shall we go see if Sleeping Beauty is awake?" Kathy said.

The entourage entered her room *en masse* and stood at the foot of the bed. Michael grabbed Jennifer's toe and shook her awake. Her eyes fluttered open, but remained at half mast. "Honey, can you wake up? There are some people here to see you."

"Oh, my goodness. How long was I out? Sorry," she said wiping some drool from her lip and chin.

"Not long, no need to apologize," James said. "Who wants to go first?" he said to the group.

Seeing the crowd, she tried to sit up but fell back to the pillow wincing with new pain. The extra morphine dose from Kathy had worn off. "What is this? The Scoobie Doo ending?"

"I'll go," Heather said taking a step forward. "We're sure glad you're gonna be okay. And we don't mean to bug you while you're still recovering, but…we have a huge favor to ask. It does involve us borrowing a little bit of money?" She said it like a question.

"To adopt? Michael told me you were thinking of adoption."

"Sort of. We have enough money to do that, but Chris and I have been looking at starting up something a little bigger. With a little more impact. We're so blessed to have our little girl." Heather started to fight back tears. "We want to help. Other parents. Like us, too," she said.

Chris took over the explanation. "We think we can pull it off, now that we've got the right location. Refurbishing and retooling are gonna cost a little more than we can manage, more than we thought it would be, even for a non-profit. We have some volunteers lined up."

"Wait. What's this all about?" Jennifer said.

"Mrs. Vickers from the school and hospital boards? Remember her?" Kathy interrupted. "Well, she probably thought she was doing me a favor, but instead I just got an enormous tax bill I can't possibly pay."

"Huh? Now, I'm really confused. Michael?"

Kathy ignored her question to Michael and continued to ramble. "Estate tax, real estate tax, inheritance tax, environmental impact studies. The government lawyers are up my ass about some stupid septic tank field. And we're not even related. I mean, we never were. Now that she's dead."

"Um, slow down Kathy. Let me try," Michael said. He sat down on the window side of the bed, then took Jennifer's hand to get her attention. She hit the button with her free hand to bring the back up so she could see better. Sitting up by herself put a considerable and very painful strain on her staples, despite the residual effects of the morphine drip.

"Okay, I'm listening."

"Heather and Chris want to start up a foster home in the old Vickers's Office headquarters. Maybe a shelter for victims of domestic violence. For women *and* men. When Mrs. Vickers died, she willed the building and property to her favorite nurse. Unfortunately, it came with some financial burdens that until now, Kathy didn't have the means to correct. Given our situation, I figured that we could help out easily, clean up the grounds, retool and redecorate and help Chris and Heather realize their dream."

Kathy had officially owned the building for years, he explained. She had tried to sell it but to no avail. Buyers were interested in the location and the square footage but no one would touch it because of the outstanding tax debt left by the Vickers. James and David had helped her with the tax burden by recommending she take a depreciation the last half dozen years, but if even if she was able to sell the building her tax burden would be more than she could afford. A charitable donation was in order.

"And what if I don't want to help? What if I think it's a stupid idea?"

"Then we'll go ahead with our charges of racketeering, money laundering, and probably confiscate the funds to build the foster home anyway," Jason said. "Maybe use the extra for a college trust fund for the little rugrats. Whoever they might be. Some sort of scholarship fund."

"In that case I think it's a wonderful idea," Jennifer said.

Heather and Chris fell into a strong embrace. James reached into his briefcase for a thick stack of papers, then thought better of it and put them back. Kathy clapped like a little girl attending her first circus. She grabbed a hand each and dragged the fireman and his wife away to plan their celebration. It was a win-win all around. Jason didn't smile, but rather, excused himself as well, saying he was glad it was all settled and he'd hate to have to put his best friend's wife behind bars.

"James? You want to give her the papers, now?" Michael said.

"Can't we wait for all that? I'm tired and I'll want to see all the numbers and know where our nest egg is going to end up."

"No, Jennifer this is something else."

"Oh, *those* papers," James said. "I've got 'em right here."

"What? After all this? You're divorcing me?"

"Well, you're not exactly the woman I thought I knew. Clearly we have irreconcilable differences. I want to help Heather and Chris with their dream of opening the shelter. That's a couple planning a meaningful future together. You can't even look the other way when I load the dishwasher."

Jennifer began to pout. "I was only making that up. I had to come up with something. I love you. I love our life together."

"I thought you always said love is ineffable. That it can't be explained, that's why you never say it to me."

"I still believe that. It's like trying to describe the color blue, or the taste of an orange. You can compare it to things, but they always fall short."

"But you say it to Hannah."

Jennifer was quiet. James started to reach into his briefcase for the papers again. "Wait, James," Michael said. "I want to hear if she's got anything to say. After all, I think her last comment to me was that we have nothing in common."

"That's not fair. You know I was just trying to protect you and Hannah. I'll try to say it more, I promise. I love you, I really do."

"Enough that Hannah and I can get a puppy?"

"Sure, whatever you want."

Michael stood up from the bed and went over to James. He whispered something in the lawyer's ear, then took the two packets of documents, one in each hand. He went back to the bed and held them out to Jennifer. "It's your choice. Take your pick."

"What's this? A divorce, or what? I already agreed to give over the money for the foster home. Or the shelter or whatever it's going to be."

"No, simpler than that. I thought you might want to change your name to Johnson. If you don't then I want to change my name to Smith, so I'll sign the other set of papers. Hannah said she's fine with it either way. Jennifer Johnson has a nice ring to it, don't you think?"

THE END

Would you like to see your manuscript become a book?

If you are interested in becoming a PublishAmerica author, please submit your manuscript for possible publication to us at:

mybook@publishamerica.com

You may also mail in your manuscript to:

**PublishAmerica
PO Box 151
Frederick, MD 21705**

www.publishamerica.com

CPSIA information can be obtained at www.ICGtesting.com
Printed in the USA
LVOW11s0817180114

369914LV00001B/6/P